By day, Jessica Strawser is editor-at-large for *Writer's Digest* magazine, North America's leading publication for aspiring and working writers since 1920. By night, she is a fiction writer. And by the minute, she is a proud wife and mum to two super-sweet and super-young kids in Cincinnati, Ohio.

ALMOST MISSED YOU

Violet and Finn are 'meant to be.' A happy couple seemingly brought together by the hand of fate, they have a gorgeous son, and are enjoying their first family holiday in Florida — until Violet returns to the hotel room to discover that her husband has left without a trace, and he's taken their child with him . . . Caitlin and Finn have been best friends since the first day of college. But friends don't ask you to hide their kidnapped son, threatening to reveal a secret which could destroy your family if you don't. Do they? *Almost Missed You* is the story of a mother's love, a husband's betrayal, connections that maybe should have been missed, secrets that perhaps shouldn't have been kept, and the spaces between what's meant to be and what might have been.

JESSICA STRAWSER

ALMOST MISSED YOU

Complete and Unabridged

CHARNWOOD
Leicester

First published in Great Britain in 2018 by
Hodder & Stoughton
an Hachette UK company
London

First Charnwood Edition
published 2019
by arrangement with
Hachette UK
London

A catalogue record for this book is available
from the British Library.

ISBN 978–1–4448–4157–2

Published by
F. A. Thorpe (Publishing)
Anstey, Leicestershire

Set by Words & Graphics Ltd.
Anstey, Leicestershire
Printed and bound in Great Britain by
T. J. International Ltd., Padstow, Cornwall

This book is printed on acid-free paper

For my children,
who manage to be both the sunshine and the stars in my universe.
I love you to Pluto and back infinity times.

1

AUGUST 2016

Violet couldn't remember the last time she'd felt so at peace. She almost felt guilty admitting this to herself as there had been so many moments to treasure in the three years since Bear was born. Becoming a mother had been many things — often indescribably rewarding, occasionally stupefying, sometimes even terrifying in the intensity of the love she felt for someone so small and vulnerable and dependent upon her — but relaxing was not one of them.

Every moment of it had led up to this, though: The blue-green southern Florida ocean sparkling before her, the gentle waves breaking, the pelicans diving into the water, and her sitting here taking it all in, a book in one hand, a piña colada in the other, and a rare and blissful stillness around her in the hour since Finn had taken Bear up to the hotel room for his nap. She smiled at the memory of Bear building sand castles earlier, making crashing noises as he plowed his dump truck through the mounds of sand he'd carefully sculpted just moments before, and of the way Finn looked at her when he offered to handle naptime today — a mixture of tenderness and something she couldn't put her finger on, as if he hadn't wanted to look away. He felt it too, the collective release of their

1

first vacation in years. Tonight, after Bear was in bed, they would take that fresh bottle of pinot grigio out to the balcony, and she'd lay her head on that perfect-fit spot on his shoulder as they settled in to watch the moonlight sparkle on the rolling water.

Life was good.

She couldn't help thinking of the day she'd met Finn. It had been on this very stretch of beach, right on the other side of the pier. They'd had that kind of instant electric connection that happens only once in a lifetime, and yet by the time she'd flopped her suitcase onto her bed back at home, she'd had the sinking feeling she'd never see him again. It had left her with a desperate empty sensation, and feeling a little foolish for pining so earnestly for someone she'd only met. She wished she could reach back in time and tell her former self not to worry. It would all work out in the end.

Dominoes. It was that intricate chain reaction of tiny movements that came to mind whenever anyone asked how they finally ended up together. There had been years of radio silence between their first and second meetings, no doubt filled with unrealized opportunities, untaken chances, unspoken words, missed connections. Even as children, they had passed each other like ships in the night. Their coupling was a story that people demanded they tell again and again. They'd be introduced at parties — 'And this is Violet and her husband, Finn. Don't let them get away from you until they've told you the story of how they met. It's a

2

bestseller!' — they'd oblige, and then would come the response: That it must have been fate. Meant to be. Kismet.

Violet wasn't sure their story was so different from any other. Ask any couple about their meeting, and you'd discover how many things had to have gone exactly right — or exactly wrong — for them to have gotten together. If so and so had been on time, and so and so hadn't been feeling sick that day, and so and so had come through with that concert ticket slash ride slash twenty dollars, and cell phones had been invented back then, and any number of other against-the-odds occurrences or nonoccurrences had or had not transpired in the hours, days, weeks, even years up until their crossing paths again and again until one time everything finally aligned, they never would have ended up together.

Fate, people liked to call it.

But Violet pictured it as dominoes.

Somehow, they'd been positioned perfectly. And at the end of the line was Finn.

Sometimes she couldn't believe her luck.

Because not only was Finn *Finn*, but Finn had given her their Bear Cub. Her most precious thing. Motherhood had wrapped its chubby little baby-lotion-scehted arms around her and would not let go, in spite of the fact that Bear's birth involved no perfect culmination of events — in fact, his was one of those stories that made people gasp in horror. There had been a postpartum hemorrhage, but not until a few hours after they'd welcomed Bear to their little world, and the doctors almost didn't catch the bleeding. She'd very nearly died.

What a marvel to wake up the next morning and see how pale Finn was, how stoic, how shaken to the core. 'I'm perfectly okay,' she told him in a hoity-toity imitation of her gram that usually made him laugh. But he just entwined his fingers with hers and lowered his forehead to their clasped hands, and she was overcome with emotion. To be loved the way Finn loved her. To have been gifted this beautiful baby boy, and to have survived his birth after all. To finally have a family of her own, something she hadn't known since her parents' accident when she was a child. Her heart had never felt so full.

Bear and Finn were her whole life now. Once Bear grew into a full-fledged toddler, Violet quit her job, a bold move she'd never imagined herself making. Her days became overrun with adventures to find exciting new leaves and rocks, with the constant challenge of trying to get him to eat anything but string cheese and chicken nuggets, with sippy cups that never had all the right parts clean, with tiny cars that always seemed to be underfoot. She brought just enough order to the chaos not to irk Finn with a complete mess when he got home from work. But mostly, she just enjoyed Bear. Sometimes after Finn had left for his morning commute, as she and Bear shared the tiny kitchen table, eating frozen waffles and watching PBS Kids, she'd look down at her pajamas and slippers and think that there was absolutely nowhere she would rather be.

Except the beach. She *did* occasionally fantasize about some time alone on the beach, a piña colada in hand, the only cries she could hear coming from the seagulls overhead.

And now here she was, right there in her fantasy, with some rare time to herself, and all she could think about was Bear.

It was useless trying to convince herself she needed more time alone. She wondered if she should be bothered by the fact that she seemed to have lost her ability to shut off her mom mode. But the thing was, the mode suited her. She *had* needed a *little* break — but really she'd been reveling in the novelty of the idea of these stolen hours far more than in the reality of their emptiness.

She was overcome by an urge to go up to the room in time to be the one to rouse Bear from his nap, to dish him up a big bowl of ice cream — something he was almost never allowed at home — and to sit on the balcony next to him watching the airplanes fly by, their banners advertising all-you-can-eat seafood buffets and two-for-one water park tickets stretching out behind them like toddler siren songs. Finn had pointed out that the tackier the advertisement on the airplane, the more Bear loved it.

'That's what it's all about, right?' she'd said, light-headed with giddiness at their first day here as a family. 'This is why we have kids!'

'I know, I know — to see the world through their eyes, with child-like innocence and wonder.'

'No. To embrace the tacky.'

It was a lame joke, but it made Finn laugh. He'd seemed a little quiet yesterday — tired, probably. He'd drunk so much coffee at the airport and on their subsequent crawl through the North Miami traffic here to Sunny Isles that he'd tossed and turned for half the night, and it had felt like a triumph to make him smile.

Now, at the sight of a giant pink flamingo banner waving behind a dangerously small red plane droning overhead, she got to her feet and stretched. She shook the sand off her decadent new Ralph Lauren beach towel, a gift from Gram for the trip, and slipped her book and empty cup into the outside pocket of the coordinating beach bag. She attempted to fold her beach chair, wrestled with the stubborn arms of the thing, and decided to just leave it — they'd be back down later anyway, and even if they decided Bear had had enough sun, Finn wouldn't mind coming to get it. He was good-natured about doing husbandly things.

Dry, hot sand puffed out behind her feet as she made her way to the resort's gated pool area. She could already picture Bear's face covered in chocolate ice cream, his adorable little dimpled grin sticky cheek to cheek.

When the elevator deposited her on the ninth floor with a ding, she paused outside their door to listen. All quiet. She smiled. He was still asleep — she hadn't missed a thing. She slipped her keycard into the slot, which for once worked on the first try, and bounded in, eyes bright.

For a second, she thought that her card had somehow worked on the wrong room. She was

6

about to call out a horrified apology to anyone who might be in the suite. This one had barely been checked into. It had none of the open suitcases and discarded T-shirts and flip-flops and drying swimsuits and sunscreen bottles and magazines and snacks and toys that had already overtaken their room.

But then, from her spot in the front hallway, she realized that the purse on the table was hers.

She stepped farther into the room and glanced into the bathroom on the right. Her toiletries were there, lined up neatly on the marble sink top, but they were all alone. Absent was the chaos of Finn's shaving gear and contacts and solution and glasses, of Bear's bubblegum-flavored toothpaste and prescription eczema cream and Lightning McQueen comb.

'Hello?'

Baffled, she walked into the combined living and sleeping area, and it was the same. Her things were just as she'd left them. But all traces of her husband and son were gone. As if they'd never been there at all. As if they'd been figments of her imagination all along.

2

AUGUST 2010

'Camp *Pickiwicki?*'

Violet didn't register the words at first. She'd moved her chair up as close to the waterline as she could without risking dousing the beach bag at her side. For a while, she'd watched, entranced, as the foam crept closer and closer to her freshly manicured toes. But then she'd been pulled back into her novel. She hadn't noticed the man walking barefoot in the surf, hadn't seen him start to pass her and then back up, doing such an obvious double take at her that there really was nothing left to do but speak.

She looked down at her faded mustard yellow T-shirt, then up at the man. He seemed to be about her age, but he was wearing mirrored sunglasses, and she couldn't see his expression. *Like a cop,* she thought. *No. A narc.*

'Camp Pickiwicki,' she said, in a tone of total agreement. You could barely make out the black letters — they'd disintegrated over hundreds of washes — but the circular logo sprawled across her shirt was still recognizable, the way the C tucked into the tree that formed the P.

'You went there?' He sounded more than just disbelieving. Suspicious.

'Picki-picki-wicki-wicki-yay!' she chanted half-heartedly. For two weeks during the summer

8

she'd turned twelve, she and her fellow campers had been cajoled into yelling the rallying cry at daybreak, before meals, after canoe races, when it was time to leave the fire circle and go to bed. If you'd been there once, it was ingrained in your mind forever.

He laughed. 'And your T-shirt still fits. Astonishing. I outgrew mine well over a decade ago.'

'Oh — this is my gram's. My grandmother's. She volunteered on the special event nights.'

'And do you often wear your grandmother's clothes to the beach?' He gave her a big white-toothed smile, and Violet could just see the arches of his raised eyebrows peeking out above his sun-glasses.

'I do not,' she replied coolly. 'But then I thought, what if someone else here went to Camp Pickiwicki? I mean, the place was only open for one summer, and hardly anyone signed up even then, and it's also in Western Pennsylvania and here we are in beautiful Sunny Isles Beach, conveniently located about a zillion miles south of the campgrounds, so you never know.'

'Indeed. I like to keep an eye out for fellow Pickiwickians everywhere I go.'

'Look out!'

A teenager on an out-of-control skimboard came barreling onto the sand, and the man leaped out of his way, knocking into Violet's beach umbrella. She grabbed the pole to hold it steady.

'Sorry!'

'Perhaps you should keep an eye out for rogue *skimboarders* wherever you go,' she suggested.

He laughed. 'Not challenging enough. They're everywhere.'

The man got to his knees in the circle of shade at Violet's side and started mounding wet sand around the pole to hold it in place, His sunglasses slid down his nose, and he pushed them up on top of his head, It hadn't been a trick of the mirrored lenses — he was good-looking. Somewhere between rugged and clean-cut, as if he'd be just as comfortable strumming an acoustic guitar as wearing a suit. *Hello, handsome stranger.* She'd be starting to get nervous right about now if her flight weren't leaving first thing in the morning. She had a tendency to get tongue-tied and ruin these sorts of things, Not that these sorts of things ever happened to her.

'It really is an odd coincidence, though, isn't it?' he said, giving the mound of sand a last pat and flopping down beside her chair. 'I've never met *anyone* who went there, let alone all these years later and a thousand miles away. I loved that place. That was, like, my favorite summer as a kid. Ever.'

'I know, I wonder if we were there at the same time? I mean, I *think* I would recognize you . . . '

He shook his head. 'We couldn't have been. There were no girls during the session my parents signed me up for, Wasn't supposed to be that way, but that's how it worked out. Or so I was told, You can imagine my disappointment.'

She laughed. 'Well, then, I am sorry to tell you

that you did not get the full Camp Pickiwicki experience, No sneaking out after dark to make out down by the docks?'

'Surely not a good girl like you who wears her grandmother's clothes to the beach.'

'Surely so.'

'Well, then it's finally clear to me what must have happened, You juvenile delinquents early in the summer ruined it for the rest of us by the time August rolled around. I *knew* the odds of no coeds enrolling that session were slim!'

She shrugged. 'That claim is unsubstantiated.'

'I can't believe my parents actually lied to me about what happened.'

'About what *allegedly* happened.'

'I feel as though you owe me an apology.'

'I owe you no such thing.'

'The least you could do is make it up to me after dark tonight.'

Violet flushed, and the man's face fell.

'That was it, wasn't it?'

'That was what?'

'The line. I'm always crossing it without meaning to. Please. Forget I said that. I was just trying to be clever.'

'No offense taken. I'd probably still be sore about it too, if I could trace my lingering virginity back to having missed out on my first tongue kiss at summer camp.'

He cocked one eyebrow at her. 'I've been accused of a lot of things in my adult life, but being a virgin is not one of them.'

'And here you were acting shocked that I was not the Goody Two-shoes little camper you

11

assumed me to be.'

'Well, in my defense, you *are* wearing your grandmother's Camp Pickiwicki T-shirt. At the beach. On an adult vacation with . . . who are you with?'

'Myself.'

'You came on vacation alone?' He looked more impressed than surprised. 'Really?'

'My boyfriend unceremoniously dumped me a few weeks ago. I've been working an insane amount of overtime at the office. I realized that I'd never spent my tax refund. So, I just booked it.'

'And how's it been?'

'Honestly?'

He nodded, and she could tell he was waiting for her to say it had been unexpectedly lonely, there were couples everywhere, there were kids everywhere, she didn't know what she'd been thinking. She'd half expected to feel that way too, before she'd gotten here.

'It's been pretty damn great,' she said, shrugging. 'I'm actually a little embarrassed at how much it suits me. I don't want to turn into one of those people who get too used to living alone, you know? But then again, maybe I just really needed a vacation.'

It was not this particular breakup that upset her as much as the fact that it was one in a long line of them in the years since she'd graduated college. Every time her phone rang and it was a friend she hadn't heard from in a while, she knew even before answering that it was another call to announce an engagement. Violet would

12

manage the customary squeals over the proposal stories and summon genuine enough happiness as she wished them well, but she couldn't do it without mentally tallying her list of engaged friends versus those whose boyfriends were getting serious. And then there was Violet, alone in the 'completely single' column, where every prospect turned out to be a false hope just a few months in. She had never been one to feel she *needed* a boyfriend, or a fiancé, or a husband to be happy, but it was enough to give anyone a complex.

'I admire that,' he said, and she braced herself for the setup of another joke. But none came. 'Independence. Half of my friends still go on vacation with their parents. Their parents! They meet a girl and you think they'll go on some couple's trip instead, but nope, they *all* go to the time-share in Marco Island together.'

She laughed. 'And who are you here with?'

'A bachelor party, actually. This guy George is marrying my good friend Caitlin. I'm more of a male bridesmaid than a groomsman, but he invited me along.'

'Let me guess. You've got eight guys crammed into a room with two double beds at the closest hotel you could find to the booze cruise dock.'

'That would be a good guess if we were on my budget. This particular guy is loaded. I mean, his family is. It's more of a penthouse. With a booze cruise in the form of its own yacht.'

Violet had seen the over-the-top Trump hotel down the strip and wondered if he was staying there. Then again, there was no shortage of

13

luxury accommodations this close to Miami. She'd been eyeing them all week in spite of herself. 'Lucky you,' she said.

'Lucky *Caitlin*. It's actually a little awkward for me. I don't really know anybody there very well.'

Violet wondered what the Caitlins of the world were doing right that she was missing.

'Well, cheer up. I'm sure next time, you'll vacation someplace far less gilded. You know, with your parents.'

She could see that she'd picked the wrong joke. He looked away from her, out to sea.

'My parents died a few years back. A heart attack and an aneurysm, respectively. I'm afraid I don't have very good genes.'

'Oh, I'm so sorry.' She touched his arm gently. 'I shouldn't have said that. I was raised by my grandmother — I should know better than to assume.'

'Don't be sorry. I set myself up for it with that joke about everyone else's parents. It *may* be that part of my annoyance with everyone else and their family vacations is that I'm a little bit jealous.' He gave her a shy grin, and she relaxed a little.

'I'm not usually too discriminating with my vacation envy,' Violet said. 'I mean, I'm *on* vacation right now, and I'm still envying your penthouse and your yacht.'

He laughed. 'It wouldn't matter if I *was* in a run-down motel — in the moment, I always think every vacation I'm on is the best ever. I go home plotting to move to wherever I just visited.'

14

'Ah, a dreamer.'

'Do dreamers go so far as to look at job openings and check rental prices?'

'At a minimum.'

'Guilty.'

'And then what happens?'

'What do you mean?'

'What makes you decide not to move? Ties back home?'

He blinked, as if surprised by the question. 'No. Nothing. I have no idea. I just get caught back up in regular life, I guess.'

Violet thought of what might be seen as her own lack of ambition. She'd always been so eager to please Gram, to not be a bother to anyone, to do the responsible and expected thing. She'd never really arrived at a logical point to pause and think about what she might want beyond any of that. In truth, she was happy enough with her duplex town house adjoining Gram's, her stable and decent-paying job, her respectably sized group of respectably close friends.

'I may be the living definition of being caught up in regular life,' she admitted, and a moment of not uncomfortable silence descended between them.

Finally, he broke it with a little laugh. 'I have no idea why I told you any of that,' he said. 'I must like you, Pickiwicki. What are you doing later?'

She felt the color rush into her cheeks and was glad of the absurdly giant sunglasses that concealed no less than a third of her face, even though Gram had rolled her eyes when she'd bought them. 'I am unable to fathom,' Gram had told her, 'how such a ridiculous trend from my own youth is back again.'

'I . . . I should tell you I'm flying home in the morning. I don't want you to waste your time with me.'

She thought she saw a beat of disappointment flash across his face, but he concealed it well. 'This is the best conversation I've had since I got here. I don't see how that can be a waste of time. Where's home?'

'Cincinnati, actually. Pickiwicki was a bit of a haul for summer camp — Gram only sent me there because a friend of hers knew the owners. You still in Pennsylvania?'

He squinted at her. 'Are you pulling my chain?'

'Um. I don't think so.'

'I live in Cincinnati now, too.'

'No, you don't.'

'I do. I went to college there, and then I stayed.'

'Prove it.'

'Well, I don't carry my license in my swim trunks.'

'Where do — '

A child's high-pitched scream from just behind them made Violet startle in her seat. Something in the tone indicated that this person was *not* playing, and she jumped to her feet. A few beach towel lengths behind her, a boy was standing with tears running down his face. 'Help, please,' he sobbed, looking frantically

16

around. His eyes settled on Violet's. 'Help!'

Her handsome stranger was on his feet now too, and together they rushed toward the child. 'What's wrong?' Violet called, trying to sound calm. 'Are you hurt?'

'My mommy. My mommy,' he sobbed, and that's when Violet saw the woman behind him in the pop-up beach tent. She was lying on her side, writhing and wheezing, her face and lips almost cartoonishly swollen.

Violet looked at her companion in horror. 'Shit,' the man said. 'A seizure? No — some kind of allergic reaction?' Then he snapped into action. 'I'll get the lifeguard!' he yelled, and took off running.

Violet fell to her knees beside the woman. 'Ma'am? Can you speak?' The woman just looked at her with pleading eyes. Violet turned and took the little boy gently by the arms.

'Did your mommy just eat something?' she asked him. He was wailing now, his teary eyes wide with primal fear. 'Think hard,' she said kindly. 'Maybe something that she doesn't usually eat? Or drink? It will help the doctors fix her if you can tell me.'

The boy pointed at a hollowed-out pineapple resting in the corner of the tent. It was one of the frozen drinks being sold from pushcarts, and it looked to have only a few sips out of it. Her brain registered a vendor walking a short distance away, and she dove for the pineapple. 'Hey!' she screamed at the vendor. He kept walking. '*Hey!*' He turned.

'This drink. What's in it? Is there some kind of

nut or something in here?'

He thought for a second, then nodded. 'Almond liqueur.'

Violet put her hand to her forehead and looked back down at the child. 'Is that a nut?' the boy sobbed. 'Mommy can't have nuts.'

But here was her handsome stranger, running back through the sand with a lifeguard. 'Everything will be okay,' Violet told the boy, hoping it was true. 'Nuts!' she called to the lifeguard. 'This vendor says there's almond liqueur in this drink, and I think she's allergic to nuts. Do you have an EpiPen? Benadryl? *Something?*' Her coworker Katie had once had a reaction to salad dressing at a business lunch, and Violet remembered the company memo that had gone out afterward, about what allergic employees should always have on hand in case of emergency. She lunged for the woman's beach bag to see if she'd brought provisions.

'Nine-one-one is on the way, just sit tight,' the lifeguard told the woman. He knelt and started rifling through his first aid kit.

'Is your daddy here?' Violet's handsome stranger got down to the boy's level and smiled encouragingly.

There was nothing of any use in this beach bag. Only sunscreen and sand toys.

The boy sniffled and nodded. 'At the pool.'

'And what's your daddy's name?'

'Dave.'

'And your last name?'

'Smithers.'

'Dave Smithers?' The boy nodded. 'Good boy.

Which pool — which hotel?'

The boy pointed, and then this remarkably in-control man was off running again. The first wails of approaching sirens sounded in the distance.

'Shit,' the lifeguard muttered, 'Shit, shit, shit. I must have used the last one on that wasp sting yesterday. I'm in for it now.'

The woman's eyes had closed, her brow furrowed as if she were concentrating very hard. She was turning blue. Something in Violet snapped just then, and she felt the weak façade she'd been putting up for the little boy crumbling. 'Please,' she pleaded to the lifeguard. 'This is this boy's *mother*. You have to do something.' The boy had returned to his mother's side and was clutching her thigh with his tiny splayed hands.

'Help is coming,' the lifeguard said, sounding unconvinced even as the sirens did grow louder. *Jesus*, Violet thought, taking him in for the first time, his sideways baseball cap and his lean, hairless chest. *He's practically a kid himself.*

'Ma'am, can you hear me?' he said loudly, lowering his face to the woman's. She didn't respond, and he put his ear to her chest. 'It's labored, but she's breathing,' he told Violet. He sat up and stared down at the woman, frozen. Whatever training he had, it had clearly gone right out of his mind.

Then, finally, three paramedics were running toward them, yelling for people to get back and give them room. Violet wrapped her arms around the crying child and stepped backward, gently

19

guiding him out of the way. She scanned the beach for her handsome stranger, for some sign of the boy's father, but all she saw was a growing circle of concerned strangers. *Looky-loos*, Gram would have called them.

It all happened so fast. The lifeguard snapped back to life and filled in the paramedics, they administered the EpiPen, loaded the woman onto the stretcher, strapped oxygen to her face, bagged a sample from her drink. All the while the boy whimpered and clung to Violet's legs.

'We have to go. Now,' the lead paramedic barked at the life-guard.

'You said someone was getting the husband?'

'The boy pointed out the hotel, but I don't see them yet.'

'Tell him to come to Aventura Hospital as soon as he gets here.' He looked at Violet. 'Can you stay with the boy?'

Violet blanched. 'I don't know him . . . I only — '

'Can you stay with him?'

The boy hurled himself at the stretcher, nearing hysterics again. 'Mommy! I want to go with Mommy!'

Violet's heart broke for him. 'Can he ride along?' she begged the paramedic. 'If I ride with him?'

'We're not really supposed to — '

The boy let out a heart-stopping wail.

'*Please*. I'll keep him out of your way. I'm really not comfortable separating them.'

The paramedic conceded with a brusque nod and turned back to the lifeguard. 'Dave

20

Smithers. If that guy doesn't show back up with him, go to the hotel yourself. Have him paged. Ring his room. Whatever it takes.'

★ ★ ★

The woman made it, just, thank God. The frantic husband did show up eventually. He'd left the pool area after agreeing to be the fifth in a pickup game in the basketball courts around the side of the resort, so he hadn't been easy to find. He didn't know the name of the man who'd come yelling for him, and though he wished he could thank him again, he didn't know what had become of him.

And as she took one last reluctant look over her shoulder the next morning, slinging one leg into the taxi that would take her to the airport, neither did Violet.

3

AUGUST 2016

Caitlin eyed the stormy sky nervously as she made her way to her cubicle. She was the first in the office, as usual, and left the overhead fluorescent lights off. She relished the isolated warmth of her monitor's glow in this first dim hour of the morning, a manifestation of her satisfaction that she was again brightly beating her coworkers to the start of a productive day. Her husband's family was a major donor to this nonprofit, and she was well aware of the murmurs that she didn't need her job or its paycheck. But she liked the work, she believed in the cause, and she wanted to have money of her own, so she'd made a point of putting her work ethic on display until the snark around the watercooler died down. She was wishing she'd been a little less ambitious this particular morning, however. It was so much darker than normal, nightlike except for an unsettling orange glow seeping around the tips of the low fingerlike cloud cover. Lightning streaked across the sky with menacing purpose, and she strained her ears for the beginning wails of the tornado siren, which always struck her as alarmingly faint.

She looked down at the keys in her hand, fighting an irrational urge to turn around and get right back in the car, pick up the twins where she'd just left them at day care, and envelop them in her arms, as if they'd somehow be safer with her, even though her office was just down the road and in the same path of the storm.

All it would take was one act of God. One error in judgment. One irrevocable mistake. And the two beings she loved most in the world could be taken from her for good. She felt this with terrifying certainty. She felt it too often. She felt it in her marrow.

Her close friends Violet and Finn had lived next door until they moved out of state last year, and Violet especially had found this quirk of Caitlin's as amusing as Caitlin did frightening.

'I don't remember you being so much of a worrier when we first met,' Violet remarked.

Well, she hadn't been. And these days, she really worried about only one thing. She just happened to worry about it incessantly, in a thousand different scenarios. Caitlin tried to keep her concerns bottled up, but sometimes the worries piled so high that she couldn't help voicing one or two.

Of course, now that Violet's own life had inexplicably fallen out from under her, it was almost embarrassing to think back on the unfounded fears Caitlin had once confided to her friend. Never much for worrying, Violet had always been the one to try to talk Caitlin back down to ground level. In Caitlin's memories of Violet's last visit — not two months ago, at the beginning of the summer — Violet seemed . . . not flippant, exactly, but almost luxuriously self-assured. Unencumbered.

23

'Now I've heard everything. Your new childproof doorknob cover seems dangerous?'

'It's just that . . . well, this cover is designed so they can't get out of their room.'

Violet had laughed. 'Right. Which was the point, remember? Because now that they're in big-boy beds, they occasionally wake up and wander the house without you knowing?'

'Well, right. But what if there's a fire or something? They'll be stuck in there!'

'Oh, come on, now.' Violet's eyes had twinkled. 'A fire *or something*? Is that the best disaster fantasy you can come up with?'

Violet knew her too well. In truth, what Caitlin was envisioning was far more elaborate. It involved a tree falling in the night, crashing through the roof and into the master bedroom, pinning her and George painfully beneath its limbs, and little Leo and Gus waking in the morning and calling and calling for her. But she'd be too weak to answer loud enough for them to hear. How long might they all remain that way? Would the neighbors see the tree and check to make sure everyone was okay, or would they see no cars in the driveway (wouldn't you know they'd finally cleared out enough space in the garage to actually park in it) and assume no one was home and things were being taken care of? Would they all wither away, she and George eventually bleeding out from their injuries and Leo and Gus slowly starving to death, never knowing that she was just down the hall, loving them, shedding tears for them, willing to give up her life if it would mean someone would come and save them? And all because of a little plastic doorknob cover to keep them from . . . well, actually from other hazards, such as drowning in the tub or gorging themselves on gummy vitamins or running into the street?

Caitlin had stared blankly at Violet, refusing to give her the satisfaction of sensing that she'd been right, and finally Violet had sighed. 'But Caitlin,' she'd said more gently, 'back when they were in their cribs, they wouldn't have been able to escape either.'

That was the same argument George had made. She'd bristled. 'But in an emergency maybe they could have climbed out! I mean, if they really needed to.'

'So just to make sure I have this right, your worry is that your children will *not* be able to defeat the safety device? When you hear it that way, doesn't it seem a bit silly?'

It hadn't at the time. But today it did seem silly compared to what Violet was going through. Caitlin immediately felt guilty. How could she be caught up in the slim odds of a tornado or a lightning bolt striking when Violet's worst fears had come true? No — not her worst fears. That wasn't right. The thing she had never had a reason to fear, something far worse. Her husband gone. Her child gone — today marked a week. The police, and now the FBI, eventually treating it as a parental abduction, presumably an interstate one (they could only hope Finn and Bear were still in the country), all the while continuing to grill Violet herself as if she were a criminal. Had she and Finn been having marital problems? Was she a good mother? Was Finn a good father? If he did in fact do what she said he had done, why on earth did he do it? How could any wife be as truly blindsided as Violet had been?

That was the question.

Caitlin had left her boys behind for the first time in their lives to drive from Ohio to North Carolina to be with Violet, who was inconsolable. Even now that Caitlin was back home — *especially* now that she was back home — she couldn't stop imagining what it must have been like for Violet that day, coming up to the hotel room in the midst of what she felt was an ordinary, enjoyable family vacation and finding nothing but her own belongings. Violet had relayed it to her again and again, until Caitlin could almost picture it as if she'd been there too. The confusion. The panic rising when she called Finn's cell phone, over and over, and over and over got the same message that it had been disconnected. The helplessness when she ran down to the parking garage and saw that their rental car was missing, when she called the rental agency and learned that the car had just been returned. Violet had done everything that Caitlin herself would have done. She had searched for signs of foul play, looking for anything out of order, checking the trash cans. She had called the front desk and come up empty. No one had spoken with Finn or noticed a man and a child acting strangely. At a loss, she had frantically hailed a taxi to the airport, running aimlessly down the flight check-in lines all the way to the security checkpoint, begging a security guard to have Finn paged, waiting with humiliation at the security desk when the pages went unanswered, when she was denied a request to have outgoing flights' passenger lists checked for their names. She had repeated the scene at the bus station, then returned to the room with some glimmer of hope that she'd walk in to find everything as it had been that morning, before the nap. Hoping that this was a bad dream, a sick joke.

It was real.

She had stood on the balcony wondering what to do next and whom to call. Finn's parents were dead. He had no other family to speak of. She had stared out at the ocean sky as the full force of her terror seized her. And then she had called the police, who reluctantly agreed to send someone out but seemed to think that perhaps she and Finn had gotten their signals crossed, that surely he and Bear would turn up. Then she had called Gram. And then she had called Caitlin.

Eventually, of course, the report had been filed, and, when it became clear Finn hadn't left an easy trail to follow, the proper authorities were notified. Gram flew down to hold vigil with Violet in Sunny Isles, but being so many miles away was torture for both of them, with no reason to think Finn and Bear were still nearby. After the first forty-eight hours, the Florida authorities agreed that it made sense for Violet to come home, and the FBI field office in Asheville took the lead on the investigation. They had already searched the home and the computers, but there was more digging to be done — so many questions to ask and so many people to ask them of — and Violet was of more use back in North Carolina.

Caitlin had immediately driven down to be with her there, and of course the FBI had wanted to talk with Caitlin too. Surely there would have been signs that the marriage was off track. Caitlin told them that she believed Violet when she said she was blindsided, and that she was just as mystified herself. This wasn't something she could imagine Finn doing. Caitlin had known Finn longer than she'd known Violet, a lot longer. Hell, she'd *encouraged* Finn to pursue Violet, a fact she now wondered if she should regret. But she'd never regretted it before. Finn and Violet were a great couple. She'd been their next-door neighbor and their landlord for years. She had come to know them both so well, to love Violet as if she were an old, dear friend too. If their night-and-day proximity and mutual fondness for Finn hadn't ensured their friendship, being pregnant at the same time had. Caitlin had given birth to the twins only weeks before Violet had Bear. The ordeal Violet had gone through then, the way Finn had held vigil at her side in that hospital room — it was impossible to imagine Finn doing this just a few short years later. What could possibly bring him to want to leave Violet, let alone take their child from her? Violet was the kind of mother every child deserved. And Finn was that kind of father. None of it made sense.

Caitlin had gone into the interview hoping

that her testimony would help Violet, would swing the agents to be more sympathetic toward her. But afterward she had the feeling that the FBI felt them both to be naïve, stupid women, either suckers or people with something to hide.

It was not a good feeling for her, so she couldn't even imagine how it must have made Violet feel.

She could only hope that where agents in Cincinnati were doing due diligence, seeking out Finn and Violet's former friends and neighbors, George's testimony would carry good weight. In politics, where the bar for an expected level of corruption was set embarrassingly low, his family's reputation was gold — almost beyond scrutiny. Maybe after talking with George, the beloved and respected senator's son, the agents would be satisfied enough to leave Violet well enough alone and focus wholly on finding Finn's trail and bringing Bear home.

The long days in Asheville were beyond awful. Caitlin felt useless, sitting at the table with Violet's grandmother, eating but not really tasting the food brought by friends — mostly Gram's neighbors from her 'independent living' center — while Vi herself lay upstairs in Bear's bed and sobbed. Caitlin and Gram took turns shooing away the few curious reporters who came by, but that didn't last long — apparently people were running off with their own kids so often that it wasn't sensational enough to draw much interest. There was some light local coverage in both North Carolina and Florida of the curious claim of the midvacation abduction,

29

but without real reason to think Bear was in danger, let alone a description of a vehicle Finn might be driving, the FBI couldn't even file an AMBER Alert. Caitlin wasn't used to being unable to *do something* to help a friend in need. She found it maddening.

Eventually, she thought she might busy herself by giving the place a good thorough cleaning, but Violet stopped her in a panic of flailing arms, shrieking that she was 'going to scrub Bear out.' The only helpful thing she'd let her do was to log on to the bank account to pay the household bills. Finn hadn't withdrawn any unusual sums before disappearing — only five hundred dollars the day they'd left for vacation, which Violet said was the amount they'd agreed they should have on hand while traveling. He hadn't withdrawn anything since. Caitlin paid the electric and the cable, but looking at the ordinary evidence of her friends' ordinary domestic lives made her feel sick. She logged off as quickly as she could, making a mental note to talk with George about lending Violet some money. Gram had already offered what savings she had as a reward for information that would lead to Bear's return. The hotel and air charges from Violet's ill-fated trip were steep, and without Finn, no paychecks would be coming in.

Caitlin left feeling ashamed of the relief that washed over her when she was belted safely in her car and pointed toward home. Caitlin and the twins had worn a path to Asheville since Violet and Finn had moved there, visiting as often as they could, usually when George was out of town, but that afternoon, she cut a full thirty minutes off her usual drive time. Caitlin ran through the door and engulfed the boys in a hug so hard they cried out in protest. 'Too hard, Mommy! You hug too big!'

'There's no such thing as hugging too big,' she told them, tears in her eyes, and then she gave each one a giant bowl of ice cream like the one Violet had told her, sobbing, that she never got the chance to give Bear that afternoon.

And now here she was back at the office. Trying to shake off the unshakable concern for her friends and move on with what was supposed to be her normal routine. Because it was the only thing left to do.

Caitlin reached her oversized cubicle and plopped down her bag, a large Louis Vuitton that George had given her last Christmas, and that she'd unintentionally and yet inevitably abused by accumulating a mess of Goldfish cracker crumbs and dried-up hand-wipes that formed a layer along the silk bottom beneath the stuff she was actually meant to be toting around in a designer purse. She turned on her cute purple mini-Keurig — another gift from George, though he would have cringed if she'd dared to bring the thing into their stainless-steel-and-gray-granite kitchen — and booted up her computer.

Even George — perhaps especially George — did not really understand why she felt the need to keep this job when he easily made enough money to give her and the kids anything they could want. Not to mention the trust his parents had set up for him, the sole heir of the Bryce-Daniels legacy. It *was* rewarding to be the brainchild behind so many fund-raisers, and she *did* love event planning, but not as much as she let on. There was no way to explain to George that she found the prospect of being one hundred percent dependent on him so terrifying that the fear got her through the aching goodbyes at the day care four mornings a week. The nonprofit was modest but well loved — it helped provide after-school programs in art and music for schools that had lost their arts funding — and George had to admit that her involvement wouldn't hurt their image if and when he decided to follow in his father's footsteps and run for office. So she'd dropped down to a reduced schedule as a compromise after the boys were born. Her assistant, Tim, was sharp enough to fill in the rest. The only loss at work she'd truly suffered was her glass-walled office; employees who were not technically full time could not take up the limited spaces available with actual doors that closed. And so she'd been sent out to pasture in the cubicle farm.

'You're back!' Tim had gossip in his eyes as he made himself at home in the guest chair positioned across from her desk. 'How's Violet? Oh my God. You have to tell me.'

Tim knew Violet from the few times she'd popped into the office with Bear to see Caitlin at lunch, and from the big annual Christmas party George and Caitlin threw for everyone they knew. He loved her, as much as anyone can love someone else he doesn't actually know that well. Everyone loved Violet in that way, really. Still, Tim had once confided to Caitlin that he made a point of staying on top of office gossip 'to fit in with the other secretaries' — no one was supposed to call them that, but if they said it themselves, so be it — since he was the only nonfemale with the job title in the office. As if they wouldn't all have been lining up to have a fun, gorgeous, young gay friend anyway.

Caitlin shot him a look. Of course the fact that she'd taken time off unexpectedly to go help a friend whose husband seemed to have left her and kidnapped their child — in the midst of their vacation — would send ripples of chatter and speculation around. But she wasn't going to add to the displaced pain and guilt she already felt by humoring Tim with fuel for the fire.

'She's awful,' she told him. 'Devastated. Obviously.'

'Oh my God. Obviously.'

He leaned forward for more, but Caitlin just rotated her desk chair to type in her login and password, then turned back to him and pulled a face. 'I don't want to know how many e-mails I have waiting for me. I didn't check my in-box even once.'

She could see him masking his disappointment at the change of subject. 'You? Not at all? Impressive.'

'Well, I don't know why it made me so nervous, but the fact that the FBI had to have been monitoring their Wi-Fi — ' Damn it. She hadn't meant to bring the topic back.

'The FBI? Oh my God.'

There was a collective sighing of power strips and overhead air vents as the electricity blinked out. Caitlin said a silent thank-you to the storm.

Tim cursed under his breath. Somewhere along the line, he'd been designated as the guy to deal with these sorts of issues — assessing snow emergency levels for early dismissals during the winter, calling in the fire department for wayward alarms, reporting dollars and coins eaten by the vending machine — probably because he was, in fact, the only nonfemale in the office with his administrative job title. 'I'll call Duke Energy. Or the building manager. Or whoever the hell I'm supposed to call.' He took his cell out of his pocket and vanished from Caitlin's space as quickly as he'd arrived.

By the time he came back, the storm had passed and the office was full, everyone milling around grumbling and fiddling with their cell phones. Caitlin could pick out the ones who didn't have anything important to do that day and were excited by the power outage, and the ones who were starting to border on panic. She probably should have been in the latter camp, but since she hadn't opened her e-mail yet, she figured ignorance was bliss.

'Listen up, people,' Tim announced, cupping his hands around his mouth. 'They don't think they're going to have it back on for hours. Maybe the whole day. Half the township is out. I called the building manager, and he recommended we close the office.'

The crowd disbursed with remarkable speed,

Caitlin gathered up some paperwork from her desktop, mainly just for show. A day with the kids after nearly a week away — what an unexpected gift! She glanced at her watch, They'd just be starting circle time — their favorite part of the morning, And George hadn't kept up too well with the groceries while she was gone. She suspected the twins had had more than their fill of pizza, Maybe she should hit the grocery store first, She could stock up on the basics, swing by home to unload, maybe throw in some laundry for good measure, and then go get the kids. They ate lunch early, around eleven, and she figured she could get there right beforehand. If the sun made an appearance by then, maybe they could hit a drive-thru and set up camp at a picnic table next to their favorite playground at Ault Park. It wouldn't be crowded on a weekday — they'd be thrilled to have the run of the place without having to take turns on the steering wheels or stand in line for the swirly slide.

Caitlin felt almost guilty about planning the day with her boys when Violet was stuck wondering if she'd ever see Bear again. She hoped Violet knew that if she still lived next door, Caitlin would be there for her every moment that she needed someone. But Violet's home was six hours away now, and she knew as well as Caitlin did that once you became a mom, kids came first. No matter how tragic everything else might sometimes seem.

★ ★ ★

Caitlin was unloading a ridiculous amount of shredded cheese and yogurt into her fridge — the boys ate it as fast as she could buy it — when she heard something upstairs. A sort of scuffling, She froze, acutely aware of her body's fight-or-flight response in action. The muscles in her neck tensed and her heart hurried its pace as she strained to hear. Had she imagined it?

No, there it was again — and a soft thud this time. She'd heard that the majority of home break-ins happened in broad daylight. Had she walked in on one? She certainly hadn't been quiet coming in, grunting as she'd dropped the twenty-four-packs of bottled water on the floor and noisily piling the plastic bags onto the counters and the island.

She grabbed her cell phone, just in case, and crept in the direction of the stairs. She didn't want to be the dumb woman in the horror movie who doesn't leave while she has the chance. But she also didn't want to overreact. It could have been nothing. Or maybe not nothing, but just a little something. A squirrel, in through the chimney? A work crew outside causing a racket that sounded closer than it was?

Then, as she reached the bottom of the stairs, she was certain she heard it: a giggle. A child's giggle, followed by some very agitated scolding that sounded to be coming from an adult male. A child came into view above, and Caitlin stopped short, stunned.

'Auntie Caitlin!' he yelled, and charged down the stairs and threw his arms around her neck.

'Bear!' Tears filled her eyes as she gripped him

as if he were her own. But how . . . She lifted her gaze and there, leaning against the upstairs hallway and looking defeated, was Finn.

'Finn! Oh, thank God.' Relief cascaded over her. 'What are you *doing* here?'

He held up a house key, one she recognized having given him years ago. 'We needed a shower,' he said in an unapologetic tone that was decidedly un-Finn, He was challenging her with his eyes, and her relief began to be displaced by an unsettled feeling that was not unlike real fear. 'You might have gathered that this is not a social call.'

Caitlin's smile faded.

4

AUGUST 2010

Being dateless for George and Caitlin's wedding wasn't a surprise to Finn. He'd never planned on taking a date, and hadn't much cared — right up until there was a specific woman he found himself wanting to have by his side, and there wasn't a damn thing he could do about it. The fact that he caught himself standing on the edge of the dance floor trying to picture what the woman from the beach might have worn to this white-light-strung evening under the stars, imagining what she might have felt like in his arms as the swing band played, *that* was the part that surprised him. What an idiot he'd been not to at least have gotten her name. All that talk about Camp Pickiwicki and not once had he bothered to ask — it was his own fault, really. He should have known better, that anything could happen at any time to derail things. If losing his parents one after the other so soon after college had taught him anything, that was it.

Caitlin had been the one to step forward and help pick up the pieces then — his male friends were relatively useless in emotional scenarios, which he understood but still couldn't help privately resenting just a *little* — and he knew he owed her wedding his full attention now. But

he'd never had much control over his daydream-
ing, and she was used to it. Gorgeous in a fitted
lace designer gown that George's family had to
have footed the bill for, breathless from dancing,
giddy with happiness, she pulled Finn aside to
chide him playfully. 'You're creative,' she told
him. 'If anyone can devise a way to locate a
mystery woman, it's you. Just devise it tomorrow,
would you? You've been standing here spaced-
out for the entire set.'

He was hopeless. For two weeks now, he'd
been unable to stop thinking about that
encounter on the beach, to stop looking for her
everywhere he went. By the time he'd managed
to locate the sick woman's husband and return
with him to the lifeguard, the ambulance was
gone, and his fellow good Samaritan with it. The
poor husband ran off in such a panic that Finn
wasn't able to ask if he might ride along. It was a
long jog back to the penthouse George had
rented — Finn must have wandered well over a
mile down the beach earlier that afternoon
before being pulled to a halt by that familiar
yellow T-shirt — and by the time he retraced his
steps, begged the keys to the group's shared
rental car, and made his way to the hospital, the
woman he'd felt so instantly drawn to was gone.

'She asked about you, though,' the husband
told him. When Finn finally came across him in
the waiting room, he was less distraught,
apologetic for having left the beach without so
much as a thank-you, and Finn looked at the
little boy asleep in the man's lap and brushed his
apologies away.

She had asked about him. Well, that was something. But it didn't help.

He knew she lived somewhere in the Cincinnati area, but what had always struck him as a relatively small city suddenly seemed impossibly vast. Whenever he had a moment to himself — sitting in traffic, waiting for a takeout order, riding his road bike, flipping through the channels on his couch alone at night — he ran over and over their conversation, looking for some clue he might have missed to help him find her. But there wasn't even a hint of what she did for a living, what kind of neighborhood she lived in, how she spent her time, anything. Just as bad, he could not think of anything he'd told her that might have allowed *her* to find *him*, if she were so inclined. How was it possible that they'd managed to have such a real connection and yet found out so little about each other?

Finn was used to returning home from vacations dreaming about going back to wherever he'd been. But this time, all he could think of was trying to find that piece of the beach that was somewhere here in Ohio with him.

The wedding ended in a blur of tossed flower petals and downed champagne, Caitlin and George left for their honeymoon, and normal life resumed, as it always seemed to. Finn's college friends had been systematically relocating to other cities since graduation — it never took much to lure bright-eyed young adults away from Cincinnati, so long as they were romantically unattached — and aside from Caitlin he mostly hung out with coworkers these days. Or with himself. There was a fine line, it turned out, between being a dreamer and being a loner. He minded it only sometimes. The week dragged by, and when a group at the graphic design firm where he worked took their summer interns out for a good-bye happy hour, Finn went along. Anything beat another solo Friday night at home. He wasn't entirely sure the students were all twenty-one, but the bartenders knew Finn and his coworkers brainstormed projects here after hours, and they weren't about to start carding people at a work function. Two pints in, Finn confessed his trouble.

'Dude,' said one of the interns prophetically. He was a frat guy type who spent his lunch breaks smoking in the parking lot and talking self-importantly on his Bluetooth. Finn had been unimpressed. 'Craigslist, dude.'

'I'm not looking for a cheap couch,' Finn said, trying to refrain from rolling his eyes. 'Or a cheap date.'

But another intern — Amanda, their hardest worker of the summer, one who'd actually helped to cover for Finn while he was in Sunny Isles — brightened. 'Craigslist's Missed Connections, he means! That's brilliant.'

Finn hated these moments when he felt out of touch. Surely he wasn't *that* old, was he? He still stayed up all night sketching some weekends, drinking Red Bull and smoking pot. He always went to the MidPoint Music Festival, and knew all — well, *most* — of the must-see bands. He didn't tuck in his shirts. 'Never heard of it,' he admitted.

The students talked over one another in their excitement to explain the wonders of the Missed Connections page, as if they'd stumbled upon a senior citizen who had never heard of Facebook. (Not that Finn was *on* Facebook — the whole principle appealed a lot less once you'd hit the find-out-who-your-friends-are crossroads of being orphaned — but he knew what it *was*.) The idea of placing a personal ad of sorts for a person you'd missed sounded simple enough. They recounted the legendary posts that occasionally went viral for their cluelessness or their poetry.

'Have you ever answered one?' he asked the group.

A chorus of nos was punctuated by an 'I wish!' Blood rushed to Amanda's cheeks.

'So people actually read these things?'

The students looked around at one another and sort of collectively shrugged.

'Right.' This time, he went ahead and rolled his eyes.

'What do you have to lose, though?' It was Amanda again, smiling hopefully.

'Dude, if no one answers, so what? You don't, like, post it under your full name. No one has to know it's you. Besides, you got a better idea?'

Finn did not. Still, he waited a few days, until the students were all back on campuses far-flung across the state, in hopes that they'd forgotten about the conversation thoroughly enough to *not* get curious and check the Cincinnati Craigslist Missed Connections page. The last thing he needed was these kids passing the post around to their roommates, laughing at how pathetic he was, boasting about how he hadn't even known what the page was until they'd told him. Finn believed in . . . well, not karma, exactly, but vibes. Good ones. He wanted the universe on his side.

Finally, on a night when the rain pelted his windows in sheets and his beer tasted like liquid courage, Finn sat down at his computer and drafted a post.

You on the beach in the Camp Pickiwicki shirt: If you're reading this, the third coincidence is the charm. Care to pick up where fate left off? My name is Finn, by the way. It's pretty obvious by now that I should have told you that.

If he had posted that, just as it was, everything would have turned out differently.

But he didn't. And it didn't.

Because as he was about to click the post through, something held him back. The words had sounded right in his head. They sounded like him. But maybe his voice wouldn't come across on-screen. Maybe she'd think he was being flippant, more friendly than romantically interested, not as genuine as he felt. Maybe he should try to be a little more romantic, less open to interpretation. Besides, maybe those interns wouldn't forget to check. They'd spot his name right away. So he wrote instead:

If you are an attractive young woman who recently returned from a vacation during

43

which you had a conversation with a stranger that ended rather abruptly, through extenuating circumstances beyond your or his control, causing that stranger to seriously question his mental wherewithal not to have gotten your name the first chance he got, then you might be the woman I can't stop thinking about, and I may be that stranger.

It wasn't the most natural-sounding thing in the world, but at least it was clear that he was being flirty, not interested in a brotherly sort of way.

He clicked Publish; he told himself there was no possible way that she would see it anyway. He went to bed.

For the next seventy-two hours, he checked his in-box obsessively, keeping his smartphone on full volume so that he'd be sure not to miss the chime announcing the arrival of what could be *the e-mail* he was waiting for. Nothing. Each time he saw that it was empty, his heart sank a little. Why did his hopes always manage to get up even when he tried not to let them? And then, on the fourth day, he awoke to find, to his complete amazement, a brief message sent through the anonymous Craigslist e-mail relay:

Okay, stranger, I'll bite. Let's see if I am your me and you are my you. Fountain Square, Saturday, 7:00?

5

AUGUST 2016

How many times had Violet sat or lay in Bear's bed with her arms wrapped around him, her fingers tousling his hair, a book open on their laps, his fortress of stuffed animals walling them in on three sides? She pulled them all around her now as she curled up as tight as she could under his Thomas the Train comforter, squeezing her eyes shut against the unstoppable tears as she tried to conjure something of him. She missed his little boy smell, always a bit sweet and a bit sour. His tiny, infectious laugh. His slow breathing when he'd only just drifted off to sleep, so dramatic that she often suspected at first that he was faking. His soft singing along with the old-timey songs she liked to sing as lullabies, 'Time After Time,' 'All of Me,' 'Moon River,' 'Walkin' After Midnight.' The faint tinkle of him calling 'Mommy' from another room.

Oh, God. Was he calling for her, crying for her now? She felt so helpless, it was all she could do not to claw the hair out of her own scalp, not to scream and scream until she had no voice left, not to heave her sobs deeper and deeper into his pillow until she couldn't breathe. Low, sorrowful moans escaped her as she clutched her fists around wads of blanket and clenched the stuffed dalmatian and alligator puppet and train pillow and polar bear and all the other remnants of her son that failed to comfort her but that she could not resist holding because she had nothing else to hold. It hurt, dreadfully, being surrounded by his things. She might have managed to get a bit more sleep — any sleep, really — in her own bed. But lying here seemed like a protest, a prayer, sent out into the universe, *I am supposed to be with Bear*, she was saying. *Bear is supposed to be with me.* Every hour of the day or night that she wasn't curled up here in Bear's place — and those hours were as few as she could make them, though Gram was starting to get more insistent about propping her up, marionetting her through the motions of a human being's day — she felt as if she was ticking down the minutes until she could return. She wanted only to bury her head and focus every bit of her energy back on the useless task of wishing with all of her heart that she would wake up to find that this was all just a bad dream.

The *physicality* with which Violet missed Bear was the most unbearable component of her pain. She felt his absence like a phantom limb. He had been cut from her without anesthesia, the act as shocking and abrupt as it was absolute, and her wound was laid so bare for the world to see that amputation didn't seem like a far-fetched comparison. She felt the space where he used to be as an emptiness that could not be described as mere yearning or longing. It was painful. It was ugly. It was unnatural. And yet in spite, of how horrifying it was, in spite of the fact that she felt nothing *but* his absence whether she was awake or asleep, somehow her cruel subconscious mind could not stop from a hundred times a day turning her head to look for him, tuning her ear to listen for him, or opening her mouth to speak to him before realizing with a start that he was not there.

She'd gone from being a full-time mom to being a mom who was unable to actively mother. She was acutely aware that *mother* was both a noun and a verb, and left without the ability to take action, the reality struck her that it was no longer possible to be who she was without Bear. Not even a little bit. Not even for a moment, let alone days, a week — how long would it be? How long could she go on this way? How long could Bear? How long could Finn?

She'd once read a description of new motherhood that had struck her, at the time that she was returning to work after maxing out her maternity leave allowance, as a beautiful metaphor for her own days back at the office. It was that mother and baby are like a ball of yarn, and when the mother leaves the baby's side, it's as if the baby grabs hold of the loose end, a tug that both mother and baby feel in their every fiber. As they both move through the hours spent apart, the string unravels more and more, and then just when each is starting to feel diminished, barely even a ball of yarn at all anymore, it's time for the mother to make her way back. Together again, they need only a bit of time to wind the string back up, and then it's as if they had never been apart, right up until they wake up and do it all over again.

Whenever Violet had picked up the infant Bear from day care, he always wanted to nurse first thing when they got home, even if he'd just had a bottle. She'd thought of this as Bear's way of winding the string back up. Where had she read that? She was almost certain it had been in a novel. She always had preferred fiction — a fact that had not struck her as grounds for self-analysis until precisely now.

As Bear became a toddler, Violet thought less and less of that metaphor. But now she knew that it wasn't something they'd outgrown. Because Violet was completely, unequivocally unwound. And the only thing worse than being unwound herself was the knowledge that wherever Bear was, he had to be unwound too. Where did he think she was? Did he understand that she couldn't get to him — not that she wouldn't, but that she *couldn't?* What had Finn told him? She'd read online that a lot of parental abductions involved the abducting parent informing the child that the other parent was dead. She couldn't imagine Finn being so cruel as to do that to either Bear or her. But then again, she couldn't imagine Finn being so cruel as to take Bear from her at all.

She had conducted her own investigation, of course, left to her own devices within the walls of their home. But they hadn't lived here long enough to amass much to go through. The fact that her husband had not brought to their relationship much in the way of worldly artifacts, and did not lead much of a digital life, had never struck her as anything other than a part of his character. Having lost his parents in showstopping medical emergencies, he'd had to sell the house where he grew up, along with, nearly everything in it, to pay the bills not covered by insurance. His relatives, all of them distant, tried to help, but his independent streak brushed them away. A recent college graduate at the time, apartment bound, he hadn't had room to hang on to possessions for sentimental reasons in any case. He loved the outdoors; he loved art; he had what he needed to be happy even when he had nothing at all. He spent too much of his days at the computer screen to spend his nights there too. He was not overly social beyond his close, trusted circle, and so why *would* social media have appealed? She had loved her husband not in spite of but in part *because* of these qualities. She resented the implication that she should have ever thought them strange.

The not knowing why he had done this or where he had gone was enough to make her feel as if she might be on the verge of something essential coming loose in her mind. And of course she couldn't let that happen. Bear would need her. Bear *did* need her. She knew it as sure as she knew that her husband was not at all the man she had thought he was.

6

AUGUST 2010

Long shadows stretched across Fountain Square as the sun streamed hazily between the high-rise buildings from its position sinking lower in the sky. The tall bronze statues showering the brick and stone with mist always reminded Finn of the iconic fountain in Savannah's Forsyth Park, and he caught himself pining for the Spanish moss-lined squares of the historic district there, instead of this one in the decidedly unatmospheric Midwest. It had become a bad habit, wishing things away, longing to be somewhere else. He reminded himself that he was here in search of someone who just might help him break it. He didn't know if he could shake it on his own. He suspected that having become so entirely on his own was part of the problem.

Finn had been hoping she'd wear the Camp Pickiwicki shirt again — he hadn't exactly been worried he wouldn't recognize her without it, but he hadn't exactly been confident he would either. Now that he was here, though, he felt certain the woman from the beach was not among the people milling about or perching around him. None of them remotely resembled her. He pressed the button to illuminate his cell phone screen: 7:20. Traffic had been awful for some unknown reason, but still, it struck him as out of character that she'd be more than twenty minutes late. He immediately recognized the thought as ridiculous. Of course he knew nothing about her character. Why would he feel like he did?

He'd been so optimistic. But he suddenly felt certain that she wasn't coming. Damn. Damn, damn, damn. There was always the more direct Camp Pickiwicki ad — he could try that one. But if the woman from the beach ever looked at the Missed Connections, she would have surely recognized their meeting in the ad he *had* placed. For the thousandth time, he cursed himself for not getting her name while he had the chance. And then he vowed that this would be the last time he'd *what if* the whole thing, period. It had seemed so meant to be — if anything was meant to be, wasn't that it? — but clearly he'd been wrong. He'd tried. There was no forcing these things.

A server carried a tray of sweating, foam-topped pints through the outdoor seating area of the Rock Bottom Brewery behind the fountain, and Finn eyed them with a sudden and intense thirst. He wasn't above sliding onto a barstool alone as long as a baseball game played on the flat-screens suspended behind the bar. There was just the small matter that if the woman from the beach was not here, that meant someone else was probably here in her place. He had two options: He could slink away and wallow in his disappointment, or he could figure out who else in the square seemed to be waiting and give her the apology he owed her.

Finn had noticed the beautiful figure seated on the far side of the fountain right away, but now he did a double take. She was wearing a sleeveless dress in a large black-and-white floral pattern, a thin red patent leather belt fastened snugly at the waistline, and shiny red heels extending her shapely petite legs. The dress and the way she sat perched on the edge of a stone bench, leaning delicately to the side, all her weight on a slender arm, with her head tilted ever so slightly up, reminded him of a Baz Luhrmann reimagining of a classic film starlet. Her long, dark curls were so glossy they were actually gleaming in the sun.

But she wasn't entirely picturesque. Each time he sneaked a glance at her, she was looking more and more annoyed. Some women might have busied themselves with their cell phone while waiting, but not this one. She wasn't a pretender, he could see that. Still, so intent was she on glaring at the people turning the corners and stepping into the square that she didn't notice his approach.

He stood just to the left of her bench and cleared his throat. 'I don't suppose you're here in response to a Missed Connections ad about meeting on vacation,' he said to the fountain, being careful to avoid looking in her direction.

'Oh, hell. Seriously?' She got to her feet, scowling. 'You know, maybe you could have been more specific.'

'I've been standing here thinking the same thing.'

'Well,' she said, 'better luck next time.'

52

She started off across the square at a surprisingly brisk clip given the height of her heels. 'Wait — ' he called, surprising himself. She turned and raised her eyebrows. He faltered. 'I mean . . . is that it?'

'What, are we supposed to small-talk now about the people we were hoping to meet?'

He cocked his head. 'Kind of. Maybe.'

'No, thanks.'

'I'm sorry.' The apology caught her just as she was about to turn away again. 'I feel awful, ruining your night — '

'Forget it. You didn't ruin anything. It's not even seven thirty.'

'Well, wasting your time, I mean.' Her anger was making him feel worse. Like he needed to fix it. 'Why don't you let me buy you a drink?'

'Are you seriously taking this opportunity to hit on me?' She squinted at him with exaggerated suspicion. 'Did you even meet a woman on vacation at all? Is this, like, your thing? Placing vague ads and waiting to see who shows up?'

'If that were my strategy, it would be a pretty painful one. I can see that it doesn't work.'

'It does not.'

He gestured across the square with his arm. 'All I'm saying is that we're here — ' She was right. It did sound pitiful. He didn't really mean it, anyway. This woman was way out of his league. And she was missing a certain faded mustard yellow T-shirt. He let the arm drop to his side with a clumsy slap. 'You know what, never mind.'

'Excuse me?' Finn turned to see a well-dressed older woman smiling at them. 'I hate to see such an attractive couple argue. Would the two of you happen to like some LumenoCity tickets? It might brighten up your night. You know, literally!' She giggled at her own joke.

Finn was about to politely decline when a voice at his side spoke up. 'LumenoCity? They ran out of tickets months ago! I entered the lottery over and over, but I never win anything.' Finn stole a glance at his companion. She was smiling angelically at this random stranger and seemed to be emphatically avoiding Finn's eyes.

'Oh, me either,' the stranger said, fingering the sheer wisp of a scarf tied at her neck. 'I mean, does *anybody* win those things? But my husband got a four-pack through his company, and the couple who was meeting us here to come along just bailed. It seems they got in an argument on the way.' She smiled. 'Must be something in the air tonight.'

'I can't even begin to thank you,' said the woman at Finn's side, looping her arm through his. 'We were just trying to decide what to do with ourselves tonight. We would *love* to go. In fact, you've settled our argument!'

Finn looked down at her, bemused. The stranger extended her arm with two tickets fanned out. 'My pleasure. When my other friends find out about this, they're going to be sick that they missed out. *Sick!* But there's no way any of them could get down here in time. Traffic is slow clear to I-275.'

Finn felt an elbow jab him in the ribs, 'Well,

thank you for your kindness,' he said quickly. 'We promise to enjoy it on their behalf!'

As the woman waved and headed off, Finn noted that the arm looped through his did not take the first opportunity to move away. 'What,' he said under his breath, 'is LumenoCity?'

7

Bear clung to Caitlin with his full body, legs and all, the way her own boys did when they were hurt or scared. She tilted her head to get a better look at his face. He did not look like a boy who had been sleeping well. His eyes and cheeks had the same puffy look as Violet's when she'd last seen her. And even though he was smiling bravely, she sensed that if she said the wrong thing, he could dissolve into tears. She thought of how Gus would go silent when he was confused or unsure about something. About how Leo would get that wide-eyed, innocent look.

'Is Mommy here?' he asked, looking at her expectantly.

'Not right this minute, sweetie, but if she knew you were here, I promise you she would be.'

'Is she *going* to be here?' he asked.

Caitlin could feel Finn's warning look without even glancing at him. 'I sure hope so,' Caitlin said carefully. 'Your mommy misses you so much.'

He pouted at her. 'I want to tell Mommy about the bus. And the train! I thought she would be at the station, but then Daddy made us get a new car instead.'

Bear was pretty sturdy — not to mention 'almost comically' articulate, as George once put it — for a barely three-year-old, but in that instant, he looked every bit the baby he had been when Violet and Finn brought him home from the hospital to their old house next door. Those days when Violet and Caitlin met almost every morning, helping each other through their maternity leaves, seemed so idyllic at the time. She'd heard other women talk about how confining those newborn days had been, how they'd spent long stretches with no reason — and no opportunity — to shower or get out of their pajamas, or paced their neighborhood streets alone with the stroller while everyone else was at work. That hadn't been her experience at all. She and Violet had nurtured their infants together. Sometimes Gram came over to give them a break, and George would instruct Caitlin to treat herself and Violet both to a pedicure or a massage. Once, they'd said they were going to spend an afternoon at the spa and instead had gotten rip-roaringly drunk on tasting flights at a wine bar. It hadn't taken much in those days. They'd sobered up over flat breads, then taken turns at the breast pump in Caitlin's nursery, giggling like teenagers, before heading next door to reclaim the kids.

What could Finn possibly be thinking? Caitlin needed to find out exactly what was going on here. And then she needed to get on the phone with Violet. Immediately.

Caitlin gave Bear her biggest smile. 'Hey, how about you check out Leo and Gus's room? They just got a couple new excavators for their construction site.'

He brightened. 'Diggers?'

'A cement mixer, too. You remember where their room is?' Bear nodded emphatically and raced back up the stairs, past Finn and down the hall.

Finn headed down the steps toward her, and as soon as Caitlin could hear Bear's 'vroom vroom!' and the hard clattering of plastic on plastic, she turned on him. 'What the *hell*?' she exploded. 'Do you know you're being accused of parental kidnapping? *Kidnapping!* Do you know the FBI is looking for you? The *FBI!*'

'I know,' he said flatly, walking past her. She followed him into the kitchen. 'I didn't mean to make such a wreck of things. I messed up.'

'You messed up?' Caitlin could barely contain her rage. 'What were you *thinking*?' she demanded.

'I wasn't,' he said simply, running a hand through his hair. 'It was the damn nap.'

She looked at him blankly, awaiting some sort of translation.

'I just couldn't leave him.'

'No one asked you to! But you could leave Violet? You were meaning to leave Violet?'

Finn opened the refrigerator, removed a can of soda, and popped the top with a hiss of fizz.

Caitlin shook her head. 'It doesn't matter. You can make this right. You just need to take Bear back.'

'That's not going to happen. At least, not yet.'

'What do you mean it's not going to happen? Do you have any idea how absolutely frantic Violet is right now? She's devastated. She can't even get out of bed. Or, more accurately, she can't get out of *Bear's* bed. What rationale could you possibly have for doing this?'

Finn faltered. 'I didn't mean to hurt her this way. I didn't think it through. I just couldn't — ' He caught himself. 'I just *couldn't*.'

'For God's sake, Finn, the woman is catatonic.' Caitlin glared at him, but got no response. 'Well, you have your midlife crisis or whatever it is on your own time. I'm calling her right this instant.'

'No, you're not.'

'Of course I am. What else would you expect me to do? Why are you even here, if not in some kind of sideways attempt to make this right?'

'I need you to set me and Bear up at the lake. At the cabin.'

'George's dad's cabin?' Caitlin stared at him incredulously, and when he nodded, a laugh escaped her lips. 'Right. I'm going to harbor a fugitive at the lake house of my retired senator father-in-law. I'm going to keep my best friend's husband and kid hidden from her while she lies there sobbing, afraid she'll never see her son again. I'm going to keep that sad-eyed boy away from his mother while I tuck my own kids into bed every night.'

'I'm sorry,' he said, and he did genuinely look sorry, 'but yes, you are.'

She gaped at him. 'Because . . . ?'

'Because if you don't, I'm going to tell George.'

'Tell George what?'

'You know, *tell George*.'

It took a moment for what he was implying to register. And when it did, Caitlin felt her blood run cold.

'Tell George *what?*' she tried again, but she knew her eyes had given her away.

'Come on, Caitlin. I was there, remember?'

'You wouldn't,' she said, inflating her voice with false certainty.

'If I have to, I would.'

Caitlin's eyes raced around the kitchen, taking in the signs of her life there — the twins' crayon scribblings held to the dishwasher door with magnets, and their little sippy cups drying in the dish drainer, right next to George's heavy steel coffee carrier mug. How many times had she gone over this room looking for hazards — installing knob covers on the stove, a childproof lever on the oven door, plastic locks on the cupboards and drawers, five-point harnesses on the booster chairs. And now the biggest hazard to her family was standing right here in the middle of it all. 'We've been friends since we were dumb kids in college, forever ago. And now you're going to show up here and threaten to ruin my life? What did I do to deserve that?'

He looked at her sadly. 'Nothing,' he said. 'I really am sorry, Cait. It's the only thing I can think of. It's my only choice. I need someplace safe I can stay with Bear without leaving any credit card records behind. You saw how he is — it's not good for him to be on the road. At first I sold it as an adventure, but he's not buying it anymore. Last summer when we all went to the lake, he loved it there. Nobody would come looking for us. It would just buy me the time I need.'

'To do *what?*'

'To think.'

Around this time last year both families had spent a week at the cabin, just before Finn and Violet moved to Asheville to stay close to Gram, who'd insisted on retiring there. 'What kind of old lady retires in the mountains, where it gets cold and snowy?' Caitlin had complained to Violet. She'd been devastated that her friends were leaving, though of course she understood that they had to go — aside from Bear, Gram was the only family Violet and Finn had between the two of them. 'The awesomely stubborn kind,' Violet had responded fondly. The whole week at the cabin, Caitlin felt like she was grasping at something that was in danger of slipping away, even as the three boys donned their little life vests and fished off the dock with their dads, even as she and Violet motored the pontoon out to the middle of the lake to sunbathe and read, even as they sprawled out with beers on the deck chairs under the stars after the kids were in bed. To her, the cabin would always be a sacred place. Not some kind of twisted hideaway.

'And if I say no, you're just going to wait until George gets home, tell him what you *think* you know that you *think* I wouldn't want him to know, then wait for the police to show up — which they will, because George will call them immediately and put a stop to all this nonsense?

You're going to take me down with you, just because?'

'I'm not going to take you down with me.' For a second, his voice was almost reassuring. 'Because you're going to give me the keys to the cabin. You're going to refresh my memory on the directions so I don't get mixed up on the back roads. And you're going to give me the code to disable the alarm on the security system.' His eyes bored into hers. 'I'll do whatever it takes, Cait. If you think you've seen me desperate before, that was nothing. This is really it.'

'Finn,' Caitlin said as gently as she could, 'you *love* Violet. Violet loves you. And not just in an ordinary way. There was a time not that long ago when if I had to listen to one more person gush about how you two were so destined for each other. I would have puked.' He didn't crack a smile. 'What's this all about?'

Finn looked away, and Caitlin settled herself onto a stool at the island, hoping he might sit down next to her, talk this through rationally. 'This is me, Finn. You can talk to me. I know marriages aren't always what they seem — but Violet is completely blindsided. What on earth happened? Even without the kidnapping charge — kidnapping! — I can't believe you'd have walked out on her at all. You two *were* meant to be.'

He leveled his gaze at her. 'Were we?' He sounded exhausted. Weary. The kind of weary that builds over time. Caitlin studied his face.

'Does it matter? You might think you've fallen out of love with her, or whatever, but she doesn't deserve this. And neither does Bear. He needs his mother. We're going to pick up the phone and call her. It's that easy.' She held out her cell toward him. 'Are you going to do it, or am I?'

Anger sparked in his eyes, and she knew she'd taken the wrong tack. 'Stop talking to me like you're a goddamn hostage negotiator,' he snapped. 'I'm not a crazy person. And stop calling me a kidnapper.' He looked genuinely hurt, even shocked, and she wondered if he was only now processing the gravity of what he'd done. Surely not? 'It's just me and my own kid we're talking about here. My own kid.'

'Also *Violet's* kid.' Caitlin couldn't take it anymore. 'I'm calling your bluff,' she said, swiping her finger to unlock her cell screen.

'You still think George is gearing up for that Senate run?' Finn's voice was eerily calm. 'His old man always did have big plans for him. He wraps up that big Hong Kong deal at the end of the year, and then what?'

Caitlin's thumb hovered over the Call button.

'It would be a shame if he ended up bowing out because something embarrassing came out — personally speaking. I bet that would go over real well with the in-laws. The fact that his wife ruined their lifelong dream for him.'

'I don't care what his family thinks.'

It was such a blatant lie that Finn didn't even grant it a response. He simply continued as if she hadn't spoken. 'And he's already invested so much in the twins' future. He can't have you slink off with them. I don't think the custody battle would be much of a battle, do you? With

63

his family's resources?'

It was a low blow, aimed strategically at the center of Caitlin's insecurity, and they both knew it. 'George loves me,' she said. 'If you insist on telling him, we'll get through it. He'll forgive me.' If only her voice weren't betraying her by trembling so.

Finn strolled to the back door and looked through the glass into the garden. 'You know those questionnaires where they ask you to describe someone or something in a single word? I always hated those, because who can be summed up in one lousy word?'

He turned back toward Caitlin. 'George can, that's who. And that word is *pride*. Heaven help the person who wounds it.'

She glared at him. 'You make him sound infallible. It's not like he's his *father*.'

'Funny you mention his father. He's kind of big on calling in favors, isn't he?'

Blood rushed furiously to her cheeks. 'You would know.'

'I wouldn't use the word *know*. I might have an inkling.' He looked down at the floor. 'But I remember you telling me once that the incident I *think* you're referring to was 'small potatoes' to him, Which leaves me wondering what the big potatoes were, I'm guessing he wouldn't want anyone looking into that, *Especially* if he has his son in mind to take his former seat.'

Her breath was caught in her throat, but she forced herself to speak. 'That would be pretty low of you, Finn. A real nice way to return the favor.'

He shrugged. 'The thing is, Cait. I didn't *ask* you to bail me out then. I probably would have been better off if you hadn't! But I'm asking you now.'

Caitlin squinted at her friend. 'Is this conversation happening? Are you completely not the guy I knew anymore, or have you just been watching too many action movies? I mean seriously, Finn, Blackmail? You? Me? Come on.'

He shrugged. She'd thought she'd seen Finn at his worst, but she'd never known him to be so cold, Suddenly it didn't seem so unimaginable that he'd taken Bear. And if he'd done that, what else might he do? 'After everything I've done for you . . . ' She was shaking, unable to form a coherent thought. 'After everything *George* has done for you . . . '

'That's an excellent impression of what *he's* going to say. To *you*.'

He was standing very close to her now, 'Mark my words, if you don't help me. I *will* tell George the thing we both know you would *strongly prefer* that George not know, I'll rekindle media interest in his father's esteemed political career, And I'll block his golden boy's chance of ever having one.' Her tears burned, and at the sight of them his expression softened. 'Please don't make me,' he whispered. 'I'm *sorry*. I don't have another choice.'

Caitlin's reeling mind grasped for something to hold on to. She had to pull herself together. For the twins, For Violet. For Bear. 'Fine. You want another choice? Money will give you plenty. How much do you need? I can get you cash. I can find a way to do it so that George won't notice.' She hated the sound of the desperation she was unable to keep from her voice. 'You name your price, and you do what you want with it, but you leave Bear here.'

'Bear *is* the price, Caitlin. This is not a negotiation,' The warning tone of his voice was too serious to defy, 'And don't think you can send me off now and then tip off the police. They show up at that cabin — or the FBI does, or Violet herself — and *I will tell George*. I *will* contact the press. No tricks. No bad directions. No wrong security code. This is real to me, and it's real to you, got it?'

She sniffed back tears, trying to hold her head high, 'Say I go along with this — for now — to protect my good name, or George's. And if a kidnapper is discovered hiding out in the family vacation house, that's not going to do any damage?'

Finn nodded, slowly. 'Guess you better make sure we don't get caught.'

A silence fell between them as Caitlin tried to reconcile the weight of the situation before her. 'I still don't understand. *Why* have you taken him?'

'He's all I have,' His voice broke. 'My only family. I just need him with me while I figure this out, okay? I can't be alone.' It wasn't an answer at all, though there was truth in it nonetheless. There'd been a time when seeing sweet, vulnerable Finn lose so much had taken a toll on Caitlin by proxy, when if Finn could have been summed up in one word, it would've been *traumatized*. Or, yes, *alone*. He was right that

66

one word could never really do. But that dark period was years behind him now. Dealt with and done with before Violet, before Bear.

Wasn't it?

'Finn, listen to yourself. He's all Violet has, too. And he's a *child*.'

'And I'm his father. You know I'd never let anything happen to him.' He stepped back, as if they'd settled something. 'Maybe it's true, what people say about us. Maybe you and I have been *too* close over the years. Let's try something new. From here on, you don't interfere in my family, and I don't interfere in yours.'

8

AUGUST 2010

A buzz of collective excitement was making its way across the dusk of Washington Park as Finn and his fellow Missed Connection made their place in the crowd, stretching their legs out in front of them on the blanket he'd overpaid for at a drugstore on the walk here through downtown. They'd managed to procure a purse full of miniature bottles of wine, plastic cups to discreetly pour them into, and grilled cheese with tomato and pesto from a gourmet food truck. Maribel — she'd called her name over her shoulder as they'd made a mad dash across Vine Street against the light — was revealed to be one of those people who are overcome with childlike giddiness the moment they become excited about something. For an instant after the stranger with the tickets left them, he'd wondered if the woman who was not the woman from the beach planned to make off with them on her own, perhaps call a friend. But she'd never acted as if it were a question that they would go together, in spite of the fact that she'd been in the process of dismissing him when the woman cut in. And so, partially out of curiosity and partially because he'd been caught so off guard, he found himself playing along.

Music Hall rose up before them in silhouette,

a massive wonder of historic brick, its arched façade and pointed towers eerie in the darkening sky. 'I hear it's haunted,' he told her, nodding toward the building. 'Built on an old potter's field.' He wasn't much into that sort of thing, just making conversation.

'Everything is haunted,' she said matter-of-factly, unwrapping the wax paper from her sandwich. 'Buildings. People. It all has to do with mistakes, regrets, missed opportunities. Missed *connections*.' Her eyes met his, and she smiled almost shyly. 'They're everywhere.'

Finn raised an eyebrow. He wasn't sure he'd ever known anyone — especially not a date — to be so *what you see is what you get* from the moment he'd met her. Except maybe the woman on the beach. 'What haunts *you*, then?' he asked.

She returned his eyebrow raise with one of her own. 'Nobody talks about the stuff that *really* haunts them,' she said. 'If you're talking about it, on some level you're dealing with it, or at least acknowledging it.' She gestured toward Music Hall. 'If those walls could talk, the stories they'd tell you might make it seem like a *spooky* place, or a *sad* place, or even a *possessed* place, but I'd be willing to bet it would seem less *haunted* as soon as the mystery was gone.'

She seemed to have given this an astounding amount of thought. He wondered what else she had her own theories on. *What an odd bird*, his mother would have remarked. A fabulously odd bird.

The white-and-black-clad mass of the Cincinnati Symphony Orchestra was filing into rows of

69

chairs arranged in a white tent set up in front of the hall. He looked around him at the people covering every inch of grass and pavement and couldn't believe he'd never heard of this event. 'How many tickets do you think they sold?' he asked. 'I mean, assuming the ghosts get in for free.'

'Everyone gets in free,' she explained. 'Tickets are hard to get, but they don't cost anything. Last year was the first year: They decided to put together something over-the-top to welcome the new conductor to town, if you can imagine *all this* happening in your honor' — she gestured emphatically around them with the triangle of sandwich clutched in her hand — 'and it was such chaos they decided they had to do something to limit the crowds. I think I heard it topped out at twenty thousand per performance.'

So this was what twenty thousand people looked like — a sea of faces and running children and lawn chairs and coolers as far as he could see. Surrounding streets were roped off to accommodate the overflow, And he'd been expecting to find the woman from the beach in a city of hundreds of thousands. What had he been thinking? Like Maribel had said, everyone here probably had a missed connection of his or her own, In that light, his encounter on the beach seemed less remarkable. He settled back on the heel of one hand and took a long sip of wine with the other. 'Well,' he said, 'thanks for letting me buy you a drink after all.'

She grinned. 'Thanks for making me look like half of an 'attractive couple.' And sorry if I was

70

rude earlier. I was just, you know . . . '

'I know. Me too.'

'So do you live near here?'

'Northside. I work for a small graphic design firm there.'

'You're kidding.' She brightened. 'I'm a designer too. I work for an ad agency, in an old warehouse down by the river.' She nodded toward the skyline. On the other side, barges and sunset cruises would be lighting up the Ohio River by now as restaurants on the banks came to life. 'It's kind of soul sucking, though — it seems like every job I do lately has to adhere to stringent 'brand standards.'' She made air quotes as best she could with a cup of wine in one hand and a sandwich in the other. 'I've been doing a lot of sketching and painting in my free time to save my sanity.'

Finn was surprised. He could usually sniff out a fellow artist. He'd had Maribel pegged as . . . what, he didn't know, but definitely some kind of other ballpark entirely. 'I'm lucky,' he replied, trying to sound nonchalant. 'We do a lot of signage, and some of it's actually really creative stuff. I draw too, though. Just sketches and line drawings, mostly, but sometimes I can get a client to incorporate them into a project, which is pretty cool.'

'Man,' she said, 'usually I can spot a fellow artist. I was way off.' Finn must have gaped at her speaking his own thoughts aloud, because she laughed. 'I feel like I owe you an apology.'

'For what? Wait — ' Finn held up a hand. 'Never mind. I don't want to know what you

71

thought I was. Apology accepted.'

The violinists were starting to tune their instruments, and the chaotic sounds added a not unpleasant backdrop to the buzz of conversation and laughter around them.

She wrinkled her forehead. 'If you're tapped into the art community. I can't believe you never heard of LumenoCity.'

'I don't come downtown much,' he admitted. 'Sometimes I go to open galleries — Final Fridays and whatnot — but usually just around Northside, Clifton . . . small neighborhoods.'

'I didn't know they *had* galleries in Northside,' she said. 'I've been a downtown girl ever since I moved here from Indianapolis. I guess I never got as familiar with the outlying neighborhoods.'

'I'm always hearing there's a lot of cool stuff happening down here. Reclaiming the bad streets, etcetera. I mean to come. I just — ' Finn could not think of a single actual reason he hadn't. He shrugged. 'Don't.'

Maribel downed the rest of her wine and pulled another miniature cabernet out of her purse. 'Tell you what,' she said, filling his cup. 'Cool stuff we know about. I'll show you mine if you show me yours.' They drank to it. 'I have to admit, though,' she said, 'I'm not sure I'm married to the place. Long term. I mean.'

'Where would you rather be?'

'Asheville. North Carolina. Have you been?'

He nodded, closing his eyes to conjure the Blue Ridge Mountains rising all around him, the low-lying clouds, the crisp air, the sidewalks filled with people who seemed to be living

72

exactly the life he wanted to be living. About five and a half hours away, Asheville was one of Cincinnati's most popular road-trip destinations. If you weren't aiming for a bigger hub like Chicago or Pittsburgh, it was one of the rare jewels you could drive to in an afternoon — but he didn't just love it the way other people loved it. He went for a weekend every time he got the chance. Made a point of stopping for a day en route to anywhere farther east or south, too.

'Just to be part of a community like that, one that appreciates art, lives art — .' Maribel sighed. 'I mean, I'd probably be in danger of becoming a total hippie, but I'd love to live there one day. And do you know Asheville is in, like, the top five U.S. cities for days of sunshine? I don't know who's in the bottom five, but my money's on Cincinnati.'

Finn laughed. 'I've thought about moving there too. Something about those mountains. It's like food even tastes better.'

'Because it is better. Their restaurants all seem to be locally sourced, organic — '

'And there's this little Irish pub where they have bluegrass and rockabilly and serve local beer — '

'Jack of the Wood! I go every time I visit, because I always end up cheaping out and staying at this fleabag motel on that end of town . . . '

'The Edge Inn!'

'Oh my God. Yes, the Edge Inn. I can't believe I'm admitting to you that I've slept in that place. You're going to think I have syphilis.'

73

'Well, in your defense — and mine, actually — it's slim pickings if you don't want to have to catch a pricey cab ride to your hotel. I just make sure I'm good and drunk by the time I turn in, and then run like hell at daybreak.'

She laughed. 'Sounds familiar. I think we'd make good travel companions.' She averted her eyes and shifted a little on the blanket, and he couldn't tell if she was regretting that she'd said it, or hoping he'd say it back.

'Well, now you've got me jonesing for a Green Man Porter from Jack of the Wood,' he said, choosing neutral ground.

'I know where you can get a fairly similar one around here. I could show you, if this doesn't let out too late . . .'

He grinned. 'Are you trying to get me drunk? Is this, like, your thing? Meeting guys from the Internet and then getting them drunk?' She punched his arm.

The darkness had settled in thickly around them by now, and the crowd was starting to quiet down. The idea that a night out with Maribel stretched before him filled Finn with warmth, and he felt himself relaxing, letting go of all the expectations he'd brought into the evening. It seemed so natural to be sitting with her this way. He couldn't remember the last time he'd felt so at ease with a stranger. Well, maybe he could. It had to have been that day in Sunny Isles. Still, this was different. It was almost —

The tent lit up in a brilliant soft white-yellow, and a hush fell over the park. Then came the opening notes as the entire exterior of Music

Hall was at once illuminated. Maribel reached over to refill his wine and clicked the lip of her cup to his. And then it began.

'It's a laser light show,' Maribel had explained back in Fountain Square. 'It uses the Music Hall as its canvas, while the symphony plays.' It sounded kind of cheesy. But this was no zigzag of neon lasers — it was itself a work of art, a complicated projection and optical illusion composed by teams with an ear for harmony and an eye for the spectacular. And the building was no canvas. As the music picked up tempo, the lights transformed the brick façade into a living, breathing thing, a larger-than-life kaleidoscope set into motion. The circular stained-glass window in its center became the spinning, twinkling focal point as all around it the building itself seemed to twist, dance, bounce, sway, then magically crumble to the ground and just as quickly reassemble itself. The crowd oohed and ahhhed, cheered, breathed as one, and finally surrendered to the genius and the beauty of the animation.

For a full ten minutes of Tchaikovsky, the lights and music sustained their dance, and then after thunderous applause, whistling, and hollering, it started up again. Finn managed to pull his eyes away to glance over at Maribel, and was almost as mesmerized by what he saw across the blanket from him. Her face was illuminated with a rosy glow from the lights and lasers, her gaze filled with a look of pure awe and contentment that mirrored his own. Even as he reminded himself that he'd only just met her, and that he'd come here intent on finding someone else, he could suddenly see, clear in his mind's eye, him and Maribel together — sharing morning coffee over their sketchpads in a sunny Asheville kitchen, sitting on their porch swing looking out over the mountains, partnering up to start their own graphic design firm right from home, walking arm in arm to local cafés, coming home at night and making love, and all the while marveling that everything they'd ever wanted was right there between them and around them.

It was unlike Finn to act before thinking it through — but the visions seemed so real, so out of nowhere and yet so clear, that before he could stop himself, he leaned over and placed.the point of his finger on her chin, tipped her face toward his, and kissed her softly, slowly on the mouth.

★   ★   ★

Finn was awakened by a headache reminding him that switching from wine to draft beer late in the night was never a good idea. And then he remembered why it had been a good idea anyway. A very good idea.

He opened his eyes. Empty. His bed was empty. The bathroom door was wide open — no one inside. He strained for any sounds of Maribel moving about the apartment but heard nothing except the annoying drone of the raspy old refrigerator he'd been begging his landlord to replace. A few minutes went by, and he was sure. Gone. She was gone. Damn.

He'd known it was too good to be true.

He closed his eyes and felt a smile stretch itself across his lips as he replayed the previous night. The surprise and magic of the symphony and the lights. The beers at the old hole-in-the-wall afterward, where they'd finished the job of getting quite drunk, until their conversation had returned finally to how their night had begun.

'The thing is,' Maribel had said, leaning forward on her barstool confessionally. 'I kind of had a feeling before I came tonight that you might not be the guy.'

'You're kidding.'

'Nope.'

'Then why — '

'I figured a fifty-fifty chance. But I kind of liked the sound of you anyway.'

'Ah. So you weren't that disappointed, then? Could've fooled me.' He grinned, remembering that she'd actually pouted. He'd never been so aware that a grown woman could effectively pout.

'Well, I wasn't sure how disappointed to be at first, so I had to err on the side of caution,' she said. 'Besides, what would you have thought of me if I just kind of shrugged and said, 'Oh, well, you'll do instead'?'

Finn laughed. 'Touché.'

'What about you?' she pressed. 'Were you actually disappointed?'

'Yeah, I actually was,' Finn said, still smiling. It was funny — that man already seemed like someone else now, someone he used to be. 'But, oh well, you'll do instead.'

Neither of them had been too drunk for the

sex to be good. So, so good.

With a sigh, Finn forced himself to swing his legs over the side of the bed. He wasn't even a little bit sorry anymore that she wasn't the woman from the beach. He was just sorry she was gone.

He scanned the rumpled comforter, the floor, the armchair in the corner for some sign of her. A forgotten accessory. A hairbrush. Anything. But every trace of her was gone. It was as if she'd never been there at all.

Coffee. The only thing to do was make a pot of coffee.

Stepping into the kitchen, Finn stopped cold. The carafe of his brewer was already freshly filled, the burner light glowing red. He stepped closer. And there, underneath a clean mug sitting ready for him, was a note with her name, cell phone number, office number, home e-mail, work e-mail, home address, office address, Twitter handle, and Facebook page. At the bottom, she'd written: 'This should be sufficient info not to miss the connection, but other data is available upon request.' He smiled, poured himself a cup, and called Maribel's cell right then.

'What took you so long?' she greeted him.

9

AUGUST 2011

Violet peered into the bathroom mirror, wiping mascara from beneath her eyes with a too-rough, too-thin square of toilet paper. This was officially a new low point, crying over a man at work, of all places, moments before she had to start interviewing candidates for the graphic design job. What a disaster.

She was becoming a pro at breakups by now. They didn't throw her the way they used to, didn't make her question what was wrong with her and wonder if she'd ever catch up to her myriad of engaged and married friends. In fact, she'd almost come to expect them before they happened — and maybe that was part of the problem. But they were usually amicable enough. 'It's just not working out,' or 'The timing isn't right,' or some other cop-out. She would gorge on Ben & Jerry's for a week or two, like a cliché, and at some point have a drunken night of sobbing alone in her apartment, or maybe at a friend's, and then, her ritual complete, she would get over it.

But this one was nasty.

She forced herself not to take the cell phone out of her pocket, not to look at the text message again. It had contained a photo of a naked woman, asleep on her stomach, a sheet draped loosely across her buttocks. She'd instantly recognized Matt's nightstand in the background, the iPod dock alarm clock she'd bought him for his birthday still in its familiar place.

'I'm moving on,' the text had read.

It would have been slightly less cruel if he hadn't sent it in the middle of a workday.

She'd known he was mad at her — she hadn't heard from him since that stupid fight had blown up Friday night. 'Why do I always get the feeling you want me to be someone else?' he'd yelled.

'That's not fair,' she shot back. 'I always go along with everything you want.'

'Yes, you're so damn easy to get along with,' he said. 'Miss Go with the Flow. You think I can't sense your disappointment? You're nodding your head and agreeing, but it's not because you really agree. It's just because *that's what you do.*'

She probably should have conceded the point. In truth, she *had* often wished he was someone else. But she didn't think anything she'd done had warranted *this*. It was *perfectly* awful, Gram would say. Not that she could ever tell Gram something that was also so *perfectly* salacious — and *perfectly* humiliating.

'Are you okay?' Katie poked her head into the bathroom, looking worried.

'Yeah.' Violet sniffed. 'Where do I find these guys?'

'Dicks R Us?'

Violet managed a laugh. She and Katie had worked together for years, and as the only two single women in the office, they'd taken to updating each other on their dating escapades as if it were a hobby. Katie had never been in favor of Matt. Of course, Katie had never been in favor of *anyone* Violet met ever since Violet came back from Sunny Isles Beach and told her the story of Handsome Stranger. Katie was convinced that he was *the* guy for Violet, and that their paths would cross again if only Violet was patient. After all, he lived *somewhere* in the sizable but not planetary Greater Cincinnati area, Outwardly, Violet always brushed this off as beyond unlikely, but in truth it was one of the few things she let herself imagine when things weren't going well — and sometimes even when they were. Her eyes meeting Handsome Stranger's across a crowded bar, Him making his way toward her, weaving through the clusters of people with increasing urgency, and when he finally reached her, engulfing her in an embrace and whispering in her ear. 'I should have done that while I had the chance.'

'Violet,' she'd say before he could ask. 'My name is Violet.'

'If it helps,' Katie said now, 'you have some time to wallow. Your first interview canceled, He called over the weekend, but apparently no one in HR checked the voice mail until now.'

Violet sighed. At least that made time for the puffiness to go down around her eyes, But that still left three interviews scheduled back-to-back, each one forty-five minutes, It was going to be a long afternoon. 'Am I allowed to be relieved? Which candidate was that?'

Katie made an apologetic face. 'The one whose portfolio you liked the best. The amazing typography on the theater signage, with all those hand-drawn elements.'

Violet groaned. 'Great. The only one who wasn't borderline underqualified. Did he say why?'

'He just found out he's going to be relocating for his fiancée's job.'

'It's official. *Everyone* but us is engaged. Even our job candidates.'

'Buck up, little camper. I slipped some of your favorite K-Cups into the conference room. The hazelnut ones.'

'You're the best.'

'You're going to want to be caffeinated when you get off work. I'm taking you out. We need to get you '*moving on.*''

'The only thing I'm moving on to tonight is my couch. With the absolute trashiest thing I can find on TV, and a bag of popcorn in my lap for dinner.'

Katie let it drop. One of the best things about her was that she knew when Violet needed to be left alone.

★   ★   ★

Hours later, back in her office as she listened to the collective sound of her coworkers packing up and chatting as they headed in intervals toward the ding of the elevator, Violet buried her face in her hands. The interviews had gone horribly. One woman had even started crying halfway through Violet's questions.

'I can already tell I'm not going to get it,' she'd

whimpered. 'Damn it. I really, really needed this job.'

She'd been right. She wasn't going to get it. Violet had shared her own pocket pack of tissues with the woman and ended the interview right there. She hadn't had the energy to fake it.

Violet checked her cell — no messages. She felt some last gleam of hope leave her, as if a part of her had been expecting a retraction from Matt. As if something like that photo was even retractable.

Sighing, she clicked through to her in-box and opened the folder of applicants. Maybe she'd overlooked someone who could be called in. Otherwise, it would be back to square one. Starred at the top of her folder was the cover letter and portfolio from the candidate who had canceled. Finn Welsh. Cool name. She'd never known a Finn before.

She opened up the PDF again. After the run of lackluster interviews, his work looked even better than she remembered. It wasn't just that his was the most balanced, the most intricate, the most high concept — there was something in it that she was *drawn* to in a way that felt almost instinctual. Maybe she could ask HR to call him back and dig around a little more, find out what his fiancée's job offer was and if there was anything they could counter in salary or benefits that would make it worth his while to reconsider at least coming in for a face-to-face.

There was a URL to view more of his portfolio online. She hadn't bothered to check it out before — his samples had been all she needed to see. But maybe something on his profile page would clue her in to what might win him over.

The page loaded, a wonder in flash animation, and there as the word cloud faded and the graphics parted to review his bio, she was staring into the eyes of Handsome Stranger.

It had been about a year since that clay on the beach, but she knew him in an instant. She *had* known a Finn before. Finn Welsh. And he'd managed to get himself a fiancée. Or maybe he'd already had one. Maybe — and the thought had never once occurred to her before — *maybe* it hadn't been any accident of fate that they hadn't managed to reconnect that day. Maybe he'd never been looking for anything beyond those moments away from his obligations back home.

Well. It didn't make a difference, did it? That was that.

Still, now that she knew his name, curiosity crept in. She looked for social media icons on his home page, but there were none. She typed his name into a search engine, but all she found were a few design credits here and there. If not through his job application, she could see no way or reason they would have crossed paths at all — not online, anyway.

She went back to the portfolio page and stared at it miserably. She almost wished she hadn't seen it. Now it would never be this mysterious thing that just hadn't worked out. Instead, she'd never again think of him without feeling silly — for a year's worth of farfetched fantasies, for allowing herself to pine over something that he probably hadn't even given a second thought.

If only he hadn't canceled the interview. She imagined herself rising from the conference room table, extending her hand, and looking boldly into his eyes. What might have happened then? What if, fiancée be damned, a part of him had been looking for her too?

But he *had* canceled. And she certainly wasn't going to beg him back in now that she knew who he was. She thought of the humiliation she'd been spared — the eagerness she would have felt when she'd seen his face, the embarrassment of inviting him to coffee after the interview only to be turned down.

Violet wasn't sure how long she'd been sitting there by the time Katie poked her head through the doorway. Her neck felt stiff. Her eyes were dry with fatigue. 'I'm gonna scoot,' Katie said. 'Don't worry — we'll just hold out for more applications. We can keep freelancing stuff out in the meantime.'

Violet couldn't bring herself to answer. Katie frowned. 'You sure you're okay to be alone tonight?'

She cleared her throat. 'I'm thinking of canceling on Jerry and Ben and making plans with Tonic and Vodka instead. You in?'

10

AUGUST 2016

Caitlin sat in the too-stiff antique upholstered armchair that usually went unused in the corner of her family room, her legs crossed awkwardly toward the wall and her glass of chardonnay held as far as she could manage out to her side and away from the action. On the area rug that spanned the gleaming hardwood floor from the couches to the fireplace hearth, the boys were wrestling with George. She'd been in the kitchen doing the dinner dishes, but they kept yelling, 'Watch this move, Mommy!' and 'Daddy, do it again so Mommy can see!' until she gave up and came to perch here, in the only spot she could find that seemed out of the path of destruction but close enough to watch and applaud their every 'point' scored. No matter that she couldn't begin to understand the rules of this utterly masculine game the three of them had devised.

At the moment, George was on all fours roaring like a tiger, one boy hanging from each side of him. He swayed dramatically, as if about to try to shake them off, and they squealed with delight and tightened their grips on his T-shirt.

Caitlin didn't often watch the three of them together this way without thinking about how lucky she'd gotten. Both Gus and Leo had chocolate brown eyes, a complexion that tanned easily — even through the SPF 50+ baby sunscreen she always slathered them with — and light brown hair that turned sun-bleached blond in the summer — all characteristics that fit with George's own childhood photos.

It was a fortunate coincidence, as he was not their father, and was also not aware of this inconvenient fact.

Caitlin was used to the fear that she'd be found out one day. That part was not new. It was just that the threat had never been this immediate, this specific.

She had not been cruising easily through these early years of motherhood as if she'd forgotten the transgression that led to their birth. Instead, she protected those boys even more fiercely than she protected her secret itself. Because she knew that she and George were not compatible in the baby-making department. Years of trying had resulted in not so much as a faint line of *maybe* on a pee stick. She had undergone a litany of not-pleasant tests and received a clean bill of reproductive health, and George, in a move that would mark the one time she had really resented him for the pedigreed haughtiness that only on rare occasions surfaced in his behavior, had refused to have his semen tested or even to discuss the matter further.

In playing his high card, George had not chosen wisely. And so when Caitlin realized it was her move, she hadn't acted with any better judgment than George had. She wasn't proud of what she'd done. And yet her choice had led to Gus and Leo, and it was hard to see how that could be entirely wrong. She did know, though, that she could never, ever again do what she'd done and continue to live with herself. And that was why nothing must ever happen to the twins. They were her two find only children. There could never be others.

Leo slipped to the ground headfirst at an odd angle and Caitlin winced. He sat up, undeterred, and again jumped onto George's back, and only when she saw the smile return to the boy's face did she allow herself another careful sip of chardonnay. She knew that all mothers worried but also that other mothers did not worry quite the way she did. She envied them that.

No one would have believed Caitlin spent much time envying anyone. She had the family she'd always wanted, the family most people wanted. She had more than she'd dared to dream of. She loved George more than she'd thought it was possible to still romantically love someone after years of silly spats and bad haircuts and countless shared pots of morning coffee and almost as many evening nightcaps and endless loads of laundry and trash dragged down to the curb and cozy pajama nights on their couch and stuffy black-tie events and exotic trips together and too-long stretches forced apart. What she had done had never been out of a faltering in her love for George — only a solution for the thing that he would not do.

And so George must never find out the thing Finn had threatened to tell him.

Nor could she let Finn go after George's family, or his career — wherever it might lead.

88

How *dare* Finn betray her this way? What gave him the right to threaten their future just because he'd so unfathomably screwed up his own? It was ridiculous, even shameful, to feel hurt by him when he'd hurt Violet so much worse. But it was impossible not to still feel the sting of his words, so deeply had they cut.

On Caitlin's phone on the kitchen counter, there was one new voice mail that she couldn't bring herself to listen to. It was from Violet, and unless some miracle had occurred in the hours since Finn left early this afternoon, it wasn't good news.

Violet probably just needed to talk. To her best friend. To her best friend who should have been calling her back right now without even bothering to listen to the message — because she was needed, obviously. But Caitlin dreaded making the call. She was not cut out for this. The guilt and fear would eat her alive — she knew that from her years of being unable to look at the boys without imagining some tragedy striking. Only this time it wasn't just in her head. It was a very real threat that not only could cost Caitlin her most treasured friendship — and her marriage, and maybe even her children, and her whole *life*, really — but also could get her into very real trouble with the very real authorities. If she were caught failing to report Finn's whereabouts, not to mention giving him access to George's family's cabin in Kentucky . . .

The potential consequences were terrifying.

There had been no picnic in the park for Caitlin and the boys this afternoon. After Finn

89

left, she paced her kitchen in a panic, running through every imaginable scenario that would reveal her crime. What if George suggested they take the kids to the lake this weekend, as he so often did after they'd been apart? It was only a couple hours' drive, but their family time together was different there. Simpler. Uninterrupted. It was the perfect place to recharge when your home life was as driven by one parent's hyperactive career as theirs was.

This time, of course, it was Caitlin who had been away, a switch that none of them was used to. If George had suggested a drive to Kentucky this morning, she would have jumped at the idea — as George would have known she would. So if he happened to suggest it now, how would she manage to decline in a convincing way?

She needed to be prepared with reasons she could not or did not want to go just in case. The problem was, she couldn't think of any. Except, of course, the one she couldn't say.

There was also the possibility that George's parents could happen upon Finn there — it was, after all, their cabin, though they rarely used it anymore. Now that they were retired, they felt less and less need to get away — unlike Caitlin's own parents, who were currently on yet another transatlantic cruise, an expense only just within reach thanks to her mother's teaching pension, her father's retired firefighter benefits, and their modest mortgage finally being paid off. The sprawling Bryce-Daniels estate was much more comfortable than the simple house on the lake. When you lived in a resort and no longer went to work, who needed a vacation?

Still, there was no telling when they might be feeling sentimental.

She tried to imagine the phone ringing, her father-in-law yelling through the line that Finn and Bear were in his house and demanding to know how they got there.

Maybe she could pretend she didn't know. It wouldn't take much acting to show surprise about this whole mess — Caitlin herself could still hardly believe it. Maybe if she just played dumb, Finn would have a change of heart and decide not to make good on his threats after all.

George crawled toward Caitlin and collapsed at her feet into a heap of exaggerated defeat. 'They got me,' he gasped, looking up at Caitlin, and though she was in no mood, she appreciated that he was trying to include her in the fun.

'Bravo, buckaroos,' she said halfheartedly. 'You slew the dragon!'

George laughed and raised his head. 'Boys, that's called a mixed metaphor,' he said.

'Mefador,' Leo agreed solemnly.

'He was a TIGER!' Gus informed her, in his bossiest voice.

'Do you know what tiger-dragon-horsies eat?' George asked the boys, leaning closer to them. 'They're very particular creatures. And they only have *ice cream sundaes!*'

'Sundaes!' the boys yelled in unison, and ran ahead of George into the kitchen.

Caitlin bit her tongue. When George was out of town for a week or two at a time, she'd spend her evenings outnumbered, struggling alone to coerce the boys into eating anything remotely healthy as they'd inexplicably shun things they'd just days before been content to eat — suddenly spaghetti was 'too wiggly wobbly,' meat loaf subject to the dissection of the minuscule translucent onion squares inside, and yogurt acceptable only if it was blue. Then George would swoop back in on a Friday night with an assortment of candy from the airport concessions. It drove her mad. He knew that treats were allowed only once in a while, but he didn't seem to realize that his splurges meant that the goodies always came from him. Just once, she wanted to be the fun one. But it hardly seemed fair to ask him to stop when he spent so much time away.

'Ice cream, sweetie?' He laid his fingertips briefly on her shoulder as he followed the boys into the kitchen.

Caitlin gestured to her wineglass, only half empty. 'No, thanks.'

Over the excited chatter behind her she heard the unfamiliar ring of the house phone. She and George used their cell phones almost exclusively. No one ever called but telemarketers, and each time the landline rang — inevitably during dinner or naptime — she was tempted to have the thing disconnected, But then she'd imagine some emergency. One of the twins taking a tumble down the stairs, or — oh God, she could barely bring herself to think about it — out through the screen of a second-story window, having defeated one of the safety latches she'd installed on every glass panel in the house. There the little crumpled body would lie, crying for her or, worse, completely motionless, and instead of holding him, soothing him, helping him, keeping him calm while she dialed 911, she'd be running around trying to figure out where she'd put her damn cell phone.

'Honey? Violet's on the phone.'

Caitlin couldn't remember having given Violet the number. Then, all at once, she did — when the two of them were on their maternity leaves together and one of them would get no answer on the other's cell, they had a code to call each other's landlines, let it ring exactly once, and then hang up. This would signify that the caller *really* needed an extra set of hands to run next door if at all possible. Potential causes included explosive diapers that had leaked all over the person changing them, conference calls that needed to be taken without a crying baby in the background, and once, an overflowing washing machine in Violet's basement.

Caitlin had never wanted to imagine a day without Violet right next door. And now she didn't even know how she would face her on the phone, with hundreds of miles between them.

Maybe Finn had had a change of heart after leaving here. Maybe talking with Caitlin had made him realize the depth of the trouble he was in, or of the pain he had caused Violet, or of the horrible position he was backing Caitlin into, or of the hypocrisy and audacity he'd had to drag George's family into this.

She took the phone from George's out-stretched hand, trying to imitate the eagerness with which she would have run toward such a call anytime before roughly ten thirty this morning.

'Vi? Any news?'

'No, no. I'm sorry for heckling you at home. I couldn't get through on your cell, and I just . . . I just had to talk to someone.'

'Did Gram leave you alone?' Gram had basically moved from her senior community into Violet's little rented house as soon as Violet had returned from Sunny Isles. She'd barely left her side the entire time Caitlin had been there.

'I made her go to the pottery workshop at the center — she's been looking forward to it forever. Only now. I can't stand being in this house alone. It's just so *quiet*. It's so quiet, it's loud — like a deafening *roar* of quiet. It almost makes me feel like I'm going crazy.'

Caitlin thought of George's primal growls as the children had giggled and clung to his back, and her heart ached. What would it be like for all that noise, all that *life* here, to just . . . disappear?

Violet sighed. 'Anyway, it's not just that I wanted to talk to *someone*. I wanted to talk to someone who would let me be angry. Everyone here is so *at one with the mountains*, you know? I mean, I love it, right up until I don't.'

Caitlin knew what she meant. Asheville was so full of free spirits it was almost impossible for them not to rub off on you. This past year, Gram had transformed into some Zen-like, earth-mother version of herself, trading in her leather purses for hand-sewn patchwork satchels, letting her bob grow out, and giving up her blond hair

94

dye. Finn had stopped shaving as regularly and traded in his sleek road bike for a heavy mountain version that all but came covered in mud. Now that Caitlin thought about it, the only one who seemed unchanged by the family's move was Violet.

'That's fair,' she said. 'You have a right not to feel *at one* with anything at the moment.'

'I think I'm officially moving from the confused stage to the pissed-off stage,' Violet said. 'I mean, how can Finn do this to me? How can he *do this?*'

Caitlin's eyes fell on the kitchen island where she'd faced off with Finn earlier. The boys were squirting Reddi-wip into their bowls, and little bits of whipped cream were flying everywhere. She'd be finding dried white splotches on cupboard doors for weeks, but George, in the custom of his forefathers, was oblivious. He lifted his eyes to meet hers and raised his eyebrows in married couple language for *Any news?* Caitlin shook her head. He adjusted his expression into one that said *Unbelievable.* George seemed as genuinely surprised as Caitlin and Violet were by Finn's disappearance, a fact that Caitlin found comforting. She loathed the idea of the two women in the room being baffled to tears and then her husband, Finn's golf buddy, swaggering in and saying, 'Oh, he finally made a run for it, did he?' as if the wives, being typical wives, had been duped all along. Caitlin and Violet weren't like those women who pretend not to know what nefarious activities their husbands are up to, or who are oblivious of behavior that doesn't fit with their ideas of a perfect marriage. And George and Finn weren't like those husbands who wait for any chance to escape the nags they married.

Were they?

'I know I don't talk about this much,' Violet went on, 'but back when my parents died — ' Caitlin stepped through the doorway into the dining room, where it was quieter. To say that Violet didn't talk about her parents much was an understatement. She *never* spoke of them. Caitlin suspected that she felt as if doing so would somehow be disloyal to Gram.

'It sounds bad to say this, but I was so young that after a while what bothered me the most was not that I missed my parents specifically, but just that I missed *having* parents, you know? There would always be these Mother's Day teas in our classroom, and father-daughter dances around Valentine's Day, and I would have this crippling anxiety beforehand that I'd be the only one without a mom, without a dad. The teachers always offered to let me stay home if I felt uncomfortable. But Gram made me go. 'You have to face it, Violet,' she'd say. 'You have to face it.' And you know what? She was right. I did. I had to face it in order to feel better about it. Because actually, those things were never as bad as I'd imagined they would be. Everyone else went out of their way to make me feel included, and it was a little embarrassing sometimes, but overall, it was actually a really good feeling. And if I'd stayed home. I would have been miserable all day. I had to face it in order to feel better about it. And I think that became, like, the way I'm programmed to deal with things now. So here I am in this situation where I just want to face Finn. I need to face him. But he's not here to face. And I'm so pissed off at him that he didn't face me, with whatever this is even about. I don't know what to do with myself.'

Something about Violet made more sense then. Caitlin had always marveled that her friend was a woman who was not only capable of vacationing alone, but content to; who not only followed the woman who raised her to her dream retirement destination, but did it without complaint, even though Caitlin had always suspected that Asheville wasn't Violet's first choice of locales. Violet didn't just face things. She faced them with resolve, with absolution.

And then there was Finn. Caitlin remembered a particular time he had barely left home for months, getting off the couch only to answer the door when she came over with food or a movie. He'd had a good enough reason, but still.

'Finn might not be the best at facing things,' she said cautiously.

'You think?' Violet retorted, and beneath the sarcasm, Caitlin could hear her anger about to boil over.

'Sorry. That was a rather pointless thing to say.'

'You know, the thing is, when he came looking for me, after all that time. I thought, here is a guy who is not going to just accept the hand that fate dealt him. Here is a guy who is going to go out and try to find what circumstances took from him, and make his own fate. I loved that! And then all these years later, for him to turn around and do this to me, as if he's trying to undo it all . . . ' Violet started to cry. 'It's too late to undo it all! We have Bear — *he* has Bear! I mean, he *has* to bring him home. He can't just disappear forever. Not with my baby boy.'

Caitlin rested her forehead against the cool wall as Violet broke down. What kind of person was she not to tell Violet where Finn was right this instant? Finn wasn't the only one who was bad at facing things. At this moment, she hated herself beyond recognition.

Her mind raced, searching for a way she could orchestrate having Violet show up at the cabin and discover Finn and Bear on her own without Finn thinking that Caitlin had given him up. If she made Violet promise to tell Finn that she'd had a key all along and had gone there on her own, would he buy it?

That wasn't a risk she could afford to take.

Besides, she couldn't tip Violet off even if she wanted to, not over the phone. Surely the FBI had Violet's line tapped. If a call came in from Finn, they'd need to be ready to trace it. If Caitlin said anything suspicious now, even an offhand remark that would lead Violet to Finn, she'd be implicated immediately. And that, too, would ruin everything.

She heard the muffled sound of Violet blowing her nose. 'If he only had come to me about . . . whatever this is.' She sniffed. 'We could have faced it together. Or at least. I could have faced *him*. If I knew where he was right now, mark my words, Cait. I would *make* him face me. Whatever it took. I would not let him leave until we talked this through. Until I figured out a way to . . . at the very least make him give Bear back. Oh God, Cait, it's so quiet here, it's deafening. I want to tear my skin off — I just *want Bear back.*'

★   ★   ★

Awake in bed that night long after George had fallen sleep, Caitlin couldn't stop thinking about Violet saying that after a while, she hadn't missed her parents in a very specific way, just the idea of them, the role they had played. If something were to happen to pull Caitlin out of their lives now, would Gus and Leo forget her? They might hang on to a fleeting memory here and there, but she knew there was no way that they'd ever know the depth of her love for them — how they filled up her days and her heart and her mind. How they were her life.

And what about Bear? How long would Finn need to keep him away before he had a hard time conjuring Violet's face, her smell, her laugh? Caitlin had watched Violet doting on Bear since birth; he had transformed her every bit as profoundly as Caitlin herself had been changed by motherhood. Every day that Bear was apart from Violet was a day that the two of them didn't have the simple but infinitely deep comfort of their bond. Caitlin knew she could not be complacent about something that grave and face herself in the mirror. And for what had Finn stooped to these depths, anyway? Why was he doing this?

Caitlin didn't know the answer, but she kept circling back to the way she could find out. She didn't like it, but there was one solution between sacrificing her own family to restore Violet's and taking the chance that Finn would disappear again.

If Violet couldn't track Finn down and face him right now, Caitlin could do it for her. She could find out what was at the bottom of this and make him see that there had to be a better way through it.

It was easy enough to take time off work when your husband was a major donor to the organization. When you commanded a token salary and still brought in more donations than everyone else combined, no one would tell you no. There was only one problem: After five whole days away at Violet's, George would never believe that she'd leave the twins again so soon. Every believable lie she could think of was just that: a lie. And in every lie there were many ways to be caught. She could say she had to go back to Violet's, for instance, that she felt too guilty being so far away from a friend who needed her. But a simple phone call from Violet would give her away. She'd called the house phone tonight. It wasn't a stretch to imagine she'd do it again.

No, best to tell the truth. To say that she was going to the cabin. George would believe that she needed a few days to recharge after the emotional fatigue of helping her friend through the ordeal. What he wouldn't believe was that Caitlin wouldn't take the kids with her.

Caitlin thought of their last family trip there, Gus and Leo finally having the go-ahead to climb into their bunk beds alone, scaring the be jesus out of her with their jumping on the mattresses and hanging over the edges.

'They're boys!' George had laughed, seeing her clenched white knuckles. 'Boys will be boys!'

And they were boys, through and through — just like George. She couldn't imagine the three of them separating, no matter the genetic circumstances. If anyone was on the fringe, it was her.

If George were to find out her secret — and if Finn were to damage the reputation of the father George so idolized, casting doubt on George's own prospects in the process — would he be angry enough to leave her? For years he'd been gently hinting that perhaps their lives were too intertwined with Finn's, but Caitlin hadn't listened. He could hold her responsible for all of this, and in a way, he'd be right. And if he were angry enough to leave her, would he be angry enough to take the kids with him? *He's already invested so much in the twins' future*, Finn had said. *He can't have you just slink off with them.* George's family had a seemingly infinite supply of money, resources, and connections, and they rarely hesitated to use them. If her kids were to grow up in a broken home, it was too easy to picture that home being one without her in it.

Finn had been right about the pride, too. George was about as nice a guy as men of his stature came, but if there was one thing he couldn't stand, it was the slightest hint that he was being taken for a fool. She had seen him walk away, pen in hand, from the rare classic car of his dreams, the exact year, make, model, and even color as the one his grandfather had driven, restored to perfection. He'd struck up an innocent enough conversation with the owner at a car show one lazy Saturday, and it turned out the thing was for sale. It was all George talked about for weeks, but when it came to one last signature at the table, the seller refused to put a part — a very minor part, in Caitlin's estimation — of their verbal agreement in writing, and that was it for George. He had never looked over his shoulder as he walked away, had never taken the seller's many calls in the days that followed, had never again so much as mentioned the incident — and he hadn't searched for a different car to buy either. George could go cold like that. And once he did, it didn't matter how hot he'd once been for whatever it was. He was done.

11

AUGUST 2011

Finn had just stepped outside onto the front steps of Maribel's apartment building when he caught sight of Caitlin heading up the walk. He knew her instantly by the way she carried herself — head held high, as if she had something to prove. She hadn't always walked that way, but her gait had changed since she'd met George. Now, even her silhouette against the streetlights looked perfectly tailored to fit. She caught sight of him and lifted her hand in a wave so excited and childlike that it transformed her back into the old Caitlin even as her other hand grasped a glittery clutch that probably cost as much as Finn made in a month.

She half jogged the last few steps to catch him in an embrace, brief but strong. Then she held him at arm's length, beaming. 'Congratulations! I can't believe this is the first time I've had a chance to tell you in person.'

Finn grinned. 'Thanks.' He took in her long, clingy black dress, accented by only a single tear-shaped emerald hanging from a golden chain around her neck. Sometimes it was still a shock seeing her this way. She'd spent so many hours lounging on the futon in his dorm room in flannel pajama pants — often she hadn't even bothered to change out of them to go to class or the dining hall.

'I know — I used to be, like, the least fancy person you knew,' she said, reading his mind. She gestured down at her outfit with something akin to embarrassment. Part of Caitlin's charm had always been that she had no idea that anyone might consider her beautiful. To Finn, that made her even more so.

'You were always fancy on the inside,' he told her affectionately. He sank onto the middle step and motioned for her to join him. All the windows in Maribel's apartment were closed tight to keep the air-conditioning inside, but the glow of the lights through the sheer curtains backlit the tiny front garden, and the sounds of music and beer-buzzed laughter seeped outside in muffled waves. 'George on the road again?'

'And miss your engagement party? No way.' She smiled. 'He's just parking in the garage. He let me off at the corner. The price of a pair of high heels is not necessarily proportionate to their comfort level, as it turns out.'

'Good,' he said. 'Please be sure to tell Maribel. If she tested that theory even once, it would drain the rest of my savings.'

Caitlin laughed. 'So the rumors are true?'

'I guess that depends on what the rumors are.'

She spread open her hand and started counting off her finger-tips. 'Let's see, you got laid off, booked a bunch of really promising job interviews, canceled all of them when Maribel got offered a job in Asheville, and are planning to start your own freelance business down there.

Oh, and I suppose the proposal came somewhere in between.'

A low, full August moon was just making its way over the top of the jarringly modern office building that stood between the historic apartments and the river. Out of habit, Finn looked up to see the stars, but could spot none through the haze of the city's own glow. In Asheville, the stars were uncommonly bright, almost close enough to touch. In a few short weeks, they'd be there, unpacking the first-floor studio space and the second-floor living space in the Victorian house they'd rented. 'Hang out a shingle,' Maribel had said, pointing to the front porch, and then, lifting her arm up triumphantly to the terrace above it, 'mix and mingle!'

'The rumors are true,' he conceded.

'I'm so happy for you.' She gave a little tug on his arm until their shoulders bumped in a brotherly way, then abruptly let go. 'But I'm so sad you're leaving! We've hardly seen you at all lately. We feel like we've already been missing you.'

'I know, I know. I'm sorry. We've been . . . antisocial.'

His eyes found Maribel through the window. She was shored up on either side by her mom and dad, and all three of them were laughing at something that someone outside the frame had said. The way her parents had embraced their news, even though they didn't know him that well, was touching — not a hint of concern that Maribel and Finn were moving too fast, or that they'd soon be moving even farther away.

They seemed genuinely happy that Maribel was so happy, and Finn took it as an honor that they would trust him so completely with their daughter. A smile spread across his face as he watched the three of them turn to greet another small circle of guests.

'I can see why,' Caitlin teased. 'You're smitten.'

'Well, you'd better be if you're going to tie the knot, right?'

'Touché.' A hint of sadness passed across Caitlin's face but was instantly replaced by one of her practiced smiles. 'You know,' she said, 'George and I never really got a chance to have that hibernate-and-be-lovey phase. He travels so much for work, and then when he is home, there's always something with his family. You would have thought when his father retired from the Senate, the all-family appearance schedule would die down. But he's still always getting some award, hosting some charity benefit, whatever, and wanting George there for 'support.''

She glanced down the sidewalk, but there was no sign of George yet. 'Really. I think his dad just likes to show him off, the prodigal son gone out to conquer the international business world. Sometimes I wonder if he wants him to run for office, too.' She gave a nervous little laugh. 'I'm not cut out to be a senator's wife. I'm still not sure how he ended up marrying me at all! A girl from the *suburbs*.'

He laughed. 'Come on. It was a *nice* suburb.'

'It was no estate on a hill.'

'You know George doesn't care about that stuff. That's what's so great about him.'

'Whether he cares about it or not doesn't change the fact that our entire first floor would have fit inside their horses' stables.'

Finn knew what she meant. And while George *didn't* care about that stuff, Caitlin's family had pulled back from her a bit once she'd become a Bryce-Daniels. Her sister and brother lived in their parents' neighborhood now, about forty minutes outside of Cincinnati, and her move to the city after college made her the odd one out even before she'd married George. His family's largesse only widened the chasm. 'I think my family is intimidated,' she'd told Finn. 'And I can't blame them, because so am I.'

When Caitlin first met George, at a black-tie function she was covering for the PR firm that had hired her out of school, she took him for a 'silver spoon snob' who'd bought his way into the Ivy League and his high-ranking job. 'He probably bought his good looks, too,' she'd told Finn, and even then he had to hide a smile, so obvious was it that this mysterious Bruce Wayne character had lit a fire in his friend. George was soon revealed to be brilliant in his own right, bitingly funny, and generous almost to a fault, and if all that didn't win Caitlin over, the way he doted on her as if she were a rare artifact did. George saw to it that Caitlin's life blended seamlessly, at least on the surface, into his. Beneath it, Caitlin sometimes seemed to be scrambling to keep up — though oddly, Finn got that sense more when George *wasn't* around.

Finn hadn't grasped the extent of the Bryce-Daniels wealth until the bachelor party in Sunny Isles last year. He grew uncomfortable, squirmy, though nobody treated him as if he didn't belong. On the contrary, it was their willingness to talk openly in front of him about their untouchable lifestyles that took him aback and made him feel like an imposter. Only then did he become fully aware that Caitlin wasn't marrying only George but also his father's legacy. He imagined joining those ranks wasn't as easy or as enviable as people thought. A mere couple days of it had left him making excuses to get away.

Meeting that woman on the beach had been like coming up for air. Sometimes, he still imagined what might happen if he were to run into her one day — loading bags into her trunk outside the grocery store, or pedaling down the bicycle trail in his direction, her Camp Pickiwicki T-shirt taut against her body in the wind. There was no denying there'd been some spark between them, so he wondered what he'd say to her if their paths ever did cross again, how he'd put a stop to it before she could even start toward him. It was almost as if he felt he owed her an explanation. 'Well, see, it's so great to run into you this way, but I have a fiancée now. She is the one who answered the ad I placed when I was looking for you, actually . . . Yes, I did. I know it sounds crazy . . . But I really love her and I apologize that it worked out wonderfully for everyone but you.'

Of course, he had no way of knowing it hadn't

worked out well for her too. He hoped that it had. After all, he owed her his own happiness. If it hadn't been for her, he would never have met Maribel.

'You know . . . ' Caitlin's voice faltered, and when he raised his eyes to hers, she offered him a sideways smile and held his gaze. 'I never really told you — '

'There he is!' George came striding up the sidewalk with a bottle of champagne in one hand and a small silver gift bag in the other, and Caitlin and Finn both got to their feet. He held the bag out to Caitlin as he leaned in to kiss her, as if it had been hours, not minutes, since he'd last seen her. That was one of the perks of spending so much time apart, Finn supposed, When George and Cait were together, they'd draw envious looks from every woman in the room — and some of the men, too — for all the affection George showered on her, how attentive he was, a rare combination of first-date politeness, old-world gallantry, and marital intimacy.

'Forgot this under your seat,' he said good-naturedly, and she turned and handed the bag over to Finn as she looped her arm easily around George's waist.

'The champagne is for everyone,' she told Finn, 'The bag is for when everyone leaves.'

'The champagne is for the everyones you really, really like,' George corrected, 'This stuff is top-notch.'

Finn was peeking through the tissue paper into the bag when he heard the storm door creek open behind him. 'There you are!' Maribel called to Finn. 'Oh — George! Caitlin! So glad you could make it.'

'Hey, love, could you come out here for a minute? With four glasses.'

'Actually, the toasts are about to — '

'Just for a minute?'

Maribel held up a finger and disappeared from view. A moment later she returned carrying four clear plastic wineglasses, which Caitlin took and lined up on the railing as George expertly uncorked the bottle with a soft pop, careful not to spill a drop.

As George started to pour, Finn handed the bag to Maribel. She reached in and removed a CD with a stunning photo of Music Hall on the front, illuminated in all its LumenoCity glory. 'The sound track to last year's show!' she gasped. 'I didn't know this existed!'

'So you can relive that night whenever you want,' Caitlin said, almost shyly. Finn realized then how little he'd let any of his friends really get to know Maribel. He'd been keeping her all to himself. There would be plenty of time to change that, even though they were moving away. If anyone had the resources to travel on a whim, it was George and Caitlin. Besides, Finn and Maribel would be back often to handle the wedding arrangements. As much as they loved the mountains and wanted to make their life there, Maribel had insisted on having the ceremony here. 'We can't *not* invite Cincinnati to the party,' she'd told Finn. 'She's family.'

'Where did the guests of honor *go?*' Finn

heard someone call from inside, but Maribel didn't flinch. She was hugging Caitlin tight, her eyes glistening at Finn over his friend's shoulder.

George distributed the glasses, and Finn raised his before anyone else had the chance. 'To the everyones I really, really like.'

★ ★ ★

The sounds of the orchestra filled Maribel's living room. The end tables were covered with picked-over trays of hors d'oeuvres, crumb-filled bowls, stained cocktail napkins, and empty glasses. 'I'm going to hire someone to clean all this up for you,' Finn murmured seductively into her ear, 'just as soon as I pick through the couch cushions to see how much spare change was left behind.' Maribel laughed and tilted her head back to look up at him as they swayed. He wasn't sure how they'd ended up slow dancing in the middle of the chaos. They'd put on the CD from Caitlin and George while they started cleaning up, and the next thing he knew, they were wrapping their arms around each other, and the mess around them seemed to fall away. It was how every day with Maribel was, really.

'I'm more worried about whether or not I'm remembering *this* correctly,' she said, her eyes bright from too much champagne. She seemed to be making a great effort to enunciate clearly, as if to conceal her level of intoxication from him, something she often did when she'd had too many drinks. He'd never let on that he noticed it, because he was afraid if he did, she would stop. It was absolutely adorable. 'Was our first kiss right around this point in the concert — ' She cocked her head as the strings reached their crescendo, then leaned in and kissed him softly on the mouth. 'Or maybe here?' she said into his lips a moment later as the percussion chimed in.

He buried his face in her shiny dark hair and breathed in the citrus scent of her shampoo. He could not remember the last time he had felt so at peace.

Life was good.

'You know, we need to give some thought to the honeymoon,' he said into her hair. 'I want to take you on a trip you'll always remember.'

'That'll be easy,' Maribel said, 'as long as the ocean's involved. I've never seen it.'

He took a step back to see if she was kidding and almost stumbled into the couch. He was a little drunk himself. 'Are you serious? Never?'

'Never, never, never,' she said, twirling in a circle with each word and giggling as she fell back into his arms.

Finn blinked at her. How was it that this had never come up? Their engagement didn't seem particularly whirlwind to him, even though there had been a fair amount of teasing from their guests tonight to the contrary. Finn knew all he needed to know about Maribel. The fact that he still had so much to learn was just . . . well, it was exciting. He couldn't imagine life with her ever becoming boring when she could manage at one moment to be the unfiltered, unapologetic woman he loved and then the next to reveal to him a facet he'd never seen before. What you saw was what you got with Maribel — but she didn't show you *everything*. He wanted to uncover the rest slowly, a little every day, for as long as he could. Forever.

Finn dipped her down in a cartoonish simulation of a ballroom-dancing move, and she smiled up at him. 'When was the last time *you* saw it?' she asked.

'George's bachelor party,' he said. 'Right before I met you.' And then he was picturing himself there, gazing down flirtatiously at the woman on the beach in her unassuming T-shirt and windblown ponytail, the sun reflecting off the water and illuminating the golden tones in her hair, even under the umbrella. He could still hear her low, appreciative chuckle when she laughed at something he said, still feel the way he'd instantly sensed that she was like him in some essential way — a kindred spirit. Someone worth looking for.

He jerked Maribel upright as bit more abruptly than he meant to. 'Wait a minute,' he said. 'How have you never seen the ocean? You answered the ad about having met a stranger on the beach.'

The symphony came to its end, and a conspicuously timed silence filled the room.

'On *vacation*,' Maribel said, looking a little hurt. 'I answered the ad about having met a stranger on *vacation*. All this time we haven't ever talked about the people we were looking for that day, and you want to start now? On this night?'

113

The light opening notes of the next symphony started, and Finn pulled her to him again. 'I'm sorry,' he said. 'You're right. I guess vacation and the ocean are the same thing to me. I shouldn't have assumed.'

A loud burst of percussion emphatically punctuated the end of his sentence, and they both burst out laughing. The moment of tension between them evaporated.

'I'd just gotten back from Gatlinburg,' Maribel said as they started to sway again. 'Hey, they've got Dollywood! That totally counts as a vacation.'

By Cincinnati standards, it definitely did. It was less than a five-hour drive away, and in addition to the campy country-icon-themed tourist traps and the Ripley's Believe It or Not!, Gatlinburg was filled with secluded mountain chalets, eclectic music, food and drink festivals, and gorgeous hiking. It was also en route to Asheville. Finn had been there himself, and he resisted the urge to ask how Maribel had met her mystery man — in the hot tub of a resort, at a bar in town, on a mountain trail. Then he thought again of the woman on the beach and felt uneasy. She'd seldom entered his thoughts this past year, and yet somehow he kept finding her there on tonight of all nights. Suddenly it bothered him very much that he could still see himself watching the tide come in with her but had never shared that experience with Maribel. He felt an overwhelming desire not just to see it through Maribel's eyes for the first time, but to be there with her, beside her, and to not picture

114

himself anywhere without her, ever again.

'We should go, then,' he heard himself saying. 'To the ocean. The honeymoon is still a year away! That's too long to wait.'

'We'll live closer once we're in Asheville,' Maribel said sleepily, nestling her face into his neck. 'Maybe we can go for a long weekend then.'

'You don't get much time off at the new job — you'll need it all for wedding planning.'

'I suppose you're right. But the wedding is only a year away. It will fly by.'

'Tomorrow.' The idea seized Finn with surprising conviction. 'We should go tomorrow! We can be outside of Charleston, South Carolina, in nine hours or so.'

She laughed. 'You're crazy. I have to work on Monday! I'm already tiptoeing around the office now that I've given notice.'

'Oh, come on. You gave well over two weeks'. You're, like, the best quitter ever.'

'Still. Any unannounced vacation days, and my boss will *not* be happy.'

'So we'll have you back by Monday. Tomorrow's only Saturday. Plenty of time.'

'Drive eighteen hours round-trip for *one night?*' Maribel twirled herself across the room and bounced down onto the couch.

Finn dove on top of her in a gentle tackle, and she let out a squeal of fake protest. 'Or two. You could catch the Finn red-eye back to Cincinnati Sunday night. There are occasional benefits to unemployment, you know. I can sleep it off while you're at work Monday.'

She made a serious face, but he could see in her eyes that she was as taken with the idea as he was. 'We really ought to start packing for the move,' she said dutifully. 'We've only got a month. And we have to load up both our apartments and combine them into one.'

Finn had already sold off a bunch of his things. Maribel's were so much nicer. He leaned his face down to hers until their noses were touching. 'You are spoiling. My grand. Romantic. Gesture.'

She looked up at him, wide-eyed. Her dark hair was splayed out on the throw pillow beneath her as if a *Vogue* photographer had arranged her that way, and a part of Finn's brain resisted the urge to run upstairs for his sketchpad to try to capture the exquisiteness of her. The symphony played on, the highest and lowest notes reverberating in a spot that had once been hollow in his chest, and he felt that the sound track seemed to do her beauty more justice than he knew his drawings ever could. 'You seriously want to go?' she asked. 'You'd really let me sleep in the car? Job or no job, that doesn't seem fair.'

He spread his hand over his heart. 'I solemnly promise that for the rest of my life, every questionable decision I make while drunk on love and champagne will be for the sole purpose of making you happy.'

'Well,' she said, and there was a hint of that slur in her voice again, 'I guess we'd better start cleaning up, then!'

★　★　★

By the time Finn climbed into Maribel's bed next to her, it was nearly three o'clock. They'd found a half-full bottle of champagne that someone had the presence of mind to stick inside the refrigerator door, and polished it off as they made quick work of sweeping the mess into trash bags, tossing them over the back fire escape into the Dumpster below, and making an assembly line at the kitchen sink. Then, buzzed anew, they'd run upstairs and started flinging things into a suitcase, giddy at their newfound sense of impromptu adventure. Finn had never technically moved in, but he had more than enough clothes and toiletries here to pack for a night or two away. Maribel made a game of tossing swimsuits and sundresses across the room to him — more than she could possibly need — as he volleyed them into the open suitcase. When they were done, he'd made love to her urgently, not bothering to turn down the covers or remove more clothes than absolutely necessary. She'd changed into his T-shirt and snuggled in happily while he brushed his teeth.

Finn downed a couple of ibuprofen before sinking in next to her. He doubted it would do much to overcome the headache that promised to overtake him by morning, but he hardly cared. Maribel's breathing was already slowing as he spooned himself around her and settled onto the edge of her pillow.

'Babe,' she said sleepily.

'Hmm?'

'If we're not really leaving in the morning, that's okay. It was still fun, just the idea of it.'

117

'It'll be even more fun when we're stuffed full of fresh crab cakes and piña coladas,' he said, smiling into the darkness.

'Mmmm.'

He would remember the way she said that *mmmm* for all of his life.

12

Violet sat obediently at the chintzy drop-leaf table that was awkwardly planted in the middle of her tiny kitchen. It was the only one she and Finn had been able to find that would fit the space here, and she hated it. She hated having to raise the semicircular leaf to make room for Bear's booster seat at every meal, constantly hauling the extra chair and booster into the pantry to keep them out of the way, always worrying Bear was going to hang on the edge and snap it right off, tumbling to the tile.

Of course, none of those steps were necessary at the moment. It was just Violet and Gram, who fit cozily across from each other at the little rectangle. Violet hated that too — the reminder that she did not need to make room for a third — or a fourth, for that matter. As she watched Gram brew a pot of coffee that the well-meaning woman insisted they share but that Violet did not especially want, she couldn't conjure any comfort from this crowded little room. Especially not when she saw Gram open three different cabinets before managing to locate the mugs.

Back home in Ohio, Gram had known Violet's kitchen as well as her own. Violet closed her eyes and pictured her sunny kitchen there — not the one she and Finn and Bear had rented from Caitlin, which was worn but beautiful, large and airy and vintage and charming, but the one in the duplex she and Gram had shared. The one that still came to mind in her most anguished moments when she longed to be in the place that felt most like home. The cheery yellow walls that were the mirror image of the ones she'd spent her childhood in, and the comforting sounds of Gram tinkering on her side of the dividing walls. The life Gram had built for herself in Asheville included Violet, but it wasn't adjacent to Violet's, not the way it so literally used to be. The only thing that had ever made this new mountain address truly feel like a place where Violet belonged was Bear. When she'd found herself getting homesick this past year, wishing she could run him next door for an impromptu playdate with Caitlin and the twins, she'd remind herself that *this* was where he'd learned to pedal his tricycle around the driveway, where he'd transitioned to his big-boy bed, where he'd soon walk to his first day of preschool down the block — and where one day she'd look down at his lanky limbs and sideways smile with wonder and realize that her baby had somehow transformed into a full-fledged kid. But he wasn't here now. And without him, it wasn't home.

Gram plunked two steaming mugs onto the table, along with a bottle of agave nectar and a small carton of organic milk. Violet made a face, stood, and retrieved the hazelnut-flavored creamer from the fridge.

'That is loaded with artificial ingredients,' Gram said disapprovingly.

'I know,' Violet said, pouring herself twice as much as she usually did. 'They're delicious,' She stopped short of pointing out that there'd been a day when Gram had consumed more of this stuff than she did. She was happy her grandmother felt so at ease here in the culture of Asheville, and at the Evergreen community where she had her own apartment with a patio overlooking the beautiful landscaped grounds of the senior center, the hazy rounded mounds of the Blue Ridge serving as a picture postcard backdrop to her days. She knew it wasn't fair to Gram that her numbness was giving way to an anger that seemed to extend to everything within reach — mild irritants suddenly becoming insufferable ills. It wasn't *Gram's* fault Finn had disappeared with Bear.

It was just that Violet wasn't sure whose fault it was, exactly. Finn was the obvious answer. But *why?*

'Katie called,' Gram said, letting it drop.

'Oh?'

'She wanted to see about driving down here.'

Violet had seen Katie only once since she'd moved to Asheville, a quick lunch date on a visit to Cincinnati. It wasn't so long ago they'd spent five days a week in neighboring offices, lunching and breaking together and sharing even their most mundane moments. How odd that that kind of closeness could dissolve as easily as you could quit a job or move away. Although if Violet was being honest, they'd probably begun to grow apart before that — when Violet had started dating Finn and so soon after gotten pregnant with Bear, and Katie had remained single, and unhappily so. Still, it was always reassuring to know that old friends were willing to be there when you needed them. Caitlin wouldn't be able to get away to come back anytime soon. A visit from Katie might be nice. Violet felt herself warming to the idea.

'I told her it was a lovely thought, but not a good time,' Gram continued.

Violet blinked at her. 'Why would you do that?' The words sounded harsher than she intended, and she checked herself. 'I mean. I can understand why you might think that, but why not let me decide?'

Gram sighed, as if she'd known the question was coming but still hoped it wouldn't. 'Katie has always taken a lot of credit for getting you and Finn together,' she said carefully.

'Well, yeah. If it hadn't been for Katie — '

'But I'm not sure it's best to be harping on how things began, dear. You don't want that to influence the decisions you make now.'

Violet's forehead knitted itself together. 'And what decisions would those be? I'm kind of at the mercy of . . . you know — ' Violet gestured halfheartedly into the air and let her hands drop to the table.

Gram let the silence fill the room, then cleared her throat. 'Agent Martin was here again earlier.'

Violet stiffened, That the FBI was a part of her life now was surreal. That they had yet to make any progress in actively helping her was unsettling. That Agent Martin made Violet anxious even though Violet had done nothing wrong was nerve-racking, 'Why didn't you wake me?'

'It was me he wanted to talk to, He went to the office at the Evergreen, and they told him I was here.'

Violet waited for Gram to continue on her own, but she did not.

'Well, what did he want?'

Gram took a long sip of her coffee, set the mug gently on the table, and began turning it slowly counterclockwise in this absent-minded way she had. Violet could see it now: She'd been summoned from beneath Bear's Thomas the Train comforter for the purposes of this talk, and not just for Gram's newly imposed face-the-day routine.

'He had more questions. About you and Finn. How things have been between you.'

Violet thumped her palms on the table in frustration, and caramel-colored coffee sloshed over the rim of her mug and puddled on the wood. 'All they've done is ask the same questions over and over!' she exploded, 'They're supposed to be finding Bear and bringing him home. Instead, they're investigating my marriage!'

Gram calmly removed a stack of napkins from the ceramic holder she'd bought for Violet at the big spring craft show and began sopping up the spill. 'Well,' she said gently, 'to be fair, I'd say the two are intrinsically linked at this point, dear, like it or not.'

'I've already told them,' Violet said, and she

felt that she sounded like a child, but she didn't know how to sound any other way. 'We don't fight. We haven't been at odds over anything — at least, not anything bigger than whose turn it is to unload the dishwasher. We moved here to be close to you and haven't met too many other people yet. So we spend even more time together than most couples, probably — and also with Bear. We both of us love our son. What else is there to tell?'

Gram looked so sad just then that Violet couldn't help but think of how Gram herself was no stranger to being blindsided. She hardly ever spoke of Violet's grandfather, or of Violet's parents, and she carried herself with such contented self-assurance that it was easy to forget she had lost her husband and then her only child in close succession, and one day had found herself faced with the unrequested task of raising her granddaughter. Alone.

'Look, darling.' Gram's voice was kind but matter-of-fact. 'I spent many, many years married to a man who I loved but was not *in love* with — and who was not in love with me. It was the same way with most of my friends. Things were different in our day. People got married for different reasons. Our expectations weren't the same. It had a lot more to do with stability than with romance.'

Violet stared. 'Where are you going with this?'

'What I mean is that I can recognize someone who is going through the motions.'

'And you're saying that's what you think Finn was doing?'

Gram didn't answer.

'Since we got to Asheville, you mean? Out of his element?'

Still, Gram said nothing.

'*All* the time he's been with me? You think he's been just . . . phoning it in?'

The old woman shifted in her chair. How long had she been looking so frail? 'I don't know about *all* the time. But sometimes, maybe so.'

'And it never occurred to you to *say* something to me about it?'

'Darling. What would you have me say, exactly?'

Violet opened her mouth, but nothing came out. Gram reached across the table and placed her weathered hand gently on top of Violet's. 'I never saw it as a red flag, dear. As I said, I recognize that look. I've seen it on your grandpa's face, and I admit I've even seen it in the mirror sometimes. It comes and goes, you know. And it doesn't mean a marriage cannot still be successful.'

'Maybe if that feeling is mutual. But Gram, you know that I've never felt that way, ever.'

'Haven't you?' Gram leveled her gaze at Violet, and an uneasy silence hovered between them as Violet stared at her, incredulous.

Violet pushed her chair back from the table, and it made an ugly screeching sound on the worn tile. 'And so you decided to say *all* of this aloud for the first time to *the FBI?*'

'Surely you wouldn't have me lie to them.' Gram looked so troubled that Violet almost wanted to take the words back, to touch her arm, to reassure her. But no. She was too angry for that. It suddenly seemed as if she was forever reassuring other people. Hadn't she reached a point where they should be reassuring *her?*

'But it's okay to lie to *me.*'

'I never have, darling. You've never asked me any of the things they asked me.'

'I never thought I had a reason to.' Violet didn't bother to stop the screen door from slamming behind her as she fled onto the back porch. *Little did I know*, she thought, tears blurring her vision. *Little did I know.*

To her surprise, Gram followed her. Usually she knew when to leave well enough alone. Violet turned on her heels. 'How could you think that?' she cried. 'How could you *say* that? I was happy, Gram. I thought Finn and I were both really happy.'

'But were you making each other happy, or was Bear making both of you happy?' Gram kept her voice gentle but firm. 'Whether you want to think about it or not, clear, something did go wrong, The investigators certainly are not going to just let this drop with your explanation that everything was perfectly fine. And neither should you. There isn't a whole lot you can do right now besides think on this, and so I think you should think on it hard. Let's assume they are going to find Finn and Bear, okay? You'll have Bear back, thank God. But what are you going to do then? You and Finn. I mean? I don't want to see you blindsided again. You need to have played through some scenarios. You need to decide how you might feel about things.'

Violet squeezed her eyes shut tight.

'Come back inside,' Gram said. 'Let me help you face this.'

She opened her eyes. 'This is between me and Finn.'

'And Bear. And the FBI. And the people being questioned by the FBI. Which includes me. Come back inside, Violet.'

Gram nodded toward the alleyway that ran perpendicular to their back fence, and Violet craned her neck for a view of the side street. Parked there was a shiny dark car with tinted windows. She turned back to Gram with disbelief.

Gram opened the screen door wide, and after a moment, Violet walked through.

Feeling despondent, she took her seat at the table as Gram moved slowly, deliberately — closing the back door, flipping the dead bolt, turning back to face Violet.

'Maybe you're right,' Gram said softly. 'I shouldn't venture to guess at anyone else's happiness. Obviously we both missed something here. Something big. It's certainly not like I saw this coming.'

Violet nodded, softening a little, and Gram seemed to take that as permission to reclaim her seat across the table. Gram leaned in, her eyes weary.

'But I'll say just one more thing, because I think it's something you need to remember. It's important.'

Violet steeled herself with a reluctant nod.

'I might not know anything about the price of

beans. But I do know you. And I know that *you* were happy before you and Finn got together. I mean, *right* before. I remember that day he materialized back into your life so clearly. A perfect morning. We'd bought out the whole damn farmers' market. We had Patsy Cline in the air, Apple pie in the making. Wine on ice. No big plans, But you were happy.'

Violet spoke through clenched teeth. 'What's that have to do with anything?'

'I don't know.' Gram's eyes were tired. 'But . . . Was he happy before he met you?'

Violet squinted, trying to make out Gram's point. 'I'm genuinely asking,' Gram said. 'I genuinely do not know.'

'Well, I . . . I guess I don't know either.'

'Maybe you should,' she said gently.

'Maybe.'

'But still, I think it's important for you to know that *you* can be happy on your own.'

Violet bristled again — she couldn't stop herself. 'Are you seriously suggesting that I would be just as well off without my husband or my son? Without my *son?*' She was near tears again,

'Of course not,' Gram said quickly. 'You and Bear belong together. But Finn isn't necessarily a given in this situation, isn't necessarily required for your happiness, is all I'm saying.'

'And that's supposed to make me feel better somehow?'

Gram didn't answer.

'That's very women's lib of you, Gram. I can see that the mountains have helped you get in

128

touch with a *lot* of things. Maybe I don't mean to *you* what I thought I did either. Maybe my whole life has been a lie. Is that what you're trying to tell me?'

Gram looked horrified. 'That is an alarmingly gross misrepresentation of what I was trying to say, Vi. You are not yourself right now, and that is understandable. I should have been more — ' Her gaze drifted to the framed photo of Violet and her parents on the wall, and Violet's eyes followed. For a moment, nobody spoke.

'Darling.' Gram sounded desperate, and Violet had to fight the urge to tell her to just forget this conversation had happened. Because even though she hated confrontation, even though she usually looked the other way at almost any cost, she knew she wouldn't forget *this*. And if anyone was going to apologize, it wasn't going to be her.

Gram sighed. 'I know this isn't something we talk much about, but I've spent no small amount of hours mulling the ways that losing one's parents so young can affect a person. It's like you're . . . well, I used to think of you as a ship.'

'A ship?'

'You'd be sailing along, and really you'd be perfectly content. You might not have known where you were going, but you were okay with that. That much, I think you got from me. And I'm proud to have been able to have taught you that, that life isn't all about making plans.'

Violet wasn't about to be taken in by some life lesson metaphor. She shrugged. 'So it's good to be a ship.'

Gram nodded. 'But then you'll see something

that looks like a safe port to you. Me. Katie. Finn. You'll gravitate toward that port and tie yourself up there, even though you were making your way just fine on your own, even though the skies are sunny. It's as if it suddenly seems like a good idea, in case a storm comes along. But maybe you didn't need a port. Or maybe you didn't need that *particular* port. Maybe if you'd kept sailing just around that bend, you would have found something even more wonderful.'

Violet sighed. 'Don't we *all* look for ports in a storm?'

'Maybe we do.' Gram shrugged. 'But let me ask you this. Before you batten down the hatches and go to sleep at night, what are you writing in your captain's log? That you saw a port and tied up to it? Or some other story, about the stars navigating you into the path of another ship?'

Violet's eyes burned. 'But I *did* cross paths with another ship. In fact, as I recall, that ship navigated toward *me*, with the big Camp Pickiwicki flag I was flying above my sails. And then when it lost sight of me, it put out a call looking for me.'

Gram was quiet for a moment. She sighed. 'Maybe you did cross paths, dear. Or maybe *you* were the port. I hadn't thought of it that way, but — ' Her voice trailed off. She cleared her throat. 'It's been a while since I've been out to sea alone, but if I were, I know I'd be prone to telling myself stories to pass the time. All I'm saying is, whatever you've been writing down for yourself in that captain's log, make sure it's honest.'

130

13

Finn stared into the empty fireplace in front of him as if there were a roaring blaze inside. They'd roasted marshmallows here last summer — he and Bear and Violet and Caitlin and George and the twins, all together — back when things had been bearable. Before Asheville. No matter that it hadn't been cool enough in the evenings to be fire weather. George had opened all the windows for the authenticity of nature's sound track and left the air conditioner on full blast. And why not? It wasn't as if he had to worry about the electric bill.

Finn wished he could build a little fire now, August heat be damned — he desperately needed to find a way to cheer Bear up. There was a huge stack of wood outside, no one would notice a few logs missing, and he'd found a bag of stale marshmallows in the kitchen. But he couldn't risk one of the far-away neighbors seeing smoke from the chimney and stopping by to say a cheery hello to George or his father. It was out of the question.

He took a sip of his coffee and grimaced. He could hardly stand the stuff without milk. He'd stopped for groceries at a supercenter midway here from Cincinnati, not wanting to be seen at the tiny market in town, and it had been too far

131

from the cabin and too hot in the car to pick up anything that needed refrigeration. He'd worn a baseball cap and outfitted Bear with one too, unsure — especially now that Caitlin had mentioned the FBI — whether their photos had appeared on the national news. But Finn had still been able to see in the shadow of Bear's cap how his tiny face fell every time Finn denied him something that wouldn't survive the journey — frozen chicken nuggets, ice cream, string cheese, those ingenious little tubes of yogurt.

Violet had once remarked that Bear could happily survive on PB&J and applesauce alone. She'd be delighted to know that Finn had proved her wrong — something she rarely was, as far as Bear was concerned — except, of course, that she wouldn't know.

She deserved to know, of course. She deserved to have her son. The problem was, Finn couldn't stand to let him go. And he could no longer see a way for them both to have him together. Nor could he see a way for Violet to remain in his life at all, not even at a distance. Not after everything that had happened. There had been a lot of things in the first place that had been done that could never be undone. Now there was one more — and it was a big one. That Violet so often seemed to be the casualty of Finn's misjudgments and mistakes seemed to be somehow unavoidable in this life, even though Finn harbored no ill will toward his wife. Not that anyone would believe that now.

Finn preferred to blame the dominoes that Violet was so fond of as a metaphor for their coupling. There had been 1,001 chances for them not to end up together; 1,001 *reasons* for them not to end up together. And there was really only one chance, and really only one reason, for it to go the other way.

Even with the odds overwhelmingly in his favor, he had lost.

Sometimes he couldn't believe his luck.

The night they had Bear — good God, she'd almost died. The pregnancy was an accident to begin with, and he couldn't stop thinking that if she didn't pull through, it would all be his fault, again, for putting her in that position. He'd sat by her bedside and thought that surely the better thing for her, if she recovered, would be for him to leave, even then. What kind of man could walk out on his new wife and their newborn son? No one would have understood Finn's reasons, years deep. But as he'd waited for morning to light the dark hospital room, he'd known with certainty that there was no telling the pain he could cause. Violet and little Bear didn't deserve to have to find out.

But then she was awake, beaming at him with color back in her cheeks, asking immediately for the baby, and his resolve faded. 'I'm perfectly okay,' she said, reaching for his cheek, and he caught the hand and squeezed it hard and lowered his head to their entwined fingers, unable to meet her eyes, to even look at her face at all just then, and he was overcome with the reality of it all in the light of day. To have ended up here with this woman. To have somehow produced this beautiful baby boy, and to have almost lost her in the process. His heart had never felt so helpless.

In the days and weeks and months that followed, he had watched her dote on Bear with as much detachment as he could muster even as he quietly grew more and more enamored with his son. He loved their Bear Cub, as they took to calling him, more than he'd thought himself capable — but Bear always saved his biggest smiles and sweetest coos for Violet, and at that Finn would find himself holding back. By the time the wondrous little creature began sitting up and interacting with them, though, Finn could no longer resist. Being a *father*, the man charged with teaching Bear how to become a man himself — how could he even describe it?

Outside the sliding glass doors, the lake sparkled in the late morning sun. Bear had never slept this late, ever — but then again, he'd been up most of the night, crying and asking for Violet. At first, taking Bear with him had been an impulse. As panic had set in at the realization of what he'd done, Finn had tried to convince himself this was something of a second chance — not one he'd ever have taken if he'd thought it through, but one he'd taken nonetheless. To start over loving someone on his own terms, without the heavy burden of the things he'd left unsaid, things that he hated himself for and that he felt sure Violet would hate him for too. To start over without the constant fear of causing further hurt, and of finally getting what he deserved — his every small happiness snatched away. Now of course he saw that that was not going to be possible. He'd been an idiot to think otherwise.

Maybe if he'd had any sort of plan at all, he would have had an answer ready when Bear first asked where she was. Maybe he would have avoided the way the little boy's shoulders heaved with sobs, the way he'd looked up at Finn last night, let out a shaky breath of a sigh, and said, 'But she's a good mommy. She's my best mommy.'

What could he have said? Bear was right. Violet was a wonderful mother. Eventually, Bear had cried himself back to sleep. He was still where Finn had left him, curled up miserably on the bottom bunk bed in the back bedroom.

It was a cold comfort that when it came to making a mess of things, this particular mess hardly even ranked at the top of Finn's life-to-date list. It probably wasn't even number two. Third, maybe. Fourth? Lucky, too, that self-hatred wasn't anything new to him — any minute now the sharpness of this fresh guilt would dull and he could brush past it as if it were merely an inconvenience, an annoyance. He wouldn't allow himself to think further of his wife. Or of how awful he'd been to Caitlin yesterday, mining her insecurities the way only a close friend could to get what he needed.

What he *needed*. That was the key to surviving it all. He was clear with himself that this wasn't about what he wanted anymore — if it ever had been — but need was key. And number one on *that* list was some kind of plan.

People did stupid things every day. And they got out of them every day. And so could Finn.

Somehow.

The unmistakable sound of the key in the door interrupted his thoughts, and Finn jumped to his feet. Shit, shit, *shit*. There was nowhere out here to hide, and he couldn't leave Bear. He started toward the back bedroom, hoping whoever was at the door might delay, but it swung open, and there, her arms filled with paper grocery bags, was Caitlin.

'Jesus,' he said. 'You scared me half to death.'

Then he saw who was behind her, and froze.

'Uncle Finn!' The twins rushed him together, each grabbing one of his legs in a hug. 'Where's Bear? Where's Bear?'

Finn felt the color drain from his face. 'Bear's not — '

But they were already gone, down the hallway, and he could hear Bear's yelp of surprise as they jumped into his bed.

He turned back to Caitlin, furious.

'Damn it, Cait, I warned you — '

'You didn't, actually.' She breezed past him into the small galley-shaped kitchen area in the corner of the open room and deposited the paper bags onto the counter with a grunt. Then, her hands freed, she began checking items off her fingers, one by one. 'You said no FBI, no cops, no Violet, no George — nothing about me.' She smiled innocently and removed a gallon of milk from the first bag. 'Want to freshen up your coffee?' she asked, glancing at his full mug on the table, and it irked him that she knew him that well, even as something like relief began to show itself in a back region of his brain. 'I've got

136

creamer, too. French vanilla.'

'But what are you *doing* here, Cait? And bringing the boys into this? Are you nuts?'

She leveled her gaze at him. 'No more so than you, evidently.'

'They won't be able to keep a secret.'

'I'm well aware of that. And I wouldn't ask them to. Any more than you could ever ask Bear to — could you?' Her pointed words didn't match the nonchalant way she began loading the groceries into the fridge — summer squash, cherry tomatoes, zucchini, blueberries, eggs, even burger patties and steaks — and Finn found himself struggling not to feel at least a small amount of gratitude, especially when another peal of giggles erupted from the back room. He stared down the hallway toward the bedrooms, his mind racing. He had to get rid of Caitlin — now. And yet, he was in her in-laws' cabin, with nowhere else to go. And Bear hadn't laughed in days.

When the last bag was empty, Caitlin folded it neatly and looked at him. 'Listen,' she said. 'We've been friends for a long time, Finn. I know that whatever you're going through right now, it's bad. You said yourself you were desperate. You said yourself you didn't feel like you had a choice. And you came to me for help. So I'm going to be understanding about you acting a little *stressed* yesterday.'

Caitlin had always been clever. Before and after he'd made the calculated decision to confront her at her house, he'd played out as many different scenarios as he could think of as to how she might react. What he'd do if she did in fact call the cops, for instance, or if he opened the cabin door to find Violet standing there. But he hadn't thought of this one.

'You asked for help,' she said again, 'so I'm here to help. I'm still your friend, Finn. I was *your* friend first, remember?' She turned away to pour a cup of coffee as she said this so that he couldn't see her face.

'But bringing the boys here — '

'I had to,' she said simply, turning back toward him and leaning against the counter. 'I just spent the better part of a week down in Asheville with Violet, my first time ever away from them.' Finn looked away, out at the lake, trying not to think about what must have gone on there, what must have been said. 'I tried to work out a way to come alone, but George would never in a million years have believed that I would voluntarily leave them again right away. He'd have known something was up.'

'How do you know he won't show up here too?'

'He's got a big project at work — doesn't he always? And he understood that I wanted a couple of days away to reconnect with Leo and Gus.'

'But you know they'll tell him that they saw me and Bear when you get home. How do you expect this to go?'

'I have no idea. But I do know that by the time I get home, whatever the boys say won't matter, because this will all be resolved by then.'

'And how do you know that?'

138

'Because you and I both know that you need to figure a way out of this. We're both in trouble now, okay? So neither of us are leaving this cabin until there's a resolution that involves you no longer being a kidnapper on the run,' She took a sip of coffee, but her eyes never left his face. 'Sooner or later, you need to face this, so let me face it with you.'

Something about the way she delivered that line made him think that she'd been rehearsing it the whole way down. The idea of it irked him.

'Face *it* with me, or face *off* with me?'

She shrugged. 'Maybe both. But like you said, you don't have any other options.'

Finn could feel his anger dissipating a little as his eyes wandered past her and out toward the lake. It was the exhaustion weakening his resolve, slowing his reaction time. If he hadn't been feeling so lost anyway, he would have been able to stay angrier. Then again, if he had *any* other ideas of what to do or where to go, he wouldn't be here. He would be . . . well, somewhere else.

'Come on, Finn. Aren't you a little relieved that you don't have to do it alone?'

In the distance, a sailboat was hoisting a tiny white triangle into the air like a flag of surrender.

The twins came stomping into the kitchen, exaggerating each step to show off their light-up sneakers to Bear and, Finn could see right away, to one-up each other. Bear padded in barefoot behind them, his hair flattened to his head on one side and spiked out dramatically on the other, his lanky little body clad in tight thin cotton pajamas patterned with surfboards and palm trees. Violet had picked them out especially for their vacation, and Finn saw Caitlin's almost imperceptible wince as she took them in. He was what they call a sorry sight.

'I'm hungry,' he announced to Caitlin by way of greeting.

She smiled brightly at him. 'How about blueberry pancakes? And scrambled eggs? With cheese?'

'Yummy!' Bear cheered, embracing her legs.

'Mommy, do we have two breakfasts?' Gus asked. 'We already had cereal.'

'Since Bear hasn't had breakfast, yes, we will have two. Boys, this is our very special visit to cheer up Bear, remember. So Bear gets to pick.'

'Bear wants to watch 'Thomas,'' Leo said, sticking out his bottom lip defiantly.

'Leo, that's not how it — '

''Thomas the Train'?' Bear asked, already smiling.

Caitlin clapped her hands together. 'Well, then!' she said. 'Uncle Finn will turn on the DVD while I get those pancakes started.'

Finn knew she was dismissing him, and he decided to let her.

14

AUGUST 2016

It had seemed safe, stepping out for only a few minutes. Violet was out of both milk and juice — two staples Bear couldn't get through a day without. She had to keep hoping that he could come home any minute. And if and when he did, she wanted it to *feel* like home. Violet was reluctant to leave the house at all just in case he did come through that door, and she knew Gram would gladly honor a request to stop at the store for her. But the grocery was a short drive down the street; she could be there and back in ten minutes. It felt important to have some kind of purpose, to prove to herself and anyone else who might be paying attention that she could still get out and function in the world — she could still function as a mother. She just needed her kid back so she could do it.

But she didn't count on running into anyone she knew. There, loading milk and creamer into his own cart, was Bear's pediatrician. Bear had struggled with a bad run of ear infections after they moved to the higher altitude, and Violet had gotten to know Dr. Saito better than any parent should in a short year. When he saw her, he let out a small 'Oh,' and simply opened his arms. She stepped into the awkward hug with a mixture of gratitude and helplessness, fighting the urge to run and hide. She felt . . . well, it dawned on her that she felt embarrassed. Her husband had left her. Dramatically. With her child. What kind of wife and mother must Dr. Saito take her for now? Violet stepped back. It felt rude not to smile but inappropriate to conjure one, so she merely stared at him blankly.

'How are you holding up?' he asked, and Violet's eyes blurred with tears at the kindness.

The fact was, she'd always had a bit of a crush on the pediatrician. It was silly, really. He was a thin, soft-spoken, spectacled man, certainly not her typical idea of sexy. She knew the only thing that attracted her to him was that he cared so well for her child, the center of her universe. That, and the fact that she didn't get out much anymore. Still, she'd entertained little fantasies of what might happen if she ran into him after hours. If Finn wasn't in the picture, of course. Which was what made the fantasy harmless. Because Finn would always be in the picture. Pending some tragic act of God, it was preposterous that he wouldn't be.

Dr. Saito reached into his pocket, removed a plastic sleeve of tissues with Elmo on the front, and handed one to her. 'This is unfathomable,' he said. 'I can't imagine what you must be going through. The FBI came by my office, asking all sorts of questions about Bear's well-being. It's just absurd.'

'Oh, I'm so sorry you've been dragged into this. I'm sure that's the last thing you have time for.'

142

'You are the last person who should be apologizing.'

'What did you tell them?' As soon as the words came out of Violet's mouth, they seemed wrong. What if he thought she was prying because she had something to hide? 'Don't answer that,' she said quickly. 'I shouldn't have asked. I'm not thinking straight.'

'I told them the truth. That you are one of the parents I most enjoy having in my office. That you always seem to instinctively know when to be concerned about Bear, and when something is just growing pains. In these days of Google and WebMD, you wouldn't believe how many parents show up every week in a certified panic over nothing.'

Violet couldn't help but think of Caitlin, and she fought off a little smile in spite of herself. 'I may have a friend like that.'

'Everyone does.' Dr. Saito rocked back on his heels. 'In fact, the few times I met your husband, I'd say he seemed like the one more prone to illogical worrying — not something I see as much among the dads.'

Violet's smile faded. 'Really?'

The doctor shrugged. 'Oh, he just seemed a little fearful that something would happen to Bear in his care. Nothing specific, just that he'd be faced with some situation where he wouldn't know what to do. Lots of hypotheticals. He asked about car accidents, anaphylactic shock . . . '

Violet started, picturing that terrified little boy on the beach. 'Anaphylactic shock?' She'd never had any inkling that it had stayed with Finn the way it had stayed with her.

He nodded. 'But as you well know, that kind of worry comes from love.'

An increasingly familiar sense of dread began to fill Violet as she headed home. Although she felt that there was nowhere else she should be, she didn't relish being trapped inside those walls again. Violet had tried to shake off the echoes of that last conversation with Gram, but she couldn't. Every time she walked into the kitchen, she heard her words again.

It was like Gram had been able to sense something that had been bothering Violet all along. Even if she put aside all her anger at Finn, even if she pretended that he hadn't been responsible for plunging her into this nightmare — that by some inexplicable trick of the universe he and Bear had vanished into thin air through no fault of his own — all of her feelings were concentrated with laser focus on how badly she wanted *Bear* back, with every bit of her being. Whether or not Finn returned was a point she would be willing to negotiate if necessary.

This never would have occurred to Violet before he'd disappeared. He and Bear together were her life — weren't they? Her ambivalence about her husband — her fairy-tale-ending husband — frightened her. It made her question all that had come before, made her question herself, At a time when she seemed to be at the center of everyone else's questioning, that was the last thing she needed.

As she pulled up to the house, she saw Agent Martin's car parked out front. He was leaning against it, waiting, sunglasses obstructing his expression, and as he raised his hand in a silent wave, Violet realized that Gram's questions might be the least of her worries.

★ ★ ★

Violet had been proud of herself this morning for pulling it together. She had taken a long, steamy shower, the water washing over days' worth of grief and grime. She had blow-dried her hair, trying not to think of the way Bear liked to drive his Tonka trucks up and down the hallway just outside the door while she got ready, the way he'd giggle when he peeked around the doorframe and she teasingly aimed the warm air in his direction, tousling his curly locks, She had put on clothes suitable for wearing in public. She had made an actual meal, an omelet and toast, and then forced herself to eat it, swallowing bite by bite over the permanent lump in her throat, before heading out to run the most ordinary of errands. Milk and juice. She had let herself believe that maybe acting normal would make a difference. That maybe she just had to force herself through the motions on her own terms, without Gram hovering over her.

But now that she was sitting here across the kitchen table from Agent Martin, who had declined her offer of coffee or tea, she worried that she looked *too* together, that he might mistakenly think she was handling things just fine — maybe even too fine.

'I appreciate you being open to me dropping

145

by,' Agent Martin said, his voice devoid of appreciation. He was not altogether unlike the FBI agents in those dime-a-dozen prime-time dramas. He wasn't as clever or as ridiculous with his dialogue, of course — no one was. But he did have the persona down, which was to say he had no bedside manner. In the many times they'd spoken over the last week, whether in a formal interview, a routine update, or a chance encounter in the agency's parking lot, never once had he expressed empathy for what Violet was going through. She didn't know if that was because he suspected her of something, or because that was just his way, but she hoped she wouldn't be needing his services long enough to find out. 'I'll get right to the point.'

Violet nodded.

'Ever heard the name Maribel Branson?'

Maribel. A pretty name. She would have remembered it. 'No. Should I have?'

'Your husband never mentioned her?'

In spite of his brusque façade, the tone of the question seemed to betray its intention. *Oh,* she thought. *Oh.* She looked at him despondently. 'Is he having an affair with her?'

The agent eyed her strangely, letting a few beats of silence fall between them. Violet held very, very still. Finally, he spoke. 'She's the woman who died when he fell asleep at the wheel of his car.'

Violet was conscious of the fact that her breathing had stopped, literally caught in her throat. 'When he — *what? When?* He *killed* a woman?' She felt dizzy. Little bright spots of color floated into the corners of her vision. She blinked them away.

Agent Martin leaned back in his chair. He looked around the kitchen and nodded to the empty room, as if letting someone there know that her surprise was satisfactory to him.

'He was responsible for the accident that caused her death,' he corrected her. 'Five years ago this month. But he was never charged. Her family was adamant about that. Just a tragic accident.'

'She was a pedestrian? Or driving in the oncoming lane?'

'She was in his passenger seat.'

Violet blinked harder.

'She was his fiancée,' Agent Martin said.

15

A FEW BLURRY MONTHS
AFTER AUGUST 2011

Finn did *not* want to go to Caitlin and George's for dinner. He knew everything about it would be perfect — the artisanal cheeses and bread Caitlin would have expertly selected from the international market, the elegant wine pairings, the elevated comfort food she was sure to serve as a main course, the decadent desserts, the married-couple banter between her and George, delicately choreographed to put guests at ease, to make them laugh, but not to raise eyebrows with any jabs that had too much truth to them. The perfection of it all was what he dreaded most. It would make him envy them, which would make him hate himself even more than he already did, which hardly seemed possible these days. But he had to go. He'd declined too many of their invitations at this point. Plus he didn't want to seem ungrateful now that they were his landlords. At least he could drink his way through the evening — the trip home was no longer a drive across town. Now it was a mere walk next door.

Fresh out of the shower, he wiped the steam from the mirror with the palm of his hand and slathered shaving cream on his face. Behind him, water dripped from the faucet into the antique tub, a constant sound that had become like a clock ticking down his moments alone in this ancient, empty house. He'd considered getting a dog to fill the space, to fill the silence, but it seemed decidedly unfair to the dog. He didn't trust himself to care for another living thing. He could barely drag himself out of bed these days. The credit for that went to Caitlin.

It was during the year he hadn't seen much of George and Caitlin — the year of Maribel — that they had bought their crumbling mansion in East Walnut Hills, restoring it top to bottom. Caitlin had fallen instantly in love with its stately façade, the semicircle of marble columns fronting the grand entrance, the brick and stone walls and arches that had withstood the years remarkably well, the fireplaces and the dumbwaiter and the gate to the storybook secret garden out back. Her only hang-up in putting an offer on the place had been the house next door — a three-story Victorian that had been converted into a multifamily years before and fallen into such disrepair that it was in danger of being condemned.

So George had bought that one too. Its renovation had focused on shoring up the structure as opposed to the cosmetics, just sufficient to bring things up to code. As for the curb appeal, it really was wondrous what a fresh coat of paint and some flowers could do. He'd planned to sell it once the current tenants' leases were up. The only ones left were up on the third floor — a couple of shaggy-haired younger guys who began and ended conversations with 'Peace, brother' and weren't home much. But then Finn's own home — his own world — had fallen down around him. George and Caitlin had called through the darkness and offered him a place to stay. Rent free, until he could find a job, get back on his feet. It was an offer he literally couldn't afford to refuse.

He would have preferred to leave entirely — leave the state, the country, even. He fantasized about the anonymity of getting lost in a faraway urban hub like London, or on one of those remote Greek islands where time seemed to have stopped decades before he'd ever laid eyes on Maribel. But he didn't have the money. He and Maribel had put down nonrefundable deposits on the historic church she'd had her heart set on for their ceremony, on the opulent ballroom overlooking Fountain Square they'd sentimentally snatched up for their reception, on the brass band she'd known right away they had to have. They'd made the most important — and most expensive — arrangements quickly, knowing that the logistics of wedding planning would be more difficult after they moved away, Her parents had offered to pay for it all, but Maribel had wanted the day to be wholly hers and Finn's, free of squabbling with her mother over the centerpieces or the menu. Finn hadn't even batted an eye as their bank accounts dipped dangerously low — they had all the time in the world to earn it back. Together. Asheville would be full of riches for them. From their happiness, the rest would come.

Finn had already downsized his possessions to

the bare minimum. What Maribel didn't bring to Asheville, they planned to buy together — or make, with their own four artistically gifted hands, in their new studio.

Instead, the meager belongings he had left he'd piled into the back of a U-Haul and unloaded here, all the while waiting to be awakened from his bad dream. He hadn't hung anything on the walls. There wasn't a photo to be found. Looking around, anyone at all could have been living here. He could almost pretend it wasn't him. If only.

The knobs of the sink squeaked as Finn drained the whisker-filled water and rinsed the basin. He wasn't bothered by the fixtures that barely worked, or the radiators that hissed, or the tile grout that was beyond the point of ever looking clean. He could understand now why people became so obsessed with the notion of other eras, even the idea of time travel. It was the stuff of silly science fiction and fantasy only until you had one day, one *moment*, you desperately wanted to go back to and stop yourself from doing the horrible thing that would ruin everything — and that you would never, ever forgive yourself for.

If one of Finn's creaky walk-in pantries or child-size built-in cupboards or understair crawl spaces would turn into a portal to another day, another time, he would jump through and emerge on the night of their engagement party. First he would relive it — Maribel in his arms, dancing after all their guests had left, drunk on champagne and love and plans for the life in front of them. Then he would erase the ill-fated, mistakenly romantic notion to drive, sleep-deprived and hungover, to the coast the next day.

He'd make sure he never dozed at the wheel. Never allowed the car to drift across that center line. Never caused the head-on collision that ended Maribel's life on the side of a lonely highway. Or if he couldn't stop it entirely, he would reach into the car with his retrospective hands and turn the wheel a few degrees to the right, just enough so that the life claimed would be his, not Maribel's. The driver, not the passenger. That was justice. That was the way it should have happened, if it had to happen at all.

Instead, Finn had walked away. Literally, figuratively. He'd been mercifully knocked unconscious, then came to in the hospital with nary a scratch. Evidently, he hadn't yet gotten around to changing his emergency contact to Maribel. Caitlin had been phoned. And Caitlin had been swift.

He supposed he was lucky that she'd never formed a tighter bond with Maribel, that rather than being sidelined by grief, her first thoughts were of him. With event planning came a certain amount of crisis management, which she now counted among her specialties. 'This could follow you forever,' she'd told him stoically. 'We can't let it.' He'd stared at her, dazed. But she'd already pled her case to George, who'd phoned his father, who'd made some calls of his own. Buried by shock and horror at what he'd done, Finn vacillated between periods of utter numbness and inconsolable hysteria. He didn't

152

have the presence of mind to ask how his name had been kept out of the papers. Or why, upon being advised by an impeccably dressed lawyer not to admit, on police record, to having dozed at the wheel, he'd never been pressed on the matter, never seen the inside of a courtroom. Never mind that he'd already told Maribel's family the truth. They hadn't wanted him charged anyway. He didn't know for certain whether their appeal would have been enough, or whether he owed an uncomfortably large debt to George's father.

As for the other driver — whose truck, rather than its passenger, had borne the brunt of the collision — he was just happy his insurance claims were settled so easily. Yet somehow none of it had cost Finn a dime.

'She told me this would kill you, after losing your parents,' George told him weeks later, when it belatedly occurred to Finn to protest. 'And my wife loves you like a brother. She's beside herself. I told her you're built of stronger stuff than that, but . . . Just let us help stop another tragedy from following this one, okay?'

The Bransons had been so gracious — too gracious. It might have been easier if they'd screamed at him the way he was berating himself. 'It was an *accident*, Finn,' her mother had said. 'Maribel loved you with all her heart. You were about to become a part of our family, and we don't want to walk away from that — you're all we have left.' They even offered to ease the burden of the money he'd lost on the wedding, to help pay for it with Maribel's small life insurance policy from her employer. 'She wouldn't want to see you buried by this,' her father told him, his hand firmly on Finn's shoulder. They were all of them so, so sad. But they weren't angry. The only angry one was Finn.

That was the most shameful part of it all. He couldn't hide his anger, nor could he allow it to rain down upon them when they were facing things so bravely on their own. He couldn't remain a part of their lives, couldn't even look them in the eye. The guilt was going to eat him alive no matter what, he could already see that. But he deserved a slow, agonizing death by guilt — anything quicker would be too kind. And staying in touch with them would only speed the process.

So he had accepted Caitlin and George's offer to move in here. Those first weeks, George was overseas for work, and Caitlin came by almost every day — after work on weekdays, and then on weekend afternoons, too, after she'd run all her errands. He sometimes wondered if she didn't have something better to be doing, some other friend to spend time with. Then again, he didn't exactly have room to talk. She'd dish up takeout for two, uninvited at the kitchen table. She'd uncork bottles of wine he didn't feel like drinking. She'd bring DVDs from her classic movies collection, pop them into his player, and deliver commentary the whole way through. He thanked her for the food but ate in silence, he drank the wine without tasting it, and he developed a fondness for the black-and-white starlets from a different era, though he never let on that he did. When the films were over, Caitlin would simply eject the disks, wash out the popcorn bowl by hand, bid him good night, and walk home. Despite his lack of talkativeness and the absence of any outward appreciation for her presence, she kept coming.

It was a new experience, sharing space with Caitlin without the two of them engaging in an unannounced, unjudged competition to see who could be the most clever or the biggest smart-ass. Sure, she'd been there for him after his parents died, but that had been more of a distract-him-from-the-sadness approach, whereby she dragged him to parties and he feigned having fun until eventually the feigning stopped. Never — not back then or any other time — had they spent so much time together and said so little. Finn was amazed that she wasn't growing sick of his melancholy. And then he began to question if she was really coming just for his sake after all. He'd never before considered that it might be lonely being married to someone like George. And when he stopped viewing her visits as sympathy calls, Finn found that he started looking forward to them rather than dreading them. It seemed as if everyone else in his life had disappeared along with Maribel. He knew he might have pushed them away — but they'd let him, easily. They hadn't pushed back. But Caitlin had. The silence between them become companionable.

One day, she brought him a listing for a graphic design job with a wedding photographer who had a storefront down the block. 'I know the idea of spending your days surrounded by photos of happy couples must be appalling,' she said, raising her arms in a don't-shoot-the-messenger gesture. 'The thing is, though, happy couples are suckers. They pay through the nose for this stuff.'

The salary *was* ridiculously high compared to the difficulty of the work. The owner wanted someone to design marketing materials for his expanding business, and to lay out custom albums for his customers. The hours were flexible. And Finn could practically throw a rock from his porch and hit the place — an advantage that could not be discounted, as he still had no car to drive and public transport here was minimally serviceable. He owed it to Caitlin to at least go to the interview. He was going to have to start paying rent eventually. It wasn't whether or not George could afford to carry him, it was the principle.

So he had taken the miserable job, airbrushing the happiest days of other people's lives, putting things in order for them, laying everything out on the pages of their albums to remind them of better days when times got tough. And they would — Finn wasn't far gone enough to imagine their lives would be perfect — but at least they'd have each other, for the foreseeable future.

The pitfalls of the job were outweighed not only by the paycheck but also by the fact that it met his lone requirement, which happened to be at odds with his line of work and overall skill set:

It required no creativity whatsoever. He could no longer have conjured his imagination even if he'd tried. At five o'clock sharp, he would walk home and sit on the wraparound porch with a beer, slouched down as if he could blend into the painted wood behind him. Winter was coming, but he hardly felt the cold. Usually, he had the whole big house to himself, though occasionally the sound of an acoustic guitar would drift faintly down from the free spirits upstairs if they weren't working one of their odd-hour, odd-job shifts. He'd watch people walk by — to and from the nearby sports bar, the cafes, the drugstore, the wine cellar — and feel both more and less lonely. They'd stroll past with their dogs or their drinking buddies or their reusable shopping bags or their steaming carriers of takeout, and their laughter looked like a luxury. He wished to be any of them, anyone but him.

Finn went into the spare bedroom, where he'd left his button-down cooling on the ironing board. Even this apartment was much too big for only him — it made his head shake if he let himself think too hard about the fact that this was only a *third* of the building that Caitlin and George had mortgaged for no reason other than to make their own house look better. He alone had three bedrooms and two baths. But who was he to point fingers at their excess? It was keeping a roof over his head. They'd reluctantly agreed to let him start paying rent, but it was way below what they could surely get for this space, Finn knew. He didn't have the energy to argue. He was happy to be giving them *something* so it didn't feel like a handout, but he knew George's pity wouldn't go away anytime soon.

Finn and Caitlin had reached this easy balance, talking but not talking, passing time together without consciously spending the time together. But it was a few months in now, and he'd still barely seen George, who had been closing some kind of big-deal acquisition. It was finally done, and he'd be around more now — not all the time, but definitely more. Hence the dinner invitation. This one had come from George himself, standing in his driveway, volleying with Finn across the lawns about the UC Bearcats' season. And that had made it harder to decline.

Finn carried the shirt back to his bedroom, where he stepped into his nicest pair of dark jeans and laced up his suede Vans. Though he already knew he was going to feel underdressed, he worried that dressing up any more would make him look like a teenage delinquent summoned to the headmaster's office for a chat. He grabbed a bouquet of flowers he'd had the presence of mind to pick up, and without bothering to lock the door behind him, headed across the lawn.

★ ★ ★

Caitlin was laughing so hard at George's story that Finn was reminded of the Caitlin he'd been drawn to back when they were in school together. The Caitlin who baked cookies for her friends when they were having bad days and brought them all homemade noodle soup when they got sick — even in the dorms, where there was a communal kitchenette on each floor that no one else ever. used — but who also would swear like a sailor and tell the raunchiest jokes of any girl he'd ever met when she got drunk. This Caitlin was sweet and generous and good at everything she did, a class act with a charming irreverent streak, but above all she was *fun*. It was jarring to him to see her laugh this way and to realize that the woman who'd been sitting subdued next to him on the couch for months was in fact his fun-loving friend just waiting for an occasion to burst back out. And apparently having George back in town and Finn over for a fancy dinner and maybe one too many glasses of her perfectly paired wine was it.

George's last trip had wrapped with a couple of days in Singapore, and he was explaining that his colleague — not one of his favorite travel companions, a guy with a 'thick, straight stick up his ass,' as George had put it — had left his sunglasses in the seatback on the airplane and ended up buying some Dolce and Gabbana knockoffs from a peddler.

'So we get into the buffet line for lunch and he slides the sunglasses up on his head and starts helping himself — some fruit, some salad, some bread — and the jackass is completely oblivious of the fact that he's got these smeared black circles where the sunglasses touched his skin. Like the old shoe-polish-on-the-binoculars trick. The spray paint on these things wasn't even dry!'

This was too much for Caitlin, who slapped

159

her knee and sank her forehead onto the tablecloth, where she was soundlessly laughing so hard she was shaking the whole big farmhouse table. Finn laughed too, more at Caitlin than at the story. She let out something between a squeak and a snort, and he laughed harder. George looked pleased with himself, as if he thought he owed it to his wife to entertain her after so many days away. Finn caught his eye, and George smiled at him the way two parents might share a glance over a child they equally adored. Finn shifted in his seat.

Caitlin raised her head and wiped tears from beneath her eyes with her napkin. She lifted the bottle of wine to gauge how much was left. It was their second, and they'd put a pretty good dent in it. 'Should we finish this up, or bring out some port with dessert?'

A fog was settling over Finn's brain just the way he liked it — enough to dull his constant pain, his misplaced jealousy toward his happily married hosts, and his guilt over feeling that way toward people who were surely better friends than he deserved. He raised his glass and Caitlin topped him off.

'What's dessert?' George asked. Caitlin never skimped on the last course — not that she'd skimped on anything. Every aspect of the dinner was impeccable, as Finn had known it would be. He hadn't had a better meal outside of a restaurant.

She clapped her hands. 'Molten lava cakes! It will just be a bit — it takes some doing.' She waved off their offers to help clear the table and disappeared into the kitchen.

The two men were silent for a moment, as if someone had hit the light switch and they had to let their eyes grow accustomed to the dark. George filled his own glass with the rest of the wine and reached behind him to place the empty bottle on the antique server. The dining room was octagonal, with tall sheer-curtained windows and layers of crown molding leading up to an opulent crystal chandelier. When Finn and Maribel had gone apartment hunting in Asheville, they'd hit a few pubs afterward and spent half their time looking up from their barstool perches, admiring the historic ceilings, the stamped tin tiles, the hand-carved wood and decorative mirrors mounted high behind the bottle-lined bars. He thought of their foursome's champagne toast that night on the stairs, the promise of more celebrations to come. Maribel would have loved this room, this place, this food, George's story about his coworker who got his comeuppance. Why had he not brought her around when he had the chance? And how could he make it through without her here, or anywhere, now and for the rest of his life?

'I know we've always been friends mostly through Caitlin,' George said, jarring Finn from his thoughts. Finn looked up, and George was looking at him earnestly, like someone in a Yale class photo. 'I was hoping to change that, now that you're right next door, but I swear I'm barely in town enough to stay married to my own wife.'

Finn laughed uneasily. He knew it was

supposed to be a joke, but he never knew how to respond to things like that — to any reference to marriage at all, let alone the idea of one on the edge.

'I do try to hit the links when I'm home on weekends, though,' George continued. 'That's kind of my one indulgence that Caitlin doesn't have much interest in. You still golf at all? There was that time in Sunny Isles, but I was nursing such a hangover that I admit I don't remember who was and was not in his element.'

'A little.' Finn shrugged. 'Not much, actually. I'm not very good.'

'Excellent. I'd like to actually win once in a while.'

Finn laughed.

'No, seriously. These guys at the club — half of them don't even have jobs anymore. They just invest. And spend their spare time on the driving range, apparently. It's not a fair fight. How about next Saturday? I usually try to get an early tee time so I can be back by the time Cait's done with the farmers' market and her yoga class. You'd be doing me a favor if you came along, honestly.'

'I'll let you know.'

George nodded, taking him in. 'Look,' he said, 'something else I wanted to mention. A lot of guys who spend so much time out of town would not appreciate their wife spending time with a single guy next door.'

Finn stiffened and turned his attention to the delicate stem of his wineglass. How had he not seen this coming? Was he so grief stricken that he

162

was blind to the social norms of the world? His mind was already racing ahead to form an apology, but George was still talking.

'I'm not one of those guys,' he went on.

Finn lifted his eyes to George's, unsure of where he was going with this.

'Caitlin could use some company. I hate leaving her alone so much of the time — my travel schedule is more intense than ever, and even though she keeps pinning her hopes on things slowing down 'after this deal,' then 'after that deal,' then 'after the next one,' it's not likely. And now that I'm mostly doing business in China, Hong Kong, Japan — even a short trip seems to take twice as long with all the layovers and delays and time zones and whatever else.' George glanced toward the kitchen doorway. Satisfied that Caitlin wasn't about to reappear, he leaned in closer to Finn and lowered his voice. 'She stayed here for me, you know. In Cincinnati. I mean. We're just far enough away from where she grew up that it's not like her old friends can meet for a quick happy hour or join the same gym, and you know as well as I do that most of your college gang ended up elsewhere, Her office is mostly these stodgy older women — she hasn't had a hell of a lot of luck making new friends.'

'I find that hard to believe,' Finn said, himself glancing at the kitchen door she'd bounded cheerfully behind just moments before. How was he learning this about his ever-present friend from her absentee husband?

'Haven't you ever noticed that women find her

a little . . . well, Caitlin has very few faults — at least on the surface. Other women hate that.'

Finn hadn't seen her in quite that light before, but he knew the second George said it that it was true, That was how she'd ended up running with him and his crew in college, To them, she'd become one of the guys. But they'd get occasional reminders — other men checking her out as they played pool in a bar, holding doors for her as they walked into the movie theater, even flirting with her at the gas station — that while she might seem like one of the guys, she definitely was not.

George cleared his throat. 'Maybe you'd rather be alone these days. I don't know.' It was the first time since Finn had moved in here that George had even indirectly referenced what had happened with Maribel, and he looked as uncomfortable as Finn felt. 'But I just want you to know that if you do like having Caitlin hanging around. I wouldn't want you to hold off on my account. Honestly, it makes me feel better, having someone look out for her — this neighborhood still has its rough spots. And I don't want her to decide being married to me is too lonely. I try to make up for the time away when I'm home, but it's never enough.'

Finn tried not to squirm in his seat. Everything about their life seemed like more than enough to him.

Caitlin breezed back in, carrying the desserts on a silver tray the way absolutely no one did anymore, No wonder Finn had grown fond of those old films she loved, Still, he felt more self-conscious than ever. He didn't know if he should be grateful for George's talk, or wary of it.

The desserts were perfect, naturally — decadent without being pretentious. Before Finn knew it, they'd polished them off, along with the rest of the wine.

Caitlin started to get to her feet. 'Let me make some decaf,' she offered. 'I'm not sure I can handle any more alcohol, but if you guys are still going, we've got Baileys or Kahlua to go with it . . .'

George placed a hand on her arm, pressing her gently back into her seat. 'You've outdone yourself,' he said. 'I'll do the coffee. I brought some cigars back with me, and I admit I'd like an excuse to sneak a few puffs out back while it brews.' He smiled at Finn. 'What do you say? You in?'

Finn held up his hands. 'I'm good. But thanks, man. Maybe next time.'

The room fell silent when George left, and neither Caitlin nor Finn rushed to fill it. He fought a stab of guilt that he wasn't doing a better job of small talk right now. It was just that —

'What's wrong?' she asked. 'You have a funny look on your face.' For a moment, Finn debated not saying anything, but he didn't have the energy not to. He kept so much else bottled in these days. 'Nothing,' he said, trying to sound casual. 'George just mentioned something about how much time we've been spending together, that's all.'

Caitlin looked surprised. 'Did he say it bothered him?'

'No.' Finn hesitated. 'Actually, the opposite — he kind of. I don't know, gave me his blessing.'

Caitlin sat back in her chair, a satisfied smile on her face. 'That's my George,' she said quietly. She twirled the stem of her empty wineglass. 'You know, I've always gotten the feeling that no one has ever believed me that you and I didn't hook up at some point. They're all like, 'Oh, come on, it had to have happened at least once!' It's like Billy Crystal's theory in *When Harry Met Sally* — that people of the opposite sex can't just be friends. But not George. He's the only one who has never once hinted at that. I used to wait for it to start bothering him that other people believed it. But it's amazing the stuff that doesn't bother George. I think he learned that from his dad, growing up in the public eye — to choose battles carefully.' She was gazing at the spot where George had been sitting, a look of such uncomplicated and complete fondness on her face that Finn's chest ached for the way Maribel used to look at him with that kind of affection.

Finn thought of what little he knew of George's father's political career. 'But when a Bryce-Daniels does go to battle, look out,' he said. 'Right?'

Caitlin tipped back her chair so she could see into the kitchen, making sure George was still outside. 'Well, they're not exactly master strategists,' she said, her voice low and thick with wine. 'But you've got to hand it to them that they're not afraid to sneak-attack.' Her smile was unwavering.

Finn cleared his throat. 'What they did for me — '

She waved him away. 'It might seem like a big deal to you, but I promise you, it's small potatoes to them. Just . . . let's just agree to never mention it again, okay?'

It was more than okay. It was what he wanted. He'd just needed to hear her say it.

'I do feel bad that I haven't gotten to know George better,' he said. 'Even after being in your wedding. That was my window, and I blew it. It's just that right after I got back, that's when I met Maribel . . . ' His voice trailed off, and Caitlin's eyes softened with the sympathy that she usually did such a good job of masking. Finn had to look away. He didn't want to end on this note after Caitlin had put so much work into this dinner.

'In conclusion,' he said, hoping to salvage the mood, 'George telling me it's cool to basically step in for him when he's not around is not one of those mind-fuck games where he says it's okay but that's really supposed to be my cue to stop?'

Caitlin laughed. 'He is only allowed to mind-fuck *me*,' she said. 'It's in our vows.'

She leaned forward and tapped a fingertip lightly on the top of Finn's hand. 'He's glad you're here,' she said. 'We both are. We asked you to come, remember? We knew that at a time like this, inviting you here meant you would become a bigger part of our lives. At least, we hoped so. We wanted to be there for you. Both of

167

us. And selfishly, yeah, I'm glad you're here for me, too.'

Finn couldn't help smiling. 'Even though I'm kind of a downer these days?'

Caitlin laughed. 'I like downers,' she said. 'Why do you think I drink so much wine?'

16

AUGUST 2016

Even before she'd had the twins, Caitlin had always noticed, and always loved, how a child could defuse the tension in a room — not necessarily putting adults on their best behavior, but simply stealing the attention from any elephants that might have otherwise taken center stage.

Take Caitlin and her mother-in-law, for example. Beverly was her name, the sort of name that people didn't have anymore and that Caitlin thought of as synonymous with old money. The two women had never exactly *not* gotten along, but they'd never been entirely at ease around each other either. George's mother was exactly the opposite of Caitlin's own, who was, if anything, overfriendly to a fault, extending her easy schoolteacher's manner to anyone within reach. Beverly always treated Caitlin with exceeding politeness, as if she were a dinner guest rather than a member of the family — and though everyone else called her Bev, she was always Beverly to Caitlin, and had never beseeched her to call her otherwise. Caitlin couldn't shake the feeling that Beverly didn't think that she was good enough for her son, didn't feel that she was *worthy* of being treated as family — though Caitlin was aware enough of her own insecurities to question whether that was just her own self-doubt or an unspoken assessment that her mother-in-law was in fact projecting.

After Caitlin had the twins, though, conversation between her and George's mother became easier, even fun. Leo and Gus were both the source and the focus of all the energy in the room. It would have been difficult for the adults to have a real dialogue even if they'd tried. And they didn't try. They were equally smitten with the boys and content to let them have the floor, as it were. Together the women would laugh over their antics, and suddenly they had something in common. They had the children. And by definition, that meant they were family — no matter how politely *Bev* might treat her, right there in front of them were the living, breathing, giggling, squirming, messy little reminders that Caitlin was the mother of her grandchildren.

It was the same way with Finn now, at the lake house. Had the two of them been alone, there would have been an immediate standoff. But they weren't, and there wasn't. With Bear and Gus and Leo commanding the room, Caitlin and Finn were left with no choice but to dance around them, and she was horrified to realize that she was almost enjoying herself.

Finn did tricks flipping burgers on the grill, while the boys clapped and cheered. Caitlin made a game of pretending not to know the words to silly kids' songs, and Finn laughed along as the boys, delighted, squealed '*That's* not how it goes!' with every mistake she made. They

170

sang 'The Itsy Bitsy Fire Truck Drove Up the Water Spout.' They sang 'On Top of Strawberries Covered with Cheese.' They raced around the living room playing, 'Duck Duck Moose!'

By the time the sun began its descent, it felt almost like old times, Finn and Caitlin trading banter as they cleaned up the kitchen, conscious that the boys were ever present, even though the kids at that moment seemed to be hyperfocused on erecting a precarious block tower in the center of the coffee table.

But of course, things were not like old times. Caitlin knew she couldn't let her guard down. Doing so could be dangerous. Maybe not physically dangerous for her or the boys — God, she hoped not. She never would have come here if she'd thought even for a second that Finn would be capable of causing real harm, though now that she was here it was clear that she was no longer sure what he was and was not capable of. What worried her most was that losing control of this situation could be dangerous for Violet. If Caitlin got careless, Finn might manage to somehow slip away with Bear. And if they didn't resurface, if Caitlin had missed the only chance to set things right, how would she ever live with herself then?

She couldn't let that happen. She had to keep them where she could see them. And so after all three boys were tucked into the room with the bunk beds, a sleeping bag rolled out on the floor for an exhausted little Bear, Caitlin took a pillow and a blanket from the master bedroom and dragged them out to the living room. Finn was sitting on the couch, elbows on his knees, a freshly opened beer on the table in front of him, almost as if he were looking forward to having Caitlin join him.

But when he eyed the bundle of bedding in Caitlin's arms, his eyes clouded. 'Thanks,' he said, 'but I told you, I'm sleeping with Bear.' Of course all the kids had wanted to bunk together, but Caitlin and Finn had already agreed to carry Bear out of the twins' room once he was asleep. At the end of the hall between their room and the master bedroom was the room George's father used as an office, and Finn and Bear could fit side by side on the pull-out couch there. Finn wasn't about to leave Bear's side any more than Caitlin was about to let Finn sleep in the room with the twins. She'd already muddled all the lines, but she had to draw one somewhere.

'These aren't for you,' she said, tossing them onto the leather recliner in the corner. 'They're for me.'

Finn raised his eyebrows. 'First you're the milkman, now you're the night watchman,' he teased halfheartedly. 'What next?' But the spell had been broken. Her mind was already turning with the possibilities she needed to head off. How to ensure there was no way Finn could sneak Bear out without waking her?

Even though the cabin was outfitted with an alarm system, she and George rarely bothered to set it unless they were headed home to Ohio. It had been years since her in-laws had stored anything of real value here, and the kids were prone to tripping the alarm, a nuisance to the adults who did not always dial in the 'all clear' code in time. But Caitlin needed that nuisance now. The problem was, she'd given Finn the security code yesterday, when he'd stood in her kitchen, making demands.

She walked deliberately to the keypad beside the front door, shielded the screen from Finn's view, and began working her way through the settings. Finally, she found the reset option. She changed the code to her ATM pin, a number she wouldn't forget and Finn wouldn't guess. The system beeped three times to indicate that it was live, and Caitlin felt a little better. If any door or window was opened during the night, the alarm would go off. Caitlin would be right here in the living room to hear it, and even if she somehow failed to stop Finn from making off with Bear, the police would be on his heels before he could get far.

Of course, if that happened, they'd be on her heels too.

She stole a glance at Finn, but he was looking out through the sliding glass doors toward the lake — admiring the last silvery glint of daylight on the water or strictly avoiding her eyes, she couldn't say. If Finn could manage to find a way to sneak out of here on his *own* — if she awakened here tomorrow to find only Bear, and not his fugitive father — *that* wouldn't be such a bad thing, would it? Come to think of it, Caitlin would prefer it if he had a change of heart and opted out of this mess. She'd still have some explaining to do, but at least she could return Bear to his mother, with minimal collateral damage to her own family in the process.

She helped herself to a beer she had no intention of actually drinking and joined Finn on the couch, curling her legs beneath her on the opposite end. She knew the bond still existed between them. It was like a habit — and if they'd fallen back into it earlier, they could do it again. If she could manage to tap back into that mutual sense of familiarity while the kids were in bed, then maybe she could use it to shackle the elephant in the room — to actually *reach* Finn.

'It's not as if I'm going to forget that we're not on a pleasure trip here, Cait,' he said, and she was unnerved that his mind-reading abilities — always a marvel in their friendship — were sharp as ever.

'Let's play that game we used to play,' she said. 'Either Or.'

He rolled his eyes, but she pretended not to notice.

'This thing with Vi. Would you say it's more about some*thing*, or some*one*?'

He tipped back his beer bottle and took a long swig. 'Someone.'

'And is that someone Violet, or not Violet?'

'It depends on what you mean by that.'

'So not Violet.' She smiled. 'Is this someone me, or not me?'

Another eye roll.

'Whew. Glad we got that out of the way. Is this someone from the past, or the present?'

'What the hell do you think, Caitlin?'

'I'm asking *you*.'

He didn't answer. Caitlin pressed her bare toes

174

into the soft leather of the couch cushion. 'Do you remember what an asshole Jake was to me in college?' she asked suddenly.

'Jake the Snake? The serial cheater? Who could forget?'

'Well, before that. I was head over heels for the guy. As I'm sure you also remember.'

'Why are we talking about Jake the Snake?'

Caitlin picked at her beer label, the way she used to on first dates when she was nervous. 'Because back when George and I couldn't get pregnant. I found myself thinking about Jake. Wondering what might have been if things had turned out differently — if he hadn't cheated. Or if I'd forgiven him. Wondering if he'd gotten married and had kids of his own. Wondering if he and *I* would have had an easier time having a kid.'

Finn gave a mirthless laugh. 'You found a different solution to that problem.'

She ignored him. 'The point is, it's easy to romanticize the past. If I can do it with Jake the Snake, of all people, if I can daydream *him* back into a suit of armor after all the shit he put me through, imagine how easily one might retrospectively transform a *good* past relationship into a *perfect* one.'

'I'm not 'retrospectively transforming' it into something that was perfect. It *was* perfect.'

'Lots of things seem perfect at first. You think Maribel was your 'one true love,' is that what this is all about? Get real! You and Maribel just never had a chance to screw things up!'

At the sound of Maribel's name, Finn's whole

body changed. Somehow his stiffened, hunched stance managed to look both defensive and defeated. Like a frightened, wounded, wild animal.

'Oh, I'd say I screwed it up beyond most people's definition of what that could even *possibly* look like, wouldn't you?' His voice was hollow, cold, and Caitlin at once realized both the insensitivity of her jab and the unreachable depth of Finn's wound. Still, Finn was used to people avoiding the topic, or apologizing or backing down when it came up. To follow his lead as he retreated into that bottomless pit would only trap both of them. She had to steer him around it.

'Wouldn't you say you're doing the same with Violet now?' she countered. 'The thing is, what happened with Maribel, everyone knows that was an accident. But what you're doing now — there's no excuse. You want to decide things with Violet are null and void, fine. I don't get it, but fine. But this is so, so far from what's best for Bear.'

But Finn went on with his rant as if he hadn't heard her. 'Never had a chance to screw things up with Maribel? I made *the* ultimate relationship-ending mistake. The only one, in fact, that you really, really can't come back from, no matter how much you want to!' Even as he was folding inside of himself, shrinking into the couch cushion, he looked as if he could pounce on her at any second, overpowering her to the ground with misplaced rage.

Sympathy welled up in her, but she fought it

176

back. 'Quit with the sob story, Finn. This isn't about that.' She was surprised by the firmness in her voice. 'A little perspective here, please. All I'm saying is that what the two of you had, it was special, but it only lasted a year, okay? I know you didn't think that was fast at the time, but think of it now. Now that you're a father, you know as well as I do, a year is like this.' She snapped her fingers. 'It's like they say, the days are long, but the years are short. And Violet's days are *really* long right now, Finn. The longest.'

Finn looked away.

She leaned forward. She was starting to feel desperate. 'Okay. So it was the perfect year with Maribel. Is it really fair to Violet for you to put a perfect year with someone else — someone you can't have anymore, as you so eloquently pointed out — up on a pedestal over *her*? Over a chance to have many years ahead of you with a real-life person who I'm sure has flaws as a wife but who loves you, and is the mother of your child?'

Finn didn't answer.

'I thought you had worked through this,' Caitlin said quietly.

He turned his eyes on her. 'What made you think that?' he snapped. 'You never asked.'

Caitlin recoiled. 'Well, gee, let's see. You, um, *married Violet*. Excuse me for assuming that meant you had come to terms with what happened with Maribel. I'm sure only *everyone else* drew the same conclusion.'

'Not everyone,' he said quietly.

'Oh, right. Not Violet. Because you never even told her about Maribel.' Her eyes bore into his

177

until he looked away and took another big swig of his beer. 'And I didn't either,' she continued, 'because I couldn't imagine her hearing it from anyone other than you. That time I asked you about it, you said you'd tell her when you were ready. I thought you were' — she rotated the beer bottle in the air, searching for alternate wording that would not come — 'working through things.'

Finn exploded off the couch so suddenly that she dropped her drink into her lap. 'In Cincinnati. I thought I could 'work through things,' okay? I thought that if I stayed away from Fountain Square, stayed away from Music Hall, stayed away from all the hole-in-the-wall bars and art galleries and brunch cafés that I equate with Maribel. I could almost do it. And I did almost do it. In Cincinnati. But I can't do it in Asheville.'

There it was. When Gram had announced that she'd be retiring in Asheville, when Violet had approached Finn about moving there, Caitlin had thought that surely Finn would finally spill his heart out to her about what had happened. When he hadn't, she'd expressed concern to George one night as they were lying in bed. He'd only shrugged. 'He's always wanted to live there,' he said. 'Why *not* move there now? He'll tell her if he wants to tell her.' *That's a male mentality for you*, Caitlin had thought. She'd convinced herself that Finn, whom she'd always known to be an artist and a dreamer and independent almost to a fault, was of the same mind as her smooth-talking country club husband.

178

She should have known better. She *had* known better, had worried that Finn was keeping too much bottled up inside, taking agonizing steps he shouldn't be taking without alerting Violet to the difficulty. And she had ignored her gut. Now look what Finn had gone and done.

He sank back onto the couch next to her, deflated. 'Asheville was too nonspecific a dream,' he said. 'The whole city, the whole goddamn *mountain range*, all of it was my picture of the life I was supposed to have with Maribel. How can I possibly be there, in any part of it, with someone else standing in where Maribel was supposed to be?'

Caitlin winced on Violet's behalf. All this time, had he really thought of his wife as a stand-in?

'I can't compartmentalize that,' he continued. 'And believe me, I've tried. It was a disaster. Clearly.'

'Maybe if you'd told Violet what was going on, she could have helped you through it,' Caitlin said. 'She loves you. She wouldn't want you to be suffering.'

'Trust me,' Finn grumbled, 'if I was honest with Violet about what I've been feeling, it would not have ended well.'

'And *this* is ending well?' Caitlin asked, incredulous. 'You left her! You took her son! You're wanted by the FBI! You've dragged me down here into this with you! How can this be the better solution than . . . than virtually anything else?'

Finn managed to ignore the crux of her response. 'I did *not* drag you down here.'

'What the hell else did you expect me to do? Really, Finn.'

'Just . . . leave me be. Give me time. Let me figure this out on my own.'

Caitlin stared at him. 'That's what I've *been* doing — for years. That's what everyone's been doing. I'd say it's not working out for you so well.' She gestured around the cabin, and her hand settled on Finn's knee. 'Look,' she said, 'this doesn't have to be that hard. Why don't we call Violet and have her come up here? I'll leave, and the two of you can talk. You tell her everything, and you work it out. Together or apart. Either way, you stop this nonsense with Bear. You tell the authorities it was a misunderstanding. Violet will back you, once she knows the truth. She's a *good* person, Finn. She's too good not to, even when you've hurt her. Badly.'

He shook her hand off. 'That would be very cozy, wouldn't it? What a happy ending for everyone — except me.' He stood. 'I told you, Cait. You say a word to anyone. I tell George, End of story, You can tell yourself I gave you no choice but to come down here, you can tell yourself you're here to be a friend to Vi, but you're really here to cover your own ass, You're here to talk me out of it, You dragged your own kids into it. At the moment, the person making the bigger mess of things is you.'

He set his empty bottle on the counter with a thud, then turned back to her, 'I'm going to go get Bear situated in the office and stretch out next to him. So don't even think about trying anything.'

As if on cue, Caitlin's cell phone burst into a melody. She looked at the screen. George. She'd texted him earlier to let him know that they had arrived safely, but never went to sleep without checking in.

Finn raised his eyebrows, knowing who it was without asking. 'Isn't he going to be wondering why you didn't call earlier to let the boys say good night?' he asked. He was right, of course, But Caitlin knew she couldn't trust the boys to babble on the way they did when they were excited without mentioning Bear or Uncle Finn.

Caitlin's thumb hovered over the answer button. 'He knows that settling in the first day here can be exhausting,' she said, trying to sound more sure than she felt.

'But how long can you keep that up?' Finn asked. 'He's going to want to talk to them eventually. What is your plan exactly, Caitlin? How long are you going to stay?'

Without waiting for the answer he knew Caitlin didn't have, he disappeared down the hallway.

Caitlin caught the call just before it went to voice mail.

'Hey, baby,' she said. She did her best to sound like she'd been dying to talk to him all clay.

★ ★ ★

Wide awake on the couch, Caitlin could just make out the twins' closed door down the hall. She wanted to join them there, where she could take comfort in the mere sound of them breathing, but resisted the urge — this was the best vantage point from which to protect them all.

She thought about the many other nights she'd spent staring sleeplessly into the darkness of the cabin. Here even more than at home she had a tendency to be plagued by fear of all the danger close at hand. She knew the comfort around her was man-made, fragile, just slim walls between them and the wilderness — the primeval forest, the deceptively calm lake.

She'd lie there and worry that the boys would fall off the dock and disappear beneath the surface of the murkiest part of the water. She could see herself jumping in after them, her panicked wails for help going unheard, her arms flailing wildly in circles through the water, her feet sinking into the mud and sludge below, unable to find them, unable to reach them in time. Just the thought of it was enough to make her heart race.

She'd toss and turn and obsess about the slight risk — but nonetheless, a possibility in this part of Kentucky — of Leo or Gus having a chance encounter with a mountain lion or a black bear. Or a venomous snake. She worried about a brown recluse or black widow climbing between the bunk bed sheets at night and leaving its mark — what if the boys called for her and she didn't see the bite? What if she didn't recognize what was wrong? Or what if they didn't wake to call for her at all, and in the morning, they were just . . . just gone? Those fears seemed as real now as they always had. She couldn't trivialize them. That would be like tempting fate.

Yet now a more immediate danger had taken up residence with its own set of terrifying what-ifs. What if George showed up? What if Finn really had lost it, and he held her and the boys hostage somehow? What if Caitlin was arrested for aiding and abetting a criminal? What if Violet found out that Caitlin was here, that she had known where Bear was for even one second — let alone two days full of thousands of seconds — and not called her?

When she'd decided to come, Caitlin had thought that sharing this roof with Finn would make her feel as if she were at least doing something for Violet, facing something for Violet. But now that she was here, breathing the same air within these walls, sharing cold beers and even a few laughs before things had turned south, all she could feel was her *betrayal* of her friend. She was swimming in it. No — drowning in it.

She had never, ever betrayed a friend before, not like this. She had only one other dark secret in her life, the one Finn was holding over her head, and that one alone had added a shadow to every minute of every new day she lived. She knew there was no way she could add another, darker shadow and pretend it wasn't there. If the roles were reversed between her and Violet, how could she ever forgive Violet for this — no matter what Violet's reasons were, no matter what Violet's rationale was? It was unforgivable.

183

Caitlin realized with a heavy sadness that there might be no salvaging their friendship — she was in too deep. And it made her hate Finn, for putting her in this position. She hated him so much that it was tempting to call the police right now, let the chips fall where they may, accept her punishment. It would almost be worth it to make sure he got his, to set things right for Violet. Caitlin might not be able to explain anything she'd done in a way that would make Violet understand, but at least she could reunite her with Bear, put something back where it belonged, even if it meant that the rest of it all came crashing down around her.

But what had she done to deserve this particular crash? Of course, maybe if she had chosen to tell Violet certain things years ago . . . but no, those things weren't hers to tell. She'd simply been dragged into the middle of this mess against her will. The unfairness of it was almost tangible.

Caitlin didn't trust herself to make any more decisions tonight — not for herself or Finn, and certainly not for the twins or little Bear. Because in spite of her years of incessant worrying, the biggest danger now was one she had not foreseen.

And that meant there could be other threats she had overlooked.

17

Violet hunched over her knees on the couch and stared at the name and phone number on the screen of her laptop, open on the coffee table. Delilah Branson, there in ten ordinary-looking digits. It had been easy to find the number as soon as she had the name. And it had been easy to find the name as soon as she'd looked up the accident. There it was in the *Cincinnati Enquirer*'s online archives: *The passenger in the car, 27-year-old Maribel Branson, was killed instantly on impact. She is survived by her parents, William and Delilah Branson of Indianapolis. Both drivers were treated for minor injuries and released. An investigation into the cause of the crash is under way.*

There were plenty of William Bransons in Indiana's white pages, but there was only one Delilah.

Violet had always been sickened by rubber-neckers on the freeway, but she couldn't stop herself from looking up every mention of the crash she could find — there'd been coverage near the scene in South Carolina, as well — staring at photo after photo of the gnarled wreckage. It was hard to believe that both Finn and the driver of the truck he'd hit had walked away from that. It was harder to believe that this

185

entire tragedy was laid bare online for all the world to see — even though Finn was mentioned nowhere by name — and yet Violet hadn't known a thing about it. In the hours since Agent Martin had left, she had been sitting here trying to come to terms with the fact that she'd been oblivious of the most public moment in the life of her own husband.

Her own husband, and the woman who would have been his wife.

One of the articles had referred to the car's driver as 'virtually unscathed.' Violet wasn't so sure about that.

She needed a drink to steel her nerves. At least, she needed the *idea* of a drink to steel her nerves. She would have only one shot at this, so it was important to have her wits about her when she called. She padded barefoot into the kitchen, where she rummaged through the cupboard above the fridge and found some vodka and an unopened bottle of cranberry juice. She filled a short glass with ice, measured out exactly one shot of vodka, and poured the tart red liquid to the rim. Then she returned to her seat on the couch and took a sip. Just a little one.

It was eight o'clock, and the sunset had reached that golden hour where the light really did paint everything it touched gold. The living room faced the street, so Violet had closed the blinds for privacy, but the white slats glowed with an ambient yellow. The house was that same deafening quiet she'd called Caitlin to complain about the other day. So much had changed since then, Gram had thrown her off balance with her doubts. Agent Martin had floored her with his questions. Bear's bed had lost a little more of its Bear smell. But the too-quiet of this miserably empty house roared its same dull, ear-splitting roar.

Violet dialed the number and waited. One ring, then two. Maybe it would go to voice mail. That would be . . . well, not easier at all, but less scary at this exact second. Then, a woman's voice. 'Hello?'

Violet cleared her throat. 'Mrs. Branson? Delilah Branson?'

'I'm afraid I'm on that Do Not Call list, though it seems as if fewer companies bother to check these days.'

'Oh, no, I'm not . . . I mean, I'm calling because — ' Violet took a shaky breath and started again. 'My name is Violet Welsh. I'm calling about Finn Welsh.'

There was a pause. 'You're his wife?'

Violet nodded pointlessly into the empty room before her voice returned. 'I am, yes. I'm so sorry for — '

'Oh my, and there's been this . . . this mix-up, with your little boy. Has he come back?'

'Not yet.'

'I'm so very sorry to hear that. To lose a child . . . ' Her voice trailed off, and Violet's eyes closed at the sound of the pain behind the words. 'That FBI agent — Martin. I think his name was? — called the other day, with all sorts of questions. I'm afraid I wasn't any help. I haven't heard from Finn in years.'

'That's not why I . . . I mean, I think I might

have different questions. If you have a minute?'
The white noise of the room's silence seemed to
have been sucked into the phone line. 'I don't
want to be insensitive — '

'Your child is missing. You're allowed to be
insensitive. I just can't imagine Finn doing
something like this. There must be some kind of
misunderstanding, surely.'

An uncomfortable pressure was building in
Violet's chest. 'I hope so.'

'I was happy to hear that he'd gotten married
and had a child. I only heard that recently
— through the grapevine, you know — and I
really did think to myself, *Good for him*. He
deserved happiness. We tried to reach out to him
after the accident, but I think it was just too
difficult for him. Some people found it hard to
believe — most of all him — but we really didn't
blame him for what happened. Maribel had been
so crazy about him, and he was so clearly
devastated . . . ' Her voice trailed off into a heavy
sigh. 'Pointing fingers wasn't going to do anyone
any good. Our pastor said maybe it would help
him if he could *feel* our forgiveness, but I don't
think he wanted to feel it. I think he wanted to
punish himself. If that makes any sense.'

'I think it does, actually.'

'We even offered to help him financially, and
he declined, though I'm pretty sure he was
desperate. If Caitlin and George hadn't taken
him in. I really don't know what he would have
done. Most of his stuff given away for the move,
all that debt from the wedding deposits — ' She
stopped herself abruptly. 'I'm sorry. Here I am

rambling on. What exactly was it you wanted to know?'

Violet hesitated. It could be hurtful to Maribel's mother to learn that Finn had never once mentioned Maribel to his own wife. She might take it as a sign that he'd put it behind him, though Violet was starting to suspect the opposite was true. Then again, she didn't want to play along, pretending this was all old news, and risk not learning some crucial bit of information that might help her make sense of what was happening now.

'Just . . . exactly this sort of thing. I'm so sorry to dredge all of this up for you. It's just that Finn didn't talk much about' — she wavered — 'about that part of his life. And I thought it might be helpful now to know what I missed. You mentioned them getting ready for a move, for instance — that was for a job, right?'

Violet could remember staring at Finn's portfolio in her office, those words from HR echoing despondently in her mind: *relocating for his fiancée's job . . . his fiancée's job . . . his fiancée . . .*

'Well, sort of. Maribel did manage to get an offer. But really they were looking for any excuse to move to Asheville. I think they would have gone even without one. Two talented artists like them, they would have figured something out when they got there.'

Violet felt as if someone had slammed on the brakes. The ice in her glass clinked, and she looked down at her shaking hand as if it belonged to someone else. When her voice

189

returned, it sounded far away. 'Asheville, North Carolina?'

'Yes. It's a beautiful town. Very individual, very artsy, Very Maribel. And Finn too, I gather. He never mentioned it?'

It was like rewatching one of those flip-the-switch movies like *The Sixth Sense* or *The Others* after you know the main characters are not what they seemed. So many scenes look different now that you know the twist, now that you're looking for the things you didn't catch the first time around. Violet could see it all: How Finn had gotten uncharacteristically quiet when she'd told him about Gram's retirement plans in Asheville and suggested they go along to stay close. How he hadn't answered that night but had agreed in the morning, then disappeared for hours on his road bike. How something had suddenly come up at his office the weekend they'd been scheduled to make the long drive to tour rental houses, and he'd insisted Violet and Gram and Bear go ahead without him. He'd just gone along with whatever Violet wanted, from the house to the furniture and décor, and she'd felt so adrift by his lack of initiative that she had ended up picking things she really didn't want at all, things that she thought might please him or suit the family but ultimately did not.

A life in Asheville was a life he had meant to be living with someone else.

She never would have suggested they come here if he'd told her. She would have missed Gram, but . . . no. If Gram had known, she wouldn't have suggested it either. They'd have gone somewhere else. Someplace they could all be happy. Unhaunted.

But he hadn't told her. And they had come here. How could Violet possibly tell Maribel's mother that she was here in Asheville now? Would she still think Finn and Bear's disappearance was so tragic if she knew the extent to which Violet had apparently taken Maribel's place?

Violet sidestepped the question. 'I'm clear on things from the point when Caitlin and George took him in,' she said. 'Before that, though — I'm trying to fill in some blanks.'

But even as she spoke the words, she wondered if she *did* know everything from Caitlin and George on. She was starting to grasp the gravity of the things that her friends had never revealed — of their loyalty to Finn over her, even if only through silence.

'Well, they were so excited about the move. Everything was all set — she e-mailed me so many pictures of the studio they picked out that my in-box practically crashed. They both just loved the town. It was one of the first things they bonded over, that night they met — one of the things that I think convinced Maribel from the start that Finn was the one, though that probably sounds silly.'

'Not at all.'

'You probably don't want to hear about this, your husband and his ex. Certainly not while your child is missing — '

'Actually, I do. I really do. How did they meet, did you say?'

'It was the sweetest thing. Meant to be, everyone used to say. They always got a kick out of telling the story. Finn had placed an ad — one of those Missed Connections on Craigslist — looking for a woman he'd met on vacation. But it was really vague, the way he wrote it, and Maribel thought the ad was for *her*. She'd just gotten back from Gatlinburg, where she'd met this guy, and . . . anyway, they arranged to meet, and obviously knew right away that they had the wrong people. He used to tease her about how annoyed she'd gotten, how she'd actually lectured him for not being more specific — Maribel was never one to pretend something didn't bother her if it did.'

Violet's mouth had gone dry. Her grip on the phone faltered and it fell into her lap. Hastily, she picked it up, pressed it to her ear, and remembered the vodka cranberry she was cradling in her other hand. She drank deeply as the room caved in around her.

It took all her reserves to summon another question.

'But he thought she was pretty?' she ventured. Maribel's pictures alongside the news reports of the accident were stunning — her cloud of dark wavy hair, her heart-shaped face, her creamy olive complexion, her petite stature and generous curvature — and had absolutely nothing in common with Violet's sandy hair and tall, thin frame. 'I mean, she was'angry, but he talked her into staying for a date anyway?'

Mrs. Branson laughed. 'Well, not exactly.'

She told Violet about the good Samaritan and

the concert tickets, and as she spoke, Violet's last bit of resolve fixed its gaze on the framed picture on the mantel. She and Finn on their wedding day, just back from the courthouse and sitting, champagne flutes in hand, in the little walled garden behind George and Caitlin's house, she in a loose sundress and fitted jacket, he in khakis and a crisp button-down, her smiling directly into the camera while he looked at her as if lost in thought. It had always been one of her favorites.

She had never felt so sure of herself as she had that day.

She had never been so wrong.

Never once had she looked at that photo and wondered what he was *really* thinking. But by the time she and Mrs. Branson hung up a few minutes later, it was the only thing she could think about.

Besides Bear, that is.

She never could stop thinking about Bear.

18

AUGUST 2012

'That night we met, you said everything was haunted, Everything.' At first, Finn had felt a little ridiculous talking to Maribel's picture, but a half bottle of bourbon later, it was coming naturally. Exactly a year ago today, they'd gotten in the car and pointed it in the direction of the Atlantic. He'd been so eager to be the one to finally show Maribel something she'd never seen before. Maribel, who somehow always knew when private galleries were opening their doors, and which unassuming pubs had the best craft brews, and when the orchestra would be lighting up the whole world out under the stars. Maribel, who had opened up his own universe to hold so much more love and magic and *possibility* than he'd dared let himself hope for. Maribel, who had miraculously agreed to be his partner — for life, Maribel, whom he'd just wanted to see for himself against the one remaining big, beautiful backdrop that he still pictured with another woman in the frame.

He'd been so ready to move on to the next phase of their lives. So ready to kick it off with a new memory on the soft sand of the beach, And so tired. So tired he couldn't even remember having fought with his closing eyelids before he drove across that double line and ruined everything, forever.

To commemorate this anniversary of his greatest regret, he'd chosen to let himself wallow. There was no other way he could fathom to function. He'd called off work. Waved away Caitlin's offer to sit with him, though he knew she meant well. Drawn the shades. Bought the bourbon. He'd stayed in bed for most of the morning and waited until exactly noon to start drinking, as if that somehow made this approach more respectable. He'd sat Maribel's picture in a club chair across the coffee table from him and poured her a glass too. Hers still sat untouched. His had been refilled so many times he'd lost count.

'I'm only haunted by what *happened* to you,' Finn told her now, running his fingers through his hair. 'I'd rather be haunted by *you*. If you could materialize here — ' He shook his head, his eyes never leaving her photograph. In it, she had just looked up from her sketchpad at the sound of him saying her name. Her hand was held midair, a piece of charcoal in her grasp, and her eyes were wide, bright, expectant.

'I guess I should be glad that you're at peace. Or if you're not, maybe you're too angry at me to show yourself here. I wouldn't blame you for that.' His bitter laugh seemed to echo under the high ceilings of the old living room. 'Hate me as much as you want. You've got *nothing* on how bad I hate myself. Show up here and yell at me. It would be so much better than this — being alone here without you. I miss you so much . . . '

Stating the obvious aloud did not make Finn

195

feel better. He'd thought he knew loneliness after his parents died. He'd thought he knew longing. He'd thought he knew regret. He'd known none of those things. It was the natural order, after all, to bury your parents, no matter how prematurely that day came. That was real, valid grief, but it only scratched the surface of the true depths grief was capable of concealing when it came not as a scratch but a puncture wound straight to the heart — efficient, yes, fatal, probably, but only after a slow bleeding out of everything that gave him life.

The room was going out of focus, and Finn's stomach churned. He couldn't even get drunk without screwing it up. He should have at least bought a frozen pizza, something to sop up the mess in his gut so he could keep drinking, prolong this haze throughout the day without ending up heaving on the cold, cracked tile of the dirty bathroom floor. This nausea that was taking over wasn't painful enough to feel cathartic. It was just an enhanced degree of the sick feeling he felt every day when he awoke and looked at himself in the mirror and thought about what he'd done and why he would be this alone forever and why he deserved things to be that way.

No. He deserved worse. He deserved to die on the side of the road, trapped in a car that was supposed to take them so much farther than just to the coastline, to the place where the waves met the earth and the sky opened up and the world seemed large and capable of anything. To a new city. A new home. A new business. A new start. All of it together. Finn hadn't even been scared of whether it would work out for him to start taking freelance clients, or if they would make friends in Asheville who'd come to mean as much to him as Caitlin did, or what he'd do if his bank account stayed as low as it was as he filled his gas tank to cringeworthy heights before they headed south from Cincinnati that day. It hadn't mattered if they failed, because they *couldn't* truly fail. They would have each other, and that would be enough to make up for anything and everything else that could possibly go wrong. Finn had been absolutely sure. He had never been so sure in his life.

He had never been so wrong.

If he had bought that damn frozen pizza along with the bourbon, he could put it in the oven now and just close his eyes. Maybe he'd fall asleep with it in there. Maybe the old smoke detectors would malfunction. Maybe he would drift away as the smoke filled the house. Maybe he would never wake up. It would look like an accident — hell, it would *be* an accident. It would just happen. No one would know what a coward he was. But he hadn't bought a pizza. He had absolutely nothing in the house to eat. And he couldn't figure out a way for *absolutely nothing* to kill him, no matter how badly he wanted it to.

'Damn it, if I could go back — if I could just go back . . . ' He was talking to her again — it was hard to stop now that he'd let himself start. A full year and he hadn't allowed himself so much as a cry uttered aloud at her grave site. He went only very, very early in the morning, or very, very late at night. He was too afraid of seeing anyone else there. Who wanted to visit their daughter's grave, or their son's, or their friend's, or neighbor's, and find standing there — or sitting there, or lying on the ground sobbing — the person responsible for her death? No one. Finn didn't even like being there with himself. If he could have found a way to abandon himself and move on as someone else, he would have done it in a heartbeat.

'I used to fantasize about going back to the night of the party, or the morning after. I used to wish more than anything that I could reach back in time to stop us from getting into that car. But I've come to terms with the fact that I don't deserve that second chance.'

He splashed more of the bourbon into his glass, clunked the bottle back onto the table, and drank deeply.

As his grief had gradually grown into something darker, he had stopped allowing himself to ask for this. And whom had he been asking? God? He felt too much like a child who had broken a favorite toy. *Please, if you get me a new one. I promise to take better care of it.*

The worst was that she hadn't been only his. She'd belonged to others too. She'd belonged to everyone. He had never even been punished for breaking her. Why hadn't they punished him — all of them? He could never punish himself enough.

'I don't deserve it,' he told Maribel again, 'but you do.'

Still, he had no right to ask God. It was a question that had to be put out to the universe. The universe understood chaos. It was prone to making mistakes. Why couldn't it right a wrong once in a while? Was that so out of reach?

He knew exactly where time needed to turn back to. He'd pinpointed the *real* root of his troubles, the one moment that if lived differently could have changed everything. It wasn't the day of the party or the morning after. It was before — a year before, to be exact. His need to go back there was intense, though he'd never allowed himself to speak it aloud. But now it was just him and Maribel, who had always indulged his dreaming. And before he could contemplate how much the words might hurt her if she could hear him now — because he didn't know if she valued her own life as much as he valued it now that he'd been forced to live his without her, because he didn't know if she'd be as willing as he was to sacrifice everything good they had ever had between them if only she could *live* — the bourbon told her for him.

'I never should have posted that ad — at least, not the way it was written. It was like you told me that first night, in Fountain Square. You were right to be angry. You should have walked away then, while you had the chance. It was too vague. It could have been for anyone.'

He was crying now. He'd been bottling it in for so long that it came pouring out, and he didn't bother to resist. What was the point of stopping it? Even if Maribel could see him now, how could she think any less of him than she

199

already did? He'd been the one responsible for the end of her life. It didn't get any worse than that.

'If you'd never met me, you'd still be alive,' he told her, sobbing. 'If I could go back and rewrite that damn ad so there could be no mistaking who it was for, you never would have gone to meet me that night, and we never would have fallen in love, or made any of the plans that I can't live without now. And we never would have gotten into that car. If I could just go back to before I posted that damn ad, maybe I could save us both.'

He swiped his glass roughly off the table, sloshing bourbon onto the worn wood. He staggered to the computer, smashing his thigh into the pointed corner of the old desk before dropping with a groan into the leather chair parked there. In his e-mail in-box, he found the folder he never let himself look in anymore but couldn't bring himself to delete. The Maribel folder. Inside was everything they'd sent each other in their year together — random love notes e-mailed in the middle of their workdays, ordinary debates about where to go for dinner or what movie to see, pictures of one or both of them. Every Monday, Maribel had sent him a candid shot of him she'd taken over the weekend — more often than not a picture that he hadn't noticed her snapping — contemplating a wine list, looking across the river to Newport, pointing to an available cab. She never captioned the photos — she never had to. He got that she was sending him glimpses of himself through her eyes. In every shot, there he was, caught unawares by her love.

The top of the folder mostly consisted of links to Asheville info, wedding DJs and cake bakeries — they'd been down to business those last weeks together, but they'd been having so much fun he hadn't even missed their other notes. He scrolled to the bottom of the folder, to the beginning of things, refusing to let his cursor linger over anything else on the way. There it was, her very first note.

Okay, stranger, I'll bite. Let's see if I am your me and you are my you.

'You were not my you,' he said softly. 'And I was not your me.'

There was one more message beneath it: the draft of the first ad he had written, the one he hadn't posted. The one he'd rewritten into the call that Maribel had answered. He opened it now and read it again.

You on the beach in the Camp Pickiwicki shirt: If you're reading this, the third coincidence is the charm. Care to pick up where fate left off? My name is Finn, by the way. It's pretty obvious by now that I should have told you that.

If he had posted that one instead, Maribel would be alive today. He wouldn't know that he had made that difference, but that would be okay. He wouldn't know what he was missing.

He might still not know what love was. He would never have met her, but she would be safe, And who knows? Maybe he would have found a way to be happy too. He never would now. Not like this.

If there was any justice in the universe, any way to right a wrong, Finn didn't believe that it would come through a portal in time. It had to come through the heart. He'd once heard someone call worrying a 'useless emotion.' That was true. But if wishing was equally useless, there was no hope for anyone. All anyone really could do was go through the motions and hope for the best. If there was such thing as miracles, maybe he would wake up tomorrow and it would be two years ago. This whole folder would be gone from his in-box. But maybe in its place would be an e-mail from someone else.

Finn finished his drink in several big swallows. It burned going down. He logged on to Craigslist and selected 'Missed Connections' from the 'Personals' menu. He copied and pasted the first ad he'd written, and clicked the post live.

He waited, as if perhaps the living room around him would be sucked up into some kind of tornadic time warp. Nothing happened. The old house creaked. His stomach churned. Angrily, Finn yanked the computer's plug out of the wall, and its fan stopped with a groan. He staggered into the kitchen to search the cupboards, the fridge, the freezer, everywhere he could think of again for something he knew wasn't there.

19

AUGUST 2012

As the late Saturday morning sun streamed through her open kitchen window, Violet hoisted the last brown paper bag of peaches onto the counter and breathed in a big, satisfying whiff of their sweetness. She and Gram had officially gotten carried away at the farmers' market. The rest of their take was spread out all around her — more peaches, early season apples, zucchini, and late-summer squash, all begging to be sliced or grated and baked. And then there was their lunch: a fresh round loaf of rosemary garlic peasant bread, a hunk of Amish cheese, a pint of this week's featured hummus. And all this on top of a gluttonous morning. As she'd watched Gram work her market magic, choosing the best at every stand, Violet had trailed along obediently and happily behind her, filling her arms and helping herself to free samples of apple cider donuts, lemon orzo salad, the last of the summer's blackberries.

Only with a partner in crime could Violet go this overboard; she always got overwhelmed at the market when she went alone. Everyone else seemed to have such purpose, but she'd find herself trying to remember why she'd come at all, when earlier it had seemed like such a perfect way to start a Saturday, She'd head home with meager pickings tucked into her reusable shoulder bag and then later pine for all the things she hadn't bought as she combed through her poorly stocked pantry looking for lunch.

Violet hit Play on the CD player mounted beneath her corner cabinet, and the voice of Patsy Cline filled the kitchen. Gram was next door on a mission to retrieve real butter (none of that 'margarine crap' Violet's calorie-counting conscience always made her buy) and her good stand mixer. They were about to have an all-day baking extravaganza — homemade applesauce, peach pie, zucchini bread — some for the week ahead, some for friends, and some for the freezer. The thought of being able to tap into the perfect, not-too-hot sunshine of this August day on some dreary weekend in November made Violet smile.

When Violet had woken up this morning, she had settled into her breakfast nook with a cup of coffee and a magazine, no particular plans in mind and no thought of making any — until she heard Gram's rap at the back storm door. Now, two hours later, Violet's day stretched out before her like a hammock in the sun, warm and comforting and full.

This sort of thing had been one of the perks of being under Gram's wing for as long as Violet could remember. Gram wasn't big on advance planning, but she believed in keeping busy. As a result, Violet never knew what to expect, but she could always bet something interesting would be in store. If it dawned on them that it was a Tuesday, they might spring for 'Bargain Night' tickets to see a classic movie on the little big screen at the Esquire Theatre. A heavy snowfall might necessitate a trip to the Conservatory, where they'd stand beneath the palm trees in the rain forest room, watching the waterfall send delicious humidity into the simulated tropical air as they tossed coins from the little arched bridge into the water below. A hot day could mean a shaded hike down to the creek at French Park, where they'd remove their shoes and wade around looking for crawdads. Gram wasn't squeamish about crawly things, and she wasn't squeamish about taking life as it came either. Violet had always observed her keenly. It was impossible to know Gram and not in at least some small way want to be like her.

The door creaked open a sliver, and a white canvas Ked poked its way through the bottom. 'A little help, dear?' Gram called, and Violet rushed over to pull the door open wide. Taking in the sight of the petite woman loaded to the gills with provisions, she couldn't help but laugh. 'You couldn't make a second trip for the wine?' she joked.

'No!' Gram shook her head with mock seriousness. 'We must uncork this immediately. It needs to breathe for a few minutes, and you know the rules. We can't start baking without wine.'

Having graduated to this level of friendship with her grandmother was one of the great pleasures of adulthood for Violet. Half the time Violet preferred her to people her own age.

'Is that because Gram's young at heart, or

because you're an old soul?' Katie had asked once. Violet didn't know, and it didn't much matter. It just was.

Together the women started wiping down the counters and setting out cutting boards and knives and bowls and Violet's pretty hand-painted canisters of flour and sugar. They moved around each other as they had hundreds of times before, Gram humming the alto harmonies on the CD and Violet singing along in her thin soprano.

'Why don't we get the apples boiling, while I set to work on the piecrust?' Gram asked in the beat of silence before the next song began, and Violet simply nodded and set to work peeling the apples over the sink.

'I stop to see a weeping willow, crying on his pillow . . . ' A third voice sang in through the kitchen window, and Gram opened the door to the little back porch. 'Katie! Come in, darling.'

Katie swept into the room and flashed Violet an I-love-your-Gram smile. 'She's the only person on earth I don't mind calling me *darling*,' she'd told Violet once. 'Not that anyone else has ever tried.' The endearments never sounded affected coming from Gram. It was just her way.

'Care to join our bake-athon?' Violet asked.

Katie surveyed the scene. 'Good God. You bought out an apple orchard. Or are those peaches?'

'Both.'

'You two are going to roast alive in here.'

'That's why we keep the wine chilled, dear girl,' Gram said, taking three glasses from the cabinet and filling them all.

'It's not even noon,' Katie protested insincerely, and then took a big sip. 'There's actually a tasting at the zoo tonight, if you ladies want to come. Wild About Wine, they're calling it. There's live music.'

'Sounds fun,' Violet said.

'I've got plans to go salsa dancing, but you girls have fun,' Gram said.

Violet opened her mouth to make a joke that it was supposed to be the other way around, them going out dancing and Gram wearing linen and heels to the zoo's botanical gardens, but thought better of it. Katie could be a little sensitive about these things.

'So. I've got news.' Katie looked excessively proud of herself, like a precocious child who was going to make them guess and guess at the answer.

'You met someone?' Violet had learned that almost all of Katie's news revolved around meeting or failing to meet someone.

'Not me,' she said slyly, walking Violet's glass over to her. 'But you really won't believe it. I was on Craigslist reading the Missed Connections — '

'And what are the Missed Connections?' Gram asked, sliding gingerly onto a counter stool.

'*Oh.*' Katie's eyes were bright. 'They're these postings, kind of like a modern twist on those old personal ads, where people write things like, 'I talked with you one morning while we were both waiting for the bus. I didn't have the nerve to ask for your phone number, and now I regret it. You were wearing a yellow skirt and knee-high riding boots and I would love to see you again.''

Gram lifted her eyes to the ceiling. 'You young people these days. You don't *talk* to one another. It's all those ridiculous devices you're always playing with instead.'

'The real question isn't the societal decline evidenced by the Missed Connections,' Violet said, laughing. 'The real question is, what were *you* doing reading them? Did you meet someone? Or — miss someone?'

'I *wish*! No, I just think they're romantic. I mean, a lot of them are actually pretty stupid — but they give me hope that people out there believe in . . . I don't know, something.'

Violet slipped a slice of apple into her mouth. 'This makes me think of an article I read the other day. Did you know that in the 1930s, most couples lived within ten blocks of each other when they first met?'

'Is that a fact?' Gram asked. 'You know, it doesn't really surprise me.'

'Well, in your day — ' Katie began.

'Watch it, young lady,' Gram teased, swatting at her with a tea towel. 'I may be an antique, but the '30s were not 'my day.''

'I don't even *know* anyone who lives within ten blocks of me,' Violet said. 'Except you, Gram.'

'I don't know,' Katie said. 'Isn't that kind of sad? That everyone would just pick the best available option within reach? Although if things

208

were still that way, maybe we'd both be married by now . . . '

'Maybe you would,' Gram agreed, and both women shot her a warning look. She raised her hands in surrender. 'Sorry. Anyway, back to these missed chances.'

'Missed *Connections*,' Violet corrected her.

'They sound like missed chances to me. I wouldn't want to hear from a man who didn't have the guts to talk to me right off, anyway.'

'What if it didn't have anything to do with guts?' Katie asked, 'What if there was some reason beyond his control that kept things from moving ahead?'

'Such as?' Violet said.

'Such as a woman going into anaphylactic shock on the beach.'

'Very funny. No one went searching for a Missed Connection there.'

'Oh, but he did.' Katie's eyes twinkled. She extracted a piece of paper from her pocket, unfolded it, and smoothed it on the counter next to Violet. 'He just took his sweet time getting around to it.'

' "You on the beach in the Camp Pickiwicki shirt . . . " ' Violet read aloud. She clamped her hand over her mouth. 'Oh, my God.'

'What does it say?' Gram asked, sitting up straighter,

'It's one hundred percent him!' Katie squealed, 'He says his name is Finn. You *know* his name is Finn, Vi.'

'*What*,' Gram demanded, 'does the damn thing *say*?'

Violet swallowed the lump in her throat. ''If you're reading this, the third coincidence is the charm. Care to pick up where fate left off? My name is Finn, by the way. It's pretty obvious by now that I should have told you that.''

'What were the first two coincidences?' Gram asked, puzzled.

'That they both went to Camp Pickiwicki, and they both live here now but met in Florida,' Katie answered for her. 'Or, wait — is that three coincidences?' Her brow furrowed. 'Well, so what if he can't count. It's him, It's *so him*!' She downed the rest of her wine in a big gulp and clinked the glass down.

Violet read the ad again. 'I don't get it. After all this time — *two years?*'

'You don't know that he didn't try to look for you before, This might just be the first note you've seen! Imagine: There could have been flyers on buses — you always drive! — and messages on the scoreboard — you never go to Reds games! — or ads in the *Enquirer* — you never read the paper! Even this, you didn't see — *I* just happen to have seen it!' Katie's excitement bubbled over into a full-out squeal, and Gram laughed in spite of herself.

Violet raised an eyebrow. 'There's also the small detail that he was engaged.'

Katie was undeterred. 'So they called it off! And he thought about the one possibility that got away. You can't hold it against him when it's so positively perfect.'

'So what am I supposed to say — that I actually happen to know his name and that he was engaged because he canceled a job interview with me? Supposedly because he was going to relocate, though obviously he's still here?'

'That was a year ago. He might not be *still* here. He might be *back* here. All that matters is that he's *here*. And you're not supposed to say anything. You know nothing.' Katie waved her fingers in front of Violet's face like a deranged magician.

'You know I can never keep a secret,' Violet said, laughing. 'I tell everyone everything. And even if I don't, they read it all over my face.'

'Keep this one,' Katie said firmly. 'I'm sure he'll tell you on his own, answer all your questions then, and the two of you can have a laugh about your near misses before fate finally brought you together.'

'I don't know if the Missed Connections page qualifies as fate.'

'Sure it does. What are the odds of someone taking the leap of faith to post something after all this time? What are the odds of you seeing it? What are the odds of you still being available and interested?'

'And when he asks if I've thought about him at all for the last two years?'

'Be honest. I mean, he placed the ad looking for you. He'll be glad to hear you've been thinking about him.'

'Honest except for the year I was thinking he was *engaged*?'

Katie shrugged, 'Be honest and play dumb.'

'At the same time?'

'Well . . . ' She smiled. 'Yeah.'

20

AUGUST 2016

Caitlin wasn't sure how long she'd been asleep, but the words woke her with the stopping of her heart. She could tell right away that it was Bear's voice, not one of her own boys', coming from down the hall, but it was in her biological programming — in every mother's organic makeup — that those words would have woken her anytime, anywhere.

'I want my *mommy*.'

That voice — it wasn't just whiny, or tired, or confused. It was heartbroken. She could hear Finn's murmurs, attempting to hush him, and more pathetic little cries from Bear that clawed at her gut until she thought she might vomit. But then she heard Finn padding into the kitchen, and feigned sleep as she listened to the opening of the refrigerator, the soft popping of the milk carton, some fumbling among the sippy cups and lids in the dish drainer, and then a second creak of the refrigerator door before his steps retreated to the sofa bed.

She waited until she could no longer hear any shuffles or sighs, not even the slightest creak from the cabin itself or anyone in it, and untangled herself from the mess of blankets on the couch. She knew now what she hadn't wanted to admit when she'd drifted off earlier.

This wasn't going to work. Talking sense into Finn was simply going to take too long. Because lying there in the darkness, hearing that tiny little *I want my mommy* playing over and over in her head, the emphasis on the word *mommy* as if it were an inalienable right he'd been denied, it became clear that another *minute* was too long, let alone hours, possibly days . . .

It was up to Caitlin to get Bear home. It was the only thing she could do to redeem herself. And even if she was beyond redemption, it was just the right thing to do.

She rose as quietly as she could and made her way down the hall and into the master bedroom, pausing every few steps to listen for sounds of anyone else awake. There were none. With both hands, she felt her way through the darkness past the hulking wood footboard of the bed and into the adjoining master bathroom, shut the door carefully behind her, and only then flipped the light switch. She squinted into the brightness of the white globe bulbs mounted above the vanity, letting her eyes adjust. Then she pulled open all three panels of the mirrored medicine cabinet and stood back and surveyed its contents.

For the first time ever, Caitlin was grateful for her mother-in-law being so uptight, and for her father-in-law always reaching for the quickest ways to keep his wife happy. They were all here — the antianxiety meds, the prescription sleep aids, It was an impressively stocked pharmacy for a second house that Beverly hardly even visited anymore. Caitlin knew that this was nothing compared to the mother lode she'd surely find at their estate in Ohio — not that she'd ever been in their bedroom there. She was still too much of a guest and not enough of a family member for that.

Caitlin herself hardly ever took medicine unless she absolutely had to. Those years of trying to get pregnant, and then being pregnant, and then nursing, she'd gotten used to suffering through cold and flu season on nothing but an occasional Tylenol. Her father-in-law had once gently joked, after Caitlin *may* have overreacted to a giant red goose egg that appeared on Leo's head while her in-laws were babysitting — the origins of which they had not the slightest idea — that Caitlin herself could perhaps benefit from an occasional Xanax. Obviously he'd never come to know her very well; the idea was ridiculous. Beneath her smooth surface, Caitlin was far too anxious to take an anti-anxiety pill. What if it affected her strangely? What if she didn't feel like herself? Or what if she liked it *too* much? What if she did something out of character in front of the boys?

No. Not for her.

Caitlin lifted the first prescription bottle timidly and read its label. Then another. And another. Her ears strained for any sounds of Finn rousing.

The only way Finn would let her walk out of here with Bear was if Finn was unable to stop her. And the only way that was going to happen was if he didn't have his faculties about him. Confusion or exhaustion probably wouldn't cut it. She was going to have to render him unconscious.

But she didn't want to harm him. It would have to be just enough for him to perhaps feel sick, to let his guard down and doze off, and to not be easily woken. By the time he came to, she might even have made it all the way to Asheville with Bear and the twins. At least, she'd have a pretty good head start. She'd never driven directly there from here, but she guessed it to be about three hours.

After much deliberation, she twisted the childproof top off the bottle of Ambien. She shook out an oblong white pill and touched it briefly to the tip of her tongue. She couldn't detect much of a taste. Some chalkiness, maybe a bit of a mineral flavor. She'd have to mask it, to be sure, but at least it didn't have the strong bitterness of, say, a Tylenol that didn't go down with the first swig of water.

Ambien it was.

She would have to slip it into his morning coffee, the first chance she got — there was no telling what else the day might bring. That meant she'd have to use enough of the sleep aid to overpower the caffeine. She shuddered at what could happen if she gave him too much — but it was risky to underdose him, too. How to determine the sweet spot in between? She knew better than to search the Web. She couldn't afford to leave any evidence of her plan, in case something went horribly wrong.

Just as when she'd gotten in the car and driven down here, she was going to have to wing it.

21

AUGUST 2016

In another universe, one where things had played out differently, Violet might have been glad — giddy, even — to find out all these years later that Finn had looked for her right away after all. That he had flown home from the beach, as she had, still thinking of their encounter, of how he might find her against the odds, of the fact that there was something unfinished between them — something that could be the start of something new, something wonderful, something real, something meant to be.

So what if he had been detoured on his path to finding the woman he'd been looking for all along?

But this was not that universe. This was a universe in which she'd learned this choice piece of her own romantic history from his dead fiancée's mother. A universe in which being grateful that she and Finn had ended up together in spite of so many things gone wrong now meant being grateful, in a roundabout way, that someone had been killed — that Finn had been responsible for the death of someone he loved. No longer could Violet look back at her life and admire the way the Fates had arranged things *just so*. Her own happiness — or what she'd thought was happiness — would not have been possible without someone else's tragedy. How was she supposed to reconcile that? How had *Finn* even been attempting to reconcile that all these years?

So what if he'd looked for her immediately after Sunny Isles? He'd found someone else, someone he loved and planned to be happy with instead. And when that blew up, and the appropriate amount of time passed, he settled for Violet. Or, at least, he tried to.

In their long line of dominoes that toppled in seemingly perfect order, there was one that had not been synchronized after all, one that had failed to fall. And that domino was Finn.

Violet's kitchen was especially gloomy after dark, with the overhead light down to just one bulb that wasn't burned out. The fixture was nearly impossible to get apart while balancing on a stepstool or chair, and she and Finn always had to tag-team it. Every time, she would quip, 'How many Welshes does it take to change a light-bulb?' and every time, Finn would grumble, too annoyed with the stubborn thing to laugh. Now she sat at the table in silence, unable to look across at Gram, and eyed the light suspiciously. How long until she was completely in the dark? And when had her life become one giant metaphor?

These long days in the house, she had either far too much space or not enough. She was getting tired of being trapped at this cramped kitchen table with people who were asking uncomfortable questions. She'd known she had to talk to Gram after speaking with Mrs.

Branson, but she would have preferred to do it in the kitchenette of Gram's comforting old lady apartment, surrounded by comforting old lady things. Violet still couldn't bring herself to leave the house, though. What if Finn came back, found the place empty, and changed his mind and left again? She knew the FBI was keeping an eye on things, but they weren't camped outside 24/7 — at least, she didn't think so. In spite of their repeated questioning, she didn't think they truly suspected her of anything other than naïveté, and she also didn't get the feeling they expected Finn to reappear on his own. But that didn't mean she couldn't hold out hope. What else was there to do?

So after she'd hung up with Delilah and watched, in stunned silence, as the last of the day's sunlight faded, she'd called Gram and asked her to come over. Gram must have sensed that something was different, because whereas before she'd been pushing herbal tea or coffee, this time she brought wine. White, already chilled. Violet had stashed the vodka back in the cupboard before Gram arrived, and she was tempted to retrieve it now that self-medication was apparently acceptable. Her wineglass sat, untouched, in front of her; Gram's was almost empty. Violet had just finished relaying all she'd learned from her visit from Agent Martin and her conversation with Mrs. Branson, and was waiting for Gram to say something — anything. Gram, meanwhile, was doing that thing therapists do — remaining silent and looking patiently at Violet as if waiting for her to say more.

Violet caved. 'The thing is,' she began again. 'I always felt like Finn *knew* me. From the very first moment, we just had this comfort level that felt . . . I don't know, almost automatic. It was like we were complete strangers who already understood each other, on some subconscious level. I *know* I didn't imagine that. But now that it turns out there's so much I didn't know, I'm not sure I even know *myself* anymore.'

Gram pointed to Violet's glass. 'Drink.'

She obeyed.

'Now,' Gram said. 'This is devastating, to state the obvious. I almost feel responsible, being the reason you both came here. Maybe if we hadn't — ' Violet held up a hand to stop her, and Gram nodded sadly. 'No point in discussing that. I suppose. But I don't want to hear any more of this about not knowing yourself without Finn.'

Gram hesitated.

'Go ahead,' Violet said. 'Say it.'

Gram sighed. 'We *did* know that you didn't know everything there was to know about him. From the day he canceled that interview, before you even met him again, you knew that he had been engaged. And when he never told you himself, you chose to let it go. I remember asking you about it once, and you said — '

'I know what I said,' Violet snapped. 'I said that it was probably just a nasty breakup and he didn't want to talk about his ex, and that having been through a few myself. I didn't blame him. Obviously I couldn't have imagined *this*.'

Gram placed a hand on top of Violet's. 'I know, darling. No one could. Let's not argue.

I'm on your side here.'

But Violet was thinking back to their first date — their first real date, after they had found each other again — and to something Finn, had said. Or rather, something he had asked her. She saw now with absolute clarity that *neither one* of them had been able to take a hint. Tears welled in her eyes.

'I'm sorry,' she said, her few remaining defenses crumbling. There were a lot of places she could rightly direct her anger, but Gram wasn't one of them. 'You're right. I never should have let that drop with Finn. And I should have known we were forcing the issue. And what you said the other day, about me being a ship? About making sure what I wrote in my captain's log was accurate?'

Violet drew a shaky breath. 'You were right about that, too. How could I have thought our story was romantic? How could *anyone* have thought it?'

Shame pooled hot in her cheeks as the tears began to fall, and she swiped at them angrily. A burst of cynical laughter emerged from somewhere deep within her.

'There are *way* too many medical emergencies in our story, for one thing,' she said, sniffing loudly. 'First, we don't get together because a woman goes into anaphylactic shock on the beach. Next, we do get together — but, little did I know, it's only possible because Finn's first choice of fiancées dies in a horrible accident. Then, just months after we're married. I almost die from my postpartum hemorrhage — no

220

wonder Finn freaked. I'd be willing to bet the *only* thing that kept him from taking off then was how bad it would have looked, running out on his wife and newborn. But none of this is normal. This cannot be the way things were supposed to be.'

Gram made a *posh-posh* kind of noise. 'First of all, life is full of medical emergencies. More than any of us like to think about. That's the way it is; we're fragile creatures. I'm an old lady, bound to have one myself sooner or later. It's inevitable.'

She refilled her wineglass and poured more into Violet's too, though she'd taken only that one sip. 'Second, Maribel was not Finn's *first choice of fiancées*. He did not have you and Maribel standing side by side and he got to know you both and then decided he liked Maribel better. He found Maribel instead of you and it worked out. Has it occurred to you that maybe she worried he was settling for *her* but still wondering what might have happened if he had actually found you?'

Violet looked at her blankly, and Gram leaned back in her seat as if she'd proved some great point.

'But he has me side by side with Maribel now, and he's choosing her.' Violet started to cry again. 'She's not even *alive*, and he's choosing her!'

Gram shook her head. 'I'm not sure that's true. He's choosing guilt. He's choosing to punish himself. Maybe even to deny himself. Maybe his love for you has always been just as

221

real as you thought, but he can't give himself over to it because he feels like he doesn't deserve it. When I said earlier that sometimes he seemed like he was going through the motions. I shouldn't have ascribed my own reasons to that. If he did have a sense of detachment, there could have been other reasons. Better reasons. And temporary ones. Things he was trying to work through — maybe still is.'

'What difference does it even make at this point? It's too late for us now. There's no way we can come back from this.'

'Don't be so sure, dear. You're a good ship captain — the best. If there is a way back, you'll find it.'

Violet shook her head sadly. 'I'm not sure how I'll ever find my way without Bear. I still don't understand . . . ' She swallowed hard, fighting emotion, trying to find the words for her confusion. 'Even knowing what we know now. I still don't understand why he took him. Why he left, maybe. But why take my son?'

The lone lightbulb above them flickered once, twice, three times with a static, electric sort of sound, and the women turned their eyes upward, holding their breaths, waiting to be plunged into darkness. But the noise quieted, the light steadied, and they found themselves staring again at each other.

'It would help if he had some discernible reason,' Gram said finally. 'But maybe there isn't one. Or maybe there isn't *just* one. Ultimately, does it really matter?'

'Of course it matters!' Violet felt instant shame

at the outburst. 'It matters to me,' she said more softly.

'Fair enough. That's your right,' Gram said, matching her tone. 'But to me? It only matters that he brings Bear back.'

★ ★ ★

Once Gram had gone — reluctantly, and only after Violet's repeated reassurances that she would be fine, that she was, above all, exhausted and in need of rest — Violet got the vodka and the cranberry back out and filled her glass at the table. As drained as she was, sleep wasn't an option. And as much as she hated this kitchen, she couldn't go back into the living room without hearing the echoes of Delilah Branson's voice over the phone, couldn't go into her bedroom without being surrounded by reminders of the stranger who was Finn, and couldn't bring herself to stoop to the low of drinking in a child's room, even if that *was* the only place in the house that felt like home. So she sat at the table alone and drained and refilled her glass. She did it again, and again, and she rethought everything she had ever believed to be true about her life with Finn.

'My name is Violet,' she had replied to Finn's ad. 'And I am free any night this week.'

It had taken him a full forty-eight hours to respond. She'd wondered if her message had been caught in his spam filter — there was no direct contact info listed in his ad, no way to reach him other than the automated Craigslist system, and she knew those return addresses were displayed as odd scrambles of letters and numbers. If she had posted an ad looking for someone, she would have been checking her in-box incessantly, at all hours of the clay and night. But maybe Finn wasn't like that. After all, he'd waited two years to post it in the first place.

But finally, there was his response, pinging into her smartphone and bolded at the top of her in-box. It was a short note inviting her to dinner and drinks after work the next day — that was all.

They met at Arthur's, just off Hyde Park Square, where even the casual spots were overpriced but the location was too perfect to argue. Tuesday was 'Burger Madness' at the little brick café — you could get as many gourmet toppings as you wanted for no extra fee. She found Finn waiting at a table in the walled courtyard out back. He was seated in a corner beneath the pergola, a ceiling fan whirling above his head, an almost-empty pint glass sweating on the table in front of him. Violet glanced at her watch. She was right on time. He must have arrived really early. A good sign.

He smiled when he saw her and stood for an awkward hug. As she settled into her seat across from him, her heart racing with anticipation, he leaned in as if to confide some great secret. 'I almost didn't recognize you — you're not wearing your grandma's clothes.'

Violet laughed, looking self-consciously down at her blousy sleeveless shirt and khaki pencil skirt. The truth was, the peep-toe heels she'd

224

chosen were the only part of her outfit that Gram herself probably wouldn't wear. She'd been going for one of those looks the magazines said could transition from office to evening, but she wasn't sure she'd exactly hit the mark. Finn was far more casual, in jeans and a faded T-shirt.

They made small talk. He ordered another round of drinks — white wine for Violet — and they rattled off their choices of toppings, which, on a list half a menu page long, were the same: Boursin, red onion, lettuce, tomato, bacon. Another good sign. They smiled shyly at each other. Finn seemed nervous in an almost reluctant way. His demeanor reminded her of someone who'd been dragged along on a double blind date against his will, which made no sense, of course. She would have to learn to read him better.

When she told him where she worked, she waited for a flash of recognition on his face, an, 'Oh. I almost interviewed there once! Funny story — at the time. I was . . . ' But none came. He merely asked if she was a graphic designer there and she explained that she was not, but that she worked with a team of them in her role overseeing communications. He only nodded.

'That's what I do for a living,' he explained flatly. 'Well, sort of. My current job doesn't involve a lot of graphics. Or a lot of design.' They laughed together then, as if this were some great coup he had pulled off.

Their burgers arrived. They bumped elbows over the condiments and politely apologized; their obligatory small talk continued. It might as

225

well have been any ordinary, semi-awkward first date. Violet kept waiting for him to bring up their meeting on the beach — and what came next, and why he'd chosen this moment to look for her. Had Katie been right that maybe he'd reached out through the universe before, and Violet had missed it? But he didn't bring it up, and so Violet followed his lead. She was here because of his ad. He was the initiator. And so she would try to stick to his script of how this should go. She would be patient — she would not rush the conversation and risk ruining things. Because if there was one skill she'd had ample opportunity to hone these past two years, it was the art of waiting. And if there was one thing she'd already known how to do even before she first met Finn, it was improvise. For that, she could thank Gram.

After dinner, they walked around the corner to Graeter's and got small paper cups of ice cream — Violet ordered raspberry chocolate chip, and when he said only, 'I'll have the same,' she couldn't hide her smile. As they stepped into the crosswalk, headed toward the small rectangular park in the middle of the busy square, a sports car sped toward them, and he took her hand, looking almost comically alarmed. When it had passed, he didn't let go. They found an empty bench and sat in silence for a moment, eating their ice cream thoughtfully as they watched the traffic go by.

Violet turned sideways on the bench and stretched her legs out across his lap. She did it without thinking, as if it were the most natural thing in the world, and only after she saw the stunned look pass briefly across his face did she realize what an intimate gesture it was. No — a *presumptive* gesture. *I know you already*, it said. *You belong on this bench next to me.*

She was about to apologize, to retract her legs and face forward again, when his face changed. She'd meticulously flat-ironed her freshly cut and layered hair that morning, and he reached out and gathered the section to the right of her chin into his fingertips. He wound it through and around his fingers as he looked into her eyes, really looked into them, as if seeing her only then for the first time.

'Now I remember,' he said softly. The veil of awkwardness lifted. The smile that came next was more genuine — the smile of someone who was a little surprised to find himself sitting next to her this way, but happily so.

Here it was, finally, that current between them — that intensity of connection that had been missing from every other masculine encounter she'd had since that long-ago day on the beach. It was there. It was real. She hadn't dreamt it. And now that this spark had again flickered, she was desperate not to be plunged back into that uncertain darkness. Now that she knew she hadn't imagined the flame, she needed to know what it was that had brought them here — and what it was that had kept them apart. She wanted to know how he'd spent every moment of every day since they'd seen each other last.

'It's been a long time, you know,' she said softly. 'Why now?' Something like fear flashed in

Finn's eyes, and, worrying that she sounded more suspicious than she'd intended, she smiled coyly and tried for humor instead. 'I mean, where *have* you been?'

She half expected some glib comeback, a battle of wits, but none came. He seemed to be considering her question seriously. She knew then that something about this man was different from the Finn she'd met on the beach. His almost automatic flirtation was gone, and in its place was something more measured. But still, he didn't drop the lock of her hair he was holding. He didn't let go. Some sort of explanation had to be given, after all, or at the very least gotten out of the way. He knew it, and she knew it.

'Did you ever think,' he said slowly, 'that maybe when we were split up that day . . . did you ever think we should take that as a sign *not* to find each other? That anything beyond that conversation just wasn't meant to be?'

She paused for only a second before answering honestly. 'No, I didn't. Is that what *you* thought?'

'No,' he admitted. He dropped her hair and gave her a sheepish smile. 'But my dad always used to say that nothing worth having comes easily. Sometimes I think I take that advice to the extreme and can't take a hint.'

His words were light, but there was real sadness in his expression. How he must miss his father. Violet felt a surge of tenderness for this man she hardly knew. She thought then that she'd been wrong — it didn't really matter where he'd been all this time, what he'd been doing. The only thing that mattered was that he was here now.

She leaned toward him. 'Well,' she said, 'if you ever miss any of my hints in the future, I'll be sure to let you know.' She inched closer still, until their noses were just inches apart, She looked at him with exaggerated eagerness, and he finally broke down and laughed — a genuine, warm sound that dissolved the moment of uncertainty. Here they were again, a woman and a man holding dishes of melting ice cream, her legs draped nonchalantly but purposefully across his lap, his arm wrapped now almost involuntarily around her knees, looking at each other so intimately that anyone walking by would surely look away.

'Would this be some sort of kissing-related hint?' he asked, touching the tip of his nose to hers.

'I knew you weren't as bad at this as you thought.'

The familiarity between them took over then — maybe too quickly, she acknowledged now, After all, it had been *false* familiarity. Without cause. But it had seemed like such a natural fit, and such a miracle to have found each other again. Looking back later, Violet would remember feeling, above all, *relieved*. Perhaps not the most romantic notion on which to build a relationship — no one ever gushed about being *relieved* when they met their spouse, though wasn't everyone relieved to stop looking for a match, relieved to stop being alone? — but it had felt good, It wasn't run-of-the-mill relief. It was a feeling that things had been restored to their natural order, To the way they were supposed to be but very nearly hadn't been. What was wrong with breathing a sigh at that?

A few months later, when she discovered she was pregnant, she wasn't even all that nervous about telling him. Sure, it was sooner than she'd imagined, and everything was out of order — but didn't that fit with the way things had gone between them? Wasn't that just one more charming bump in the story of their love?

When he heard the news, though, he got quiet. And when he went home from her little duplex that night, rather than staying over as he usually did on Fridays, she cried herself to sleep, hoping Gram couldn't hear her from her side of the walls.

But he was back in the morning, with her favorite cinnamon-sugar-crusted bagels and seasonal pumpkin spice lattes, decaf for her. 'I guess we should get married,' he said, smiling apologetically, and it wasn't really a proposal, but that was okay. It was them. They weren't fancy. They just . . . they just were.

They arranged things hastily. Neither of them wanted to make a big deal. Violet once tried to suggest more, but Finn looked so troubled that she thought it had been insensitive of her. Of course he'd be bothered that he had no family to invite. Surely there must be aunts or uncles or cousins somewhere, but when she asked, he just said, 'Not really.' She let it go. She didn't want to cause Finn any pain. He was fond of Gram, and his closest friends were already becoming Violet's own, and of course that was enough for Violet. It seemed to be more than enough for Finn.

And so that's how it was: George and Caitlin were there, and Gram. The last weeks of November could swing between Indian summers and snowstorms in Cincinnati, and the day they'd chosen fell somewhere in between. They spent a chilly morning at the court-house, but later, as they celebrated with a spread at George and Caitlin's house, the sun made a brilliant appearance, and the day turned warm enough to sit in the courtyard out back, even to remove their jackets.

For their honeymoon, they drove east, deep into Amish Country, to the Murphin Ridge Inn, a spot recommended by Caitlin. It was billed as a place to unplug, but with a luxury take on rustic — the inn served dishes by award-winning chefs who sourced their ingredients from adjacent farms, and the private accommodations were designed so that you wouldn't miss the TV. In their chalet fringed by woods, the centerpiece was a deep Jacuzzi and a 360-degree fireplace. The room came well stocked with books, cards, and board games. They took breakfast and dinner at the inn, and snacked in between from a basket delivered daily to their door. With the excuse of being pregnant, Violet ate heartily. At night, the innkeepers built bonfires on a large stone patio and she and Finn settled into Adirondack chairs under the stars, she with hot cocoa and he with something stronger. It was a communal atmosphere, with other couples also drawn to the circle, but most of them kept to themselves, paired up in their own little worlds, lost in the roaring blaze.

That first night, as they admired how wide the sky stretched above and beyond them, how bright the stars were here, how they could actually see the haze of the Milky Way cut its swath across the sky, Finn lowered his eyes to hers, and she saw something there that she only then realized she hadn't seen from him before: hope. 'Maybe nothing has to be as complicated as we make it,' he said. 'Maybe life really is this simple.' Violet didn't know what to say, so she just squeezed his arm in reply and looked back to the sky, and a moment later she felt his gaze leave her face and follow.

She hadn't known that he found things complicated, but it wasn't such an odd thing to say given their circumstances — planning so suddenly for a baby, and her move out of her duplex and into his more spacious apartment next to George and Caitlin's house. She was sad to leave Gram, and sorry not to have her next door to help when the baby came, but Finn's rental had more bedrooms, a better yard, and a bargain price. It made the most sense. Gram would be only a short drive away and could stay over anytime — there was a guest room she could use as often as they wanted. And Caitlin was pregnant also, with twins. It would be fun, Violet thought. A new start.

Complicated? Maybe. But as Finn said, it was really pretty simple. It was just what you do when you fall in love with someone — you go with the flow, as the cliché says. It seemed to Violet that she and Finn were pretty good at riding those tides as they came.

But if she'd known that it would lead her here, to this miserable little table where she'd come to sit alone, drinking well into the night, her husband and her son vanished, her world turned upside down by an FBI agent and a stranger on the phone, she would have navigated those waters differently.

22

BEYOND AUGUST 2012

Caitlin loved Violet from the start. She'd always loved Finn, but had rarely seen him in love. Until she'd met George, her boyfriends always felt threatened by the fact that her best friend was another guy, always suspected there was something more to their relationship. There never had been, at least not outwardly, but it also was true that Finn had spent the majority of those years single. He wasn't one of those guys people were always looking to fix up. Not because he wasn't a great catch — he was — but because he just seemed uncommonly content to be alone. It wasn't until he lost his parents that Caitlin saw a change in him, a hint that he might be longing for someone or something after all. Still, she'd once teased Finn that it would take a sign from the universe to pin him down, and though they both had laughed it off, it turned out she hadn't been far from the truth.

The year Finn fell for Maribel, he almost disappeared entirely from Caitlin's view, under-standably preoccupied with new love in spite of her attempts to keep him close. She missed him, missed seeing what that version of Finn was like. She still wondered about it sometimes, still wished she had more memories of him and

Maribel with her and George — double dates, weekends away, all those things they'd said they should do together but hadn't followed through with before it suddenly had been too late. It seemed ridiculous to Caitlin that she'd met Maribel only a handful of times when her loss had had such a profound effect on one of her oldest and closest friends. She mourned Maribel, of course, but she mourned her on Finn's behalf. And she mourned Finn, too. Because Finn was changed. Her efforts had done nothing to shorten the shelf life of his grief. Caitlin felt sure, though, that if anyone could bring him back, it was Violet.

'I was drunk when I placed the ad,' he confessed the day Violet's response landed in his in-box. Caitlin could still picture him, hands over his face, his bottle of beer from her fridge already sweating in the August heat, as he sat awkwardly forward in one of the. whitewashed Adirondacks on her massive front porch. 'I almost forgot I even did it. How did she see it? What are the odds that she actually would have seen it?'

'Slim,' Caitlin agreed. 'Still, that is usually the idea behind those ads. You know, the hope that the person it's written for might actually see it. If it didn't ever happen, I suppose they wouldn't exist.'

He looked at her skeptically. 'Fad diets exist. Penis enhancers exist. Plenty of things that never work exist.'

She rolled her eyes. 'Fortunately, what we're dealing with here are real people going about

235

their lives in the natural world, and not something that was manufactured to make a dirty buck.'

'What if I don't reply? This might just . . . go away.'

'Why on earth would you want that?'

'Cait.' He looked up at her desperately. 'Forget the fact that I'm not even close to ready for a relationship, that I can't imagine ever being ready again. This is the woman I was searching for when I met Maribel. How can I ever look at her and *not* see Maribel?'

She didn't understand then what he really meant — that he believed that if he'd found Violet in the first place, Maribel would still be alive. She wouldn't understand that until it was too late. And so what she said next was not what she would later wish she'd told him when she replayed the conversation with the benefit of hindsight. But on that day, it was from the heart.

'You can and you should, because she isn't Maribel. She has nothing to do with Maribel. She's a fresh start. She's a second chance. She's someone you bothered to search for in the first place, years ago. And so what if you've found her now by accident? Doesn't that still count for something? Doesn't that count for *everything?*'

They didn't discuss it again. But a few weeks later, he brought Violet by for the first time. And that was the first sign Caitlin saw that maybe Finn would be okay. He wasn't the old fun-loving Finn, but nor was he the new grief-stricken one. He was someone else. Not someone in between, but someone off to the

236

side, maybe. Someone who at a glance looked like the Finn she knew but upon close examination wasn't exactly. Still, George didn't seem to notice, and Finn acted as natural as this version of Finn could, and Violet didn't know the difference, so Caitlin decided that this was probably fine too. Good, even. This was probably what moving on had to look like. Not backward, and not forward, at least not yet — just an almost imperceptible step to the side.

For her part, she wasn't going to let him disappear into the relationship this time, the way he had with Maribel, the way some people did with *everyone* they dated. This time, she'd stay close. Finn wasn't the only one who'd had a fragile year. In the long stretches of George's absence, she'd found herself pining for a baby more strongly than ever before, curling up into herself with every unsuccessful attempt, envisioning with something close to panic the periodic loneliness of this life stretching out for all the years before her. Failure was unfamiliar to Caitlin. At the moment, George's otherwise good grace only infuriated her. It was sallow Finn whom she instead found to be some kind of a comfort. And so this time she would not sacrifice him so readily to another woman. It would be much easier to keep hold of him now that he was right next door. She would learn to love Violet, she would embrace her into their circle as if she'd been there all along, she would support Finn in whatever ways he needed her. She would not lose him, nor would she allow him to lose himself.

The best realization of all was that Violet reminded her of the person Finn used to be, the person Caitlin had been drawn to in part because he was so very different from her, in ways that she couldn't help but admire and, if she was being honest, maybe even envy a little. Violet wasn't much of a planner. Violet wasn't much of a worrier. Violet had lost her parents even younger than Finn had, but the role had been filled so well by her grandmother that any damaging effects were hidden from view. She seemed to like her job, was good at it, but not so much that she lived it. She was close enough to Gram to appear grounded and stable, but not so much that she came across as dependent. She seemed content on her own but drawn almost irresistibly to Finn. Anyone could see she adored him. And the way he looked at her, as if she had just fallen out of the sky and landed in front of him, to his astonishment and often amusement — it gave Caitlin hope that Finn could be truly happy again.

And Finn had a right, she thought, to this fresh start. Even though she had reservations when the weeks and then months went by and it was occasionally obvious from something Violet said or didn't say that Finn still hadn't told her about Maribel, Caitlin didn't press him. She asked him about it exactly once, and when he brushed her off, she didn't argue. Nor did she take it upon herself to tell Violet what Finn wasn't yet ready to. Long before Violet had come into the picture, Caitlin and George had arrived at a sort of truce with Finn, an unspoken agreement that he was the only one who would speak Maribel's name *first* in any conversation. It put him in control of when he wanted to be reminded of what had happened, or to discuss it. And he almost never did — which was fine with Caitlin. She didn't like to be reminded of it either, of the way Finn had slipped into shock as if it were a new skin, of the way he'd looked at her when she told him George's family would help to quietly extricate him from the wreckage of the crash. His look had not been one of gratitude, but rather . . . what? Resentment? Disgust?

It nagged at her at first, the idea of Violet not knowing something that was such a big part of who Finn had become, but as Violet and Finn quickly became one of those inseparable couples who hardly did anything apart, and as all four of them found themselves miraculously pregnant and due around the same time, Caitlin gave herself over to the promise of *finally* becoming a mother and worried about Finn less and less. So he really had started over. He'd left that tragedy behind. If he'd had to do that on his own terms, then so be it. Why be the one to mess that up for him by rocking the boat?

23

AUGUST 2016

Finn wasn't Catholic, but he still felt a little as if he'd been instructed to recite Hail Marys until he had repented his sins.

The Hail Mary did seem an apt metaphor — in sports terms, anyway. He'd sensed Caitlin's desperation as she had instructed him, in that half-kidding tone that really wasn't joking at all, to leave the syrupy breakfast dishes and sugared-up boys to her, and instead go down to the dock and focus on 'one happy memory with Violet.'

'What are you, my therapist?' he'd grumbled. But Caitlin only raised an eyebrow as if to indicate that some therapy, might have come in handy. It was easy enough to go along with her request, or at least pretend to, if only to get her off his back. Obviously, she had no way of knowing what the hell he was really thinking about down here. He could see her through the cabin's large picture windows, moving around the kitchen. Once in a while he caught a flash of a giggling child running by the sliding glass doors. He'd eaten his share of the banana pancakes standing up, evading the awkward silence still between him and Caitlin from the evening before. Upon waking, they'd wordlessly agreed to a cease-fire, but he knew better than anyone that pretending everything was fine was a temporary solution, and an ineffective one at best.

The truth was, he still couldn't shake the feeling that he was halfway glad she was here. It was ridiculous. Her being here was a disaster. It couldn't end well for any of them. And yet . . . Finn needed a friend. He couldn't help it. And though it was complicated in this case for that friend to be Caitlin, it was also fitting. They'd been through the worst together before. But of course that had been before Violet, and long before Bear and the twins.

Even though she claimed she was here to help him out of it, he knew that really meant she was here to try to *talk* him out of it. And even though he also knew there was no way that was going to work, he still couldn't help feeling some small relief not to be alone in this corner he'd backed himself into. And that relief was dangerous. Caitlin was not to be underestimated. He couldn't let his guard down.

Back in school for graphic design, his professors were fond of cautioning students never to jump at the first fix for a design problem. 'Think of five solutions, and then discard them,' they advised. 'Then dig deeper for a *better* one.' That was when the real creativity kicked in. But in this case he'd already picked a bad fix to start. It was as if his very wiring had short-circuited, and when the power came back on he'd blinked into the light and was surprised to find Bear at his side. From there he'd chosen all the wrong moments to hesitate. He should have taken the money Caitlin offered when he confronted her in Cincinnati — but she'd stipulated that he leave Bear. By then he'd already accepted that he couldn't go back to that moment of the power surge, and he wasn't about to give him over easily — the boy was all he had left of love. He had to find some other way out.

'Do you want me to come up with a happy Violet memory for you?' Caitlin had asked with mock innocence. 'I can think of several . . . '

'Don't be ridiculous,' he'd snapped. And before he knew it, he was pouring himself a cup of coffee and stalking down here. As beautiful as the lake was in the morning light, he wouldn't turn his back on the cabin. He didn't think she'd be so bold as to try to run out the front with her boys *and* Bear, but this was uncharted territory for both of them, and he didn't know how she might react any better than he knew what *he* was going to do next.

The air at the water's edge smelled mildly fishy, and of wet leaves, the overeager ones that had detached and allowed themselves to fall prematurely. He breathed deeply, trying to block out the sounds of the boys whining up on the cabin's deck. It was something to do with wanting more juice. No matter how many just-this-one or just-one-more treats they got, no matter how many times he or Violet or Caitlin or George bent the rules in the name of a moment of peace, they never seemed satisfied. *It starts in childhood*, he marveled. *Nothing is ever enough. Why can't we just learn early on to be satisfied with whatever we have?*

Funny how a smell could conjure a memory like nothing else. All at once he could see himself pedaling his bike alongside the river one long-ago autumn, Violet hunched over her handlebars out in front of him. He'd been trying *not* to picture her since the day he'd left her at the hotel. But now he could see her so clearly, he might have reached out and touched her.

That first season together, they'd ridden every chance they got, evenings, weekends, claiming the paved railroad tracks of Southwestern Ohio's Rails-to-Trails network as their own, following the river through cool, damp ravines and old run-down mill towns as the leaves fell all around them. Maribel had never really been into that sort of thing; she'd been so conscientious about focusing her free time wholly on her art. But Finn's creativity had always needed a physical outlet. Violet came along with a love of trail riding, and Finn, who'd mostly been using his road bike on neighborhood streets, found it easy to love it too.

There was something meditative about the trail stretching out in front of them, the woods flashing by on both sides, the speckled sunlight coming through in patches from above. Finn would find himself zoning out to the patterns of shadows on the pavement, but Violet had an uncanny gift for spotting hidden remnants of the old railroad that was no longer functioning there. She'd point out a rusted train crossing sign overgrown by vines. A cracked block of concrete where a station platform used to stand. Tall lights that no longer blinked.

Open your eyes, she seemed to be saying. The world is still here, all around you.

As she was the slower rider, he'd always let her lead to set the pace — and there was no denying that the view never got old. He'd catch himself admiring the tone of her legs as they pumped up and down, the lean muscles pulled taut across her back as her shoulders hunched forward, the narrow swath of her waist perched effortlessly above the seat, even the windblown ponytail that streamed out from beneath her helmet. By the time they got back to his apartment or hers an hour or two or sometimes even three later, it would have been hard for any man to resist reaching for her after they showered. He was only human. And she was so warm, and active, and healthy, and alive.

Afterward, they'd lie with their limbs intertwined and talk, compensating for their hours of companionable silence on the trail. They traded stories of their childhoods, of the highlights before and after Camp Pickiwicki. She told him about Katie's awkward stream of dating disasters — she was on an ill-advised kick of dating their coworkers by then — and he relayed the antics of the most difficult customers in bridal photography. There was certainly no shortage of them, and it felt good to laugh about the job that had been adding to his misery for the better part of a year. She always had something sweet and homemade in her kitchen — peach cobbler, pear crisp, peanut butter cookies — and she would bring bowlsful to bed, warmed and topped with vanilla ice cream. She didn't care if they dripped on the sheets.

Damn Caitlin and the power of suggestion. Those *were* happy memories, and more than one. Reconnecting with Violet, to his surprise, had been like the warm sun on his face after so much time hiding indoors. Not that he'd ever thought it could last. But then had come the news that she was pregnant with Bear.

She'd almost succeeded in masking her hopeful expression as she made the announcement, waiting for him to be the one who'd determine whether or not this news was good. He could recognize in her something that he'd felt inside himself upon meeting Maribel's family, when they'd seemed so willing to adopt him as one of their own, knowing he had none. *I'll do anything you like*, that something seemed to say, *as long as you let me stay*. In Violet, he understood it as a side effect of being raised by Gram even as he knew that Gram had never done anything to make her feel unwanted or like a burden. And he didn't want to take advantage. It was just that it was so hard to turn away from the kind of love that is so eager to find you.

And he'd been so lonely when he met her.

How could he ever tell her that the last person who'd loved him, he'd *killed*?

The morning after her hemorrhage, she'd been ghostly white. That was when Finn had first realized the magnitude of his mistake. But he couldn't see a way to back out then. And he'd made a hell of a mess of it now.

When was it ever a good time to leave a

relationship, especially when the other person didn't see it coming? She wouldn't have been blindsided if she could have read his thoughts these past years. He almost wished for it — a world where he wouldn't have to try to explain everything that was so inexplicably wrong about how things had turned out. Where she would have just known.

★   ★   ★

Finn heard a rustling behind him and turned to see Caitlin approaching. In her hands were two thermal carriers of coffee, one light pink and one navy blue. Anyone happening by on an early-morning hike through the woods or paddle around the lake might have taken Finn and his friend as two halves of an ordinary his-and-her equation.

She held the blue mug higher as she approached. 'Peace offering,' she said, gesturing toward it with her head. 'These lids work great for keeping the gnats away down here.'

Finn looked down at the ceramic mug he was holding. It was almost empty, and sure enough, a gnat was floating on the surface of what was left, still circling its wings in a futile attempt at escape.

'Thanks,' he said, bending to set his mug down on the dock at his feet. But when she reached him, she didn't hand over the thermos. She pivoted back toward the cabin, and he followed her gaze to the kids. They were kicking a large orange air-filled ball around the grass

246

beneath the deck, following it in a little pack of three, laughing.

'Juke!' Bear yelled, dodging between the twins. 'Juke! Juke!'

Finn had taught him that. Because while Finn had never been the fastest or the strongest or the best shot on his own youth sports teams, he'd always been good at staying out of dodge.

'Remember how little they all were when we were here last summer?' Caitlin asked. 'I remember sitting in this exact spot with Violet, talking about how big they'd already grown. If we'd only known then — '

As her own words registered to her ears, she stopped short. 'I'm sorry. I didn't mean that we couldn't have imagined that a year down the road you'd be such an ass. I mean, you *are*, but . . . ' He watched her search his face for a sign that her attempt at levity had worked, but he wouldn't give her one. She sighed. 'I just meant that neither of us realized they'd keep getting so damn big so damn fast.'

'I knew what you meant. And it's okay. I do realize I'm not the victim in this, you know. I'm not *that* far gone.'

'Bear was doing that clingy thing where he wanted to be carried everywhere,' Caitlin continued, caught up in the memory. 'Never mind that he was capable of outrunning the twins if he wanted to. He was skittish about new places. And do you remember how *patient* Violet was with him? He'd lift up those little arms and she'd bend down and tote him wherever he pointed, up to the deck, then back down here, then up again, even though he was getting too heavy for anyone's back to handle that all day. Whatever Bear needed, she never let it show if she was too tired or not in the mood. She's so amazing that way — and I don't only remember watching her and thinking that. I remember watching *you* watching her, and knowing you were thinking the same thing.'

Finn forced a shrug he didn't really feel.

She looked down at the mugs in her hands as if surprised to find them there. 'I'm not going to be able to talk you out of this, am I?'

Her words caught him off guard. Caitlin wasn't one to give up on anything — or anyone — once she'd set her mind to it. She was persistent to a fault. *That's a fund-raiser for you,* George was fond of saying when she wouldn't let up.

She gazed out over the water without really looking at it, her eyes moving back and forth as if she were engaged in some inner dialogue, trying to talk herself into something. Or out of something.

'I disconnected my cell phone,' he heard himself say.

Caitlin turned to Finn, her jaw suddenly slack. 'What?'

'I could have left it in the hotel room. I could have tossed it in a trash can. But I didn't want there to be any mistake about what my intentions were. I didn't want her calling it over and over again, with false hope, or wasting time looking for it. And I didn't want to cost her a penny more, on the next bill.'

'Very considerate.'

He closed his eyes. 'You know what I'm getting at. I had to disconnect from Violet, Cait. All the way. I don't expect you to understand, but I *had* to. And yet I can't bring myself to disconnect from Bear.'

'There are other ways to go about this. Divorce. Shared custody. Pursue this any further, and you risk having your rightful half reduced to supervised visitation. Or less. Because you'll be a felon. You'll be disconnected from *everything*.'

When he didn't answer, she looked at him for a silent moment before finally handing him the coffee she'd brought. Then, without a word, she turned on her heels and walked back up toward the cabin.

24

Caitlin stood at the kitchen sink, ostensibly watching the kids play just outside the window. A few minutes earlier they'd been running in a herd behind that big inflatable ball, but now they were taking turns belly flopping on top of it and then rolling off into the grass. Their maniacal giggling and choruses of 'Watch this — boom!' 'Watch this — flop!' 'Watch this — oof!' floated through the screen of the open window like a pleasant distraction.

Caitlin wasn't watching with her usual vigilance, though. She was trying to force herself to breathe. She couldn't believe she'd actually done it. She'd crushed up the pills, stirred them into the coffee, and then, in a last-minute paranoia that Finn would detect an off taste, poured in as much French vanilla creamer as she thought she could get away with. She'd walked, determined, down to where Finn was standing at the dock, but even then had stalled, throwing him one last bone, looking for some sign that he might decide to redeem himself after all. And then, when that sign hadn't presented itself, she had handed the thermos over, as coolly as she could.

But now, her lungs were betraying her, constricting in fear. She had no idea if this would actually work, or if it did, how long it would take or exactly what it would do. But there was no turning back now — her plan was in motion. She had to stop holding her breath. She had to force calm. She had to be ready. For anything.

She startled at the ringing of her cell phone on the counter. With a shaky hand, she lifted it and saw her office number flashing across the screen. She had promised, upon taking the days off so hastily, to make herself available as needed. She had to take it.

'This is Caitlin.'

'*So* sorry to interrupt your time off. You know what they say: Don't shoot the secretary.'

She smiled at the sound of Tim's voice. He sounded so *normal*, businesslike but friendly with a hint of mischief. Then, just as quickly, her smile faded. Back home, it was just an ordinary day. She should be there too, doing ordinary things. Not holed up with a kidnapper. Not being blackmailed. And not, for the love of God, in the process of drugging someone's drink. She was just as normal as Tim. How on earth had she ended up here?

Caitlin forced her eyes back to the window; the boys were now wrestling in a heap, the forgotten ball rolling toward the tree line. She willed herself to harness their levity, to force it into her voice. 'No worries. I always welcome calls from my *administrative assistant*.'

'Not this call. This is . . . well, it's a little *awk-ward*.' Tim sang out each syllable in a too-obvious attempt to set her at ease, and she braced herself. 'You know that logo Finn designed for the Autumn Art in the Park event?'

She cringed. She hadn't even thought of all the ramifications of Finn's crime yet. She'd been hiring him for freelance projects ever since he moved to Asheville. Although he'd easily found work with a firm there, the pay wasn't great, and he didn't want to have to ask Violet to go back to work when she was so devoted to raising Bear.

'That came in last month — we're good.'

'We *were* good. But now the boss wants revisions. *Less autumny, more arty.*'

'Tell me that's not a direct quote.'

''Fraid so. Sponsors are lining up for this one, so they've decided to do one every season. They want something they can adapt for Winter Art in the Park and Spring Art in the Park and have it still look branded.'

Caitlin heard the scrape of the sliding screen door in the living room behind her. Finn must have come up the stairs on the far side of the deck, opposite from where the kids were playing. Was he already feeling sleepy? Disoriented? Sick? Had he tasted the pills? Had he come to confront her?

She turned to face him. He was sliding the door shut as if everything were normal. The thermos was in his hand. She gestured to the phone and put her finger to her lips.

'Well, that *is* a problem. Clearly I don't know how to reach Finn to request a logo revision at this particular moment.'

Finn froze at the sound of his name.

'Of course not. Oh my God. And I realize this is not at the top of your list of Finn problems, what with poor Violet and all . . . ' Tim paused, and she knew he was hoping she'd launch into a Violet update. But her eyes had locked with Finn's, rendering her silent. After a beat, Tim cleared his throat. 'It's just that . . . well, what do you want me to tell them?'

Caitlin kept her expression neutral even as she forced herself to turn back to the window to check on the kids, 'That he's not available, I guess. We're going to have to get someone else.'

'I tried that, but it didn't go over too well. Revisions are included in the project fee we paid him. There's no budget for a new designer.'

Caitlin groaned inwardly. As if Finn hadn't already caused her enough trouble. 'Look, this sounds like a reasonable request for a rework. If I knew how to reach him, obviously I would . . . '

She risked a glance over her shoulder at Finn, who had the decency to look chastised, He stood awkwardly by the door, looking down at his feet, and Caitlin quickly turned back so he wouldn't see her frustration mounting. She didn't want to argue now, to get him fired up. She needed him complacent. She needed the drink to do its job.

How much of it had he had?

'I'll hold them off for now,' Tim said. 'Just . . . if you find out that he's turned up, let me know?'

Sure, right after I explain how he's happened to turn up at my in-laws' cabin.

'Of course. But if he turns up, he might be . . . '

'In custody?' Tim's voice was hushed with scandal.

And I might be there with him.

She swallowed. 'This is embarrassing. I'll take responsibility. I'll find the money to hire someone else.'

'You don't have to — '

'I hired him. It's my responsibility.'

The room behind Caitlin was heavy with silence as she hung up, Outside, the wrestling match was turning decidedly less friendly.

Finally, Finn spoke. 'I'm sorry. Did you need me to — '

Caitlin lifted a hand, 'Least of our worries.'

'Right.'

Normal. She just had to act as normal as she could and let this play out. There was no turning back now. She had to be brave.

'Careful, boys,' she called out the window. 'Be gentle! Play nice!'

Everyone knew that for Caitlin, calling out a worried warning was as normal as normal gets.

She heard Finn step into the kitchen. He reached around her to turn on the faucet, then rinsed out his coffee mug — the ceramic one he'd been drinking from earlier. She caught sight of a gnat in the milky dregs as they swirled down the drain. He switched off the water and plunked the mug onto the counter behind her.

'Don't think I'm ungrateful,' he said. 'I like French vanilla creamer as much as the next guy. But I also like a splash of coffee in there.'

Caitlin's cells seized with fear. She forced herself to pivot, just in time to see Finn unscrew the top of the thermos she'd given him and pour half of his caramel-colored drink into the ceramic mug. He then topped off the thermos straight from the coffeepot and took a sip.

'Ah. Much better.'

Damn it. Damn, damn, damn. There'd been five pills in there. Now he was down to, what, two or three? With the caffeine on top of it, would that be enough to take effect? She'd have been better off adding a normal amount of creamer and having him think the coffee tasted a little off. He probably would have drunk it anyway.

She realized then that he was noticing, almost with amusement, that she was eyeing his abandoned mug. She swallowed hard.

'It won't go to waste,' he said, and another surge of fear gripped her before she realized he was only talking about the coffee. 'I'm going to need more than a couple of cups to keep up with Bear today. I haven't been sleeping much.'

'Neither has Bear,' she said, before she could stop herself. She couldn't ignore the echo of that *I want my mommy* any more than any other living breathing parent of a tiny human being could.

'You heard that.' It wasn't a question. Finn sighed heavily. He joined her at the window and took another long swig from the thermos.

He'd left the lid off, and she was standing so close she easily could knock into it with her elbow, spilling the whole pharmaceutical mess into the drain. When she'd returned from the dock moments ago and closed the door behind

255

her with shaking hands, she'd thought things had been irreversibly set into play. But they hadn't. Not yet.

'I'm sorry,' he said. 'It always amazes me how you moms are all programmed to wake up at every little thing.'

She narrowed her eyes, keeping them on the boys. 'There's nothing *little* about a kid crying for his mom that way,' she said. 'It's heartbreaking.'

No. She would not knock the mug into the sink. She was not the one who had a wrong to right. *Drink up*, she thought.

'I know,' Finn said quietly. Honestly. She glanced at him in surprise.

The boys were clomping up the stairs to the deck. They'd burst in any minute now.

He shrugged at Caitlin. 'Like I said. I didn't exactly think this through.'

'Mommy!' Leo came running through the door first, and beyond him she caught sight of Gus extending a hand to help Bear up the last step. They were like brothers, the three of them. Even if Caitlin's plan to get Bear home worked, would Violet ever allow the boys to be friends after this? Her heart ached.

'Can we do the tent? We want to do the tent!'

The tent had been a gift from George's parents over the Fourth of July holiday. The boys had used it that weekend in their grandparents' backyard — if you could consider acres of untouched Ohio countryside a 'backyard' — but not since. They'd insisted on bringing it along when she was packing them up yesterday. It was still in the trunk. She'd forgotten all about it.

Caitlin sighed. It was amazing how kids could fail to retain the things you wanted them to remember — look both ways before stepping into the street, ask before helping yourself to a cookie, wash your hands before you eat — but when it came to something you didn't really want to deal with, they had memories like little elephants.

Finn was shaking his head. No tent in the yard. It was too far outside the controlled area of his experiment.

'Maybe just here in the living room,' Caitlin said wearily, hoping they'd lose interest.

'Yay!' the three shouted in a chorus, 'Camping!'

Gus encircled her knee with his arms, pulling on her Bermuda shorts. 'Can we have a campfire and marshmallows too?'

Caitlin laughed. 'It's too hot for a fire, Gus. Look at you guys! You're covered in sweat! But maybe tonight. If we have marshmallows, I mean . . . '

Finn opened a cupboard and tossed a half-full bag of marshmallows onto the counter. 'Found these earlier,' he said. 'A little stale, but they'll work!'

He was trying to act cheerful for Bear, Caitlin could tell. And Bear seemed happy enough. So she went to get the tent out of the trunk. Maybe setting it up would distract Finn from any of the early effects he might be feeling. Maybe it would ensure that he'd keep downing that coffee and still have room for the refill that was waiting for him on the counter.

★ ★ ★

Caitlin's bare feet sank into her in-laws' luxurious bath mat as she stepped out of the shower, In spite of the August heat, it had felt good to turn the water on as hot as she could stand it and let it steam-clean her mind, just for a minute, But she couldn't stay in any longer, She questioned her judgment in leaving the kids with Finn even momentarily, though she had activated the security system again at the keypad while he was busy helping them haul blankets and pillows into the tent they'd erected in the center of the living room floor.

But the shower was a calculated move. She sensed that Finn was less likely to let his guard down while she was hovering around. Once the boys were situated at their 'campsite,' they'd asked for a DVD, and she'd purposely chosen the one about the trains at the rail yard turning in for the night — the one that bored her to tears but that she often suffered through solely because it seemed to have a sleep-inducing effect on the twins, Maybe it would work on Finn too, Maybe he'd just . . . just not wake up until after Caitlin had returned Bear to Violet's side.

As Finn had settled onto the couch and started the show for the boys, she'd risked a look into his thermos on the end table. It was empty. But on the counter, the other half of his oversweetened drink remained untouched, cold, forgotten, She just hoped he'd ingested enough to take effect. Thank goodness she'd gone with the five pills and not just one or two.

Caitlin toweled off as quickly as she could, straining her ears for signs of giggling or talking from the living room, All she could hear was one of those dreadful sing-along Island of Sodor songs. 'Let's pray to God they tire of this show by the time they can read lyrics,' George had once said, echoing her own thoughts exactly. But instead of agreeing, Caitlin had grumbled that he didn't have to sit through half as many episodes as she did. If she got herself out of this mess somehow — if she got all of them out of this mess somehow — she'd be kinder. There was no reason for bitterness toward George. Even though his job took him away too often, he had their best interests at heart. And he was on track to do what his father had groomed him to do. She'd never aspired to be a senator's wife, or even a high-powered businessman's wife, for that matter, but now that Finn had threatened George's future prospects, she felt defensive of her husband's hard work. She should never have allowed herself to be anything but proud, even on her most tired days.

She pulled on drawstring khaki capris, comfortable for the long car ride that with any luck she'd be taking today. *Please let this work. Please. Let this work.* She buttoned up a sleeveless cotton sheath and slipped her feet into canvas deck shoes. No time to mess with hair or makeup — she ran a brush through the wet, tangled mass, twisted it up, and secured it with a clip. She poked her head into the hallway, and when she still didn't hear anyone, crept toward the living room.

Finn was stretched out on the couch away from her — she could see only the top of his head. He didn't stir. She inched closer, then closer still, and finally came around the corner, her breath in her throat, a cheerful greeting ready on her tongue. But his eyes were closed. She watched his breathing closely. It was slow, heavy, the sleep of someone who hadn't really rested for days on end and was badly in need of a deep, undisturbed slumber, one he would've kept denying himself if he had anything to say about it.

But he didn't.

She must have stood there for a full minute, watching the rise and fall of his chest, checking that his cheeks still had color, which they did, and scanning him to see if she could spot any signs of distress, which she couldn't. She said a silent prayer that she hadn't given him enough to hurt him. Then she said another that he wouldn't wake up until she was long gone.

Caitlin peeked her head into the tent. Bear and Gus were sound asleep too, in a tangled mess of blankets, Bear curled up with his thumb in his mouth — the fetal position had never seemed so appropriate as it did now — and Gus slack jawed, his legs thrown almost protectively over Bear's. Poor little Bear. He looked even more exhausted than his father did. But not for long. Her plan was under way, was going to

260

work. She'd have him back to his mother in hours.

She hadn't allowed herself to think much about what would happen next. She dared to hope that in person, she could talk Violet into coming here, confronting Finn on her own — assuming Finn was still here to confront by then — taking one last chance to talk things through on their own terms without the authorities calling the shots. Maybe there was still *some* way out of this, however unlikely, for all of them. But then again, maybe not. Maybe Vi would insist on calling Agent Martin right away. Maybe Finn would be taken into custody and follow through on his blackmail threats. Maybe he'd escape, and she'd be accused of letting him go.

The price Caitlin might pay . . . well, she'd just have to face it.

But where was Leo?

'Boo!' he shouted, springing up from the pile of pillows against the back wall of the tent. Leo erupted into a fit of giggles as Caitlin's hand went to her throat. Her eyes darted toward Finn, half expecting him to sit up. He didn't move, Miraculously, neither did the other boys. Caitlin went down onto her knees and opened her arms, and Leo sank into her hug.

'I was hiding!' he said proudly, his voice muffled by her shoulder.

'I can see that. You scared me!' She could always count on him for a good snuggle, no matter where they were or whom they were with. She knew that would change one day, but she

261

hated to think of it. She held him close for as long as he'd let her and tried to think of exactly what she should do next. She had to disable the alarm, grab the essentials — pull-ups (she'd learned the hard way that the boys couldn't always wait for the next exit on a long drive), clothes, snacks — and rush the kids out to the car. She'd need to grab Bear's car seat from that clunker Finn was driving — she still didn't have the slightest clue where he'd gotten it, or how — and figure out how to install it in her own. And she had to keep the boys relatively quiet while she was loading up — she wasn't sure how soundly she could bank on Finn sleeping. But if she could just get the car moving in the direction of Asheville, and everyone strapped in, she'd be home free.

Well, neither home nor free, actually. Her own troubles would just be beginning — but Bear and Violet would be together and safe. And that was what mattered.

Leo pulled back and grinned up at her, the kind of goofy grin full of unencumbered love that only the youngest kids can give. And the kind of messy grin that comes only from those who have yet to learn to use a napkin. She had to laugh. 'What on earth is all over your face?' It looked like smears of chocolate, and something stickier. Leo had been getting into everything lately. It was the age, people told her, and she had to bite her lip to point out that Gus didn't seem to have any problems staying out of trouble. She couldn't stand the idea of people categorizing the twins in the way that she knew

262

they eventually would: the troublemaker and the mama's boy, the old soul and the wild child, the brawn and the brains.

'Hot chocolate.'

She glanced around for a mug but didn't see any. She didn't even think they *had* any hot chocolate.

'Hot chocolate? Did Uncle Finn make you that?'

Leo didn't answer. He buried his hands in the front of her shirt and started pulling on the fabric, the way he did when he thought he was in trouble. 'It's okay, little man. Mommy isn't mad. We just need to clean you up.'

He looked at her with so much gratitude she regretted all the times she'd been less patient, less understanding. 'I wanted marsh-mallows,' he explained, as she took his sticky hand and led him toward the kitchen.

And that's when she saw. The bag of marshmallows open on the counter. The stool pulled up next to it, The puddles of French vanilla-flavored coffee that had sloshed over the sides of Finn's mug from this morning. And the fact that hardly a drop was left inside.

She scooped Leo into her arms and crossed the rest of the distance to the counter, trying to remain calm. She pointed at the mug. 'This is what you drank?' He nodded, and something inside her keeled over. *No. It couldn't be.*

'This isn't hot chocolate, little man. It was Uncle Finn's coffee. Coffee is a grown-up drink. It didn't taste funny to you?'

He shrugged. She looked again at how much

was spilled onto the counter. It was hard to judge. She forced into her voice a calm she didn't feel. 'Did you actually drink it, or did you just dip marshmallows in it?' He didn't answer.

If only she had dumped it out — if she hadn't been so careless to hold on to some lingering hope that Finn would polish it off after all . . .

Her heart pounded, yet she moved slowly — if she set off a tantrum, if he felt he was in trouble, she might never get the answers she needed. And the consequence could be deadly serious. She touched the tip of her nose to his, a move she reserved for when she needed his attention most. 'You drank it, or you just dipped marshmallows in it?' she repeated.

'I wanted marshmallows,' he said again. Then, with another sticky grin, 'It *tasted*, like hot chocolate!' Caitlin had a flash of Gus and Bear, still sleeping in the tent. She set Leo on the floor at her feet and took him by the shoulders as gently as she could manage with her pulse racing.

'Did Gus and Bear drink some too?'

He shook his head.

'Are you sure? Not even a little bit?'

'I didn't want to share,' he said.

Caitlin fought against the growing sense of panic that threatened to overtake her. She couldn't let herself get frantic, not now.

'Honey, do you feel sick at all? Do you feel sleepy?' Leo looked at her strangely. She glanced over her shoulder at the tent, at Finn asleep on the couch. No one stirred.

'Let's go into the bathroom, sweetie,' she said

soothingly, taking Leo by the hand. She pulled him down the hall and he followed reluctantly. Back in the master bathroom, she washed her hands and his at the sink. Then she led Leo gently over to the toilet and knelt down beside him.

When he was younger, he had an underdeveloped gag reflex, one that used to make every little head cold miserable for the whole family' by causing him to throw up without warning — all over his bedsheets, or the couch, or his car seat — when he coughed with any force at all. She prayed he still had it. Without a word, she wrapped an arm around his midsection, bent him over the bowl, and pushed her index finger as far down his throat as she could. Leo made a loud, startled gagging noise, and she pulled her hand back. He cried out, and then began to wail, tears of hurt and surprise instantly streaming down his face. He did not, however, throw up.

She did it again, to no avail. She gave him a moment to catch his breath, then tried again. Each time, he wailed louder. By the time her fifth attempt failed, she was crying too. She sank onto the floor, wrapped both arms around him, and pulled him close. His little shoulders heaved and she held on tight.

'I'm so sorry, baby,' she said. 'Mommy's so sorry.'

'You're — ' Leo was sobbing so hard he could barely get the words out. 'Scaring — ' Another sob. 'Meeeee . . .'

'Mommy's so sorry,' she said again and again, rocking him back and forth on the tile. Poison

Control. Should she call Poison Control? They'd want to know, of course, how many pills he'd had. Could she safely tell them half the amount she'd given Finn? It seemed possible that the powder might have hovered near the bottom of the thermos. So maybe Leo hadn't gotten much. Then again, maybe he'd gotten more than his share.

Even if she ventured a guess, invented a story as to how he'd gotten into the pills, even if Poison Control said he would probably be fine — even if they brushed it off as a common accident, even if this sort of thing happened to *other* parents all the time, even if they asked her to just monitor him for any concerning symptoms — could she ever take that chance, not knowing how much of the drug he'd actually ingested? She knew the answer already. Besides, she couldn't stay here now that she'd managed to knock Finn out, and she couldn't observe Leo properly on the road to Asheville. There was no way around getting him to the emergency room.

She *had* to get them all out of here without waking Finn. If he woke up, this would all be for nothing. She would have *put Leo in harm's way* for nothing.

If the hospital said Leo was okay — and if by some miracle they didn't arrest her for child endangerment — she could take Bear straight to Violet as planned. If not . . .

She couldn't think about that. She wouldn't.

Leo was sniffling quietly in her arms now, heaving the occasional shaking sigh like she herself did after a good cry. She tilted his face up to hers. It was hard to tell after he'd been crying, but did his eyes look glassy? Groggy? His lead lolled against her chest and he looked at her lethargically.

She had to grab the other kids and go. They had to go *now*.

25

AUGUST 2016

The morning following her call with Mrs. Branson, Violet didn't leave the house. She didn't want to see anyone, if she could help it. Lying rumpled in Bear's bed, cell phone in her sweaty hand, she made up excuses to evade Gram, then preempted Agent Martin's daily visit with a phone call to check in.

'We have a lead on a car Finn may have bought, from a mobile home park in walking distance of an Amtrak station in Tennessee,' he told her.

Her heart stilled. 'When was it sold?'

'Four, five days ago.' He sounded preoccupied with the information, which she took to be a good sign. 'Hard to say whether the guy just wants the reward, but we're sending someone to look into it.'

Violet had almost forgotten about the reward Gram had offered for vital information. The chances of the missing persons report drawing interest had seemed so bleak.

'Thank you,' she told him, sincerely, willing her brain to wrap itself around this new, small hope. A car would mean a license plate, and that might mean they could issue an AMBER Alert after all. It might mean there was a trail to follow. Her eyes watered with gratitude. 'I won't keep you, then.'

'As always, let us know if you think of anything else,' he said, clearing his throat. 'In light of new information.' He was referring to the bombshell about Maribel, of course. Would he think it strange if he knew that she'd phoned Mrs. Branson? She hated this new lingering sensation of always feeling as if she might be doing something wrong. But perhaps it wasn't entirely new after all. Perhaps it didn't feel as unfamiliar as it should have.

He said he'd come by the next morning, unless there was something to report in the meantime, and she hung up feeling oddly off the hook. She reverted to not bothering to shower. She stayed in her pajamas. She didn't eat breakfast, even though her stomach was roiling with a hangover from the night before. She left Bear's bed only to down some ibuprofen and — though the morning sun streamed through his blinds, and her own room across the hall was invitingly dark — she nestled back in among his stuffed animals, as much because she missed Bear as because she couldn't stand the thought of being in the place where she'd spent so many nights lying next to the stranger who was Finn. She tried to picture Bear now. An Amtrak station. A train, then. A walk to a mobile home park. An unfamiliar car. Tennessee. It wasn't much, but it was something. She closed her eyes against the daylight, but she did not sleep.

Nor had she really slept the night before. Because even surrounded by so many sweet, soft reminders of Bear, even having downed enough vodka to make the room tilt until she had no choice but to close her eyes, unconsciousness had evaded her. She'd been unable to stop thinking back, memory by painful memory, on all that had transpired with Finn, from day one through the nightmare of today.

No, she wasn't thinking of it — she was *rethinking it.*

She was trying to rewrite the story of her life. The story of *their* lives together. She was trying to discover what an objective passenger might have written in that captain's log — or, perhaps more to the point, what Finn would have written there. The problem was, she wasn't sure. Everything was a big question mark now.

Just days ago, she would have welcomed any distraction that would keep her from obsessing about Bear every second of every day and night. Now, in the revelation about Maribel, she had one — but it was a distraction that only made her feel even more helpless, more clueless, than she could have imagined possible.

That confusion, though, was juxtaposed with an odd sense of clarity that overtook specific memories — particularly the recent ones.

Violet had never been able to figure out, for instance, why Finn had insisted on flying rather than driving on their vacation. It would have been so much simpler to choose a beach in the Carolinas that wouldn't have taken more than a day's drive. It would have been so much easier to transport their ridiculous amount of little kid gear that way — the car seat, the stroller, the portable booster for meal-times, the overflowing diaper bag she still kept on hand in case of accidents. It would have been so much cheaper to bring their own beach chairs, and umbrellas, and sand toys, rather than buying it all when they arrived, only to have to throw it out at the end of the week. Violet had argued all of these points, but their fights never got very far — whichever one of them was less determined or less upset, and it was always one of them, would soon cave rather than draw out the agony.

In this case, Violet had conceded. She'd thought Finn was being romantic, wanting to return to Sunny Isles, to the spot where they had first met, wanting to go there *with* her this time, wanting to add to their memories of the spot with Bear. The fact that he was willing to go to extra expense and more inconvenience to make that happen couldn't be anything but sweet, could it?

Now she thought differently. She no longer knew when Finn had stopped being in love with her — or if he'd ever really loved her at all. But she did know that the last time he'd embarked on a road trip to a Carolina beach, someone had died. Someone whom he most definitely did love. Of course he wouldn't want to take that route again.

And if he'd planned all along to leave Violet there — she didn't know if he had, but *if* that was the case — why stay closer to home when he could give himself a head start on running away? How much more thorough to strand her so far from everyone and everything she knew, without even a car.

What kind of marriage was that? She'd seen the smugness of the question on Agent Martin's face yesterday. *This guy didn't even tell his wife he had a fiancée before, let alone that he caused her death. Not so shocking all of a sudden that he ran off with his kid, was it? No telling what a guy like that might do.*

Of course, Violet hadn't admitted to the agent that she actually *had* known all along that Finn had been engaged — that as those first days of their courtship had stretched into weeks and then months, she had waited for the moment he would take her hands in his, say softly that there was something he had to tell her, and then gently explain that he had had a fiancée once, but that it hadn't worked out for one reason or another, and say that he was so very glad it hadn't, because all along he'd been thinking of her and wishing things had ended differently on the beach that day. And she also hadn't volunteered to Agent Martin that when that moment never came, she decided to just try to move forward as if she didn't feel a piece of his history was missing from what they'd shared. Because who knows? Maybe her company's HR department had gotten his reason for canceling the interview wrong in the first place. Maybe they had misunderstood, or mixed him up with a candidate for another job opening.

There was no way to know. Because after months of waiting for Finn to bring it up, how could she possibly be the one to do it? 'Hey, remember when you applied for this job with my company, but canceled your interview at the last

272

minute? How do I know that? Well, funny story . . . ' He'd want to know why she hadn't asked him about it earlier. There wasn't an explanation that didn't peg her as a coward, afraid to hear the answer. Which, deep down, she had been. And apparently with good reason.

She could still hear Katie's parting advice that day she'd brought Violet the Missed Connections ad. 'Be honest and play dumb.'

Right.

In a way, she was just as guilty as Finn. Maybe not guilty, but not guilt*less* either. Admitting that to Agent Martin would have meant she would have had to admit it to herself. And Gram. And Caitlin.

Caitlin.

She hadn't called to check in, nor had Violet tried her again since catching her on the house phone days ago. And that was just as well.

Caitlin had to have known Finn's history. All of it. And she, too, had never seen fit to mention this to Violet, as if it were something that might be important for Finn's wife and the mother of his child to know, Not only that he had loved before, and been responsible for the death of that love, and planned to start a new life with her in the very place that Violet found herself now, but that it wasn't clear how or whether he'd found a way to make peace with any of that.

Caitlin had said nothing when she and Violet first became friends. She'd said nothing when the two women were bound by their forays into motherhood and grew just as close as Caitlin and Finn had been all those years before. And she'd said nothing when Finn disappeared with Bear and she herself came to sit in this very room with Violet and cry with her.

Alongside Gram, Caitlin had been the first one here when Violet returned from Sunny Isles — was it really just a week ago? — broken-hearted and confused and empty-handed. She'd seemed appropriately devastated and outraged and mystified on Violet's behalf. But now all of Violet's memories were being called into question. Who was to say whom she could trust? Or whom she should?

Had Caitlin been more loyal to Finn all along? Had Violet been blind to the true feelings of *everyone* she felt close to?

Even if she still couldn't see it in looking back, she now knew that while Finn had appeared sturdy enough on the surface, he'd been crumbling at some key structural components underneath. And if the foundation was that shaky, there was no way anything they built on it could ever be stable. Violet could slather on as much mortar as she wanted; she could redecorate their relationship to mirror a glossy picture that she liked; she could patch and prime and paint until she'd exhausted the available resources and then some. But none of it would ever fix the real problem, none of it would stop the whole crooked thing from sliding to the ground.

It wouldn't have been so catastrophic if what they'd built had housed just the two of them.

In spite of everything she'd learned, none of it changed her disbelief that Finn would want to hurt her this way by taking Bear. Maybe he'd panicked and hadn't thought it through. Maybe he regretted it. Maybe even as she was lying here miserably now, he was looking for a way to bring Bear back without digging himself in deeper.

If there were a way for Finn to return Bear without himself being charged with kidnapping, would he take it? There had to be a way, if she had anything to say about it — but how could she let him know?

And how had they spent so many of the years since they'd met wanting to reach out to each other but unsure how to cross the indeterminable distance between them?

26

AUGUST 2016

Caitlin had pictured this moment countless times — the moment she would do irreparable harm to one of her children. But she'd never pictured it like this. Watching the national news or reading parenting magazines, she'd feel physically ill at the stories of parents who'd forgotten their sleeping children in car seats, who'd thought their handguns were stored out of reach, who'd sworn they'd gone back inside just for a second while the child was playing in the front yard. She knew everyone else was thinking, *What awful parents. Who could be so irresponsible?* But Caitlin felt only fear. *Who was she to judge? What if she were to one day make some crucial mistake that brought on that kind of heartbreak and self-loathing from within, that kind of wrath from all around?*

Once she'd made it with the boys out of the cabin, past a mercifully unconscious but evenly breathing Finn, the full force of her terror set in. She'd hastily squeezed and strapped Bear's car seat between the twins' as best she could with shaking hands, and peeled out in a crunch of gravel and a cloud of dust. The whole drive here to the hospital, she'd silently begged — whom, she wasn't even sure. *Please,* she pleaded, over and over, as her eyes flicked wildly from the rearview mirror, where she could see Leo slumped over, eyes closed, in his car seat, to the curvy road ahead, and back again. *Please don't let today be that day. Please don't let this happen to Leo — my beautiful, perfect, energetic, miracle baby Leo. Please don't let it happen to Gus, his brother who needs him, or to George, who didn't ask for any of this, or to Bear, who just needs to go home. Please don't let it happen to me.*

There was also the small matter of entering a hospital with a kidnapping victim. There had been some coverage, though it was light, in Asheville and Cincinnati, but Caitlin wasn't sure about here in Kentucky, smack between the two. Were health care workers trained to keep a lookout for kids who were missing in the region?

Ultimately, it was futile to try to calculate the risk. She had no choice but to take it.

She told the boys they just had to make sure Leo wasn't sick. She called it an adventure. And she found, in a stroke of luck, a pair of zip-up hoodies that she'd stashed in her trunk. They were ninja sweatshirts, the kind with flaps sewn in to transform the hoods into pull-down eye masks, gifted to the twins by her mother-in-law a few months ago. Caitlin thought them ridiculous. Not only was she tired of Beverly indulging them with overpriced boutique items that cost more than most outfits she'd worn in the earlier years of her own adult life, but the boys didn't even yet know what ninjas were. Into Caitlin's trunk the gift bag had been stashed that day, and there it had stayed.

She told Gus and Bear they could be hospital superheroes, and they pounced on the idea — no matter that it was pushing 90 degrees. Everyone knew that kids this age love to dress up, and besides, the car and the hospital were both air-conditioned. If Bear kept that little mask flap down, maybe it would be enough for him to escape recognition on the off-chance that anyone *did* remember his face.

The ninjas were sweeping around the tiny waiting room now, 'rescuing' each other from under the rows of chairs. The three of them had been led to this smaller area behind a maze of corridors off the main ER, and no one else was here at the moment. Caitlin could tell that the occasional nurses and orderlies cutting through knew better than to pass judgment on unruly children. Not a single person gave her a dirty look, and for that, she was grateful.

Even though Leo had been out cold by the time they arrived, only mumbling and fluttering his eyelids when Caitlin tried to rouse him, even though she'd let down her calm façade in that moment she gathered him into her arms and burst through the lobby doors, Gus and Bear seemed remarkably nonplussed. They were mostly just excited to be at the hospital, and at worst curious about where Leo had gone. Thank goodness they were too young to understand — she could only hope there wouldn't be any serious explaining to do later.

'From what you've told me, it sounds like he'll probably be fine,' the admitting nurse had said, laying a warm hand on Caitlin's shaking arm. Of course, what Caitlin had told her was a variation on the truth, but one that approximated the amount of Ambien he may have had. 'Try not to panic. We'll take good care of him.' Somewhere in the maze of hallways off this fluorescent-lit waiting room, they were working Leo over, hooking him up to monitors, running blood-work. They'd assured Caitlin she could come back to his side just as soon as they knew his status.

'But he's sleeping so soundly — ' Caitlin had started, the tears welling up again.

'Of course he's sleeping soundly. He had a little Ambien. It's what it does.' The nurse had looked past Caitlin to the boys. 'Would you like me to call someone to sit here with you? To help with his brothers? Cell phones aren't allowed back here, but there are courtesy phones in the waiting area.'

'Thank you,' Caitlin told her, wiping the tears, trying to pull herself together for the sake of Gus and Bear. 'I can handle it. I just . . . I blame myself.'

'Things happen,' the nurse said sympatheti-cally. She nodded toward Gus and Bear. 'I can see you have your hands full. We can't watch them every second of every day, can we? Now you sit tight, and I'll let you know as soon as we hear something.'

She seemed so genuinely kind. But Caitlin didn't know if that was just good bedside manner or a smooth line to evade giving any hints that child services would be notified.

Caitlin knew she should call George. His son

was in the emergency room, after all. But she was clinging to the hope that the doctor would come out and say Leo was completely fine, no harm done, they could go home, and then Caitlin could proceed with her original plan and George would never have to know about this terrifying gaffe. Well, she supposed he'd get the hospital bill, but by then . . . well, either the cats would all be out of the bag anyway, or she'd have had plenty of time to come up with a more reasonable explanation.

If she were to bring George into this, she might as well put Finn's blackmail plan into action for him.

But what if he's not fine? A battle waged in her head. *If his father misses his only chance to be at his side, he'll never forgive you.*

She had to believe it wouldn't come to that.

A wail from across the waiting room snapped her back to attention. Bear had tripped and was picking himself up off the waxed linoleum, crying. Caitlin could tell he was fine, just a little bruised and annoyed that his fun had been interrupted. She shuddered to think about the germs on the hospital floor, though, Autopilot kicked in and she swooped over, collecting a dollop of hand sanitizer from the wall dispenser along the way. She gave him a hug, reassured him that he was okay, and rubbed the foam into his little hands as best she could, Gus, who wasn't typically jealous when she doled out affection to Leo or anyone else, hovered over her shoulder, resting his chin there and peering at her through his long eyelashes, These boys were

280

tired. They were off their routines and out of their element and while they didn't know enough to be scared here with Caitlin, they must have sensed something wasn't quite right. Bear quieted down to a whimper, and she led them both to a table spread with crayons and photocopied coloring book pages of doctors and nurses and ambulances. *You'd think they'd want to get the kids' minds off this place*, she thought. *Just Elmo or some Care Bears would suffice.*

'Let's see how well hospital superheroes can color,' she said, hoping her words might encourage them not to lift their masks.

'I want to make a picture for Mommy,' Bear said, choosing a red crayon. Caitlin's eyes filled with tears. Damn it, they were supposed to be in the car on the way to Violet's right now. If she hadn't been so stupid . . . 'She hangs them on the 'frigator,' he told her solemnly.

Maybe there was still a way to set things right. Assuming the FBI had Violet's phone tapped, Caitlin couldn't tip her off outright. But if she could get her down here — maybe she could still go through with something close to her plan, and redeem herself with Finn too, by giving him one last chance to make good before the authorities swooped in.

'Boys, I'm going to make a call at this phone right over here.' Caitlin pointed. She needed to be sure Bear would not yell out to her while she was on the line with Violet. 'Can you color three pictures? One for me, and one for Leo when he's feeling better, and one for Bear's mommy, when we see her again.'

'What about Daddy?' Gus asked.

'Of course! One for Daddy. That makes four. Four pictures.' She counted out the sheets for each of them.

'What about *my* daddy?' Bear asked, wide-eyed.

'And Uncle Finn! What was 1 thinking?' Lord help her. 'Five. Five pictures.' She gave them each one more. Then, when she was satisfied that they were busy at work, she crossed the room to the courtesy phone and dialed Violet.

The hopefulness in her friend's 'Hello?' was almost too much for Caitlin. Of course. She was calling from an unknown number. Violet would be hoping it was Finn.

'Vi, it's me.'

'Oh. Cait.' Violet did not sound happy to hear from her. Downright unhappy, in fact. Caitlin told herself it was just the initial disappointment that she was someone other than Finn.

'Are you okay?' Caitlin asked. 'Your voice sounds kind of funny.'

'How am I supposed to sound when my husband and son have gone missing?' The iciness'was unmistakable.

Caitlin looked over at Bear. 'I'm sorry.'

'Or when I realize my best friend never saw fit to tell me about my husband's dead fiancée? Or their plans to move to Asheville, where I unwittingly dragged him against his will?'

So that was it. 'How did you find out?' she asked, her mouth dry.

'From the FBI. You know, the way everyone wants to find out key information about their spouses that it turns out their friends have known all along.'

Tears filled Caitlin's eyes. What little resolve she'd had left was gone. 'I always thought he'd tell you, in his own time . . . '

'Right. Or he could snap and do something different 'in his own time.' Like disappear with our *child.*'

'If I had ever in a million years thought — '

'Where even are you?' Violet cut in. 'I don't recognize the area code.'

'I had the boys down at the cabin, and I . . . I mean, Leo . . . ' Her voice broke. Even with everything that was going on, she realized that a part of her had been longing to hear Violet's voice. She needed a friend right now. She was so scared and felt so alone. She was desperately trying to fix this. Violet had every right to be upset with her, but just . . . just *not right this minute.* Right this minute it was going to make it impossible for Caitlin to do what she had to do.

Violet sighed heavily. 'What *about* Leo?'

Caitlin sniffed. 'He got into some pills. Some Ambien.'

'Oh my God.' And just like that, the sarcasm in her tone changed to concern. Because Violet was, above all, a good person, a good friend, a good mom. She didn't deserve any of this. 'Is he okay?'

'I think so. I mean, they don't know yet, for sure. But I think so. We're at the hospital.'

'Jesus.' Violet's anger was softening. 'Wow. So that really does happen. I mean, you hear on the news about kids doing that sort of thing, but I

283

always think, *Really? How?* I mean, pills are gross. I can't get Bear to eat half the good stuff I put on his plate, let alone stuff he's not supposed to touch.'

At the sound of Bear's name, Caitlin felt the blood draining from her face. 'He was also eating marshmallows,' she said weakly. 'They were both on the counter.'

'You take Ambien?'

'No, George's mother. She left them in the cabinet.' Caitlin stuck to the story she'd told the nurse. 'I wasn't sleeping well, and I got them out because I thought about taking one but I . . . I didn't.'

'We just have to be so careful about every little thing the kids can reach, don't we?' Violet got quiet then, and Caitlin imagined the agony of wondering if you'd ever need those little parenting reminders again. Even her position in the emergency room was probably enviable to Violet right now. *If she only knew.* 'Are you okay?' Violet asked after a moment.

'I . . . ' Caitlin's original train of thought had derailed. 'Actually. I was wondering if you could come down here. Sit with me? You know how awful hospitals are.' Violet didn't answer right away, and Caitlin stole a glance over at the boys. They were intent on their work, heads down. Bear's tongue was protruding from the corner of his mouth in concentration.

'George isn't there?' Violet said finally.

'He's working. In Cincinnati this week. I came alone with the boys.'

'Well, that's not that far.' Violet sounded

284

satisfied. 'He could be there in a couple hours.'

Caitlin's mind raced after another lie, but it came up with the truth. 'I can't face him,' she said. 'This is all my fault.' She choked back a sudden sob, covering her mouth quickly with her hand. She turned away from the boys so they wouldn't see and willed herself to pull it together.

'I thought you said Leo was going to be okay?'

Caitlin fought back another sob. 'He is — ' She sniffed hard. 'I mean, I think so — '

When Violet spoke again, her words were thick with emotion. 'Caitlin, under any other circum-stances, I'd come and sit with you anytime, day or night, anytime you need a friend. But you have to understand — I sit here and I wait for Finn and Bear to come through that door. It might sound dumb, but that's what I do. There's nowhere else I can be. I can't drive to Kentucky and risk missing them. That's too much to ask of me. Especially right now, when I have so many questions for you. I'm sorry, but no.'

'We could talk about Maribel,' Caitlin blurted out. She knew she was grasping at the air, about to plummet into the abyss. But what else could she do? She would say anything it took to get Violet here — where Bear was. If she could just tell her, if she could just think of some hint that might get by the wiretap . . . but her mind, torn apart by worry, was failing her now.

'In person,' she added. 'The way I should have told you in the first place. I can explain — '

'No offense, but I'm not sure a hospital is the best place for me to hear that story. I've already heard it, anyway. From Maribel's mother.'

Caitlin didn't know what to say to that. She couldn't imagine Violet talking with Mrs, Branson after all these years. What had been said?

'Well, we could talk about Finn, how he was afterward,' Caitlin said, sounding as desperate as she felt. 'Maribel's mother wouldn't know about that.'

Bear is here! She wanted to scream. *I've got him for you!*

'You know I love you, Cait, and I really hope and pray that Leo is okay, but even if I did want to leave Asheville, which I don't, I'm not feeling ready to see you right now. I'm sorry. I kind of can't believe I'm the one apologizing here, but I *am* sorry.'

'But just — '

'Call your husband, Cait. At least you know how to *reach* yours.' And the line went dead with a definitive click.

27

It was all because of that damn nap.

Finn had never understood why Violet made such a fuss about them. She'd be nearly frantic if they ran late at the store, or if someone had the gall to invite them to anything that took place in the midafternoon. 'He *can't* miss his nap,' she'd moan. And then she'd go on and on, all the while Finn thinking, the kid will sleep if he's tired. Or not. If he's fussy later, we'll put him to bed early. What's the big deal? 'Maybe he would fall asleep in the car on the way?' she'd say, wringing her hands. 'Or maybe we could leave a little early so that when he *does* fall asleep in the car, we could drive around for a while so he could at least get a power nap in? Even twenty minutes would help ward off the hangry crankies . . . '

Hangry crankies was a term of her own devising that could just about send him over the edge with its redundancy. *Hangry* already reflected a blend of *hungry* and *angry*. There was no need for the addition of crankiness, which seemed to him to actually trivialize the implied fury of the *hangry* rather than emphasizing it. But hangry crankies she had dubbed them and so hangry crankies they had become in their household. Why argue about something so meaningless?

In truth, it was often better not to argue because she would turn out to be right. Bear did need the naps, for instance. Without one, he'd be so overtired by bedtime that he not only couldn't manage to fall asleep but would aggressively battle any suggestion of it. She would meet Finn's eyes as they worked together to wrestle pajama armholes and skinny cotton legs onto the human tantrum flailing on the ground between them with a raised eyebrow that said, *What's the big deal, huh?* To her credit, she never said it aloud. To his, he started volunteering to do the afternoon nap duty.

Which was part of the plan on the day of no return. Essential to the plan, in fact. Violet would be soaking up the beach and Bear would be snuggled on the sofa bed of the hotel suite and Finn would be climbing into a taxi on his way to buy a one-way ticket to Not Home. It had actually seemed kinder to do it this way when he had conceived of it, though he was starting to doubt that once the moment was upon him — once he could picture her bouncing through the door, pink and happy from the sun, and stopping dead in her tracks at the sight of Bear here alone. Still, he could have left her in the midst of their messy life, bowls with milk-hardened O's cemented to their sides lining the sink, dirty play clothes piling ever higher on the laundry room floor, plastic Mega Bloks carpeting the living room. Surely it was less depressing for his wife to be left in a tropical paradise, where the palms would shade her face, the pool would distract her son, and the brightness of it all would show her that things back home were sort of bleak anyway. This was where it had begun, and as it never should have gone any farther, this was where it would end. It would be cleaner for everyone to leave it full circle, rather than going wildly off the mark, as he knew things would if he didn't have the grace to extract himself.

So Finn had insisted that Violet remain lounging in her beach chair, enjoying her book, soaking in the rays and listening to the waves, while he put Bear down for his nap. He'd even bought her a pineapple-encased piña colada from a pushcart vendor, though she claimed those drinks gave her bad memories of the day they'd met. She took it with a smile, and with one sip he could see that she wasn't going anywhere.

Bear had been sleepy from the sun but also punch-drunk from the excitement of the sand and sea and wanted a story. As Finn read, Bear fell into this odd state that used to send them running for the camera when he was a baby, where his eyes appeared half open but he was actually sound asleep. Finn hadn't seen Bear do it for months, maybe a whole year. But he did it now, and he conjured for Finn the memories of his earlier days as a father, when he'd still had hope that maybe he could work things out.

And so Finn sat holding him and looking into those slits of elsewhere eyes and brushing back the golden wisps of hair that fell into his face — Violet said she couldn't bear to cut those curls, even though anyone could see they were driving the kid crazy — and thinking of newborn

Bear, charmingly leaking milky drool onto Finn's bare chest those first days home from the hospital. The newborn had grown into baby Bear, learning to sit with his pudgy little legs stretched out in front of him in a triumphant V, banging a plastic spoon into a colander with unabashed glee until he lost his balance, tumbled to the side, and then gave up and dozed off right there on the floor. Then had come mobile Bear, cruising from one piece of furniture to the next in clumsy but determined caveman steps, licking his first popsicle, pushing his little plastic mower along the bumpy sidewalk, and waving excitedly as Finn pulled into the driveway, home from work. These days, a swift runner and dangerously good climber, and already talking better than many older kids he knew, he was their Bear Cub. The nickname was so perfect you would have thought he and Violet had planned for it all along. Strong, cuddly yet fierce, learning to make his way through the forest.

How could any father want to forget?

Finn packed his bags as silently as he could so as not to disturb the nap. From his wallet he removed the sealed envelope containing the letter he'd written, the one that asked her to raise Bear alone and not tell him what a coward his father was. He stood there holding it for a long minute, eying the kitchen counter where the letter should go, and then looking back at his blissfully oblivious son, the only good thing he had to show for his life, his only proof that something good could still, somehow, come from a string of mistakes. And then damn it if he didn't pocket the envelope, pack up the boy's clothes and toys too, and carry Bear's sleeping form out to the backseat of their rental car in the dim hotel garage. Car seat laws seemed like more of a suggestion down here in this land of frozen cocktails with breakfast and smoke shops 'for tobacco use only' and no-shirt-no-shoes-no-problem and pirate flags and barely-there bikinis and anything goes. So he didn't think much of hitting the road with his sleeping son not exactly strapped in, any more than he thought about what would happen after he woke up.

28

AUGUST 2016

As Caitlin stared at the courtesy phone receiver in her hand, she couldn't escape the sting of Violet's words. *Call your husband, Cait. At least you know how to reach yours.*

Worse, though, was the sting that she had failed to convince Violet to come.

Damn it all to hell.

She turned back to the boys, who had grown restless with the crayons and resumed their game of superheroes, climbing up and down the slick vinyl chairs. It was only a matter of time before one of them got hurt again. Or complained of being hungry. Or needed a nap. It really wasn't feasible for Caitlin to be here alone with two barely three-year-olds when another was lying in a bed somewhere down one of these hallways and needing her desperately.

Where *was* that nurse? What was taking so long?

She glanced at the clock. They had already been here for ninety minutes. She had no idea how long she could count on Finn sleeping off the Ambien. If he woke to find them gone . . . What were the charges for hiding a kidnapper and then basically just setting him free? Would anyone even believe her that she'd gone to extremes to escape with Bear, that she'd meant

292

to give Finn and Violet a last-ditch chance to work this out before their lives were irreparably ruined in federal court? Would anyone believe that her intentions had been good?

She'd feared that she could lose her family as she knew it if Finn made good on his threats. But now she feared that they all could lose everything. Once it was discovered that she had done this, all of it, George would be ruined, whether Finn opened his mouth or not. He could never run for office. His father's legacy would be stained. All because of her, the ordinary girl from the suburbs whom George had exercised poor enough judgment to marry. And the boys — they might have to grow up with their mother behind bars. What kind of shameful life was that? How could that reality ever in a million years become hers?

'You made bad choices, Mommy,' Gus had chastised her one day after he was less than enthusiastic about the lunch she'd served. Caitlin had laughed, caught off guard by his grave tone. She guessed he had picked up the phrase at day care. It was a very politically correct way of handling things when a child needed to be disciplined — break it all down to choices. Out of context, though, the 'bad choices' line could actually be quite astute.

Now she really had made bad choices. Important ones. She couldn't unmake them — she could only try to stop herself from making more. So she braced herself to do the thing that she knew she had no choice at this point but to do, no matter the consequences for her life, her

293

marriage. With a shaky hand, she picked up the phone again. She had to call George.

'Mrs. Bryce-Daniels?'

The receiver clattered back onto the hook

She hadn't heard the doctor come up behind her. His voice sounded young, vibrant, but as she turned, she came face-to-face with a man old enough to be her father. He had on a white lab coat, and his hands were clasped behind his back. 'I'm Dr. Avery. I didn't mean to startle you.'

'Leo,' she breathed, her throat clenching. 'Is he . . . how is he?'

'All of his lab work came back within normal limits, and his vital signs have remained steady.' He dropped his hands, and she saw that one of them was holding a clipboard. Leo's chart. 'We'll monitor him until he's awake, but it's likely he'll be fine once he sleeps it off.'

'Oh, thank God,' she said, blinking back tears of relief. Over the doctor's shoulder, she could see the boys watching her curiously. She couldn't let emotion get the better of her now. 'Can I see him?' It was all she wanted. To wrap her arms around him and feel him breathing, to press her ear to his chest and hear his heart beating.

'In a few minutes,' the doctor said. 'He won't know whether or not you're there, anyway — not for a few hours at least, I'd guess. He's out pretty good.'

Caitlin's eyes widened in alarm. 'Just heavy sleep,' the doctor assured her. 'It was sleep medication, after all.'

'Right,' Caitlin said, flush with humiliation.

But as ashamed as she was to be in this position, nothing could override her gratitude. 'Thank you for taking care of him, Doctor. I can't tell you how truly grateful I am.' Her voice broke as the tears threatened to spill over again.

Dr. Avery looked away and cleared his throat. 'Yes. Well, we do need to ask you a few more questions — you know, about how this happened. To go over it again.' He seemed uncomfortable, as if he'd drawn the short straw in coming out here to deliver the news. Maybe this kind of thing didn't happen that often after all.

Caitlin felt thrown off balance by the intense roiling of emotions — such dread on the heels of such relief. 'Of course,' she said, willing herself to ignore the sound of the blood coursing through her ears, the dots beginning to creep into her peripheral vision.

The doctor looked over at the kids. 'Is there someone to watch over them?' he asked. 'Do you want me to designate a nurse?' Caitlin felt dizzy. His words came to her through a tunnel.

'I was actually just about to call my husband,' she stammered, gesturing toward the phone behind her. 'George. I — ' She needed a better explanation. 'I tried to reach him earlier but I couldn't get through.'

'Why don't you go ahead and place the call,' Dr. Avery said. She watched then as he hesitated, doing a double take at the top sheet on the clipboard. 'Your husband is George Bryce-Daniels? From Ohio?'

'Yes,' she managed to answer. Cold water. She

needed a drink of cold water.

'Oh my word,' the doctor said, clucking his tongue. 'I didn't realize! Of course. I used to play golf with his father, at the lake club. He owns that cabin down here, you know . . . '

Something like a glimmer of hope was presenting itself to Caitlin. She had to sit up and take notice. She couldn't succumb to the light-headedness or the encroaching panic. 'Yes,' she said, smiling as demurely as she could. Sometimes it paid to be the wife of a senator's son. *Please God*, she thought, *let it be one of those times.*

'The cabin is actually where this happened, where we are staying,' she explained. 'It was my mother-in-law's Ambien. I thought it was out of reach — he's never climbed on the counter before — '

She didn't fight the tears this time when they started to come. Better for him to see them.

'Oh, her insomnia,' he said, nodding. 'Augustus used to talk about that.' His tone softened, and he placed a gentle hand on her forearm. Caitlin felt almost guilty. She didn't deserve his sympathy, she really didn't. But Leo and Gus needed her. And at this moment, so did Bear. And Violet.

'Why don't you call George,' he said, handing her a tissue from the end table at his side. 'Then we'll talk. Never fear — this is all routine. Nothing to worry about.'

Caitlin nodded, dabbing at the tears with the rough fabric. 'When do you think Leo can come home?' she asked. 'George will be asking, I'm sure,' she added for good measure.

'Provided that he remains stable, that depends on when he can be roused. Could be later today. Could be tomorrow morning.'

Caitlin nodded, not trusting her voice to speak again.

Maybe the powder had settled at the bottom of the thermos after all. If Leo hadn't had enough to cause any alarm, there was a chance Finn had had more than enough. Which simultaneously renewed her hope that he wasn't likely to wake anytime soon and her fear that she might have slipped him too much. She couldn't think about the latter. The important thing was she might not be out of time to try to fix this unfixable mess.

'I'll give you privacy to make the call,' he said. 'I know these times are not easy. Being a parent never is.'

And then Caitlin was left alone with the receiver, and only one thing left to do. She would call George, and he would come. And if she managed to walk out of this hospital untouched today — and if Leo managed to walk out unharmed — she would have gotten better than she deserved. And she would pay it forward by doing what she should have done all along, no matter the consequences.

29

AUGUST 2016

It wasn't that Violet was ungrateful for Gram's support. It was just that she desperately wanted her to leave before she witnessed any more of her unraveling.

Gram was there, dropping off yet another casserole from the ladies at her living center, when Caitlin's call came in. Gram had let herself in, dragged Violet out of Bear's bed, announced that she looked like 'death warmed over,' ordered her to stop torturing herself, and informed her that what she needed was a meal to settle her stomach and clear her head. It was lunchtime, after all. Standing disheveled in the center of Bear's room, Violet told her what Agent Martin had said about the possible lead on a car, and Gram clapped her hands so enthusiastically, yelling out, 'Now we're cooking!' that Violet couldn't help but follow her to the kitchen. Violet was scooping coffee grounds into the filter, Gram squinting at the dial to preheat the oven, when the phone rang.

Violet took the call in her bedroom, and when she returned a few moments later, she was determined not to tell Gram what had happened. But Gram saw through her, like she always did, and before Violet knew it she was repeating the conversation practically word-for-word.

An odd thing had happened these past few days. Gram had gone from encouraging Violet to open her eyes and stop telling herself the stories that she *wanted* to believe about her life, to trying to convince her that things weren't as bad as she made them out to be.

When Violet admitted that she'd basically hung up on Caitlin, leaving her to wait alone in the emergency room, Gram's eyes filled with tears. 'I know you've just had shock after shock,' Gram told her. 'But that doesn't mean you have to do a complete about-face on everyone in your life. It might seem easy to blame Caitlin, but try to put yourself in her shoes, how caught in the middle she must have felt.'

Violet's hands were still shaking from the sickening combination of high emotion and low blood sugar, and she steadied them on the counter while she waited for the coffee to brew. 'But — '

'I'm not saying she was *right* not to tell you the things that she didn't tell you, but that doesn't change the fact that for years, she's been your closest friend. And I'm not sure this is a time when you should be pushing people away. If Caitlin needs you — '

'You know what? Spare me the lecture,' Violet snapped. 'Maybe I should have gone. But aren't I allowed to be a little selfish right now? Can't I stay in self-preservation mode if that's what it takes to get through the day without Bear, without even knowing where Bear is, or if he's okay?'

Gram dropped it then, but she didn't leave.

Instead, in true Gram form, she served up the casserole to Violet, had only a few bites for herself, and then set about baking a cheesecake neither of them had any desire to eat.

Violet perched at the kitchen table, nursing her hangover and watching. Even in her exhaustion, she couldn't seem to quiet her mind, couldn't shut off the dizzying strobe light shining in flashes over her best and worst memories. She had to bite her tongue not to talk at Gram, rehashing everything all over again.

Violet had never been one to overanalyze, and she'd once seen her more even-keeled approach as an asset. She'd tried not to dwell on the things she and Finn might not know about each other as intimately as they should. She'd tried not to worry about worst-case scenarios with Bear the way Caitlin did with her twins. She'd never convinced herself that any of his ordinary colds were meningitis, or that if she looked away for an instant at the playground he'd fall off the slide and break a bone, or be snatched up by a sex-trafficking ring.

Now, of course, it was hard not to view what she'd once seen as levelheadedness — or a faithful trust in the natural order of the universe — as a fault.

It didn't take much stretching of the imagination to see that a little more analysis at certain points along the way might have prevented all of this in the first place. If she'd allowed her wildest fears to have free rein, some of them might not have been too off the mark.

But now that she couldn't stop herself from

frantically turning things over in her mind, she hated the sensation that came with this obsessing. It was as if she were spinning along with her thoughts, over and over, until she felt physically sick, but she didn't know how to hit the Off switch on the ride.

Last night's vodka had been as close as she could come.

For too many days she'd been behaving as if Bear would walk through the door at any minute. She had tried to be responsible, a mother ready to start mothering again at the turn of the doorknob. She had forced herself through some motions and allowed herself to be forced through others. And when she was still reeling that the roof had blown off, and the floor suddenly crumbled out from under her too, the first thing she did was to calmly place a phone call to Maribel's mother, seeking a sensible explanation where of course there was none.

After she'd hung up with Delilah last night, and sat with Gram for a few more hours, and then sat awake drinking for a few more, something in Violet had become unhinged. Something dangerous. Something she wasn't ready to put back in its place.

Even now, she couldn't bear to let herself place too much stock in the lead Agent Martin had mentioned. He'd cautioned her that the tipster might just be after a piece of the reward, And even if the lead panned out, they'd still be four or five days behind Finn on the trail. She didn't think an AMBER Alert would do any good if Finn had made it to Canada.

When Gram suggested that Violet take a shower, she ignored her. When she fussed over the cheesecake, Violet wrinkled her nose. When she asked cheerfully for a hand drying the dishes, Violet poured herself another cup of coffee and returned to her station at the table, When she suggested a movie, Violet lied and said the DVD player was on the fritz. And when she asked one more time if Violet might like to call Caitlin back and make sure Leo was okay, Violet looked right past her, like an unruly child.

But when Gram mumbled reluctantly that she might as well go, Violet quickly got to her feet, returned all the right niceties, opened the door to a wall of humidity and late afternoon sunshine, and waved good-bye. Then, even before the sound of Gram's old Buick had faded away, she went and poured herself a stiff drink.

★ ★ ★

The Internet was always changing — redesigns, relaunches, old Web sites vanished, new ones in their places — but the Missed Connections page on Craigslist looked exactly as it had years ago.

Violet appreciated that. At least *something* was the same.

The screen vibrated in front of her, It was finally dark enough outside that Violet's drunken state didn't feel out of sync with the rest of the world. 'I could go down to Jack of the Wood and blend right in,' she slurred aloud to the room. Not that she was going anywhere. She just liked the idea that others out there were also drinking

302

by now. The imagined solidarity.

Wherever Finn was, he probably wasn't online. Or was he? Was he reading up on his own crime — 'parental kidnapping'? Did he even know there was a name for it, or how common it was? Did he sense the weariness the federal agents would bring to the search, the look in their eyes that let Violet know how often these cases went unsolved?

Violet almost wished she had learned something that had made her stop loving Finn. She was heartbroken at what he had been through with Maribel, and disappointed that he hadn't told her, and hurt that he'd gone along with the move to Asheville without sharing his reservations, and maddened that he'd let things go so far as to leave her without having clued her in to their problems that she didn't even know they had. Above all, she was furious that he had taken Bear.

But in other ways, learning Finn's secrets had actually deepened her compassion toward him and her regret that things hadn't somehow turned out differently between them. If only he'd given her a chance.

She had no idea if she could ever trust him again, if he would even want her to — it seemed far-fetched to think of it, pathetic. But she couldn't shake the feeling that on some level she actually *did* know Finn. And that of all he'd been through, the most pivotal thing was what *hadn't* happened to him.

He hadn't talked to anyone. About any of it.

He hadn't acknowledged that he couldn't cope

with his guilt and grief alone.

He hadn't gotten any help whatsoever.

Post-traumatic stress disorder. She'd looked it up on the Internet, and there, in the four main categories of symptoms, found what she imagined to be a pretty decent description of Finn:

1. Intrusive memories
2. Avoidance
3. Negative changes in thinking and mood
4. Changes in emotional reactions

Every article she read said that symptoms often started within months of a traumatic event, but sometimes they did not appear or magnify for years.

There could be triggers. Not just people, but also places.

And so when Violet was done reading what she could on the Mayo Clinic site, and Wikipedia, and WebMD, she closed all those windows and replaced them with one.

Missed Connections on Craigslist.

And even though she didn't have enough left in her to earnestly hope that Finn was out there reading, she downed the rest of her drink to steel herself, and then she began to type.

30

Finn was waking up groggy. At least, he was trying to wake up. Never had he had such a hard time coming out of sleep. Just when a thought would start to form, he'd feel himself drifting off again, against his will. Then, a few minutes later, he'd start to come to and repeat the cycle all over again. Or was it hours later? He'd lost all sense of time. How had he even come to fall asleep here on the couch, anyway? How could he have been so stupid as to let his guard down like this? He needed to find Bear. It had gotten so quiet, it was deafening. He wasn't used to quiet, not even for sleeping. There was always the fuzzy sound of the baby monitor he couldn't convince Violet that Bear was too old for, and Violet's own soft snoring, which had begun during pregnancy and never stopped, and the light car and foot traffic through their Asheville neighborhood. Nothing like the solitude of this cabin. Only this wasn't supposed to be solitude. Bear should be here, and Caitlin, and the twins. Where were they?

He must have drifted off again because when he became aware of the voice, it was in the middle of a one-way conversation — on the phone with someone, he could tell. The voice sounded like George. But George couldn't be here; that couldn't be right.

Not that Finn was going to go through with any of his threats, of course, but still — he was sure he had rattled Caitlin. His rookie attempt at blackmail, or at least the threat of blackmail, had worked. Well, it had also sort of backfired, but — surely she wouldn't have asked George here. Unless . . .

What if George had just shown up? What if he'd decided to come on his own?

Finn fought to open his eyes. He could just make out the form of George standing outside on the lakefront deck. His back was to Finn, his profile illuminated by the bright screen of the cell phone he held to his ear. It was dark out — Christ, it was really dark, and Finn was positive he had fallen asleep in the morning. The sliding glass door was cracked open just enough so that Finn could hear snippets of conversation, but not the whole thing.

'You ran out of here so fast . . . We could hardly talk in front of the kids . . . '

George sounded frustrated, impatient, but not unkind. Could it be Caitlin on the other end of the line? But that would mean she wasn't here . . .

'Thank God it was Dr. Avery . . . I suspect he pulled some strings to get us all out of there . . . If he does tell my father, I'll handle it . . . '

George backed up to lean against the side of the cabin, and his voice came clearer through the door.

'I promise, he's fine. I've been looking in on him every forty-five minutes or so, like you

306

asked. That stuff must really work, if he slept most of the day and is going to stay out all night too. Do you know my mom complains it isn't strong enough? She's so full of it . . . '

It *had* to be Caitlin. George wouldn't dare talk about his mother that way to anyone else. Finn yawned, fighting to keep his eyes open. *Slept all day . . . out all night.* Was George talking about him?

'I still don't understand how a three-year-old can choke down coffee, of all things. I don't care how much creamer is in it.'

Finn squeezed his eyes shut, then opened them, then tried it again. His blurry vision refused to clear.

'All right. Well, look. We were in agreement that you had to go, but when you get back, you are going to have to tell me what Finn could possibly have said or done to make you come down here and get involved like this . . . '

Finn's ears strained at the sound of his name, trying desperately to stay focused, to fight the fqg of sleep that still wanted to creep back in and overtake him.

'I know. Later. It's just the small detail that I happen to be in the cabin with the man unconscious on the couch. You do know this could ruin us . . . '

Finn cringed. George was never supposed to get dragged into this. Neither was Caitlin. Finn didn't want to ruin any more lives. He had only wanted the damn cabin key. He'd remembered about the alarm system — otherwise he would have just driven around down here until he found the familiar road, broken in, and hoped for the best.

'No, no, I'll handle it. He's sound asleep with the other kids. I know you wanted to take him with you, but I think it's better this way. Our only shot at getting out of this. If we can just make her understand . . . Right. We'll figure it out. We have to.'

George was hanging up, coming back inside. For a moment, Finn thought of feigning sleep. Maybe if George went into one of the back rooms, Finn could sneak away. Maybe he could still escape from this trap he'd unintentionally walled himself into. But that would mean going without Bear. Where was he? A fresh wave of unease washed over Finn. George had mentioned something about a doctor. But also about the kids being asleep.

Finn wasn't sure he felt sturdy enough to venture out anyway — not even into the car, much less into the woods. His legs felt almost too heavy to move, and his stomach churned as if he'd had too much to drink. So he didn't see any sense in pretending. He'd done enough of that. Too much. His eyes remained open and fixed on George as he stepped into the living room and slid the glass door closed behind him.

'Hey there, sleepyhead.' George spoke with uncharacteristic sarcasm. 'Welcome back to the world of the living.'

'How long have I been out?' Finn asked. 'And where did you come from?' Finn attempted a good-natured laugh, but it sounded strange to his ears, and George didn't smile in return.

'Figured you'd be starving,' George said. 'I made you a snack.'

Finn struggled to sit up while George crossed the room to the kitchen counter and picked up a plate. Seconds later, he plunked it down on the coffee table in front of Finn.

'Peanut butter crackers,' he said apologetically. 'If there's one thing you can count on us to have, it's kid food.'

Finn didn't bring up the groceries Caitlin had unloaded into the fridge yesterday. He *was* starving, but now did not seem like the time to request a three-course meal. 'Thanks,' he said. He shoved the first Ritz sandwich into his mouth in a single bite. It was delicious, he had to admit.

The men locked eyes, each daring the other to speak.

Finn took another cracker and chewed self-consciously as George stood over him, watching.

'Well, this is cozy,' George said finally.

'It's not what it looks like,' Finn said, averting his eyes.

'Oh, come on. It's exactly what it looks like.'

Finn strained his ears for any sound of life in the bedrooms behind him. He heard none. 'Where is everybody?' he asked, his anxiety growing as the jolt of sustenance helped clear the fog from his brain.

'I don't think you are in a position to be asking questions here,' George said. 'No offense,' he added, and Finn found himself fighting back a hint of a smile. George really was one of the most amicable guys he knew. It sometimes seemed at odds with the fact that he was also one of the most powerful. He'd observed this dichotomy dozens of times watching George halfheartedly attempt to discipline the twins — though he suspected that had more to do with his absentee parent status than with a lack of backbone. Still, now that Finn was at his mercy, it didn't seem outside the realm of possibility that he could get off the hook somehow. Caitlin had always been the tougher one to crack.

But if she wasn't here, where *was* she? Finn's eyes darted around the room as if expecting to see something he had missed, but everything looked basically as it had before he'd fallen asleep. The kids' tent was erected in the middle of the floor, empty save for a stack of pillows and blankets. Finn cringed at the sight of chocolaty-looking handprints all over the nylon dome and hoped they didn't belong to Bear, Here he was making a mess of his friends' lives, but he was still worried about his son making a mess of their stuff.

'Milk?' George asked. 'Juice?'

Finn was tempted to ask for something stronger, but knew it wasn't a good idea. What he needed now was a clear head. 'How long was I out for?' he asked again, George only stared at him.

Finn's mouth was dry. And his blood sugar felt off. Once he was steady on his feet, then he would figure out what to do. 'Juice,' he said softly. 'Thanks.'

Was Bear asleep in the bedroom, with the twins? Is that who George had talked about

310

looking in on? He wanted to ask so badly, but he hesitated to speak his son's name. Was there any chance at all that George did not know the extent of what he'd stumbled into?

I know you wanted to take him with you, George had said, *but I think it's better this way. Our only shot at getting out of this.* Had he been talking about Caitlin taking Finn, or Bear?

George appeared before him with a glass, and Finn gulped the juice as if he hadn't had a drink all day — which, he supposed, he hadn't. Not since that coffee this morning. And he hadn't even finished the rest of it —

Finn was midswallow when something else George had said came back to him. Something about a kid drinking coffee. *I don't care how much creamer was in it . . . That stuff must really work.* And Finn, who'd drunk the cream-loaded coffee himself, had been asleep all day. Slowly, he raised his juice glass to eye level and peered into the liquid, looking for any sign of something that shouldn't be there. Abruptly, he set the glass on the table.

'Do you mind telling me what's happened?' Finn asked. 'Don't make me beg it out of you, George. Seriously.'

'First, why don't you finish your juice,' George said. He was still standing, hovering over Finn in a way that made him nervous.

'I don't want the juice.'

'Yes, you do. You must be incredibly thirsty. Drink up.'

'Maybe later.'

George lifted his sport coat open to one side,

just wide enough so that Finn could see what was at his hip, a tan leather holster. George was carrying a gun.

'Drink it.'

'Oh, come on. You're not going to *shoot* me.'

'What makes you so sure?' George smiled. 'You mean because of my image? Because I'm an upstanding citizen? Last time I checked, upstanding citizens are within their rights to confront intruders in their homes. Especially when those intruders happen to be wanted on federal charges. And when they show up at a remote cabin driving a car that's registered to some redneck in a trailer park in Tennessee.'

So George had been here long enough to do his homework.

'I have the pink slip,' Finn said, feeling oddly defensive. 'I just haven't, you know, gotten to the BMV yet.' He gave George a wry smile.

'Do you want me to drive you?' George asked, with exaggerated sincerity.

'Would that be before or after you shoot me?'

'Just — don't make me do it, okay? Drink the damn juice.' George actually did manage to look like he meant business that time. Then, true to form, came the clarification.

'I'm no murderer, obviously,' George said. 'But I can make it so you can't run out of here. And I'm not going to be too swift at calling an ambulance either.'

'Where's Caitlin?' Finn tried to keep his voice calm.

'That's always the question, isn't it? Where's Caitlin?' George's façade dropped, his voice gently mocking. 'Don't you *ever* get tired of my wife bailing you out of things? Because I have to say, I think I've finally reached *my* limit.' He smiled disingenuously at Finn. 'We had a helluva run, though, didn't we? You're lucky, you know, that she means enough to me that I let her talk me into caring how much *you* mean to *her.*'

Finn wasn't sure how to reason with this new George, but clearly he'd taken the wrong tack. 'How about a truce,' he suggested. 'I get myself a glass of water from the tap, and you set the alarm, and no one goes anywhere until Caitlin comes back.' George didn't correct him, so Finn figured he had guessed right. She wasn't here, and that had probably been her on the phone. But did she have Bear with her?

George leaned his weight onto the arm of the leather recliner opposite Finn and sighed heavily. 'Sounds like a reasonable request. Thing is, that would mean I have to figure out what to say to you while we wait. And I'd rather not deal with the hassle.' George gazed out toward the lake, where the moon was sparkling off the water like an image from one of the glossy brochures at the Visitors Center down the road. 'It was so quiet here while you were asleep. Peaceful. I don't get much time alone with my thoughts, you know. Always rushing around from one airport to the next, and then when I get home, the boys are there waiting. You know how it is, being a father yourself.' He looked pointedly at Finn, and Finn thought he saw there something darker than anger over Bear — something deeper.

'Look,' Finn said. 'You win. Just tell me where

Bear is, and I'll drink the damn juice.' Maybe he could go into the bathroom and throw it up.

'You know who really wants to know where Bear is?' George asked. 'His *mom*. Your *wife*. Remember her? Thinking of the state she must be in right now, forgive me if I'm not feeling charitable.'

George removed the gun from its holster and held it gently in his palm. 'You're drinking the juice. You are not in a position to negotiate here, Finn. Too bad you didn't make it out on the golf course with me more over the last few years. If you had, you'd know by now that these days, when I take aim, I rarely miss.'

31

AUGUST 2016

When she heard the knocking at the back door before the sun was even up — was it early morning already? — Violet's first thought was that Gram had come back. She was curled under an afghan on the couch, and even before she threw off the cover she was fantasizing about yelling through the closed door — '*What* does it take to get a little *head space* from you?' — and then flinging herself back into bed. Never mind that she was already feeling guilty for behaving like a child — albeit a child who'd only wanted to be left alone to get drunk — the day before.

The buzz was wearing off, and Violet's head was starting to throb as she peered at the clock. It was not morning. It was 1:30 A.M. She'd fallen asleep disorientingly early — it couldn't have been past 9:30 or 10:00 — logging off Craigslist and throwing herself onto the couch with all of the drama but none of the grace of Scarlett O'Hara. She guessed that was what happened when you started drinking in the afternoon. She'd never had much practice with it before.

The back door . . . the middle of the night . . . She bolted upright on the couch. A confused, drunk person walking home from a bar to the wrong house, or someone else? Agent Martin, having located the car? Finn? Bear!

She flew off the couch and into the kitchen, breathless. With a twist, the dead bolt was freed and Violet yanked open the door.

She stared.

She had never seen Caitlin look so awful.

This couldn't be the Caitlin she knew, the Caitlin who had once shown up at a different back door of Violet's wearing a sparkly V-neck shirt that read I WOKE UP LOOKING LIKE THIS.

'Very funny,' Violet had said, nodding at Caitlin's chest and rolling her eyes. It wasn't that she begrudged her friend her perpetually flat-ironed hair and manicured nails and powdered skin and designer everything. It was just that sometimes she wished they could stand a little farther apart so she wouldn't feel so underdone by comparison.

'You think it's actually funny?' Caitlin had said, sounding a little too hopeful. 'George bought it for me.'

'It depends on who's wearing it, On me, people would be like, 'Well, yeah, we can see that.''

But looking at Caitlin now was more like looking in a mirror. Reflected there, she saw exhaustion, worry, guilt, shame. 'Oh God,' she said. 'Is it Leo? What are you doing here?'

'Leo is fine,' Caitlin said. 'They discharged him, though we're keeping a close eye. Just to be a hundred percent sure.'

'Doctor's orders?'

'More like Mom's orders.'

Violet looked past her into the darkness, but no one was there. 'Who's watching him?'

316

'George.' She took a deep breath, 'I'm here about Bear, I . . . I know where he is. I came to take you to him.'

Violet blinked at her, disbelieving. Opposing tides of relief and fury clashed within her, turning her instantly into a dangerous whirlpool.

'If you know where he is, why isn't he with you?' she cried. 'Why did you waste time driving here, rather than calling the FBI? What's *wrong* with you?'

'Because we were afraid if I brought him to you, you wouldn't come with me,' Caitlin said, jutting her chin stubbornly into the air. This was unfamiliar territory for her, Violet knew, being called out on anything at all, let alone something so awful. And Violet could see it on her face as her voice turned pleading. 'I need you to come with me. No matter what happens next, you've got to come talk to Finn first.'

'*We* were afraid?' Violet repeated, incredulous. 'Who is *we*? You and *Finn*?'

Caitlin shook her head. 'Me and George.'

It was all Violet could do not to shake Caitlin by the shoulders. 'Where are they?'

'The cabin,' Caitlin said, and Violet drew back. All along, she'd been picturing Bear being dragged along on the run, spending the night in seedy hotel rooms, even sleeping in his car seat as Finn drove and drove him farther and farther from her. But relaxing at George's family's vacation home, in the place where Violet and Bear and Finn themselves had vacationed the summer before? With what, with Caitlin there too? Grilling dinner, laughing around the campfire?

317

'How long have they been there?' she asked.

'A couple days,' Caitlin admitted.

'*Days?*' The relief she felt that her little boy was safe and accounted for was displaced by a blind rage. Her eyes burned.

Caitlin started to cry. 'Vi — '

'I'm calling Agent Martin *right now.*'

'I swear to God, I don't know where they were before that! I was just as shocked as you when they showed up.' Caitlin's words came rapidly, desperately, almost incoherently through her sobs. 'It's not like Finn called me, or knocked on my door. He broke into my house while I was at work. I came home and found him there — but then he *blackmailed* me. And I've been trying to figure a way out of it, trying to figure a way to get Bear back to you, trying to figure a way no one gets hurt, but *everyone* got hurt. Even poor Leo — '

'And you *left them there* and drove down here?' Violet felt her own panic rising. 'What makes you sure they'll be there when we get back?'

'George is keeping watch. There's an alarm. And Finn is . . . he's asleep.'

'*Asleep?*'

'I slipped some Ambien into his drink.'

Violet stared.

'Leo didn't exactly just get into the pills. I was careless — ' She was heaving such gasping breaths that Violet worried she was about to hyperventilate.

'Calm down, Cait,' she heard herself say.

'All I did was make everything worse! It's so

318

scary having the FBI involved, and George still doesn't really even know what the hell is going on, but of course he's furious, and I know I'm in trouble, and I just want to do the right thing. I *need* to do the right thing before I pay the consequences, okay? So after we get there, you can call the cops, the FBI, whoever, but please, come with me first. Some part of me still thinks that if you and Finn just talk . . . '

Violet's mouth opened, but she was unable to summon any words. Caitlin turned to look over her shoulder, into the darkness of the backyard, then back at Violet. 'Are they watching right now?' she asked, as Violet started to grasp the weight of everything she'd been saying. Finn had dragged Caitlin into this. Caitlin, who maybe could have helped avoid this whole thing if she'd just told Violet about Finn's past from the start — but who had children of her own. Children who called Violet *Auntie Vi*, and whom Bear loved like brothers. 'I wanted to tell you when I called from the hospital, but I was sure your line was bugged. I was going to bring Bear to you, but then Leo got sick and George had to come and we all went back and Finn was still out of it and George thought it would be better this way, for me to bring you there, so maybe we could all sort it out together — ' She cut herself off abruptly. 'Are they watching you right this minute?' she asked again.

It seemed a maddeningly audacious question, but Violet was too shocked to do anything but answer. 'I don't think so,' she said.

'Good,' Caitlin said. 'It only took me three

hours to get here. Three hours more, and you will be back with Bear.' Her eyes filled with tears again. '1 know you hate me for this,' Caitlin said. 'You have a right to. Just please, get dressed, get whatever you need, and get in the car. I'll explain the rest on the way.'

32

Caitlin had once had the misfortune of breaking up with a college boyfriend on the hind leg of a road trip. *Better to know now*, she'd told herself, *that we don't make good travel companions. What's life if not one big journey?* They'd driven the route back to campus in near silence, until they'd been caught in an intense rainstorm, and the rubber of the windshield wipers on his rusty old Volvo kept detaching from the metal as they scraped across the flooded glass in nerve-shattering, useless swipes. They had to keep pulling over to reattach them, getting more and more soaked each time, and eventually ended up waiting out the storm on the side of the road, screaming at each other all over again, which was almost better than the silence.

It was Finn whom she'd cried to after she got home. 'On the bright side,' he'd said, 'at least you've gotten that out of the way.'

'What?' she'd asked miserably, reaching out to accept the beer he offered.

'The most awkward silence you'll ever share trapped in a car with another human being.'

She shuddered now to think of the laugh they'd shared. Finn had been wrong about so many things.

She knew Violet had questions. But her friend

321

seemed determined not to ask them — or not to *have* to ask them. Rightly so, perhaps. But Caitlin wasn't sure where to start. So she just drove, every few minutes stealing a glance at Violet, who remained staring out the passenger window, lips pursed, eyes glassed over with lack of sleep and the threat of tears.

Quit being stupid, she told herself. *Just be honest*. She cleared her throat.

'I guess I have a lot of explaining to do,' she ventured.

A muscle twitched in Violet's neck, but she didn't move.

'You have to believe that the second Finn showed up, I was going to call you. I was so relieved to see that Bear was okay, and so glad for you, and then — '

'And then what?'

'He threatened me. Finn threatened me.'

'You're scared of Finn?'

'No. Yes. He knows about something I did — something I'm not proud of. He threatened to tell George if I didn't hand over the keys to the cabin, give him a place to take Bear and get his head on straight. I tried to call his bluff, but he upped the ante, calling out something else that could ruin George's father, and George too, and — ' She faltered. It all sounded so unimportant when she said it out loud. So unworthy of what she'd sat by and let Finn put Violet through. She tried again. 'These secrets, they're bad, Vi. They would wreck my family.'

'So you just let him blackmail you and wreck my family instead.'

322

'No!' Caitlin fought to keep her eyes on the road. Up here in the mountains, even the interstates were steep and winding, and had to be navigated carefully. Especially in the middle of the night. 'I didn't. I followed him down there. I thought if I could convince him to do the right thing, I could avoid the whole mess for George and me *and* get Bear back where he belongs — with you. It's just . . . Finn didn't come around.'

'And now?'

'I couldn't wait him out any longer. I had to do the right thing, even if it means that he'll follow through on his threats. I probably deserve it anyway.'

A beat of silence filled the car. 'But you said George is there now. With Finn.'

'Yeah.' Caitlin took a deep, shaky breath. A sharp curve was just ahead, and she tightened her grip on the wheel. 'I guess if Finn hasn't already told him, I'm probably going to end up having to do it myself. I dodged his questions earlier to run out and get you, but he's none too pleased about being pulled into this mess.'

For a moment, Violet didn't answer. Then she tilted her chin in Caitlin's direction, though she still wouldn't look at her. Caitlin's face burned with shame. They were climbing now, and the fog was thickening — she could scarcely see any farther than her headlights. She scanned the highway's perimeter for deer, which too often managed to jump over the high concrete walls and into traffic. Why they'd go to so much effort to get to a place they clearly weren't meant to be was anyone's guess.

'You going to tell me what it was? Or is? That he has on you?'

Caitlin knew that without a real explanation, there was no chance of salvaging her relationship with Violet. Besides, there was no point in not telling her. She'd likely find out soon enough.

'Do you remember that party you and Finn threw, not long after you started dating? The cookout at the old house next to ours, before you had moved in there?'

Violet nodded. 'We wanted all our friends to meet.' She paused, as if reconsidering the memory. '*I* wanted all our friends to meet,' she said more softly, and the pain in her voice made Caitlin's heart ache.

'Well, by that point, George and I had been trying to conceive for a long time.'

'You never told me that.'

'I never told anyone. Until the day I broke down and told Finn.'

Even then, Finn had heard only part of the story. Now, Caitlin told it all to Violet. It was her first time saying any of it aloud, and she carefully recited the details she'd been trying so hard to forget.

After the first year of trying to get pregnant, Caitlin had made an appointment with her ob-gyn. They ran some tests and could find no obvious cause for infertility. The doctor told Caitlin that meant one of three things. One: They were overlooking something that only deeper evaluations would turn up. Two: The problem was with George, which they would need to rule out before ordering any more involved testing on Caitlin. Three: There *was* no problem and they just needed to keep trying.

But George was not interested in getting his sperm count tested. In fact, he was adamantly opposed, and when Caitlin asked why, he gave no reason, only clammed up and changed the subject. She would let it go, then wait a month and try again. As the months piled on top of one another and the ovulation kits became a daily ritual and half the time he was overseas on her fertile days anyway and still her period kept coming, she tried everything to cajole him — it was noninvasive, a simple test, so why not just take it so they could pursue the real root of the problem? — but he refused to go.

Having children was not something that Caitlin could take or leave. Not only did she continue to want what she'd always wanted, and what George had always known she wanted — a family — but she wanted it more than ever. She was tired of being alone so much while George was off working. She wanted a purpose to the days that dragged on while he was away. And if that involved George jerking off in a cup so the doctors could find out what it would take to get her pregnant, Caitlin really didn't think that was too much to ask. She didn't ask much of George at all, in fact. He had given her so much just by choosing her as his wife that she'd been hesitant to ask for anything. That he would deny her this one request ate away at Caitlin. That she could not persuade him made her think of him as selfish, and thinking that of her otherwise generous husband made her like herself less, which only made her resent him even more.

Finally, with no other options that she could see, she went to Finn and begged him to try to talk some sense into George.

Finn frowned when she explained what was going on. 'Weird. Those tests are no big deal.'

'I know. I don't get it.'

'I mean, they're *really* no big deal. There's this guy I used to work with, Kevin — he teaches in the graphic design program at UC and would hook our firm up with co-ops when we needed them. Anyway, one day a bunch of us go out for beers and he starts telling us that he volunteered for this study the med students were doing on campus. He gave samples, like, once a week for an entire summer, and it had to have been easy, because it's not like this guy really needed the extra cash.'

'He just happened to mention this?'

Finn laughed. 'He was *bragging*. He found out he has an abnormally high sperm count. I guess sometimes that can actually be a bad thing, because they don't have enough room to swim, but he had a high volume of fluid too, and . . . anyway, I guess he was the shining star of the study. Super Sperm, we were calling him. Seemed appropriate, because the guy will sleep with anything that walks.'

She rolled her eyes. 'Appropriate, or dangerous?'

'Exactly. Dangerous, probably. But I always did wonder if there was some kind of correlation there. Would you say George's sex drive seems a little low?'

'Absolutely not.' She punched him in the arm. 'And also, none of your damn business.'

So the next time George invited Finn to go golfing, Finn accepted. He promised Caitlin he'd broach the subject, let George know that it was no big deal, that it was a small thing to do that would mean something big to Cait. When they returned home that afternoon, she came out to the driveway to greet them, calling out cheerfully that she'd made a fresh pitcher of Tom Collinses and put up the patio umbrella.

Finn was unloading their golf bags from the trunk of George's SUV, one slung over each shoulder. As he reached to close the heavy rear door, his eyes met Caitlin's and he shook his head almost imperceptibly.

'I don't know why,' he told her later. 'Are you sure George *wants* kids?'

'Of course I'm sure. Why? Did he act like he didn't?'

Finn raised his hands, palms up. 'I honestly didn't get that vibe. But he was pretty opposed to the test, and I couldn't figure out why. He seems to think it's unnatural or something, that it will happen on its own if it's meant to be. And maybe it will, Cait. How long have you guys been trying?'

'Since our honeymoon,' she said quietly. 'Years.'

Finn put his hand on her arm. 'I'm sorry.'

And then, a few weeks later, Violet and Finn threw their party.

George was out of town on business, as usual. She'd let him go without argument, without reminding him that the trip fell across the fertile days in her cycle, that they'd be skipping yet another whole month of trying. She was tired of arguing.

So Caitlin went alone to Finn and Violet's party. Actually, thinking back now, she knew Violet was right to have corrected herself earlier — it was Violet who'd been so enthusiastic about the idea of the party, and Finn who had grudgingly gone along with it. Secretly, Caitlin had worried that he felt awkward about friends who'd known Maribel coming to a party to meet his new girlfriend. His social pool had diminished, anyway, after the tragedy — Caitlin never knew how much of that was his own doing, him keeping everyone at arms length, and how much of it was them avoiding Finn because of what he'd inadvertently done. In any case, Finn invited hardly anyone to the barbecue in his own backyard. There was Caitlin, of course, and the wedding photographer he worked for, and a handful of former coworkers, but no one, Caitlin noticed, whom he'd ever been particularly close to.

Violet, however, seemed to have invited everyone she knew. She often joked that practically all her friends had gotten married in the past couple of years, and Caitlin could see now that not only was Violet not exaggerating, but that the group of them had moved on to phase two — never had she seen so many pregnant women in one place. Caitlin got drunk out of belly envy. And in that drunkenness, she grew from being confused and hurt by George's behavior to being angry, really angry, with George — George who was so far away right now, with a baby or a stupidly easy sperm count test the farthest possible things from his mind, when they wouldn't stop weighing on Caitlin's own. It all suddenly seemed impossibly unfair. And when Finn introduced her to Kevin, the assistant professor at the university, a lightbulb of recognition went off in her brain. Super Sperm. And that lightbulb turned flirtatious. It was almost too easy. *He will sleep with anything that walks*, Finn had said.

In the kitchen as the guests started to leave, Finn pulled her aside. 'Do not do this, Cait,' he said quietly. 'Go home.'

And Caitlin did go home — with Kevin trailing behind her through the grass to her back door, Finn watching them out the window with his forehead creased in ugly frown lines.

The funny thing was that not once did Caitlin think of sleeping with Kevin as true infidelity, as an act of intimacy beyond her marital bed. She simply thought of him as a means to an end. If George's sperm would not do the job, eventually the two of them might need to seek a sperm donor anyway — which is what Super Sperm was. In fact, if he'd participated in that study for three whole months, and if his sperm really was so legendarily 'super,' wasn't there a decent chance that if she ended up at a sperm bank, the DNA would be his anyway?

It was never all that hard to rationalize your

way through doing something wrong when it was a way to get what you wanted.

She didn't stop to think about the ramifications of getting pregnant with someone else's child. She didn't think about the baby who would not be George's and how she would live with that secret — if she could keep it a secret — for the rest of her life. She thought only about how she wanted to be a mother and didn't want to miss her chance just because George had too much macho pride to get a routine test done.

It was indeed fortunate that she had not, for once, whined to George that he was going out of town during her fertile days, had not begged to tag along and been denied. Because he believed that she got pregnant the next week, when he got back. His count was off by only a few days, not enough that he ever questioned the timing of her first ultrasound at six weeks to confirm the pregnancy. And when she saw not one but two tiny heartbeats blinking on the monitor, she couldn't resist, just for a split second, a flash of satisfaction that Super Sperm had lived up to his name.

As far as she knew, Finn had never told Violet what had happened. And she presumed, thank God, that he'd never told Kevin about the result of their little indiscretion either. If he had, Kevin must not have cared, because he'd never shown up at her door.

And Caitlin and Finn had never discussed it. Not until the day he stood in her kitchen, his kidnapped son playing in the twins' room upstairs, and demanded she give him the keys to the cabin with the words she could hardly believe she was hearing.

'If you don't, I'm going to *tell George*.'

Caitlin confessed it all to Violet, point by point. The cabin was still a couple hours away, and nothing could be worse than that accusatory silence between them, so Caitlin spared no detail. By the time she got to the part where she'd returned from the heartbreaking days at Violet's, had the power outage disrupt her first day back at work, and gotten home to find Finn and Bear in her house, her eyes were filled with guilty tears. But there was nothing she could do but hope that *something* in her friend still had the compassion to understand.

When she finished, the silence resumed. Caitlin squirmed in her seat. The worst was that there was more to come. That she hadn't even gotten into what George's father had done for Finn, after the accident, and how Finn had threatened to use it against him, against them all. That wasn't a conversation she wanted to have — there was so much other air to clear about Maribel. But she would. She just had to finish this one first.

'Say something,' she pleaded.

When Violet finally spoke, her voice was cold and incredulous. '*That* is the reason you didn't tell me — or the FBI, or anyone — you knew where my son was *days* ago? Days that I've spent curled up in his bed and *crying*, thinking my life was over? Days that *he's* spent crying for me?'

'I know it sounds selfish.' Caitlin started to cry again. 'I know. It's just . . . this isn't just any male ego we're talking about here. It's George. His father has plans for him, you know, and he has plans for his sons . . . ' Her voice trailed off, but she knew Violet knew their family well enough to know the rest. With the long history of the Bryce-Daniels name, it was important to have a lineage. That was a part of the reason she'd never understood George's refusal to undergo testing. But it was also a part of the reason she knew that he could never, ever find out about what she had done. It wasn't just the infidelity that would turn him against her — sometimes she even wondered if he half expected that, traveling as much as he did, though her own thoughts of the opportunities he must have had on the road were usually fleeting and easily dismissed. They loved each other. But if he were ever to find out that the twins weren't his, and if his parents were ever to find out, or if the media were ever to find out —

'Caitlin.' Violet didn't just sound furious, she sounded annoyed. 'George already knows the twins aren't his. For God's sake.'

33

AUGUST 2016

Finn raised the glass to his lips, then hesitated. George seemed unhinged enough that Finn didn't want to test him. Yet he knew that if he allowed himself to go under again, there was no telling what he might wake up to. 'Before I drink this,' he said. 'Just . . . thank you.'

The hand holding the gun didn't move. 'For?'

'For not calling the cops. Yet, anyway. I know I messed up. I never meant to put you in this situation.'

'To which situation would you be referring?'

Finn was taken aback by the solid ice in George's voice. He gestured to the cabin around him, indicating the obvious circumstances at hand.

George stood and paced across the room, then back again. 'I know what all of you think of me,' he bristled. 'That I'm just this entitled rich kid. But I didn't get to where I am because of my dad. I happen to have a good head for business. My clients trust me implicitly. My colleagues would say I'm smart. Which is why it amazes me that when I'm not on the clock, everyone else seems to think I'm so stupid.'

Finn squinted at George in confusion.

'I don't think 'everyone' thinks of you that way at all,' Finn said carefully. 'Not me. Not Caitlin.'

'Oh, *especially* Caitlin,' George snapped. 'And you. You know what, I wasn't going to get into it — I was just going to wait the two of you out, like I always do. But you have the audacity to *thank* me? Do you think if it were up to me, I would even be here right now? Don't you think I would have turned you in the second I found out about all this nonsense?' George gestured wildly with the gun. 'I wanted to call the FBI from the hospital!'

'The hospital?' Finn tried to keep the alarm from his voice.

George went on as if he hadn't spoken. 'But it's not only up to me. I have to look out for Caitlin. And the boys. I might be at my limit as far as how long I can go along with this ridiculous charade, but that doesn't mean I want them growing up with their father in jail.'

Finn wished the drug would clear from his brain. This mess he'd made was a lot of things, but was it really a *charade*? 'I won't let you go to jail, George. If I get caught — ' George opened his mouth to speak, and Finn held up a hand. 'I mean, when you turn me in, I'll tell them you didn't have anything to do with this. I'll tell them I threatened Caitlin. Which I did, by the way. I'm sorry. I never expected her to follow me down here . . . '

'Why the hell not? Do you think she's going to just let you disappear on Bear and the boys?'

'You keep saying 'the boys.' This doesn't have anything to do with the boys.'

'STOP already!' George's voice thundered through the high-ceilinged living room. 'It has *everything* to do with the boys.' His eyes were reckless, unfocused.

Finn raised both hands, as if he were under arrest. He had to hold off whatever this was until Caitlin got back. 'Whoa, man. Listen, forget the juice. Why don't we have a drink together, okay? Relax for a minute.'

'We aren't friends, Finn. We never were.'

Finn cringed. Of course George wouldn't take this lightly, Finn getting his wife and sons involved in his own mistake. Still, something deeper seemed to be fueling his fury. Something dangerous. He'd never seen George quite like this, like something pent up under pressure was about to burst loose. He had to keep him talking.

'You only drink with friends?' Finn asked, keeping his voice jovial, calm. 'Those are pretty stringent standards.'

George's eyes rested on a framed photo on the mantel. In it, he was a teenager, and his dad's face was tanned and smooth, and the two were wearing matching fishing vests down at the dock. 'My dad always said, 'Never drink to feel better — only drink to feel *even* better.''

'Oh, come on. That sounds good on paper, but I can think of plenty of times you haven't followed that.'

'I think I'll start today. Because this is going to be the day all the nonsense stops and we start doing things the Bryce-Daniels way. No more going along with whatever imaginary rules the rest of you keep putting into play.'

Rules? Finn tilted his head. 'George, I have to tell you, I'm feeling a little lost here. It's like we're dancing around some kind of elephant in the room, but I honestly have no idea what the elephant is. You care to enlighten me?'

'Why don't you tell me. I'd like to hear you say it.'

Finn took a breath. There was so much he hadn't ever said aloud. So much he probably should have. George had chosen the right words after all. His whole life was a *ridiculous charade.* 'I ran out on my wife? I appear to have abducted my son?' Finn began ticking off points on his fingertips. 'I should have been charged with involuntary manslaughter — or negligence, or *something?* I should have been convicted? I can't seem to stop being in love with my dead fiancée? I feel guilty every time I catch myself feeling *happy* with my wife? I don't know how to live a life I don't deserve?' He raised his eyes to George. 'Which thing?'

'An impressive résumé. You just forgot a line.'

Finn threw up his hands. 'References?'

'The part where you fathered my children.'

34

AUGUST 2016

'What do you mean George *knows*?' Caitlin felt sick, but also skeptical. Violet was hurt. It would be natural to lash out with the first thing that came to mind. That didn't mean it was true.

'He told me himself. I mean, not about Super Sperm — God, what a stupid name. Honestly, Caitlin, I expected something classier. But that the boys weren't his.'

'*When?*'

'Years ago.'

Caitlin's mind raced. Then a furious thought pushed its way in. 'Does *Finn* know that he already knows?'

'I have no clue what Finn does or does not know. Which should be more than obvious right about now.'

Caitlin checked herself. She had to tread carefully here. Violet was the one being wronged. Except — all of a sudden Caitlin didn't know where she stood either.

'Where was Finn when George told you this? Where was I?'

'Not there, obviously.'

'When were you alone with George?' Caitlin heard the accusation in her voice and didn't bother to mask it.

Violet sighed heavily. 'We tend to romanticize

those early days, when the kids were babies: It was so much fun to be on maternity leave at the same time, and blah blah blah. But do you remember how *exhausted* we were? I mean, I came to understand why they use sleep-deprivation as a form of torture. And you had the worst of it, with two newborns on different feeding schedules.'

Caitlin nodded irritably. Of course she remembered. But she'd been so happy to have the twins after lonely years of failing to get pregnant that she'd felt as if she had no right to complain — and so mostly, she hadn't.

'Well, one night George was trying to let you get some sleep. It must have been midnight, or later. I'd just gotten Bear settled back into his crib and went outside to dump out the diaper pail — it was stinking up the whole house — and George was coming up the side-walk with the stroller. The boys were asleep in there, but as soon as he stopped to talk to me, they woke back up. I was kind of beyond sleep myself at that point, so I got us a couple of beers and walked up and down the driveway with him, keeping him company. It was the only way he could get them to stay down.'

'And that was such a bonding experience that after one beer he decides to spill his guts that he doesn't think he's the father of his kids?'

'It was two beers. And the added factor of no sleep. But yeah, basically. He sort of mentioned it as if I already knew, as if it were something I myself had to have come to terms with too. I remember that striking me as odd. He seemed surprised, almost apologetic that he was the one telling me.'

'What did he say, exactly?'

'That he was 'shooting blanks.'' Violet made little air quotes with her fingers. 'Now that I've heard your side, I gather that's why he never wanted to have the test done. He said he'd known since he was a teenager — some kind of sports injury turned it up.'

'A teenager? So his *parents* know?'

'It didn't sound like it. Maybe he was eighteen, an adult? He said he was afraid that you wouldn't marry him if you knew. And then after the fact, his fear was that if you adopted, his parents would be disappointed about the Bryce-Daniels line ending. He seemed pretty humiliated about the idea of anyone knowing. I tried to tell him that was silly — it's not like it's anything he can control.'

'So all those years, he knew we couldn't get pregnant, and he let me keep on hoping? I mean, he *knew* I wanted to be a mother, and he married me without telling me that he couldn't father children?'

Caitlin reeled. Through the fog, her high beams illuminated a sign for a rest area two miles ahead. She was going to have to pull over. She didn't feel safe driving with this tornado swirling around in her head.

Violet's voice softened a little, 'He said he hoped that if he stalled long enough, you might change your mind and decide you didn't want kids. But then you got pregnant with the twins. And of course he knew they couldn't be his, but he just — ' Violet shrugged, 'He just played along. He said as sad as he was to think of you having an affair, in some ways he was actually relieved. You would have what you wanted, his family would never know about his shortcomings, and he would get to continue being your husband and even become a dad.'

But Caitlin's racing thoughts had stalled. 'He was hoping I'd change my mind? So he could blame our childlessness on me? So his parents could resent *me* instead of being disappointed in *him*?'

She slowed the car as the off-ramp for the rest area approached, It was as if all the insecurities she'd ever had about not being good enough for George's family were coming to a head. Of the whole hoity lot, her own husband would have been the one to throw her under the bus.

'I don't think that's what he meant, Cait. He probably just figured it would be easier to tell people the two of you had decided against it.'

Caitlin's very skin was tingling with embarrassment, That Violet had known all this and had never told her — what Violet must have thought of her, of George, of their marriage . . . And yet even as her fury built, there was something as bizarrely comforting as it was disturbing about the fact that George had known all along and *had stayed*. George had stayed. Every time Caitlin had imagined him finding out and leaving her, she'd played it out wrong. That was one nightmare, at least, that would never come to life. At least, not the way she'd pictured it.

'If you had any idea what it would have done

for me if you'd just told me this — if you'd been enough of a friend to tell me this — ' Caitlin could hear the hypocrisy in her words even as they escaped her mouth, but it was too late. Violet's face changed. Caitlin had rarely seen so much as a hint of sadness, or resentment, or remorse, or even wistfulness from Violet before Finn disappeared with Bear. Now, here it all was — years' worth, condensed into one searing, disbelieving, mocking, frozen glare.

Caitlin swung the car into a spot near the restroom and switched off the ignition. 'All the wrong people know all the wrong secrets here,' she said, her voice small in the suddenly silent space. She tried to manage a nervous laugh, but even to her own ears, it sounded more like a whimper from a wounded animal.

'Sometimes I wish I'd never met any of you,' Violet said quietly.

35

AUGUST 2016

The part where you fathered my children.

Finn actually laughed — until he saw that George was serious. 'Whoa,' he said, his smile fading. 'Whatever you think you know, you've got it wrong.'

'Oh, it's wrong, all right. Like I said, we're not friends.'

'We were. We are.'

George's arm went flying, palm splayed, and caught Finn's plate at the edge of the coffee table. Peanut butter crackers rained across the room; the dish shattered on the brick hearth. Finn jumped. 'Jesus, man, if the kids are sleeping back there, they won't be for long.'

'So now that the cat's out of the bag, you're going to start acting like their father? Way to step up.'

The shock of George's accusations dissolved the lingering fog of Finn's deep, drugged sleep, and an anger of his own filled him with surprising intensity. He hadn't managed to devise much of a plan these long days on the run, but this was so far from how he'd wanted things to go. This was, in fact, the last thing he needed.

'Look,' Finn said. 'No offense, but if I wanted to fuck Caitlin, I would have fucked Caitlin, okay? It's not like you would have been in the way. You're *never* there.'

'At least I don't sit around wallowing in self-pity! You *kill* someone, and instead of being there for her family, or honoring her memory in some meaningful way, all you do is feel sorry for yourself!' George was yelling now, his face pink, a vein throbbing at his temple. 'I might not be the perfect husband, but *you* are not even *close* to good enough for Caitlin! Or Violet.'

From the counter, George picked up a tablet computer, pressed the button that brightened the screen, and shoved it into Finn's hands. 'Look at that,' he said. 'Does that seem to you like it was written by someone who's worthy of your kind of 'love'?'

Finn recognized the Missed Connections page of Craigslist instantly from his own ill-fated posts there. But this one was dated today — or yesterday. He didn't know what day it was anymore.

Papa Bear: I can see that we shouldn't have ended up here. But here we are. We can do things your way, or no way at all. I'll go along with whatever you want. And no one has to know. The choice is yours. The choice was always yours. Just please, bring our little cub home.

Papa Bear. Little cub. Clever. The investigators would never recognize Violet in this post, but Finn couldn't miss her. And what he saw triggered an intense yet familiar wave of

343

self-reproach. He raised his eyes to George. 'How did you find this?'

'I've been checking every day, waiting to see if one or the other of you would post. It seemed obvious to me — the one place in your history that was plain to both of you but where the authorities wouldn't look. Do you know, I actually thought it was more likely that I'd find an olive branch from *you* here? I already could picture how I'd be the one to crack the case, spotting your message and showing it to Caitlin, who'd call Violet, who'd get her little boy back. But I was giving you way too much credit. As usual, it's the women around you who have the courage to step up, even when you don't deserve it. And little did I know, Caitlin already knew exactly where to find you!'

'Violet, she's — ' Finn couldn't think of what to say. He hadn't thought enough about Violet. He hadn't let himself.

George let out a cruel laugh. 'That about sums up your thoughts on her, doesn't it? Can you imagine someone taking your child, and you having the grace to post that you would do *whatever they want* to make them happy? That you would let them off the hook they had hooked *themselves* on? Of course you can't! You're too stuck on the irrelevant fact that Violet isn't Maribel.'

Irrelevant. George was smart, smart enough to conjure the word that was *supposed* to fit — or so Finn had been trying to tell himself, for years. There had been moments when he'd almost listened, when he'd allowed himself to forget, just for a flash, and give himself over to life in the uncomplicated now. Violet, tipping her face up toward the stars on their honeymoon, the bonfire glowing on her skin, her fingers entwined with his. Violet, dancing with infant Bear in their living room, her hair wavy and loose, her laugh inviting and warm. Violet, sleeping the half sleep that mothers do, that worn Camp Pickiwicki T-shirt draped around her frame, her features steeped in the unassuming beauty that comes with contentment.

George kicked at the coffee table leg, jolting Finn. 'News flash,' he said. 'You weren't good enough for Maribel's love either.'

Finn shrank back into the leather of the couch cushion. With the force of George's words came the routine gut punch of other memories. The genuine shock that would come on the sleepiest mornings upon waking to find Violet, long and lean where Maribel had been curvy and soft. The awful ways he'd tried to prod Violet out of being so easy and accommodating, longing for a flare of Maribel's stubborn, strong will. The time Violet had looked up at him from his art desk and he'd had to run from the room, gasping, so sure had he been that it was Maribel sketching one of her beautiful vignettes there rather than Violet scribbling a meaningless shopping list.

Seeing that he'd hit his mark, George pressed on. 'Thank *God* Maribel didn't live to see you this way. She never would have agreed to marry you if she'd known you could be remotely like this. Self-indulgent. Selfish. Manipulative. Incapable of being happy with what you have, with what's right in front of you. I might not have known Maribel that well, but I know enough to say with utmost certainty that's not someone she would have related to — and it's not someone the old Finn would have wanted to know either.'

Even in a rage, George still managed to speak articulately, smoothly, and shrewdly on point, as if he were overseeing a high-stakes business meeting, or taking his turn at the podium in a debate. He'd always been a hand talker, something they'd teased him about having inherited through some politician genetic code, but now each gesture seemed menacing as the gun clasped in his hand rose and fell with each phrase, catching the glow of the kitchen light. He began to pace the cracker-strewn floor. 'When I first told you I wasn't bothered by your friendship with Caitlin, I meant it,' he said. 'For you to turn around and betray me that way — '

'How many ways do I have to tell you?' Finn was yelling now too, trying to block the words from his ears, to push the images from his brain, to regain control, to turn the focus. 'I am *not* their father. You have it all wrong. I know who he is — ' At that, George stopped midstride and snapped his head around to glare at Finn. 'But you should hear that from Caitlin, not from me. Where is she?'

George didn't answer.

Finn got to his feet, and the men stood eye to eye. 'She loves you, you know,' Finn said. 'Odds are you'd be happily raising your *biological* children together if you'd just gotten that stupid

346

sperm count test. Why didn't you get the test, George?'

George looked away.

'Oh my God. You knew you were going to fail, didn't you?'

Silence.

'Well, aren't we high and mighty, accusing *me* of not being worthy of my wife's love.'

George turned his gaze back on Finn, and what Finn saw there made his blood run cold. He took a step back. 'Look, we've all done things we're not proud of — '

'Don't put me in the same camp as you.' George was practically growling now.

'You're right. I'm the worst offender, by *miles*. But of all the things I'm guilty of, you're after me for the one thing I didn't do.'

George shook his head. 'Even if I believed you — which I don't — you say you know who the father is. And all these years, you've watched me play the part, thinking I was some chump. Not saying a word.'

Finn nodded. 'Just one question back at you. You seem to be quite taken with Violet's unsuspecting role in all this. Why didn't you tell her what *you* knew? Why didn't *you* tell her about what happened with Maribel?'

George just stared.

'Exactly.' Finn knew he was pressing his luck, but he felt he had no choice but to risk it. 'Caitlin will tell you I'm not the father. Tell me where she is. Is she getting the police? Is she getting Violet? Is Bear with her, or is he here, in the bedroom with the twins?'

George looked down at the gun in his hand curiously, as if someone else had put it there.

Finn felt defeat wash over him. All these agonizing nights of indecision, of looking for a way out, and now he knew that Violet had reached out and offered one. She would have let him return Bear and go. She would have let him disappear, no questions asked. She would have let him get away with it — with so much — at the cost of his son. At the cost of the only thing he had left.

Would he have taken her escape hatch and paid that price if he had the chance? Would he have given up Bear if it meant he could at least try to save himself? It didn't matter now. Because George had trapped him here. And he could see that he wasn't going to talk his way out of it. What he wanted was not on the table for discussion, nor would it be. He had lost. And he deserved to lose. He'd known that all along. George was right.

Finn turned and headed for the front door. Without the possibility of taking Bear with him, there was nothing keeping him here. George had gotten Violet's message to let him go. George would return Bear to his rightful place. Finn would disappear into the kind of fugitive life that no one could take any pleasure in — the kind of life he deserved. He wouldn't look back. He wouldn't say good-bye. This was how it had to end. His strides grew longer, more sure of themselves. He reached for the door.

He registered the sound of the gunshot and the stinging in his leg simultaneously. But before the pain truly hit him, his first and last coherent thought was not of himself, or of Bear, or Violet, or Caitlin, or Maribel.

He did it, he thought, as he crumpled to the floor, his hands instinctively going to the wound that was already oozing blood. *The son of a gun really did it.*

A chorus of frightened wails came from down the hall. Finn thought he could make out Bear's cry alongside the twins'. So the boys were all there, after all.

'They *are* mine, regardless,' George said. 'And they come first.' He headed down the hallway, leaving Finn to fend for himself.

36

Caitlin opened the front door and stopped where she stood. Finn grimaced up at her from the floor, shivering under one of her in-laws' thick Native-American-patterned blankets. He looked as if he'd been there awhile, long enough to attempt to make himself comfortable, though why he would have chosen this spot at her feet was not immediately clear. Behind him, George was standing in the middle of the kitchen, looking as if he'd been caught eating someone else's leftovers.

'What's wrong?' Caitlin asked George, and when he didn't answer. she turned her gaze back to Finn. 'Why are you on the floor?'

Violet didn't wait to find out. She pushed past Caitlin without so much as a glance at Finn and ran down the hallway toward the bedrooms, toward Bear. Finn watched her go, looking sad and deflated. And then Caitlin noticed something on the blanket. A dark stain. She knelt down, lifted the edge, and gasped. Finn's pant leg was soaked in blood. A tourniquet had been tied around the top of his thigh with an old leather belt. The dark center of his wound almost looked like —

'Oh my God!'

'So much for *no one needs to know anyone*

did anything wrong,' Finn quipped, trying to manage a smile through his pain. It came out as a downlike wince.

Caitlin stepped toward George, confused. 'You *shot* him?'

'I deserved it,' Finn said weakly. 'Just not for the reason he thought.'

'And what was *the reason you thought?*' she yelled at George, but he turned away from her, his hands over his face. Her thoughts raced, frantic, disbelieving. Hours ago she had signed her son out of the hospital after accidentally poisoning him. Now they'd be rushing back again because George had *shot* a man? This couldn't be happening. There wouldn't be a way out of it this time. And Finn, her oldest friend . . .

Caitlin dropped to her knees. 'Are you okay? Has an ambulance been called?'

'Not yet,' Finn said. 'I think we were waiting for you.'

'George!' He didn't turn around. She saw the glint of something in his hand. 'George, for God's sake, put down that gun!'

Finn couldn't see into the kitchen from his vantage point on the floor, and his eyes went wide at Caitlin's words. 'Tell him,' he said, his voice hoarse.

'Tell him what?'

'Tell him the boys aren't mine, That I'm not their father.'

Oh God. Violet said he'd known the twins weren't his from the start. But had he thought it was Finn all along? Had he thought it was Finn and gone along with *that* for years too?

Caitlin stood and slowly moved toward her husband, the way she might approach a wounded animal. When she was finally close enough to reach out and lay a hand on his shoulder, he flinched.

'The boys are not Finn's, George.'

He wheeled around to face her, and his eyes were so unfamiliar, she took a step back. 'Well they sure as hell aren't mine,' he said, and his voice broke. Tears filled his eyes.

'To me they are,' she said. 'To me, they *are* yours. And to Gus and Leo, you are their father, and they love you. And I promise, they aren't Finn's.'

'He's lucky I thought they were,' George growled. 'It might be the reason I shot him, but it's also the reason I didn't turn him in the moment I found out he was here.' He pulled at his hair with his fists, the way Leo and Gus did when they were trying to calm down from a tantrum. Caitlin had never noticed the gesture in George before.

'The idea of me not being their biological father, I've tried to accept that. But the idea of their real father being in prison, because I helped put him there? That I didn't think I could live with.'

'But you could live with shooting him?'

'In the leg! It's not like I was aiming for his head! I was just stopping him from running away from this.'

'But he — '

'For years, I've waited for you to tell me, and

nothing. You think I'm just going to accept the first explanation you give me?'

'And you've been nothing but honest? Omitting the tiny detail that you were infertile?'

He froze.

'We'll get Finn a paternity test,' she said, her voice shaking. 'Then you'll see. You didn't have to *shoot* him! What the hell are we supposed to do *now*?'

George pounded his fist onto the counter, and Caitlin jumped. Behind her, a whimper came from Finn. 'Right, so this is all *my* fault!' George exploded. 'At least I didn't try to shoot him and hit Leo instead!'

Caitlin burst into tears. She turned and saw Finn dragging himself out from behind the leather couch and into the open, where he could see what was going on.

'Look at us!' she screamed at him. 'After all that we've done for you, after we tried to be there for you, no matter what you'd done — look what you've done to *us*!'

37

AUGUST 2016

Violet fell to her knees on the bunkroom floor and scooped up Bear into her arms, sleeping bag and all, hugging him to her as tight as she could. Tears of relief and elation and anger and sadness poured down her face and into his baby-soft curls. He mumbled something into her chest, and she pulled back enough to let him tilt his face up to hers and open his sleepy eyes.

'Mommy,' he said, smiling, and closed them again as his little arms wrapped around her — just as they always had, right where they belonged.

'Oh, baby, I missed you so much, *so much*, so much . . . '

'Mommy, why are you crying?'

She buried her face in his hair. She had to keep it together, for Bear. He probably didn't understand what had gone on, or where she'd been. Who knew what Finn might have told him? And she didn't want to wake the twins if she could help it.

'I just . . . I couldn't find you, Bear Cub,' she whispered. 'A lot of people have been helping Mommy look everywhere for you!'

'I was with Daddy.'

'I know you were, sweetheart.'

'I was missing you.'

She blinked away fresh tears. 'Me too, little man. Me too. But it's okay now. I'm here.' She rocked him back and forth, and he clutched her tighter. 'I'm not going anywhere,' she promised him. 'You're staying with me.'

Violet could hear faint sounds of shouting coming from the living room. For too many days, she'd been determined to have the chance to be face-to-face with her husband, to confront him head-on. And yet now that she was here, all she wanted to do was curl up in this sleeping bag with Bear and let the rest of the world just fall away.

Even as Bear clung to Violet, his eyes were rolling back into his head. There was no telling how exhausted he'd been and for how long. Now that he was safe in her arms, he drifted back to sleep as if it were the most natural thing in the world — and it was. Even with the twins starting to stir in their bunks. Even with the yelling down the hall. Even though Violet knew that soon the cops would be on the way, and the feds, and they'd take Finn away, and Bear's world would be changed forever.

Violet had to talk to Finn first, whether she wanted to or not. That was why Caitlin had brought her here instead of carrying Bear to her. And though she wanted to hate Caitlin for it, she also knew in some back corner of her mind that Caitlin was probably right. This could be her only chance to talk to Finn in private, to try to get real answers to her questions. She'd been willing to let him walk away if that was the only way she could get Bear back. But now that she was here, now that Finn didn't have a choice in the matter, she wasn't going to dissolve their life together without at least an explanation. He owed her that much.

She pulled at a blanket that had been tucked into Bear's sleeping bag and wrapped it around him, discarding the bag on the floor. She stood, and his head rolled easily onto her shoulder, his legs wrapped around her middle, his arms loose around her neck. He shouldn't hear what was about to be said, but he was going to have to come with her anyway. She wasn't about to let him out of her sight. She just hoped he'd sleep through the worst of it.

She forced her legs to move, one foot in front of the other, down the hall, to the place where the living room met the kitchen. There, she stopped and stared in horror. Finn was cowering on a blood-smeared floor. His pants were soaked through. Seeing Bear in Violet's arms, he rushed to cover his legs with the blanket that had been draped over him when they'd walked in. Caitlin was standing, sobbing, midway between him and George. She swiped angrily at her tears with the backs of her hands.

'Oh my God,' Violet said, her eyes widening as she caught sight of George setting a gun on the kitchen counter. He backed away from it as if it might attack him on its own. 'What *happened*?'

Finn looked at Violet as if she were some foregone conclusion he'd been avoiding. 'There was a . . . misunderstanding,' Caitlin said. She turned away, still sniffling, took George by the elbow and pulled him toward the sliding glass doors. 'We're going to go outside and let you talk. But you don't have long. We need to call an ambulance.'

Violet stared in disbelief as the door shut behind them. An unnatural silence filled the room. She crossed to the couch and gingerly laid down Bear, who tucked his hands under his chin and curled up into a ball without waking. Reluctantly, she turned back to Finn.

'I know we have to talk, but he stays with me,' she said quietly. 'I promised him.'

Finn nodded, and she stood looking down at him, trying to bite back her rising concern. How long had he been like this?

'I guess you know everything,' he said with a grimace, and she couldn't tell if he was bracing himself against the pain of his wound or against whatever she was about to say.

'What's *everything*?' she asked, careful to keep her voice calm. 'How would I even know the answer to that?'

I don't know anything! she wanted to scream. *We promised to love each other forever, and I don't even know if you ever loved me at all!*

When he didn't reply, she sighed and lowered herself slowly onto the floor next to him. 'I think I got the basics.'

He nodded, but still did not speak.

'For one thing, I'm thinking moving to Asheville was a bad idea,' she said.

'It didn't help matters,' he admitted.

Would you have been able to love me somewhere else? Could we have been a family?

'You should have told me. All of it. Any of it.'

'I know, I'm sorry.'

Outside on the porch, she could see Caitlin try to put her arms around George. He shrugged her off and walked into the darkness, and Caitlin followed.

'Did you ever even *try* to tell me? Did I . . . I don't know, miss something?'

'No.'

This sullen teenager routine was only making Violet resent Finn more. But she also knew that eventually, the intensity of that resentment would fade — didn't it always, no matter who did the betraying or how bad things seemed? And then what would she be left with, besides unanswered questions?

She tried again. 'I guess I don't get why you didn't feel like you could. If not at first, then before you checked out. I admit I might not have reacted well, but anything would have been better than *this*. How can I ever trust you again?'

Finn was trembling. Shock must be setting in, 'You don't have to. We won't be married anymore. And I'll be . . . wherever they send me.' He said 'they' as if he were talking about some all-encompassing hypothetical and not a very real federal agent who had been sitting at Violet's kitchen table not forty-eight hours ago, telling her that her husband might as well have been a stranger. And yet, the most unexpected thing now, seeing him like this, was that he was not a stranger at all. He was still Finn. And for the moment, at least, she was still his wife.

'Last time I checked, you're my son's father. Tell me again why I don't have to trust you?'

Finn looked properly chastened, but he didn't backpedal. 'For starters, I think Uncle Sam is going to have a big hand in my parenting moving forward.'

'I get the feeling Caitlin wants me to tell them this has all been a big misunderstanding.'

Finn stared at her, and she saw something there. Hope? Despondence? She couldn't tell.

'Was it?' she asked. 'A big misunderstanding?'

'Not really,' he said. Then, seeing her face fall, he added, 'The Bear part, maybe.'

Violet's attempt at empathy faded — she was running out of time — and the fury she'd been suppressing bubbled over.

'*The Bear part, maybe?*' she repeated, incredulous. 'Why don't you start with the part where you got me comfortable in a beach chair, stuck a drink in my hand, made me think everything was great, and then just *disappeared?* Do you know what I've been through? Do you know that *I've* spent hours being questioned by the *FBI?* Do you have the slightest idea what it's been like for me, missing Bear with every bone in my body, so bad I could hardly stand it?'

Her tears threatened to spill over, and she blinked them back. She wouldn't cry. Not yet. 'Forget about what happened with Maribel, or what you decided not to tell me, or why. Why would you do that to me? How could you?'

To her surprise, Finn's eyes filled with tears too. 'Oh God, Vi, I didn't mean to hurt you. I thought you'd be better off.'

'Better off? How could *anyone* be better off after that?' Her voice was louder than she intended, and Bear stirred on the couch. She pressed her lips closed tight and leveled her gaze at Finn.

'That day of the accident, the day I fell asleep at the wheel and killed Maribel' — Finn's voice was barely above a whisper — 'I talked her into that drive to see the ocean. And part of the reason was that *I couldn't picture the beach without picturing you there.* I was going there with her to erase the image of you and replace it with her. And instead I erased *her*, forever.'

Finn pulled the blanket tighter around him, and Violet could see that the pool of blood on the floor was still expanding. He needed help. Soon.

'We had absolutely no business being on the road that day. It was the morning after our engagement party. We'd been completely whacked the night before. We'd hardly slept.'

'Her mother said you were trying to be romantic.'

Finn blinked at the mention of Mrs. Branson but then shook his head. 'That's the outside story, smoothed over by my inner PR guy, and by people who want to think the best of me. It's a nicer story for her that her daughter loved me and it was a whirlwind romantic trip gone wrong. The truth is that our heading to the beach that day was just me being stubborn, feeling disturbed that I'd been reminded of you on the night of our engagement party and wanting to make sure Maribel was the *only* woman I thought of from that moment on. It seemed so ridiculously urgent. But it wasn't. We had our whole lives . . . '

His voice trailed off, and when he spoke again, it shook. 'And no matter how hard I try, I can't get it to go away. The guilt. The pain. The feeling that nothing ended up as it was supposed to. And then all these years later I found myself there at the ocean again, with you, trying to live my life, even though I don't deserve it, trying to be *happy*, even though I don't deserve it, and I realized I *still* wanted to erase the picture of you and replace it with her.' She winced, and he did too, aware of the pain he was causing. But there was no point in holding back now.

'I couldn't force myself *not* to feel that urge to rewrite things. Not even while we were standing there on the beach together that first day of our vacation, watching Bear see the ocean for the first time. It should have been this moment of complete joy, and it wasn't — only I was the only one who knew that it wasn't. And I couldn't stop thinking how unfair that was to you. And what a horrible person I was for thinking that way about my own wife. And all of a sudden I swear to God it honestly seemed like the kind thing to do, to leave you there without me.'

Violet reeled. Intuitively knowing some things were worlds away from hearing them spoken aloud. She clenched her jaw and swallowed hard. 'And it seemed kind to take my son with you?'

'Of course not. Hardly. God, Vi, I didn't plan on it, I swear. I thought I could walk away, but when the moment came — ' Finn's eyes were agonizing pleas. 'Bear's was the only love I could think of that I hadn't royally screwed up. I think I felt like . . . '

His words trailed off, and he sighed. 'It doesn't matter. The thought of being so alone again — and of the added agony of missing him — something in me snapped. I just didn't want to let go.' He shook his head. 'Bear deserves to be with you. I know that. Everyone knows that. But you don't deserve to be with me.'

It did matter. It mattered to Violet what he had felt, and it mattered to her that she hadn't been allowed to have a say in who deserved what. But it wouldn't change the outcome now.

'So maybe I'm not your soul mate after all,' she said finally. 'Maybe our whole story — how we ended up together but almost didn't — maybe all of it's bullshit. Maybe everyone's story is bullshit. That doesn't mean we couldn't have had some kind of love, an understanding. That doesn't mean we couldn't still have been parents together to Bear.' Even to her own ears, the words sounded pathetic. A futile, desperate attempt at catching a ship that had already sailed.

'Look,' he said gently, 'I found Maribel when I was looking for you. But I've spent every day with you looking for her, and I can't seem to stop. It's my penance for what I've done, and it's not fair to any of us. I think maybe a part of me thought if it was just me and Bear, I could love somebody the right way, without all this . . . history, fate, weight. But I know that's not right. That's only punishing you both for my own mistakes.'

'You would never have married me if I hadn't gotten pregnant,' Violet said. It wasn't a question.

'I tried to do the right thing. I thought I could handle it.'

'We wouldn't have made it more than a few months otherwise, would we?' It probably should have been her clearest revelation when she first found out about Maribel, but for some reason, it was just hitting Violet now.

'I don't regret Bear,' Finn said. 'He's the only good to come of any of this.' The pure pain on his face just then laid bare the heart of it all: *This* was why he'd failed to walk away from their son, even when he could no longer bring himself to stay, even when there was nowhere else to go.

'Why did you even look for me at all?' Violet had to know. 'The second time, I mean. After she died.' When he didn't answer, her anger flashed again. 'Why couldn't you just *let me be?*'

She could see that the words stung him, and that he was surprised that they did. She didn't wish them back, but she didn't take any satisfaction in them either. She was just so *tired*.

She looked past Finn and could see the faintest hint of a glow on the horizon where the sun would soon appear. 'It wasn't meant to be,' she said, more to herself than to him. 'How funny that everybody believed so strongly that it was. I mean, people used to beg me to tell the story to the point where I got sick of telling it. I guess I should have enjoyed it while it lasted.'

'I'm sorry,' Finn said again.

Violet steadied herself with a deep breath.

363

'We're going to have to call now,' she said. 'The ambulance, the feds. No way around it.'

As if on cue, the faint song of a siren sounded in the distance, just as it had on the day she'd met Finn and lost him. She was about to lose him again. Caitlin must have already called. Violet's eyes met Finn's. Some connections couldn't be undone just because someone said so.

'Don't tell them to go easy on me,' Finn said.

'I'll tell them the truth,' she said. 'That you need help. You should have talked to someone about all this a long time ago — and I don't mean me. I mean someone who knows what they're talking about, someone who can help you.'

'Ah. The insanity defense. Why didn't I think of that?' He looked so pale, so clammy, and in spite of everything, Violet was afraid for him.

'What happened with Maribel was an accident, Finn. It's like Gram used to tell me, when I spilled something or broke something — they're called *accidents* for a reason. You don't have to live your life as if you're a murderer.'

He nodded, though whether or not her words had had any effect, she couldn't tell.

'Of course, there is the small detail that now you're a *kidnapper*.'

Finn forced a laugh. Violet hugged her knees to her chest. Together, they watched Bear sleep until the ambulance arrived.

38

AUGUST 2017

Bear pushed the bright orange Tonka bulldozer in figure eights around the thick pillars of the pier. Violet had been assigned back-hoe duty. Her job was to fill the dump truck with sand, at which point Bear would stop what he was doing, gleefully dump the truck's load onto the sizable pile they'd accumulated, and instruct her to do it again. The brittle plastic of the backhoe's scoop was not exactly smooth in its response to the toy's levers and gears, and so now and then sand would fling into the air and rain down on Violet's warm skin, already sticky from sunscreen and bug spray. But she didn't care. It felt so good to be away from things, just her and Bear, hours and hours from home. The tide was going out, and the foam rolling gently beneath the tunnel of the pier was a hypnotic piece of vanishing-point-perspective art.

After Finn had been taken into custody, Gram had announced almost immediately that she didn't know what she'd been thinking, retiring in the altitude, and would prefer a warmer climate. Violet knew Gram was putting the rest of the family's needs above what she really wanted, and yet she didn't argue. Finn would always be a part of Bear's life, though in what capacity they didn't yet know, and Asheville was too connected to his most painful memories. Violet wasn't exactly feeling nostalgic about her time there either. And so she helped to find another independent-living facility, one farther south but surrounded by eclectic artists and historic homes not unlike those Gram had so loved in the mountains.

They settled in Beaufort, South Carolina, right on the coast, where Gram's new seniors' community was steeped in Low Country charm and afforded breathtaking views of the sunset over the marsh. Violet found a rental nearby, a two-bedroom in a newer complex where the living room and kitchen were adjoined, and Bear's tiny room shared both a wall and a bathroom with her own. The close quarters suited her just fine, and the sleek, freshly tiled kitchen with its built-in breakfast bar was a welcome change from the old awkward space she'd so loathed in the Asheville rental. Although Violet knew Gram's heart hadn't been in coming, she seemed to genuinely like her new home too, making fast friends with the exceedingly polite Southern belle retirees and flirting shamelessly with the men — she couldn't resist their thick Carolina accents. Not to mention the cobblers, the pies, the fresh crops of peaches and pecans — Gram's culinary skills fit right in here, and any lingering guilt Violet felt quickly eased.

'This is what's best for the whole family,' Gram said firmly the one time Violet dared to ask if she was really okay with the move. 'And that means it's best for me.'

Finn wasn't the only one who'd pictured

Violet every time he thought of the beach. She'd always seen herself there too. Looking out at the ocean made her feel connected to something bigger, in rhythm with something constant. She needed that in her life right now. And she liked the idea of raising Bear with that kind of perspective.

'A few more minutes, Cub, and then I thought we could drive into the old town and watch the boats come in. Maybe this time we could have a picnic by the Castillo.'

St. Augustine's massive open harbor was nothing like the glassy waterways of Beaufort, and it mesmerized Violet just as much as it did Bear. They'd ended every day of their vacation there so far this week. Gram had called Violet a ship, and maybe she'd been right. Violet couldn't help but feel a kinship with them as they glided in from the uncertain open sea.

Bear's eyes lit up. 'Will there be fishing boats again?'

Violet nodded. 'But *I* like watching the sailboats best.'

'*I* like watching the *cargo* ships!'

'*I* like watching the pirates come in!'

Bear giggled. 'There *are* no pirates, Mommy!'

'Well, there might be today. You never know.'

'If there are, I will save you with my sword!'

Violet didn't want to mourn this August, the anniversary of things gone so horribly wrong. She wanted to celebrate it — an August with Bear, on the heels of an August without. For years now, it had been a month of almosts, starting with that first meeting with Finn, and with him looking for her and finding a different love instead. The next August, he'd lost that love, and himself along with it. He'd reappeared a year later on Violet's own August calendar, with the excitement brought by the ad she'd almost missed, the first date marked by the questions she'd almost asked. The following Augusts had been consumed by Bear — sharing those infant days with Caitlin, watching him become a toddler, vacationing together at the cabin before their move to Asheville, reveling in things briefly coming together before they fell apart again.

But there was nothing *almost* about this August. She had her Bear, and things set right with Gram, and a new start. She'd had to let go of so much that had happened, but more than that, she'd needed to forgive Finn, and Caitlin, and, most of all, herself. Finally emerging on the other side of all that felt good — like the delight of coming across something forgotten but treasured, something she'd misplaced long ago and eventually given up looking for.

And so she'd loaded Bear into the car and driven the three hours down here to the top of Florida, where she knew Bear — who'd gone a bit pirate crazy these days — would be amazed by St. Augustine's Castillo. The first day, she bought him an old-fashioned wooden sword in the souvenir shop, and he'd been carrying it with him everywhere since.

She loved the old-world feel of the gated city's pedestrian walkways, the way they transported anyone who walked there to another time. Bear hopped down the cobblestones with abandon, and she could let him without fear of traffic or losing him in a crowd. He was transfixed by the lighthouse, whooped every time they drove across the long bridge toward St. Augustine Beach, and astonished her daily with how much he had grown in only a year. He asked a never-ending string of questions, and she took her time to thoughtfully answer every one.

'Wait until you take that sword home,' she told him. 'Your friends at preschool are going to think it's *so cool*.'

He nodded, then turned serious. 'Except Emma. Emma only wants to play Who Wants To Be My Puppy?'

In moments like these, when Violet had to stifle a laugh, she missed having another parent there to meet her eyes and share a look over Bear's little head. But in general, she was happy with just the two of them. And though she knew he missed Finn, Bear seemed happy too.

For Bear, it sometimes seemed almost as if the incident last August had never happened. He'd been so young. It was a big change, of course, to live with Violet alone, and to see Finn only during supervised visits, which would have been few and far between even if Finn hadn't been taken so far away, back to southern Florida, the scene of his only true crime. Violet tried not to think of what it was like for Finn at the treatment center, aside from being glad that her own wishes had been taken into consideration, and that he was receiving treatment rather than strictly punishment. It seemed to her that he'd been doling out punishment to himself for years, only making things worse, But just because she was glad he was getting help didn't mean she had to be a part of it. Gram took Bear on his visits there — always efficient, flying down and back on the same day — and Violet didn't ask many questions, trusting Gram and their case workers to tell her anything she needed to know.

She gathered that Finn was doing well — deeply repentant for what he'd done, learning ways to try to let go of his guilt, and wanting only good things for Violet. His year of mandated inpatient treatment had sped by, and though he still had years of therapy and probation ahead, she was glad that he'd have another chance at a way forward. Eventually, the restrictions on the visits with Bear would lessen, though Violet had no idea how that might work or what it might look like. She wasn't quite ready for that yet — but it no longer seemed unfathomable that down the road she would be.

At home, on an everyday basis, Bear proved remarkably resilient. The child psychologist assigned to their case had assured Violet that it would be so, and to her surprise, it was. He rarely brought up the time they'd spent apart just the year before, He didn't cling to Violet, nor did he seem shaken by his visits to his dad. He accepted the straightforward explanation that Finn was sick and doctors were making him better, and he answered the social worker's questions as if they were doing a fun quiz.

For Violet, the incident still shaped her days more than she wanted to admit. She did cling to Bear — emotionally if not outwardly. Her eyes rarely left him, whether they were at home or out somewhere, and sometimes, she still slept in his bed, But she did it out of love, not fear.

She'd had to go back to work, of course. She now managed communications for a chain of day cares at their headquarters, which adjoined one of their own centers. Bear enrolled in preschool there for a fraction of the tuition, and Violet knew how lucky she was that her funds weren't nearly as tight as other single moms'. She never could have forgotten that, anyway — that she was one of the lucky ones. She'd gotten her son back. And she liked the aspect of her job that involved telling parents not to worry, that their children would be in good hands there — because she could see for herself that it was true.

Violet loved that her new workday included 'Bear breaks' when she'd pop in to his class. Somehow she always ended up with a crowd of three- and four-year-olds gathered around her to play the high five game — 'up high, down low, you're too slow!' She loved how uncensored they all were, how they'd just yell out whatever was on their minds. After too many years of secrets, she found it refreshing that Bear had entered such an honest age.

Caitlin wrote to her, about once a month. Old-fashioned letters sent in monogrammed envelopes. Violet sometimes contemplated discarding them, unopened, but curiosity always got the best of her. And the truth was, she was happy to hear that Caitlin and George were working things out, that he was traveling less, that he was probably not going to run for office after all, though it still wasn't out of the question. He'd come out of the situation at the cabin well — too well, for anyone who valued the truth over the trumped-up version of the story. The media had hailed him as a hero for wounding the fugitive to keep him from running — *imagine the Bryce-Danielses' shock to come upon a family friend who'd been trying to hide out at their vacation home!* — and for reuniting a mother with her child in the process. That Caitlin had first driven to get Violet before calling the cops had been an error in judgment, certainly, but not a crime. And George had simply done what anyone would do when he caught Finn trying to make his escape. It was the story Finn had told, and Violet didn't mind it. She'd gone along with so much, unsuspectingly — what was one more thing? But she had to keep it at a distance.

Agent Martin, she was pretty sure, hadn't swallowed what they were feeding him as eagerly as the press had — but there wasn't much motivation to dig deeper once Finn was in custody and Bear was home. Violet couldn't help thinking that the universe seemed to be constructed so that things would work out for the Georges and Caitlins of the world. She didn't begrudge them that. But she never wrote back.

'Can we take this sand home too, Mommy?' Violet laughed. The sand at St. Augustine Beach was fine and white, a closer cousin to fairy dust than to the brown, shelly mix that lined the barrier islands outside Beaufort. This was just the vacation they needed. She'd invited Gram, but Gram had declined, saying that Violet needed to do this on her own, to 'get it under her belt,' as she put it, and erase the bad taste of the vacation that had come before.

'I have a feeling we're going to whether we want to or not,' Violet said, turning the dump truck upside down and trying to shake it clean enough to go back in the beach bag.

'*Daddy!*' Bear was on his feet in an instant, running toward a figure walking in the wet sand. Violet squinted through the sun at the man and was amazed that Bear had recognized him. He was wearing a decidedly un-Finn shirt, a linen button-down instead of his usual graphic T. His mirrored sunglasses masked his expression, but not the eagerness with which he bent down to scoop Bear up into his arms. He looked tan. Well fed. Healthy.

She checked the surge of involuntary happiness that overtook her at seeing the two of them hug, offering a baffled half smile as he splayed his fingers apart in a wave and carried Bear toward her. She hadn't seen Finn since that night in the cabin, not wanting to cause either of them, but especially him, any further unhappiness. The divorce papers were signed and delivered through couriers and lawyers.

Finn deposited their son in the shade of the pier, and Bear began to jump up and down wildly, kicking sand onto Violet's feet. 'Did you come to watch the ships with us?' he yelled, bubbling over with excitement. 'Did you come to look for *pirates*?' At that Bear began an invisible sword fight, slashing his arms through the air, and Finn grinned at Violet, an apology forming in his smile.

'A free man,' she said, clapping her hands in silent applause.

'A probationary man,' he corrected her. 'But a weekend away is allowed if you tell them where you're going and stay in the state. It helps if your therapist thinks it's a good idea. And if it's free. A guy in my program has a condo here — he's letting me use it.'

'How did you know we were here?' she asked.

'I didn't.' He pushed the sunglasses onto the top of his head. 'Honest.'

She watched him take her in — the long crepe sundress, draped with strands of freshwater pearls she'd picked up at a touristy boutique in the old town. Her hand went self-consciously to her wind-blown braid.

'I might have wished for it, though,' he said softly.

She waited for him to look meaningfully at Bear, but he didn't. His eyes were on her.

'And you didn't know *I* would be here?' he asked.

Violet raised her eyebrows. Of course there was no way she would have known.

'So we're meeting again,' he said, 'on a different beach, by accident.' He held her gaze. 'Again,' he repeated.

Violet looked over at Bear, who was jumping in and out of the pier's pillars now, hiding and chasing invisible pirates, showing off. 'Yaaarrrr!' he yelled. 'Shiver me timbers!'

'Imagine if this were the first time,' Finn said.

374

She nodded. Things could have been different. 'I'm not wearing the right shirt,' she said finally. 'You wouldn't have stopped.'

'Oh, I don't know about that. You have Camp Pickiwicki written all over you.'

'Is that so?'

'It's just that you look so wholesome — and yet, I can't help but wonder if you might be the type who'd sneak out after dark and meet me by the docks.'

Finn smiled, and there it was — that effortless, kindred warmth that had drawn her in from the start. The one that she hadn't seen again the second time around, but that somehow still felt familiar. It didn't make any sense. Finn had been a stranger then, and in some ways he was even more unknown to her now. Violet wiped the perspiration from her forehead with the back of her hand.

'Imagine if,' she repeated. She'd liked the sound of the words when he said them. They sounded so much better than *almost*.

Acknowledgments

Thanks first and foremost to my husband, Scott, who has proven to be unfailingly good-natured about me saying, 'Can I just have twenty minutes alone with my laptop?' and then sheepishly emerging from my office an hour or two later to find him cooking dinner with a hungry child dangling from each leg. And to the aforementioned children, who remind me every day that life is full of big magic and little miracles, two of whom — by some incredible stroke of luck — live under my roof and call me *Mommy*. Being wife and mother to these three beautiful souls is the greatest honor and purest joy of my life.

My agent, Barbara Poelle, believed in me when my faith in myself was wavering, and that is the single greatest gift that anyone — no matter who you are — can give to a writer. The list of things for which I owe her thanks starts years before that and continues today. In my mind, she'll forever be wearing a superhero cape and clutching a fabulous Kate Spade bag. Thanks extend to the entire Irene Goodman Literary Agency team.

My editor, Holly Ingraham, not only made this publication possible, she made this book better — and I can't think of anyone more delightful to work with, Gratitude, applause, and awe to the entire team at St. Martin's Press:

Jennifer Enderlin, Jennie Conway, Lisa Senz, Katie Bassel, Danielle Christopher, Robert Allen, and a whole host of dream-makers behind the scenes.

With appreciation for invaluable feedback at earlier stages of this manuscript: all-star beta readers and friends Amy Fogelson, Orly Konig-Lopez, Amy Price, and Megan Rader, For thoughtful critiques of my previous works: Donald Maass, Katie Merz, Joe Stollenwerk, and Lindsay Hiatt, For mentoring my editorial career from the very first, Jack Heffron; for putting so much trust in my abilities, Jane Friedman.

For kindly lending their expertise for the factual details of this novel: former FBI Assistant Special Agent in Charge Toni Chrabot, who generously took time away from her important work at Confidence LLC to answer a cold call from a new writer; pharmacist extraordinaire Jamie Mitchell; and my old friend turned wonderful nurse Amanda McDaniel-Price. All are incredibly busy people who patiently answered my many questions, and any deviations from fact or procedure are mine alone, for the sake of the story. (Speaking of which, I should note to my fellow Cincinnatians that I took creative license with the timeline of LumenoCity, which did not start until 2013, as well as a few other minor details — but I hope you'll find the city's spirit and its landmarks intact.) At one point Violet mentions a beautiful metaphor for new motherhood involving a thread connecting mother and baby — she doesn't remember where she heard it, but I do: Thanks to Maggie

O'Farrell and her wonderful novel *The Hand That First Held Mine* for the flash of inspiration.

For always telling me I could be whatever I wanted when I grew up, and for tolerating the constant presence of a book in my hand: my parents, Michael and Holly Yerega, and my brother, Evan. For welcoming me to your clan: Marty and Terry Strawser and the rest of the crew. For years of sisterly cheerleading when you probably would have rather talked about something else (anything else!): You know who you are. An extra wink to Erin Nevius, Marcie Holloway, and the much-missed Jackie Skukan.

Finally, I'll forever be grateful to my *Writer's Digest* family — the colleagues past and present who've been so enthusiastic about this endeavor (with special thanks to Brian Kleins, Zac Petit, and Phil Sexton) — the talented contributors and author interviewees who keep me steeped in insight and motivation during my working hours — and the readers who share the dream.

Other titles published by Ulverscroft:

SHE CHOSE ME

Tracey Emerson

After twenty years abroad, Grace returns to London to manage her dying mother's affairs. Taking a temporary post teaching English at a local school, she rents a rundown flat and travels to the care home on weekends. But the people in Grace's life are not what they seem to be . . . When she receives a blank Mother's Day card in the post, she is confused and unsettled. Who could have sent it to her, and why? She isn't a mother. Another Mother's Day card arrives, and then come the silent phone calls. Haunted by disturbing flashbacks, Grace starts to unravel. Someone is out to get her. Someone who will make her face the past she has run from for so long . . .

OPEN YOUR EYES

Paula Daly

With six unpublished novels, it feels to Jane like her writing career is going nowhere. Her husband Leon, on the other hand, is a successful author. Jane is happy for him, but it doesn't make the constant rejections any easier. She prefers to focus on what's going well, on the good things in life. But it all changes on Leon's forty-sixth birthday, when he is attacked by an unknown assailant and ends up in a coma. As Jane tries to deal with the fallout, she wants answers. But what she ends up with is more questions. She can't pretend everything is fine anymore. Everything is *far* from fine. Will Jane finally get uncover the truth, and the secrets that have been kept from her? And will she be able to handle what she hears?

ALL THAT WAS LOST

Alison May

In 1967, Patience Bickersleigh is a teenager who discovers a talent for telling people what they want to hear. Fifty years later, she is Patrice Leigh, a nationally celebrated medium. But cracks are forming in the carefully con-structed barriers that keep her real history at bay. Leo is the journalist hired to write Patrice's biography. Struggling to reconcile the demands of his family, his grief for his lost son, and his need to understand his own background, Leo becomes more and more frustrated at Patrice's refusal to open up. Because behind closed doors, Patrice is hiding more than one secret. And it seems that her past is finally catching up with her . . .